DEATH

on

LILY POND

LANE

DEATH
on
LILY POND
LANE

A Hamptons Murder Mystery

By
CARRIE DOYLE

DUNEMERE
Books

NEW YORK
SAN FRANCISCO

Published by Dunemere Books

Copyright © 2016 by Caroline M. Doyle
Cover illustration © 2016 by Jill De Haan
Book and cover design by Jenny Kelly

ISBN: 978-0-9972701-5-0

DEATH

on

LILY POND

LANE

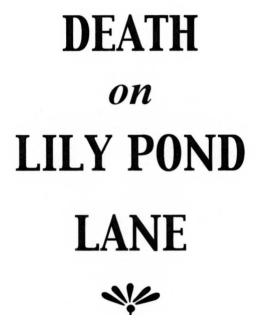

1

MONDAY NIGHT

Warner was too stunned to think clearly. He stumbled out of the bathroom in a frantic effort to reach his cell phone. His heart was pounding and his hands shook as he tried to dial 911.

"Come on, come on," he coaxed.

The call wouldn't go through. Why the hell was it so hard to get service in East Hampton?

He hurled his phone on the bed in frustration and ran out of the room. Warner knew he was in a race against time. He was about to make a left to try the landline in the maid's room when he heard the back door slam in the kitchen right below him. He paused and cocked his ear, his heart thumping wildly. Suddenly, he heard footsteps on the back stairs.

Shit. He's coming.

Warner changed tack and raced quickly down the hall towards the master suites. He made a left into Eleanor's room and his eyes searched frantically for a phone extension, before zeroing in on a portable phone on the desk. He grabbed the receiver and moved into bathroom, crouching down next to the toilet. His entire body was shivering with terror. He couldn't believe this was happening; couldn't believe what he had just witnessed.

The cold tiles felt like ice against his feet and his wet hands shook so violently that it was an effort to even punch the numbers. Warner only managed to press 9 before he sensed a presence at the door.

He glanced up in fear, raising his hands in an ineffective gesture of protection, calling out "No!" just before a massive blow landed on his head.

Then it all faded away.

2

TUESDAY

*E*ast Hampton has come back to life; there is no doubt about it, thought Antonia Bingham with excitement, as she maneuvered her blue Saab out of the Main Beach parking lot. The morning sky was a palette of milky pastels. Soft shades of baby blue, faded pink and a blush of pale yellow smeared into each other like a child's water color painting that has been held up before it could dry. It made Antonia recall one of the first things someone had told her about East Hampton: the American impressionists had chosen it as their place of work and residence because the light so closely resembled that of Giverny, its European counterpart. Here, nature's sparkling hues came to life, shimmering and essential. The winter had been frigid— replete with temperatures hovering near freezing, gusty winds, and icy sleet. But now it was a distant memory, replaced by spring's burgeoning foliage blossoming on the trees. When she made the left onto Lily Pond Lane, Antonia was thrilled to see the bright yellow forsythia bushes blooming, speckling the landscape with much needed color. In a few more weeks the hedges would thicken, gradually making it more and more difficult to peek into the multi-million dollar properties that lined this notable road.

On this early morning, the still-bare branches of the sycamore trees waggled in the breeze and few people were out. That was to be expected on a Tuesday in mid-May. Most of the residents in this part of town ("South of the Highway") used their houses primarily in the summer or on weekends. Their six-to-eight-to-ten bedroom "cottages" were in fact second homes that were occupied less than half the year. Antonia didn't live in this neighborhood. She owned the historic Windmill Inn on Main Street across from the cemetery, and inhabited the cozy ground-floor apartment in the back. She actually preferred her location; there was something thrilling about being in the center of what was arguably the most picturesque village in the United States. Her street was dappled with historic windmills, lovingly restored century-old houses, small—mostly one-story—meticulously maintained storefronts, and two equally distinguished yet stylistically divergent churches—the regal stone Episcopalian with its traditional English gothic architecture and the white clapboard Presbyterian church whose spire loomed high above the treetops. In the center of the village green was a sparkling pond that permanently hosted a family of swans. Antonia loved the small town familiarity of her neighborhood and had grown accustomed to the everyday busy hum of people driving by on their way to and from work. This leafy enclave was the destination of power players in the summer, but in the off-season it was merely a quaint historic town where people led normal working lives with the occasional celebrity spotting.

This morning Antonia had just completed her morning walk along the beach. When she had moved to East Hampton roughly a year and a half ago, she promised herself to make it a daily ritual to do so every morning, and it was a definite challenge for her to force herself outside on colder days. At least it had been until she met *him*— but Antonia quickly erased that thought from her head. She couldn't think about her friend from the beach. It was a waste of time. A stupid fantasy.

She drove by a distinguished-looking older man walking a red-leashed Wheaten Terrier and waved. He gave her a nod and a look as if he were trying to place her before she sped by. Antonia passed him each morning but didn't know his name. At this time of year, she'd wave to everyone she saw, as the population dwindled in the absence of the summer people. But when the season commenced and the second homeowners and tourists poured in, waving at strangers on the road was no longer the norm. Everybody was rushing about, determined to get in their share of beach time, tennis, golf, biking or whatever was their fancy, and waving to strangers was not part of the plan. That didn't matter to Antonia; she still did it anyway. She refused to be "pocket friendly" as her mother would say, which was her funny way of describing the act of putting kindness deep in your back pocket rather than on your face.

In addition to owning the inn and serving as chef for its

well-reviewed restaurant, Antonia also moonlighted as a 'caretaker' of sorts for two sprawling houses in East Hampton. Business could be slow at the inn during the off-season and she had enthusiastically embraced the opportunity to supplement her income. She also didn't mind looking after houses; the work was fairly easy. Her role was to visit each house once or twice a week and confirm that nothing was amiss. And it was always a pleasure to have a reason to visit this part of town, with the beautiful houses that mostly stood empty.

Despite the absence of cars on the road, Antonia clicked on her right blinker to turn into the Mastersons' gravel driveway. She was surprised to see that Warner Caruthers's BMW SUV was still parked in the driveway. Warner, a friend of the Mastersons' son Luke, was staying at their house while he filmed a documentary about the Hamptons. He was supposed to have left by now. He had even called her the previous evening to ask her what he should do with the keys, and she told him to leave them on the counter next to the telephone.

Hmmm, Antonia wondered. *Why is he still here?*

Antonia turned off the ignition and glanced at herself in the rear-view mirror as she applied some lipgloss. Big blue eyes reflected back at her. Her cheeks were flushed from the beach wind; red and rosy. If she were to analyze her looks, Antonia had always believed that a first, quick glance of her produced the best impression. She had glossy black hair (inherited from her Italian-American mother), creamy white skin (from her English father) and plump red lips. There was something youthful about her appearance, despite her thirty-five years. It was only when one took a further look that the cracks appeared. Lines were marching across her face, particularly on her forehead. Her nose did not produce the best profile. And she was a good fifteen pounds overweight, (okay, twenty) which she carried primarily in her mid-section, the part of her body that she ironically referred to as 'the bread belt'.

It is what it is, Antonia always told herself. She snapped her lip-gloss shut and exited the car. Time to find out why Warner hadn't left.

The Mastersons' house never failed to take her breath away. The mega-cottage had been built a hundred years ago, and was fitted with the standard design elements that were fashionable at that time—shingled façade, gambrel roof, wraparound terrace, multiple chimneys and functional shutters—features that have been heavily imitated along the Hamptons coastline in recent years. Situated one leafy road from the beach and enclosed by a weathered split-rail fence, the house glowed in the vibrant reflection of the well-manicured landscape that surrounded it. It was so lovely, and exactly the sort of architecture that appealed to Antonia. She was originally from Southern California, the land of schizophrenic structures and oversized eyesores. But it had never felt like home to her. So, at a particularly low point in Antonia's life when her friend Genevieve announced she was quitting acting and leaving L.A. to return East to the place where she had spent her childhood summers, Antonia decided to make a radical change and follow suit. It had paid off; she adored the place. Sure, it had been a little bumpy in the beginning, well, a lot bumpy with a homicidal bookkeeper who wanted kill her in order to take over the Windmill Inn, but that was in the past, thankfully.

When Antonia closed her car door there was movement in the side yard that caught her attention. Turning to her right, she scanned the grounds. She didn't see anything out of the norm. Perhaps it had been a deer. The town was now overrun by these brazen beasts who seemed determined to chew up everyone's landscaping.

After unlocking the back door to the house, Antonia stepped into the immaculate kitchen that was equipped with every possible appliance.

"Warner?" asked Antonia into the empty room.

The hum of the refrigerator was the only response.

Antonia flicked the lights on and looked around appraisingly. The room was spotless, as usual. Per Antonia's recommendation, the Mastersons employed two of the same cleaners that Antonia used at the inn: Angela and Rosita Diaz. Not only were they excellent housekeepers, they were also excellent people. Antonia's bond was greater with Rosita because they both shared an unfortunate marital history: they had kicked violent ex-husbands to the curb and survived. But that was part of the past that Antonia tried not to dwell on.

There was no sign of Warner in the kitchen or the mudroom.

"Warner? Are you here?" asked Antonia into the emptiness, knowing that she was talking to herself. "Are you sleeping?"

Antonia had met him only on two brief occasions when he stopped by the Windmill Inn, and found him to be charismatic and charming. A tall, slight young man with a mop of strawberry blonde hair, an aquiline nose and thin lips, he possessed the same optimistic exuberance and naïve arrogance that she had found in most twenty-somethings fresh out of college.

With a sigh, Antonia hastily walked through the pantry towards the dining room. She stopped and abruptly retraced her steps. A white paper bag perched on the edge of the counter near the bar had caught her eye. She carefully opened it and found a cold untouched slice of sausage pizza.

"Interesting breakfast," murmured Antonia.

Unless it was a discarded dinner? In any event, it meant that Warner was still around. She was a little dismayed that he had breached his agreement with the Mastersons and overstayed his welcome.

She did a hasty sweep of the living room and dining room, which revealed nothing out of the norm. There was a tacit understanding between the Mastersons and Warner that he would not use the formal rooms on the ground floor or the family's bedrooms upstairs. As far as she knew, he had adhered to this agreement. She wondered why he hadn't adhered to the plan to be gone by yesterday.

Antonia stopped short at the foot of the grand front hall staircase. Her palm gripped the edge of the mahogany banister and instantly felt clammy. She wasn't sure why, but something gave her pause. She glanced around. The grandfather clock ticked softly. Its pendulum was the only movement in the room. Her eyes moved to the front door but she could see it was still locked. The outside lights were off. Shaking her head, Antonia continued up the carpeted front staircase to the second floor.

A clicking noise sounded. Startled, Antonia whipped around.

"Hello?" she asked.

She was met by silence. Then just as suddenly, a burst of hot air rushed forth from the vent above her. Antonia smiled. It was only the heating. The temperature was always set to maintain 60 degrees.

At the top of the stairs, Antonia took a left towards the guest quarters. If Warner were asleep, she would rouse him and send him on his merry way.

There was a hall door between the guest quarters and the family's bedrooms. It was closed, which was unusual. Joan Masterson liked to keep the doors open for air circulation. The door was somewhat warped from the sea air, so Antonia had to bang it on top to loosen it before turning the door handle. If he hadn't been awake before, he would be now, Antonia mused.

"Warner, it's Antonia."

She didn't want to surprise him. She glanced right into a maid's room and bathroom and confirmed that they were untouched. She made a left to enter the room Warner was staying in.

"Yoo hoo?" Antonia asked.

The bed was made, and with such precision that Antonia guessed Warner hadn't slept on it since the cleaners were here yesterday. She'd be very surprised if he could make a bed as well as Rosita. Antonia glanced left and noticed a black monogrammed duffel bag propped against the wall on the floor. It was unzipped, revealing a jumble of wrinkled and discarded shirts and pants.

Resting on the desk was an open folder. Antonia cocked her head to glimpse at it (a little peek never hurt anyone.) One side of the folder was stuffed with loose notes, pages ripped out of a white spiral notebook and scrawled mostly in a black ballpoint pen. On the other side was a typed cover sheet that stated in over-sized font: Too Rich To Behave: *a documentary by Warner Caruthers (with Hayes Rutherford)*. Tantalizing title, thought Antonia. She wondered what it was about.

She left the guest quarters and made the long walk down the narrow hallway, past the framed family portraits, to check on the bedrooms.

"Warner?" Antonia asked.

But there was no response.

Antonia glanced into the bedroom that belonged to Eleanor, the youngest Masterson child, and at once felt something didn't seem right. Her eyes flitted past the king-sized bed to the lacquer desk that held a computer and a telephone. When she found nothing amiss, she glanced at the skirted vanity. Poised atop were the usual knickknacks: various makeup bottles; monogrammed jewelry boxes in varying sizes; an old watch in a ceramic dish alongside a Tiffany china piggy bank. Antonia wasn't quite sure what was giving her pause.

She ventured a step into the room and turned to face the back wall. She glanced around again; the bookshelves gave no indication of tampering. Everything in the room was the same as it always was. That is, until Antonia looked down at the pink carpet. Bingo. In the thick fluffy surface, there were impressions—footprints.

Warner's? Antonia wondered. What was he doing in here, when he was specifically told not to use the master suites? But then who else? Rosita, who was responsible for cleaning upstairs, was very particular about marks in the carpet. She would leave no trace of her existence after she vacuumed, in essence, vacuuming herself out of the room. Antonia's eyes followed the footprints to the door of Eleanor's bathroom, which was closed.

That was odd.

Antonia walked to the door and hesitated.

"Warner?" she demanded.

She was met by silence.

Antonia hesitated before turning the handle. She watched the brass knob twist, as if in slow motion. She pressed open the door cautiously, tentative of what she might find behind. Her eyes first met the rack of yellow towels hanging on the wall. Eleanor's initials were embroidered into them in a swirling white font. Antonia pushed the door open further and caught her own reflection in the mirror. She stared at herself before pressing on the door until the toilet was revealed, then the shower, and finally the bathtub.

It was there that she saw him.

He was naked. The top half of his body was bent back in a half-filled tub, while his legs were splayed: one of them dangling over the side, the other weirdly contorted underneath him. There was a stream of dried blood that had dribbled down from the back of his head and pooled in the now bloody pink water. His left hand rested atop the shower curtain, which was yanked off several rings, the fabric gathering around his head and torso. His right arm, on which he wore a Rolex watch, was submerged in the water. His eyes looked heavenward, unblinking; his face was bloated and puffy.

Antonia felt her heart sink. There was no doubt about it: Warner Caruthers was dead.

3

STILL TUESDAY

Hours later as Antonia pulled out of the Mastersons' driveway, a man stepped from the shade of the trees and in front of her car. Antonia jammed on the breaks. She lurched forward into her seatbelt and fell back into her car seat. Disoriented, she glanced around. Her eyes narrowed into hostile slits when she realized who had stopped her.

Larry Lipper gave her an obnoxious smile. He slowly walked around to the driver's side and tapped on Antonia's window. She reluctantly rolled it down.

"I've been waiting for you to get out of there."

"I almost killed you."

"You would never kill me, Antonia. We still haven't had sex yet."

"And we never will. Why did you stand in front of my car? I could have run you over."

"Ah, but I knew you wouldn't." Larry walked over to the passenger side of Antonia's car and got in.

"What are you doing?"

"We need to talk," said Larry. "Pull the car to the side of the road, we don't want to get into an accident."

"Oh, now you tell me."

After being detained most of the morning with the police, the last thing Antonia wanted was to deal with Larry Lipper. Each officer had grilled her as they arrived on the scene, forcing her to retell her discovery ad nauseam. She'd repeated countless times that she saw no signs of forced entry, nothing was amiss other than the fact that Warner was dead in Eleanor's bathroom, and she had no reason to believe it was foul play, or anything more nefarious than simply an unfortunate accident in the bathtub. There were so many cops that they all blended together, with the exception of Sergeant Flanagan. She could tell he was good at his job because he was the only one who seemed to sense that Antonia was not being entirely truthful when she insisted she had not removed anything from the crime scene. The fact was, she *had* removed something. It was so unlike her to do anything like what she had done, and quite honestly, she was stressed about it. The whole situation made her sick. But the only thing that gave her sanity was that she knew it had to be done. It's like a white lie—sometimes you have to tell a lie in order to make everyone feel better. Nonetheless, she had been tempted to confide in Sergeant Flanagan—it was literally on the tip of her tongue—but then she remembered her past experience with the police. And although Sergeant Flanagan seemed decent enough, he was a cop, and as far as Antonia was concerned, cops couldn't be trusted.

"Alright, lady. I'm ready for you," said Larry.

"You know, you're really infuriating," said Antonia, her voice rising.

"But you love me," he responded smugly.

"I know you think that's true," responded Antonia.

Larry Lipper covered the crime beat for *The East Hampton Star*. He was excellent at his job and she knew he would squeeze her for information. To Antonia, he was not unlike one of those annoying yap dogs that keeps barking and barking at everything and everyone until you tune them out and grow totally immune to their noise. Antonia attributed it to Larry's short stature: he stood about five feet two inches high, which was amazingly small considering the powerful personality that lurked inside.

"Thou doth protest too much. Always telling me how you don't like me when every interaction between us is simmering with sexual tension."

"Simmering with queasiness is more like it," said Antonia.

She recalled the time in November when she had (reluctantly, after much cajoling) agreed to attend an event with him socially. They were standing watching the concert one minute and then the next he had shoved his tongue down her throat making a break for her esophagus. It was so revolting that it took her a second to regain her senses; when she finally did, she glanced down and saw that Larry was standing on his tippy toes. Antonia had pushed him away in disgust. Larry shrugged off her rebuff, always taunting her that she would come back for him. She was amazed that he thought so highly of himself.

She would feel *slightly* flattered if he didn't have this weird rapport going with several other women in town. He was hedging his bets.

Antonia put the car in park and turned and stared at him.

"What do you want from me? I'm tired and late and have to return to the inn."

"You found the body. This is your lucky day. I want to hear all about it."

"I have nothing to add."

"That's not going to work. I've already lined up Page One."

Antonia sighed. "I can't go through this again."

"Quit your complaining! A little murder now and then spices up everything in this dreary town."

"You just want to get a book deal."

"You know I'm relentless. And this is a major story! A suspicious death on *Lily Pond Lane*? This is not some domestic dispute in Springs or some loony nobody killing local innkeepers. This is rich people, the most expensive real estate in the United States, the most beautiful beaches in the world. This is the stuff of TV movies."

"That's gross."

"You know it's true. It's '"Lifestyles of the Rich and Famous"' over here. And anything about them is a juicy read and you know it. We locals love them and hate them. They're our bread and butter but they also have so much entitlement when they waltz into town and take up our parking spaces and gobble up all the beach permits."

"I don't feel that way . . ."

"Of course you don't! You own an *inn*. You rely on these vultures. But there are a lot of people who resent the summer people."

"You make it sound like '"West Side Story".' That's hardly the case. People are annoyed by traffic for sure, but I can't name one local who has that sort of anger towards a summer person."

"Because you're not looking."

"So you're saying some disgruntled Bonacker killed Warner? He didn't even live here. He was a guest."

"I don't know who killed him. Right now it's game on. This guy wasn't popular with anyone. I've already got enough shiz on this dead A-hole to write a book."

"He wasn't an 'A-hole,' Larry."

"That's not what I hear."

Antonia was genuinely surprised. She shook her head. "I don't believe you."

"Whoa, you two must have been pretty tight for you to be so defensive. Were you sleeping with him?" Larry leered.

"We weren't tight," Antonia corrected him. "Or sleeping together, for God's sake. But he was best friends with Luke Masterson, who *is* a fantastic kid. There was no way Luke would be friends with a jerk. And my *limited* interaction with him was very pleasant."

"Maybe he was pleasant to you, but he was a problem."

"How so?"

"Oh, *now* you're not so tired," said Larry with a maddening smile. "Well, tit for tat, lady."

"Then you go first."

"It's not even noon and I've already tracked down a whole bunch of people that were pissed off at him."

"Really?"

Larry started to rattle off his information. "Warner Caruthers and Sidney Black loathed each other. In fact, they both filed restraining orders against each other."

"Hang on a second. Sidney Black? Who's that?"

"Some corporate raider who makes Bernie Madoff look like Santa Claus. He owns Black, Black and Kendall. Swoops into little family-owned companies, promises to help, then destroys them."

"What does he have to do with Warner?"

"Has a house out here. Warner claimed Black was harassing him. Black denies it, filed charges against Warner saying *he* was harassing him."

"Does it have to do with the documentary?"

"Yes. What do you know about this documentary?"

"The police asked me the same question. But the fact is I really don't know anything about it other than Warner was convinced it would be a big deal. I admit, I tried to gently cajole him into telling me what it was about, but he was pretty tight-lipped. I think if I had a little more time with him, I would have gotten him to talk . . ."

"Now that he's dead, I'll let you in on the secret: it was about embarrassing the rich people in East Hampton. Making them say ridiculous stuff. Now granted, they are responsible for their actions but this guy had one agenda: to make them all look like assholes. They probably deserve it, but talk about biting the hand that feeds you."

"Are you sure?" It was hard for Antonia to reconcile the animated and enthusiastic young film student with a cynical, nefarious mini-Michael Moore.

"Yes. Warner had been bugging everyone. Just the other day, security threw him off the grounds of the Dune Club. Members caught wind of what he was doing and shut him down. They do not like that sort of thing there."

The Dune Club, established 1899, was one of the oldest and most exclusive clubs on the East End of Long Island. It had an eighteen-hole golf course, twenty grass tennis courts, an Olympic size swimming pool and a big chunk of beachfront. Antonia had only been there once in January after it had closed down for the winter when her friend, Len Powers, the head of security, gave her a brief tour.

"I'm sure private clubs nail people all the time for trespassing."

"There's more," said Larry, licking his diminutive index finger and turning the page of his notebook. "I've also got a pool guy two houses down saying he saw Warner sneaking through the neighbor's hedge."

"Really? That seems weird."

"Makes total sense to me. The guy was a voyeur."

"Pot calling the kettle black."

"I'm a reporter," said Larry defensively.

"A nudge, more like it."

"This is a murder case, fair and square."

Antonia remained silent. The police hadn't confirmed anything, but Antonia had been around cops enough to know they would look at all the angles. Nothing would be determined until the autopsy, but perhaps that's why they had pushed her so hard with their questions. She made a mental note to ask Len Powers what happened with Warner at the Dune Club.

When Antonia didn't respond, Larry continued. "Warner was making problems, poking around houses, going through people's garbage, no doubt, looking for incriminating stuff. Someone got tired of it, and took action."

Antonia sat for a minute, digesting this information. She was still quite certain that Warner's death was an accident, and she had proof of that. But the fact that Warner had a set of powerful enemies here in town was a new twist. A knot formed in her stomach. Maybe she had been hasty removing something from the scene if it really was a crime scene? Antonia couldn't believe it.

"I don't know, Larry. Just because Warner annoyed people doesn't mean they would kill him."

"Sure it does. Karma is a bitch." Larry turned and gave Antonia one of his obnoxious grins. "So, now tell me what you saw. And start from the beginning."

*   *   *   *   *

Antonia was stressed out by the time she returned to the inn. Just as she was pulling into the driveway her cell phone rang. She slid into her parking spot, turned off her car and answered.

"I'm FREAKING out."

It was Genevieve. Of course she had heard; it was hard to keep anything quiet in a small town, let alone, a possible murder. And Genevieve did always claim to be "the eyes and ears of the Hamptons." Antonia was so relieved to hear her voice, a friendly buoy bobbing in the midst of such an awful day. She slid back in her seat.

"I know. I'm still shaken. I mean, I can't believe it! It's surreal. What a nice guy . . ." Antonia let her voice trail off.

"I know! And so hot. I mean, without his shirt on, mamma mia."

Antonia thought back to Warner in the tub. She hadn't even noticed his body, so horrified was she by the fact that he was dead. "I guess."

"Oh no, I'm telling you. Rocking bod."

"I'll take your word for it. I wasn't really looking at that, I was more shocked by the whole thing."

"I'm shocked, too. After three solid weeks of pursuit, I crept into the house and got him."

Antonia felt her stomach drop. "Wait, what?"

"Let's just say that when I was through with him he was naked and not moving. Not even breathing!"

Antonia shot upright. "Genevieve, what are you saying?"

"Oh, I forgot, you're little miss conservative. Don't always be so prissy, Antonia."

"Genevieve, what did you do to Warner?"

There was a pause. "Warner? You mean that guy who was staying at the Mastersons'?"

"Yes, the guy whose body I found dead in their bathroom this morning."

"WHAT?" screamed Genevieve so loud that Antonia had to hold the received away from her ear. "He's dead?"

"Yes, isn't that who we were talking about?"

"No! I was talking about Carl!"

"Carl?"

"Carl? That hot guy I met at Citta Nuova? The one who works in real estate? I've only been obsessing over him for two weeks. What the hell happened to Warner?"

Relief flooded Antonia's body. It was a classic Genevieve and Antonia misunderstanding.

"You almost gave me a heart attack, yet again, Genevieve," said Antonia.

They were unlikely friends: Antonia, the maternal, mature and organized mother hen type and Genevieve, the free-spirited, childish and disorganized party girl type. But when they had met as fellow caterers years before in Los Angeles something had clicked. Genevieve made Antonia laugh and despite generally being flighty she had been a rock in Antonia's darkest hour; in return Antonia was the eternal stable presence in Genevieve's life.

After filling Genevieve in on everything that had transpired with Warner, an emotionally wrought Antonia returned to Genevieve's news for a happy distraction.

"So tell me about Carl."

"He's awesome. Took me to dinner last night at 1770 House."

"Fancy."

"I know. Then we went to the Talkhouse and shut it down. Didn't sleep a wink all night, if you know what I mean, then he left around nine for an appointment to show a house. Not until I ravaged him one last time, though. He literally had to escape my clutches, I didn't want him to go!"

Antonia frowned. Genevieve always came on a little strong and scared the men away. "I hope you played a little hard to get, Gen. You know what happens . . ."

"No, this is different. I can tell he's into me because he wants to take me to dinner tonight! I suggested your restaurant, so make sure there is a table."

"For you, always."

"Thank you. Now I have to go shower and make myself get to work. And sorry to babble about myself, are you sure you are okay? I can't imagine what this is like for you. Do you think he was murdered?"

Despite their closeness, Antonia didn't want to reveal to Genevieve that she had taken something from that bathroom that would prove that Warner had fallen. Genevieve was not the most discreet person when it came to information like that. And Antonia was now becoming increasingly afraid that she had really messed things up. If only she could leave things alone. But that wasn't her character. "I hope he just fell. What I really hope is that maybe he had an aneurysm or a pre-existing heart condition. Something that nothing could have been done about anyway, so it wasn't an accident . . ."

"Or murder."

"Right."

"I guess. I'll see what I can find out today around town."

"I'm sure you will," said Antonia.

After hanging up the phone, Antonia made her way through the reception area and dropped her handbag on the desk in her office. She quickly scanned her messages before walking down the hall to the mudroom. The Windmill Inn, built in the late 1840s, was a rambling white-shingled house framed by green shutters. It stood three stories high and boasted eight guestrooms, as well as one suite and several public common and dining rooms. The décor was cozy and inviting, and the architecture full of nooks and crannies where guests could curl up with a great mystery novel and spend hours relaxing. Antonia tended to spend most of her time in the kitchen, which is where she was supposed to have been hours ago.

In the mudroom, Antonia exchanged her Merrells for a pair of pink Crocs. She could almost hear Genevieve groaning. Genevieve insisted Antonia would never land a man if she walked around town in those 'ugly excuses for footwear that completely cancel out your great boobs." Antonia would retort that she had "no interest in landing a man right now, thank you very much."

As she reached for a double-breasted chef's jacket there was a soft stirring outside the side door to her left. It led to a little used patio that backed up to the corner hedge. Antonia moved towards the door and listened. Only the soft chirp of birds could be heard. But suddenly she heard the sound of footsteps on gravel. They were becoming fainter. Antonia whipped open the door and looked to her left. No one. She glanced right. She saw someone turn the corner quickly, but all she could make out were dark pants and a dark jacket. Perhaps it was a lost guest? She wasn't going to sweat it. Today had been full of enough anxiety.

When Antonia entered the kitchen, Marty, her sous chef, already had things underway with assistance from Kendra, the station chef and Soyla, the prep cook. As Executive Chef, Antonia's responsibilities included menu creation, plating, and management. Marty was her second in command. He was a cantankerous old goat who drove her crazy; still, he did a fabulous job.

"Where the hell have you been?" he demanded.

"You're not going to believe it—I found . . . Did you meet that young man, Warner Caruthers? He came here a couple times. Well, I found him . . . dead."

Soyla and Kendra glanced up with surprise.

"What?" exclaimed Kendra, eyes ablaze.

"You okay?" asked Soyla nervously. She was Rosita's cousin and her husband Hector was the head gardener, who also helped with maintenance. "You want to sit down?"

Marty shrugged. "Ah, come on. Cry me a river. You've seen one dead body, you've seen them all."

"Well, I had never seen one before," Antonia announced.

"Congratulations! Let's buy you a goddamn medal," snapped Marty. "Now while you were out earning your First Dead Person badge, I was here making the unpleasant discovery that those idiots from that goddamned organic green grocer you insist on using forgot the freakin' ramps and artichokes! Oh, and not only that, but that fish recipe that Kendra came up with? It's goddamn disgusting. That's why you can't take suggestions from a fattie who likes to eat everything."

"I love you too, Marty," shouted Kendra before returning her attention to Antonia. "Who was Warner?"

Kendra crinkled up her pug nose and waited for a response. A small gold stud protruded from her left nostril. Antonia wondered for the hundredth time why Kendra would want to draw attention to the least attractive feature on her face.

"A guest at one of the houses I look after."

"How'd he die?"

Antonia paused. "It looks as if he slipped."

"That's a good way to go," Marty exclaimed. "He can't complain."

"Well he was only twenty-five!"

"Ya win some, ya lose some," Marty barked.

Antonia shrugged. She felt as if in a daze. She walked over to her mise-en-place and glanced around the kitchen. "So, everything is running smoothly," said Antonia, eager to change the subject.

"What are you talking about? I'm in the goddamn weeds here!" snapped Marty.

Antonia knew that Marty's grumblings meant nothing and the kitchen was under control. She wondered sometimes if her presence was superfluous. That was good to know; if anything happened to her, everything would carry on. Antonia rolled up her sleeves and went to work, zoning out their banter. For the next two hours she methodically peeled shrimp, simmered broth and chopped vegetables. Flashes of Warner lying in the bathtub danced in her head. She thought of Larry's information that Warner was reviled. And there was the peculiar fact that Warner was in Eleanor's bathroom. What was he doing there? As far as she knew, he had used the guest bathroom provided for him. It was so strange.

At five o'clock Antonia put down her knives.

"Break time," she announced.

Kendra and Marty went outside for cigarettes while Soyla kept working. Antonia could never get her to take a break; the woman had more energy than anyone she had ever met.

Antonia set off to meet her friend Joseph in the parlor. As with most of the inn, the cozy parlor was royal blue with burnished mahogany paneling. Over the past few years, Antonia had returned the antique windows and door fixtures to mint condition, reupholstered plush armchairs of varying sizes in batik and ikat fabrics, and refurbished the bathrooms with imported Moroccan tiles and converted marble top sinks. Her vision was to create a British style country manor with a modern twist, and as a result, she amassed a collection of mostly English antiques—dressers, sleigh beds, writing desks—as well as rare leather-bound books to adorn every room. Antonia's accountant had desperately tried to reign in her spending but to her it was the little details that mattered most: the rare hand-cut crystal vases with fresh flowers; the gold-framed maps of Long Island from the 1900s that lined the stairs; and the brass and crystal lamps that graced every table in the dining room. She wanted people to feel like they were at home.

And to Joseph Fowler, it was in fact home. He was the permanent tenant of the two-room suite on the second floor that was accessible by a private elevator. The sixty-four year-old widower was an author of some renown, whose historical fiction was intensely research-based and literary. A dapper gentleman, always impeccably groomed and donning custom fitting blazers and a bowtie, he was Antonia's closest confidante.

"Here are the print-outs," said Joseph, motioning to the stack of papers on the antique side table. "I started in as soon as I received your email. I'm sorry you had to spend all that time there."

"So am I. But thank you for pulling these articles. Anything good?" said Antonia, plopping herself into a chair next to the open window. She picked up the papers.

"Google comes through every time."

"I know it works for you, but it just sends me down the rabbit hole every time I search for something. I'll go on to look up a new recipe for crepes and the next thing you know I'm on a page reading about some obscure French artist. I don't know how that happens."

Joseph sat patiently while Antonia read. This morning, while she had waited to be interviewed for the zillionth time by the police, she had sent an email to Joseph asking him to do a little research for her.

"Looks like it's not uncommon for people to fall to their deaths in bathtubs," said Antonia. "Did you find any lawsuits?"

"You'll see there were several. Usually, it's people suing hotels because they didn't have the proper matting, things like that. There is the possibility that the Mastersons could be open to a lawsuit if Warner's family is the litigious sort."

Antonia put the papers down and leaned back in thought. "That's what I was worried about. And it looks from these papers as if there is precedent."

"You look like you need a drink."

"A drink? Heck, I need an IV rack of alcohol hooked up to my veins. But I'll get it."

"Don't be silly."

Joseph, who was mostly confined to a scooter due to the side effects of a childhood bout with polio, slid himself off his chair and on to his scooter. He buzzed over to the bar and poured Antonia a full glass of red wine. He handed it to her and she took a big gulp. He slid back into his chair. Antonia knew he liked to be active, so she never tried to protest when he did things for her.

"Better?"

"Infinitely."

She closed her eyes and felt the soft cushion behind her head.

Joseph watched Antonia carefully. "There is another article that I found."

"I'm sure you did."

"An interesting one," said Joseph.

Antonia opened her eyes.

"Don't taunt me. Bring it on."

Joseph held a sheet of paper in his hand.

"There was a recent case about a bathtub that you may recall. It was all over the news. The wife of a police officer in the Midwest went missing, and the general conjecture is that he murdered her. Upon further investigation, they discovered that his previous wife had died in a bathtub. At the time it was ruled accidental, but when the next wife disappeared, they reopened the case. Turns out it was made to look like a fall. They charged him with homicide."

Antonia nodded and took a sip of her drink.

"You don't think he was murdered?" asked Joseph.

Antonia stared at him. "I know for a fact that it couldn't be true."

"Oh?"

Antonia leaned towards him.

"Joseph, I have a confession."

"Of course you do."

"What's that supposed to mean?" Antonia asked with faux exasperation.

"It means that I know you very well. It is impossible for you to be a passive participant in any sort of drama. I'm certain you stuck your nose in somewhere you shouldn't have."

Antonia frowned at him.

"I resent that."

"Ah, but it's true. What did you do now?"

Antonia took a sip of her drink that placed it down hard on the coffee table.

"I thought it was the right thing to do, but now I'm really

scared." She paused to look imploringly into his eyes before adding softly, "I took something from the crime scene."

Joseph looked nonplussed. "Proceed," he said calmly.

"A can of disinfectant."

Joseph arched his eyebrows questioningly.

"I know, it sounds really bad. But let me explain."

Antonia rose and walked over to the fireplace. She poked the logs before retreating to the windowsill where she perched with her back to the window, wringing her hands.

"So, I found Warner and then I called 911. All by the book, mind you, before you accuse me of anything. Well, you know how out here it doesn't exactly take the police two minutes to arrive on the scene. So I went back to the bathroom to check on Warner. Obviously, I knew he was dead but it didn't seem right to leave him up there alone. I stood there for maybe five minutes. It was strange. It was so quiet and the room felt heavy with death. I stood there, taking it all in . . ."

She glanced up at Joseph.

"But then?"

She smiled at Joseph. He knew her well. "But then my eyes fell on this can of Lysol that was lying on its side next to the bathmat, way back behind the toilet. It had clearly rolled there. And suddenly it dawned on me: Warner had probably slipped on the can, and that's what had caused him to fall and hit his head! And my mind went crazy. Lawsuits. Liability. Then it dawned on me that Rosita would be the one who was blamed!"

"Rosita?"

"Our cleaner!"

"Of course I know Rosita but why . . ."

"She also cleans the Mastersons' house. *I* got her the job!"

"But if it was an accident, she wouldn't be in any trouble . . ."

"I would hope so. But you never know. We live in a litigious world. And Rosita has enough problems. She's got this terrible ex-husband. Let's just say I can identify with that. And she has some visa issues. I don't want her to get deported or dragged into any sort of investigation. I think it would kill her. She could lose her job or even her kids, if things got really out of hand. Not that the Mastersons are like that, but you never know when something like this happens. And bottom line, I don't want the Mastersons to have any problems either. They're good people."

"So, you were trying to protect them?"

She nodded. "I didn't want there to be any blame other than he just slipped in the tub. At the moment I was thinking all this, I heard the sirens. Then I just sort of sprung into action. It was impulsive, but I grabbed the Lysol. And I went downstairs and put it in my handbag just as the police were pulling in the driveway. And when they asked me if I had taken anything, I said no. I choose to look at it as a white lie."

Joseph paused before speaking. Antonia knew his concerned look and thought he was about to deliver a verdict she didn't want to hear but instead he surprised her.

"Don't worry, you did the right thing."

Antonia sighed audibly with relief. "You think so?"

"Yes. It's just a can of Lysol. I'm sure it means nothing that you took it. Totally inconsequential."

"Oh my gosh, I'm so glad you agree."

"A preemptive strike."

"Right. As you will recall, past faith in the justice system has never worked in my favor."

"I remember."

Once upon a time Antonia had trusted the police. Like everyone, she revered them, and regarded them as protectors and caretakers. That was until she married a policeman. Philip was a wolf in sheep's clothing. She thought she had found someone to give her stability but instead he traumatized her. They had been married for five years, the last four of which were full of increasing abuse. His brothers in arms closed rank around him and were deaf to her pleas for help. One night he kicked her father when he tried to intervene on her behalf, and two weeks later her father died of the complications. After that, she realized nothing held her in California any longer, and with Genevieve's prompting, she moved to the East Coast to start a new life and used the settlement that she won from him in civil court to purchase the inn. The only external trace of Philip was the scar he had caused above her right eyebrow, but there was much greater internal damage to her heart and soul.

"I'm sure it's over-compensation, but it took me a while to stand up for myself and I want to make sure I stand up for others."

"That's what Margaret would have liked about you: your fighting spirit."

Margaret was Joseph's late wife. After she had died of cancer, Joseph had been living alone in their house on Buell Lane. One night he had a terrible fall, which resulted in a trip to the hospital. At the urging of his son, who wanted to be able to keep an eye on him, Joseph had reluctantly been considering a move to the city when Antonia had offered him accommodation at the inn instead. Joseph had quickly agreed, and the arrangement worked out perfectly for both of them.

"I bet she was an amazing woman."

Joseph's smile faltered. It was still difficult for him to talk about Margaret, the loss still raw. He took off his glasses and wiped them carefully with his handkerchief before changing the subject. "What's on the menu tonight? It's prix-fixe night if I'm not mistaken? That always brings in the crowds."

Antonia felt the breeze picking up, causing the leaves in the yard to stir so loudly it sounded as if someone were walking outside the window. She rose and after giving a log one last poke, she turned and faced Joseph. Antonia and Joseph had a routine when they met for drinks before dinner. She would tell him what was on the menu, and he would interject his commentary. For her, cooking was a form of performance, and having a welcome audience made it all the more rewarding.

"Come on, my dear, the show must go on," he gently coaxed.

Antonia smiled. He was right; not only the show, but also life must go on. She stood up, assumed a professional stance and began speaking in a very theatrical manner.

"For our first course this evening, we have a choice of roasted red pepper soup with a lobster wonton; frisee and fava bean salad with pecorino cheese and pears; or warm Vidalia onion and pancetta tart . . ."

"Did you make the soup yourself?"

"Of course," said Antonia with a smile. They both knew she made all of her dishes from scratch, so this was part of their shtick.

"Then that's what I'll have."

"Very good."

"And the main course? Better be some red meat in there."

"We do have a filet mignon with potato leek gratin and sautéed mixed mushrooms . . ."

"Delicious. Save me a piece . . ."

"But for a gentleman who has been advised by his doctors to reduce his cholesterol intake, there is also a potato crusted Sea Bass with mixed spring vegetables . . ."

"What is 'mixed spring vegetables'? Did you open a bag from the frozen food section and dump them in?"

"Of course not, what sort of an establishment do you think this is?" asked Antonia with mock horror. "We don't do Birdseye here, sir. We have local asparagus and fava beans in a lemon sauce . . ."

"Boring . . ."

"And there is also the option of shrimp risotto with English peas and cherry tomatoes."

"Will the doctor let me have that?"

"Just this once. Don't forget that shrimp are high in cholesterol."

"But worth it."

"True," said Antonia. "And I might add that the shrimp are very plump and sweet, as are the cherry tomatoes. You won't be disappointed."

"Do I qualify for dessert?"

"Berries and fresh cream?"

"Or?"

"Pear pithivier with caramel ice cream and toasted almonds?"

"You're getting warmer."

"Warm strawberry rhubarb pie?"

"From scratch too?"

"Yes, sir," said Antonia. "Everything is from scratch."

"Then save me a slice," said Joseph with a wide grin.

Just before Antonia returned to the kitchen, Joseph handed her an additional stack of papers. He had done a full background check on Warner Caruthers.

"It feels kind of morbid to look through them," said Antonia with a shake of her head.

"Just take them," he advised and pressed them into her hand. "You may need to refer to them later."

4

The dining room was more crowded than usual for a Wednesday night. All of the dozen freestanding tables were taken, even the least desirable one in the front next to the maitre d's station, which suffered due to its proximity to the entrance and the kitchen. In addition, two of the four cobalt booths in the back of the restaurant were filled to capacity and the eight barstools at the dark azure lacquered bar were taken.

"We're *so* busy tonight," Glen, the maitre d', whined on a trip into the kitchen. A tall, slightly angular fellow who Genevieve accurately described as 'pointy,' Glen was handsome but cheesy, with over-gelled luxurious black hair and a thick Long Island accent. "I mean, it's great that we're almost full, and I give myself full credit for suggesting these prix-fixe nights, but it's a little too much with the skeleton staff we have off season."

"They're not here for the food tonight, Glen, sorry to burst your bubble. Everyone wants to hear about the dead guy," said Kendra.

Antonia jerked her head up from her station. "You think that's why they're here?"

"Are you kidding?" asked Kendra, wiping her brow. "A dead body in a mansion in the estate section of town is just too irresistible! People are here for the gossip."

"Well, they're not getting any from me. First and foremost, Warner's death is a tragedy. He's not just a 'dead body in a mansion.'"

Although Antonia enjoyed being apprised of everything that was happening around town, she was, as a rule, disdainful of gossip. She liked to regard her own quest for news as more of an information gathering rather than something as meretricious as small town tittle-tattle. The truth of the matter was she was always eager to hear it, but parsimonious when it came to dispensing it. Perhaps that is why people confided their most personal things to her; they knew their secret was always safe.

It was not until nine-thirty when Antonia was able to extract herself from dinner service. Before she headed out to the dining room she decided to run to her office to check for any messages. As soon as she entered her office she stopped short and inadvertently emitted a loud gasp.

She heard footsteps, and Jonathan, the manager of the inn appeared at her door, his face awash with concern.

"Are you alright, Antonia?"

"Yes," said Antonia. She turned and faced him, blocking his view into her office. "Sure, sorry."

"I hope it wasn't a mouse," said Jonathan swiftly. His eyes glistened behind his horn-rimmed glasses. He possessed the kind of long eyelashes that women claim are wasted on men, and a round face that would look eternally youthful.

"No. Not a mouse. My purse fell over. I was horrified to see how much junk I have accumulated in there."

Antonia motioned to the pile behind her.

Jonathan chuckled. "Alright, well, if you need anything I'm next door finishing up the details of the wedding party that will be staying here this weekend."

"Oh right, I forgot about that."

"Yes. The wedding is late on Saturday night. They expect they won't return until after midnight. I've arranged to have some sandwiches and beverages laid out for them in the parlor in case they have the late night munchies."

"That will be fun: drunken revelers returning home at two in the morning."

"True. But you will recall we agreed to this because they are paying extra for every room."

"Right. They're funding the new gutters."

"Exactly."

"I remember this couple now. The groom has those bushy eyebrows?"

Jonathan laughed. "Yes."

"I think we were betting on them not making it. She was pushy and he was nervous, swallowing every five seconds. We were thinking maybe she was forcing him towards the altar with a pregnancy or something, right?"

"I don't know, Antonia," he said, shaking his head with a smile. "You are much better than me at figuring out what goes on behind closed doors with our guests."

"You mean I'm the snoop and you're the gentleman who discreetly welcomes people to the inn without psychoanalyzing everyone who comes through the door."

"You said it, not me!"

Antonia appreciated that Jonathan was meticulous and personable at his job. His smooth British accent and unassuming manner won over even the most difficult guests, and he had that wonderful ability to make himself scarce when need be. She knew little about his personal life, as he was very private, but she had quickly come to depend upon him when it came to matters regarding the inn. She had hired him after her previous manager/bookkeeper Lucy had been arrested for murder.

As soon as he left, Antonia quietly shut the door. She had been less concerned about the bag falling than she was with the fact that the Lysol can had rolled out and was in plain view. Not that anyone would know she had taken it from the Mastersons', but she still had to be more careful.

"What a mess," Antonia grumbled to herself.

She bent down and stuffed all the contents into her bag. She looked over at the window. It was slightly ajar, but not enough for a large gust of wind to knock down her heavy bag.

Something caught her eye, and Antonia stood up. Resting on her ink blotter was a standard issue white envelope with her name written on it in black cursive. There was no stamp.

"Hand delivered," murmured Antonia.

She slit open the letter with a silver opener and pulled out a white sheet of paper. Antonia unfolded it. There in black ink was written the following:

Are you looking for someone?
Sometimes the obvious is right in front of you.

Antonia turned it over and upside down. There was nothing else on the paper. She picked up the envelope again to confirm that it was addressed to her, which indeed it was. What the hell did this mean? It sounded like something she would find in a fortune cookie. Antonia was confounded until it dawned on her.

"Genevieve."

Antonia shook her head and threw down the letter on her desk. Genevieve was always trying to coerce Antonia out into the dating world. She tried all sorts of tactics and no doubt this was her latest effort: a cryptic message. And it would be typical of Genevieve to knock over Antonia's bag and not bother to pick it up; Antonia shook her head in disappointment. As she knew Genevieve was dining at the restaurant that very moment, it all made sense. Time to confront her.

Antonia turned to exit when she noticed a middle-aged man in a suit and tie standing on her threshold. He had receding brown hair and a lantern jaw and the type of big sharp features that a caricaturist would have a field day with. His gaze was neither warm nor cold, and it was clear to Antonia at once that he was all business.

"Antonia Bingham." He asked but it was more like a statement.

"Yes, can I help you?"

"You can help me and I think we'll need privacy."

He entered her office without invitation and carefully closed the door behind him. She noticed now that he carried a briefcase. Not the sort of thing you see people toting around East Hampton. He placed it on the chair but kept a firm grip on it.

"Okay," said Antonia cautiously. She was more curious than offended by his audacity.

"I'll get right to it. My name is Terry Rudolph," he said while simultaneously shoving the standard rectangular vanilla business card into her palm. She glanced down on it only to learn he was an attorney.

"How can I help you?"

"I work for an individual who would like to purchase something from you. In regards to compensation, you can be assured that we will make it worth your while."

"What is it?" asked Antonia with surprise. She couldn't imagine what this man was talking about.

"We want the footage from Warner Caruthers' documentary."

"The footage . . ." Antonia trailed off. She had not expected this response. "I have no idea where it is."

The man gave her a small smile. His teeth were so white they were off-putting.

"In the interest of time, let's not do this. We both know for a fact that you are in possession of it."

Antonia was more stunned than offended that the man was accusing her of lying.

"Me? I have nothing to do with the documentary . . ."

He continued as if he hadn't heard her. "We are eager to make this transaction quickly. It is of the utmost importance that this does not fall into the wrong hands."

"Are you sure it's in *any* hands? The police must have it by now. I believe they took anything of importance from the Mastersons' house."

"They don't have it," he said flatly.

"But you can't be sure . . ."

"The source of my information is very reliable."

Antonia shook her head in confusion. "Well, I have nothing to do with this matter."

"Ms. Bingham," he said in a tone that suggested impatience. "I can assure you that this matter will be dealt with discreetly. No one will have to know. And it will be beneficial for you as well. No more money issues. You have a beautiful inn."

"Thank you."

"But your overhead must be extremely high for your returns. Not to mention that you have expensive taste . . ." he motioned at the antiques that filled the room.

"Everything is paid for," bristled Antonia. Well, at least the furniture. Sure, she was trying to renegotiate the terms of her mortgage, but she was certain it would be worked out. Or at least she hoped. The settlement from her ex-husband had been completely depleted and she was a little too promiscuous with spending the income from the stocks that her father had left her.

He smiled. "Ms. Bingham, my employer is well-connected to everyone in this town as well as most towns. You do him a favor, he won't forget it. His power reaches far and wide."

"What is that supposed to mean?"

He paused. "Nothing. But I am happy to present to you a lucrative offer, making this arrangement mutually beneficial. My employer is willing to pay you $50,000 for your time and brief effort. Cash."

"Are you joking?"

The man blinked twice but his expression didn't change. "I'm completely serious. Now, shall we do this now?"

Fortunately, she didn't even need to hesitate. She didn't have the footage and had no idea where it was.

"I'm sorry I can't help you. I don't have it. And if I did, I believe it belongs to Warner's family."

The man appeared as if he had expected this answer. He picked up his briefcase. Antonia observed that he had incredibly large hands with rather well-groomed nails. His response came in an unctuous tone. "You don't have to decide now. I'm sure it has been a very difficult day for you. A friend has died, and I am sorry for your loss."

Antonia didn't correct him and allowed him to continue.

"I'll let you sleep on it and be in touch tomorrow."

He turned and left.

Antonia slumped down in her desk chair and took a moment to recover. Who was this man and his mysterious employer? And why had they come to her with the utmost conviction that she had Warner's footage? It was absurd. And who was his 'reliable source'? It was probably all a misunderstanding. Someone had told them that she had found the body and they confused her with someone else. She was sure she would never hear from them again it.

With resolution, Antonia made her way to the dining room to find some friendly faces. Joseph was on his way out when she ran into him.

"Excellent as usual, Antonia," he said with a wide grin, but then noting Antonia's worried look, he inquired, "Everything okay?"

Antonia briefly filled him in on the lawyer while Joseph listened pensively.

"Any idea why they think you have the footage?"

"No! It's so strange."

"I wouldn't worry about it, my dear. If he's a lawyer then he is professional. He'll figure out you have nothing and leave you alone."

"Yes, but if he's working for that corporate raider Sidney Black, the one Larry Lipper told me about who hated Warner, then he may make my life hell. He did say, and I quote, *his power reaches far and wide.* How sinister is that?"

"I'm sure he wanted to inflate his position as a negotiating tactic."

"I don't know."

"Remember what my late wife always used to say," said Joseph. Antonia smiled. "Don't borrow trouble."

"Yes, and I think you should take her advice right now until you have a reason to think differently."

"You're right," said Antonia. "You're totally right."

Antonia continued on to the dining room. As the evening had drawn to a close, the bustling atmosphere in the restaurant had diminished. Now only a smattering of tables were still occupied with guests engaged in muted conversations. She knew or recognized most of the guests this time of year. There were locals who frequented the restaurant, as well as some guests staying at the inn. In the summer it was more of a mixed bag. She noticed her friends Len and Sylvia Powers at a corner table. She remembered that Larry had told her that Len had recently thrown Warner out of the Dune Club. She was eager to know more and made a beeline towards his table.

After briefly discussing the meal, it was obvious that all three of them were itching to discuss the elephant in the room.

"So, Antonia I'm surprised you're even standing. You had quite a shock today," said Sylvia, sympathetically. Sylvia taught third grade at John Marshall Elementary and had that wonderful cozy and maternal aura about her that made you want to fold into her arms for a big hug. Big boned, big breasted and with a big blonde beehive and pink stained lips, she was like your favorite grandmother.

"It was pretty terrible," confessed Antonia.

"I can't even imagine," admitted Len. He was in his early sixties, and boasted a thick mop of steel gray hair that curled around the nape of his neck as well as a stomach as big as Santa Claus'. His skin was weather-beaten as if he had spent a lot of time in the sun, which he had, and he had milky blue eyes that smiled when he talked.

Antonia gave them a brief rundown of the morning's events before directing her attention at Len. "I heard you had met Warner, and that it didn't go that well."

Len nodded. "I didn't get a good impression of that kid."

"Len thought he was a punk," added Sylvia.

"I'm really surprised by that. I had a totally different impression," said Antonia.

Len looked thoughtful. He was someone who carefully chose his words. "Oh, I'm sure he could be charming. He was slick. He tried everything to get my permission for him to film all around the club. Said it was the off-season, no one would know. Offered me money . . ."

"Can you believe that? Offensive," said Sylvia.

"No, he obviously doesn't know what kind of man you are," said Antonia.

"In the beginning, he was friendly. Nice," said Len, his eyes squinting as if he was remembering. "But when it became clear that I wouldn't give in, he got smart with me. I didn't like it. That's when I could see his true colors."

"Wow. That's too bad," said Antonia.

"But still, I think it's a sad ending," said Len. "What a waste. He was still young, could have come out okay at the end."

"People change," said Sylvia. "I've seen it. He could have changed."

After a few more pleasantries, Antonia moved on in the dining room. Her eyes flitted from an elderly couple to an attractive young woman lingering over her cappuccino. Her name was Bridget Curtis. She had checked into the inn two days ago. To Antonia's right, busboys were clearing china from abandoned tables. At the far end of the bar a man was nursing a beer and talking with the bartender. Antonia squinted to catch a better glimpse of his face but Genevieve's voice interrupted her.

"Over here, Antonia!"

Antonia turned and smiled with relief. She tried to brush the last ten minutes out of her mind while she approached her friend.

Antonia observed that Genevieve had worn her latest purchase, a sexy low-cut purple dress that she called her "come hither gown." She insisted that this was the dress that she could get lucky in, but Antonia thought it only accentuated Genevieve's flat chest.

"Antonia, this is Carl," said Genevieve with excitement.

"Nice to meet you," said Antonia.

Carl stood up and shook her hand firmly. "I really enjoyed my dinner, particularly the shrimp."

"Thank you."

Antonia eyed him appraisingly. He was medium height, thin and lean (what Genevieve must consider to be a 'rocking bod') with slightly wavy brown hair and hazel eyes. At first blush he could be dismissed as average, but Antonia discerned that upon closer examination that he had very good bone structure and was indeed handsome. Genevieve had said he was her age, which made him thirty-four, but he had an intensity about him that made him appear older.

"Thanks for the cookies. But you know I didn't need

them," said Genevieve, motioning to the plate Antonia had sent out earlier.

"I can't let you leave without dessert."

"Have a seat with us," said Genevieve.

"I don't want to interrupt."

"Please, Antonia, sit," sat Carl with conviction. "I'd like you to join us. I've heard a lot about you."

Genevieve wiggled her perfectly plucked eyebrows with delight and threw Antonia a look as if to say she couldn't believe her luck. Genevieve's face was always in a constant state of animation. In repose she was absolutely stunning, but when everything was fluttering and moving and wiggling, her features looked as if they didn't really co-exist peacefully on her face.

"Alright," said Antonia. "I could take a load off."

"I told Carl all about your horrible day," said Genevieve, before turning to Carl. "Of course she is such a rock star that despite everything she manages to throw together a kick ass dinner."

He nodded gravely. "Right, right. Are you very shook up?"

"I've had better days, I'll admit. It was not exactly what I was expecting to find this morning."

"And in that neighborhood no less. You generally don't see a lot of police activity on Lily Pond Lane," said Carl before adding, "my grandmother lives not far from the Mastersons . . ."

"She does?" asked Genevieve.

"Yes, that's what brought me back out here. When I was young we spent every summer at her house."

"Me too!" exclaimed Genevieve. "We were in Northwest Woods."

"I didn't even know that part of town existed when I was young," said Carl, taking a sip of his wine.

Genevieve smiled slyly. "Oh, excuse me. I forgot. You were in the fancy part of town. Everything else beneath you."

"It just wasn't on my radar. I had no reason to go there."

"Right. You could walk to the beach. We had to pack all of our stuff and drive down there. I still remember the smell of baloney sandwiches in the cooler. Gross."

Carl leaned back. "East Hampton was so great back then. It was quiet. You could actually go see a movie in the summer whereas now it's a mob scene! Not to mention there were actual stores in town, not all these empty designer showcases."

"I know, do you remember the Cheese Cupboard? And Engel Pottery?" asked Genevieve. She loved talking about old East Hampton to anyone who had been there before the eighties.

"Of course, I remember. Everything was very different. There used to be a liquor store on Main Street now it's some fancy boutique selling junk. And all of the farmland is being eaten up by these horrible McMansions." Carl stopped and looked at Antonia. "You must hate it."

"I wasn't here twenty years ago. I only moved here a year and a half ago, so it's all the same to me and doesn't change how much I love this town," confessed Antonia.

"Yes, but you must resent all the crowds coming in and taking over," insisted Carl. "I mean, doesn't it drive you crazy to have all these tacky hordes of people come crashing in every summer? On their cell phones, with their shopping bags, grabbing lattes at Starbucks! This town is like a suburb now."

"They're my bread and butter!"

"Of course."

"No, but I do like the energy they bring. It can get very quiet here in the winter," said Antonia. "In fact, it's a little trick I have. I like to think of the summer crowd as the flowers that have bloomed. Eventually they will fade away, but we can just enjoy them while they are here," said Antonia.

"I admire your attitude but can't find it in myself to agree," said Carl. "Nor can my grandmother stand it. She says the town has gone to hell in a handbasket. Had she known, she would have bought up more houses just to keep all these people away. They never should have expanded the Long Island Express-way," said Carl.

"It's funny, most of the people I know who lament the development are summer people," noted Antonia. "I mean, of course I want to preserve the integrity of the town. And I too, don't want the land gobbled up by all of these redundant houses. I would like to see the farmland sustained, and I have been working hard with the Historical Society and the Peconic Land Trust to preserve what we can. But I don't feel any more ownership of East Hampton than the people who are only here for one season a year. They pay taxes also."

"Not the renters," said Carl with a touch of disdain.

"True, but a lot of people own houses."

Genevieve could see that both Carl and Antonia were becoming slightly heated, so she tried to veer the conversation in a different direction. "Your grandmother sounds like a hoot. I'd love to meet her some time."

"You will, of course," said Carl firmly. "She used to split her time between here and Florida, but this year she didn't make it down. She's getting old. That's why I moved back here, to help her out."

"That's really nice of you," said Genevieve, stroking his arm. She looked suddenly alarmed. "Wait, did you check on her? What if there is a killer on the loose in her neighborhood? You have to make sure she's okay!"

"I did. I stopped by early this morning. She's fine. In fact, she's so determined to be independent that she *insisted* that I stop looking in on her. Told me she has a very large social calendar and could I please make an appointment next time."

"She sounds like a character," said Antonia.

"To say the least. As feisty as they come. But strong as an ox. I told her I would wait several days before I returned. And call first."

"But what about the guy who killed Warner? He could be roaming around the 'hood stalking his next victim!" exclaimed Genevieve.

"Genevieve, you have an active imagination," said Antonia.

"But, how do you know I'm not right?"

Antonia sighed deeply and shook her head. "I don't. But I wouldn't worry so much. I don't think Warner was murdered."

"Don't be so sure," said Genevieve wiggling her eyebrows.

Carl returned his attention to Antonia. "Are the Mastersons in town?"

"No," said Antonia, shaking her head. "After the police got a hold of Warner's parents, they called to inform them, and then I briefly talked to Robert Masterson afterward. He was pretty devastated. Warner was like a son to him."

"That's awful."

"The police think murder," Genevieve stated confidently.

"The police haven't made any statements yet as to what they think it was," said Antonia, her patience draining. "I think they're not drawing any conclusions until they receive the autopsy results."

"But it's murder for sure."

Antonia shook her head. "Genevieve."

"It's true. It's because of the documentary."

"Ugh, you sound like Larry Lipper."

"I have proof. You remember my friend Tanya?"

"Vaguely . . ."

"Well she is a personal assistant to Edward Hamilton, this rich old guy. Tanya told me that Warner convinced Mr. Hamilton to participate in his documentary and then totally made fun of him and accused him of all sorts of stuff. She said Hamilton was furious, mad as hell. He is all about protecting his family image."

"That doesn't mean he'd murder him, Gen," said Antonia with a weary smile.

"I agree, but what if he uncovered a dark secret that someone didn't want exposed? Something so bad that murder is the only option? Warner created a shit show the past two weeks. People kill for less."

"Come on," said Antonia.

Antonia had what she called a 'Genevieve filter" which

meant that everything Genevieve said had to be taken with a grain of salt. Although not intentionally deceptive, she was dramatic and often exaggerated for effect. Talking with her was often like playing a game of telephone, where if you told her a story, by the time it got back to you it would be completely distorted.

To Antonia's surprise, Carl concurred with Genevieve. "I think Genevieve's theory is entirely possible. You hear of all those people killing themselves because something they have done has been exposed, some secret life, that could also translate to murdering someone. I don't know if what happened to Warner was murder, but I'm sure the police are looking good and hard at those people who participated in the documentary."

Antonia didn't want to conjecture anymore upon Warner's death, especially now that a nagging feeling was growing inside Antonia. She thought of the man who had just offered her money for the tape. Did he work for Edward Hamilton? To what extent would his mysterious "employer" go to obtain it?

Fortunately, the conversation drifted to Carl's background. He'd had an interesting life from the sound of it. He had done everything from working as a trader on the Asian stock exchange to captaining a private sailboat for a Russian oligarch. He explained that he wanted to see as much of the world as possible, have as many adventures as he could, before returning home and starting a family. And he definitely alluded that East Hampton might be his final stop, although not his current "shack" in Springs. He mentioned several times that it was temporary until he found his "dream house." Carl chose his words carefully, speaking with such proper diction that Antonia was sure he had been well educated; he gesticulated languidly with his long fingered hands to emphasize a point. He was nice enough, but Antonia wasn't sure exactly what to make of him. He was definitely a snob and uptight. How that would mesh with Genevieve's character was beyond her. But on the other hand, maybe it was better than the usual slackers that Genevieve seemed to attract.

Carl and Genevieve were wrapping up the story of how *exactly* they met (at a bar; he was celebrating his return to town; he bought her a drink. Not much to tell in Antonia's opinion, but as they were in the giddy throes of new romance she kept a smile plastered to her face) when they were interrupted.

"Excuse me, sorry to bother you."

Antonia wasn't sure what she would expect when she turned around but certainly not the chunk of manhood that she found herself face to face with. In a strangely primal experience that was not the norm for Antonia, she noticed his scent first. It was musty and clean, like soap and other things she couldn't possibly place. But whatever it was, it hit her like a ton of bricks. The tall and muscular man looming over her had close-cropped reddish hair and nicely lashed green eyes. The two-day growth of beard enhanced the intense masculinity that he exuded.

"Can I help you?" asked Antonia.

"I had to meet you while I had the chance. I'm Sam Wilson."

"Nice to meet you. I'm Antonia Bingham."

"I know; your reputation precedes you." He broke into a smile.

Antonia was surprised. "Oh?"

"Yes. You've managed to charm some of the toughest critics around. Most importantly for me, my two buddies Jack Palmer and Stephen Henderson. They have been raving about your food ever since they came here. I'm also in the biz; out here helping my cousin open a restaurant. Palmer and Henderson said I couldn't leave town without coming here."

He was referring to two well-known chefs who had been guests at a wedding at the inn the week after Thanksgiving. It had been one of those magical nights where everything in the kitchen had gone spectacularly well, and Antonia was euphoric. She had no idea that she was cooking for two James Beard award winners until they came into the kitchen and applauded her after the dinner.

"It was the candied bacon jam," said Antonia.

"The candied bacon jam?" repeated Sam, raising his eyebrows.

"It was a last minute thing. I added it to the local bay scallops. The pairing, along with the side of bitter greens, was a complete success."

Sam smiled. "That must be it. Bacon always seals the deal."

"It had *me* at hello," said Antonia, with a smile.

"Would you like to join us?" asked Genevieve.

Sam's eyes broke away from Antonia's as if it was the first time he noticed that she was not seated alone.

"No, I'm sorry to interrupt," he said quickly. "I just had to meet this lady. Unfortunately, the kitchen was already closed by the time I arrived, so I didn't have a chance to sample the food. But meeting you is even better. You're a rock star."

Antonia stood up. "Let me please bring you something from the kitchen, I can't let you leave without tasting the food."

Sam put his hand up. "No, really. I will come back."

"Then at least have a cookie," said Antonia. She held up the plate in front of him and he smiled and selected one. He took a big bite.

"Delicious."

Antonia sat back down.

"What kind of food do you cook?" asked Antonia, embarrassed at the attention.

"I like BBQ, spice, grease."

"Sounds good, where can we get that?" asked Carl.

"It'll be open this summer in the spot where the bagel store was."

"I look forward to that," said Antonia.

"Yum! We'll all go," added Genevieve.

Sam barely glanced at her. His eyes remained on Antonia.

"I'll be back for dinner. For sure."

Antonia hoped that was true. "Let me know and I'll make you some bacon jam."

* * * * *

After Genevieve and Carl called it a night, Antonia realized the dining room was empty, except for Bridget Curtis, who was still nursing her coffee. The room felt strange and eerie, as if the air had been sucked out. Antonia had been so distracted with her conversation about Warner's death and then with that handsome chef Sam introducing himself that she realized she never had the chance to confront Genevieve about the note on her desk. Oh, well, maybe later. Antonia walked over to Bridget and put her hand on the chair across from her.

"How was everything this evening?"

"Great, thanks," said Bridget quickly, not meeting her gaze. Antonia looked at her carefully. She was really extremely pretty, with long, dark hair and big, blue eyes. Antonia guessed she was in her early twenties.

"Are you enjoying your stay in East Hampton?"

Bridget was still not facing her, fumbling under her chair for her clutch. "It's been okay."

Antonia waited for her to continue, but when Bridget turned and looked up at her, she realized she would not. Bridget was staring at her carefully, her eyes both sad and confused. A split second passed where Antonia had a peculiar feeling.

"Is everything okay?"

Bridget hesitated but then smiled brightly.

"Sure, why do you ask?"

Antonia didn't believe her but knew it wasn't her place to say more. She was tempted to pull up a chair and ask Bridget to unload her problems, as she had done with many a guest in the past; but something about this girl held her at arm's length. And with Antonia's friends hinting about her nosiness, perhaps it was best not to meddle.

"I just wanted to make sure your stay with us is pleasurable."

"Infinitely," said Bridget.

Antonia locked eyes with her before glancing away.

"Well, good night then," said Antonia.

Bridget looked away. "Good night."

Antonia walked along the dining room, picking up used glasses, the rims stained with lipstick marks, and several napkins that had fallen on the carpet underneath the table skirts. When she pushed open the kitchen door, Antonia felt an odd sensation. She turned slowly. Bridget was standing at the other end of the room at the entrance, staring at her. Antonia was about to say something, but Bridget quickly hurried away.

5

Antonia nestled under her fluffy comforter and picked up the stack of papers that Joseph had printed out for her earlier. It was an Internet retrospective of the life and times of Warner Caruthers. According to Warner's Facebook page, he had 843 friends and had graduated from Union College. He was a fan of Quentin Tarantino, The Onion, Hooters and Girls Gone Wild, and a member of Baba Booey (the Official Gary Dell'Abate Fan Club.) There were pictures of him and his friends with a pyramid of empty beer cans in front of him, as well as snapshots of him and bikini-clad girls on a beach somewhere. In one of his final postings he had ominously written: *Something major is about to happen.* If only he had known.

She scanned for clues that might tell her something about his death but there was nothing. But then what did she believe, that his Facebook page would explain why he was in Eleanor Masterson's bathroom? Of course that was wishful thinking.

Antonia tried to think back to anything Warner had said about Eleanor. There was nothing. She didn't think they were a couple. Eleanor had been dating the same guy, Teddy, for three years and was madly in love (at least that is what she told Antonia when she met them over Christmas break.) And judging from the pictures it didn't appear that Warner had any shortage of girlfriends. Had she missed the connection? Already Antonia was mad at herself for not picking up on the fact that Warner was causing problems in town with his documentary. Out of loyalty to the Mastersons, she might have tried to talk to him about it. She knew her powers of persuasion were very solid. Now it was too late.

Antonia yawned and put down the pages on top of her nightstand. She contemplated finishing the *New York Magazine* crossword puzzle that lay half finished next to her, but decided against it. Instead, she flicked off the lamp and put her head down on her pillow. Almost simultaneously the phone rang. Startled, Antonia sat bolt upright in bed and fumbled for the receiver. A quick glance at the alarm clock on the nightstand indicated it was 11:45. Who was calling at this hour?

"Hello?"

"It's Scan Security. Is this Antonia Bingham?" inquired a deep baritone voice.

Antonia shot up in bed.

"Yes."

"You are listed as the contact person for the residence at 1111 Egypt Close. Can you please provide the password?"

"733."

"That is correct. Ma'am, an alarm was activated in the zone one region, which is the front door."

It was the Felds' house. Antonia worked as their caretaker as well.

The security man continued. "We tried the 631 number on our call sheet but there was no answer. We sent a cruiser over but he did not see any sign of a break in."

Antonia glanced at her cell phone, which was turned off. Bad.

"I'll be right there."

"I don't think that's necessary. We've deactivated the alarm. The police believe a potted plant tipped over by the wind set it off. They have moved it out of the way and secured the area."

Antonia relaxed a little. "Okay, thank you."

A potted plant was the culprit. That was unfortunate, especially because now the Felds would be charged $250 for the visit from the cruiser. Antonia felt guilty; she should offer to pay. Her cell should have been on. And shouldn't she have noticed that the planter appeared unstable? Wasn't that her job? She prided herself on being meticulous. With a sigh, Antonia rose and walked into the bathroom. It was her favorite room in her apartment because it housed the hundreds of creams, bath products, fancy shampoos and conditioners that she adored. Antonia was a sucker for any and all beauty products, particularly the "free with purchase" ones. She took a large clot of firming cream and began slathering it all over her legs, an attempt to utilize some of her nervous energy. The possible benefit for a stressful day was at least she'd get softer skin.

A sudden wave of anxiety shot through Antonia. First the Mastersons' house; now the Felds'? Was there more to this than meets the eye? Was she just paranoid because of what happened this fall with someone she deeply trusted turning out to be a killer? She wasn't sure. Antonia put down the tube of cream and marched out of the bathroom. She had no choice. She'd have to go check on the Felds' house. After pulling on a cashmere sweater, a long prairie skirt and slipping on her Uggs, she was ready.

Antonia walked through her tidy pink living room and flipped on the light in the kitchenette. Her bag was on the counter. Antonia stopped. The illicit Lysol can was still inside. She had to deal with it. It was not exactly the thing she wanted to be walking around with. She opened the kitchen cabinet under the sink and placed it inside next to her a bucket full of sponges, dishwashing gloves and Windex. It would look right at home. After grabbing a fleece, she closed her door.

The backyard of the inn was empty. Antonia's eyes fell on every corner but they revealed nothing out of the norm. The gusty, stinging air was a shock after the warmth of her cozy apartment. She rubbed her hands together. The wind was zipping though the maple trees and the branches were flailing in frantic little jerks. Antonia glanced up at the inn, but all the bedroom windows were dark with the exception of Joseph's. He was a night owl, often working deep into the early morning hours. She was tempted to enlist him to accompany her, but she didn't want to bother him. She knew he was on deadline for a manuscript. Her eyes moved across the other windows and stopped suddenly. She could have sworn she saw movement in one of the darkened windows. She did the math in her head and realized it was the one that Bridget was staying in. Antonia squinted but saw nothing. She must have been mistaken. Bridget had made her feel uneasy. The girl was troubled. She'd have to keep an eye on her.

After flicking on her iPod and allowing Stevie Nicks' voice to fill the silence, Antonia backed out of the inn's driveway and headed east on Route 27, towards the center of East Hampton village. She promised herself to make this as quick a trip as possible. She would have a brief glance at the Felds' house, everything would be okay, and she could return to bed.

Antonia passed the graveyard dotted with headstones dating back to the seventeenth century. She remembered that the first time she'd visited the town she'd been struck by the fact that the cemetery was front and center, boldly marking the dead. In California, cemeteries were tucked away and hidden. Here it was part of the mosaic of the town. Antonia often saw tour groups being led through and children doing grave rubbings with their teachers. She liked the fact that the past was integrated with the present. Somehow it was comforting. But tonight she had a quick flash of Warner being lowered into a grave and it made her recoil. She pressed on the pedal. She passed Mulford Farm and other historic buildings with expansive yards where fairs and antique shows were held throughout the year. The village green, a broad lawn where cattle once roamed freely when East Hampton was a farming town, was now on her right followed by Guild Hall, the cultural performance center where she often attended plays with Joseph. She was looking forward to summer's upcoming schedule. In fact, she was looking forward to everything summer.

What had bothered Antonia most about living in California was that nothing ever seemed to change. It was like the movie "Groundhog Day" where every day is exactly the same. It was hard to punctuate memories when the sun is eternally shining and people are always doing exactly the same things. There was something to be said about the hardship of the seasons. Winter, when the village green was blanketed by snow and the trees were bare, was for hibernation. It meant what little free time Antonia had was spent doing cozy reading at the library, sampling restaurants where she could never secure a table during the high season, and the occasional stolen trip to Buckskill Skating rink where everyone plopped inside for hot chocolate and marshmallows by the fire afterwards. There was also a lot of downtime, and waiting. January and February were particularly quiet. Most businesses closed during those months because it made more financial sense to shut down during that time. The land was gray and dark, the days very short; on the plus side, her fewer customers came earlier and drank more. But all this had made Antonia all the more appreciative when spring arrived. It had still only been her first full winter there so there was the novelty effect. She wondered if that would change if she were here for several years.

Antonia glided down Main Street. Most of the storefronts were empty, having been closed for the winter. The "For Rent" signs had come down and it looked as if some of the "pop up stores"—boutiques like Hermès and Michael Kors that opened exclusively in the summer—were starting to stock their shelves again. At this late hour, the shiny boutiques stood idle, the expensive clothes and jewelry in their windows ignored. The town was dead.

Antonia put on her right blinker and turned down Fithian Lane, a one way street near Citarella. She drove to the stop sign and made a right and then a left onto Egypt Close. Down the block, she pulled into the Felds' driveway. The house was dark.

"Well, let's do it," Antonia said, tapping her fingers on the steering wheel.

The Felds were amongst the first people Antonia had met in East Hampton. An energetic couple in their mid-fifties, they were fine dining and travel enthusiasts, much like Antonia. They had been introduced at a wine tasting at Morrell's and hit it off after debating the merits of South Fork versus North Fork wine. Impressed by Antonia's knowledge and wit on the matter, they invited her to join their wine club, which was filled with an eclectic group of foodies and connoisseurs who instigated emphatic debates. When the Felds discovered she had taken on the job of looking after the Mastersons' house they asked her to check on their house as well, and paid her much more than she deserved.

Antonia opened the car door and made her way up to the slate path. The Felds' house was smaller than the Mastersons', and could not have been more different structurally. They had employed a modern architect to "reimagine" a country barn. They used the actual oak frame from an 18th century structure in Pennsylvania, and attached a modern silo cylinder with a conical roof. The house's windows were large-paned and enormous. A giant red front door, huge enough to allow cattle to enter if ever the need arose, loomed in the front exterior like a rosy red mouth on a twenties film siren. Antonia glanced at the offending potted plant and slid it even further away from the house. There, that would take care of it. She dusted off her hands and unlocked the door and paused on the threshold. Silence and a rush of stale air greeted her.

Antonia quietly entered. The alarm started beeping and Antonia quickly entered the code on the panel to silence it. She decided to follow her usual route, as if it was just another day of checking to make sure everything was in place. She flicked on the overhead light in the front hall. The downstairs was almost completely one large open space, making it very easy for Antonia to ascertain that nothing was amiss. Exposed oak beams crisscrossed the ceiling and flowed down to the stained cherry wood floor. The centerpiece of the room was the large fireplace with a river stone mantel on the north wall. The furniture was mission style; simple wooden chairs that were more function over comfort (she knew this first-hand because every time she sat in one her ass hurt) and square tables. The simplicity highlighted the various wall hangings, ceramics and sculptures from the Felds' impressive collection of works from the Arts and Crafts Movement. It wasn't exactly Antonia's taste, but she appreciated their commitment to it.

She ascended the steep wood stairs to the balcony of the great room and made her way through the three bedrooms with en suite baths. The beds were sturdy and plain, with wooden headboards and antique quilts in rich geometric patterns neatly tucked around the mattresses. There was nothing to distinguish the master bedroom from the additional bedrooms with the exception of a large bookcase filled with a carefully curated pottery collection.

By now, Antonia probably knew the Mastersons' and the Felds' houses better than they did. To her, it wasn't as if the life was extinguished when the denizens left town. The houses were their own entities. It sounded strange, but she had come to understand the rhythm and pulse of them better than anyone.

She wandered back downstairs before stopping to check on the back door by the kitchen. She confirmed that the door was locked. A glance around the kitchen revealed nothing out of the norm. Antonia glanced up at the gabled skylight. The murky blackness obscured all vision of the sky.

With a sigh of relief, Antonia walked back to the front door. Perhaps it was because she was approaching from a different angle, but this time Antonia noticed that something was under the doormat. As she grew closer she could see that it was a manila envelope. With curiosity, Antonia picked it up. She thought it might be one of those real estate newsletters that agencies stuff into mailboxes or shove under their door alerting them to the latest sales in their neighborhood. The Felds would have no interest in that. It wasn't sealed or even closed, so Antonia felt little remorse pulling out the pages inside.

She felt herself grow weak as she read the contents.

"Oh my God!" she said, extending a hand to steady herself, and ultimately leaning on the closest object, which was the shoulder of a large statue of a Native American in full regalia. Hopefully his fierceness would rub off, since the envelope did not contain a real estate listing. Not at all.

Antonia pulled out her cell phone. She prayed Joseph would still be up.

"Am I waking you?" she asked when he answered.

"Of course not, my dear, is everything alright?"

Antonia filled him in on the alarm that led her to the Feld's before disclosing the contents of the manila envelope. "I thought it was a real estate listing, one of those things that they slide under your door when a house in your neighborhood is sold . . ."

"Hmmm . . . I don't think they do that in East Hampton," said Joseph.

"I know. That should have been my first clue, but I wasn't thinking. They did it all the time in L.A. But that's beside the point. Inside the envelope was . . ." She paused.

"Antonia, are you still there?"

"Yes. It was a dossier. About *me*."

"What did it say?"

"It's . . ." she hesitated. "It's a file on me. They have everything. Medical files. Do you remember the time I told you about when I was in the hospital as a teenager?"

"Of course."

"Well, that's in there. How did they find this all out? That was supposed to be sealed."

"It's hard to keep anything secret."

Antonia gulped. She didn't even want to think of that part of her life. Joseph was the only person who knew about it, and they never discussed it. It was all devastating. She continued flipping through the file.

"There's so much about Philip. The articles on what happened at the end of our marriage . . ." Her voice broke. She hated to think about the violent last night where everything came to an end. "And there's more. There are current pictures of him. Coming out of what must be his house. It's so creepy. I don't want to be reminded of any of this!"

Joseph paused before answering. "You think it's the lawyer? The man with the briefcase?"

"I don't know. But my instinct says yes. If his 'employer' is powerful enough, he can buy anything."

"This is very troubling."

"I know." Antonia paused to flick through the current photos. Philip looked the same—tightly wired and tense. Only slightly older. But still mean.

"Well, you can find anything out on the Internet, as we well know."

"I guess," said Antonia. "But I had Philip's last name then. And I didn't go out much during my marriage, because remember, I was a virtual prisoner. So, it's not easy to find many people who knew me. The scary thing is that Warner has been dead only twenty-four hours and they already have all this stuff on me in order to blackmail me."

"If it is the lawyer," said Joseph.

"You think it's someone else?" asked Antonia, her voice rising. "That's even scarier."

"No, don't worry. It's probably him. Of course you can't prove anything; couldn't even go to the police if you were so inclined. But don't worry. If that man comes calling again, I want to be there."

"What do you think he expects to do with all this? It's not something I want out there but it's not like I'm hiding it. It wouldn't change my mind or make me take money to keep this a secret."

"I think he probably wants to show you he's in control. These are serious people you're dealing with."

"Great."

"We can handle them. Now, it's time to come home and have a good night's sleep."

"Okay."

"I'll watch for your car lights."

"Thanks, Joseph."

Antonia pulled out of the Felds' driveway aggressively and made a left onto Egypt Lane. Where she first felt alarm, now she felt anger. What could be so important about Warner's footage that someone would want to destroy her life for it? And why did they think she had it? Antonia shuddered. She hadn't seen the envelope when she was on her way in, and she thought it was because of the angle of the door as it opened. But what if it hadn't been there? What if the lawyer had followed her and slipped it under the door when she was upstairs? She shuddered.

Antonia stared hard into her rear view mirror. Was the lawyer following her? Should she be concerned? There were no cars behind her but the thick darkness and the scarcity of streetlights made it difficult to see. In front of her, heavy fog rolling off the ocean spread out against her windshield and curled itself into the corners. The air was dense. Antonia slowed down, realizing she was speeding. Suddenly, she blinked rapidly. She thought she saw a figure walking along the road. It appeared that the person was dragging something. When Antonia approached, she saw a woman in a thin trench coat pulling a black suitcase. The woman glanced at Antonia stealthily and quickened her pace. Antonia was about to continue on, but reconsidered. She glanced at the clock on her dashboard and it said 12:23. She shouldn't leave this woman outside in the middle of the night if there were people like the lawyer with the briefcase lurking around. Antonia rolled down the window.

"Do you need a ride?"

The woman looked startled. She quickly shook her head. "No, thanks, I'm just going to Spaeth Lane."

If she had been driving, or even walking in the daytime, Spaeth Lane was an acceptable distance. In the middle of a pitch-black night, it did not seem that close.

"Are you sure? It will only take me two minutes to drive you."

The woman hesitated. She was pretty, Filipina, with a round, pretty face; approximately in her early thirties, her dark hair was neatly pulled back into a small knot. Antonia could see that underneath her coat she wore a black maid's uniform, the very formal type that Antonia had only seen in movies that took place in grand manors. She looked tired, but was obviously unsure if she should accept a ride from a complete stranger.

"I'm Antonia Bingham. I own the Windmill Inn, and I promise, I'm very safe. Although saying that makes me seem strange. Sorry. We can keep the windows down so you can jump out at any time."

The woman squinted, and walked closer. Antonia must have appeared harmless because the woman finally nodded.

"Okay, if it's no bother. Thank you."

"You can put your suitcase in the back seat."

The woman opened the door and placed her black roller suitcase inside. She sat in the passenger seat. "Thank you. My name is Francine."

"Francine, it's really late to be walking around by yourself. Where are you coming from?"

"I took the Jitney out from the City."

The Hampton Jitney was the commuter bus line that ran between Manhattan and the Hamptons. It was fancier than your average Greyhound, offering free magazines, beverages and snacks, as well as complimentary bestselling books during high season.

"And no one could pick you up?"

She shook her head. "I can't call my boss. He would not be happy. I was to take a taxi but there were none. I can walk. It is a nice night and I sat so long on the bus."

Antonia noted that her boss must be a bit of a jerk if he let her roam around this late. She started driving slowly, for fear there were others like this woman walking down the road and she may hit them. She put on her left blinker when she reached the stop sign.

"Do you live out here year round?"

"No, I work in the city, but my boss is out here for a few weeks to put his boat in the water for the season. I came to help. I usually go back to New York on my days off. It was supposed to be Friday but yesterday afternoon my boss said, "Go, go!", so I went. He had a private meeting at the house. I heard him talking. He did not want me there. But he wanted me back tonight. He's going sailing tomorrow."

"Ah, a sailor. I know nothing about sailing. I like the idea of sitting on a boat for about ten minutes but then it makes me antsy. It's not really my thing."

"Me neither. My boss loves it. He also plays golf. He wants to join the Dune Club but they won't let him in. He's trying very hard."

"It's a difficult club to get into," agreed Antonia. They were passing it now, although it was too dark to see the lush greens.

"Yes. I know. My boss is very mad he can't play there. He lives almost next door, and they won't let him in. I don't understand why. He has a lot of money."

Antonia smiled. "Money can't buy everything."

"He says his ex-wife is to blame."

"Bitter divorce?"

"Yes. He left her for another woman. She was very angry."

Obviously, Francine was a chatty bird, thought Antonia.

All too ready to spill her employer's secrets. "That's too bad," said Antonia.

"Yes, Mr. Black hates his ex-wife. I'm glad they don't have kids."

Antonia felt as if she had received an electric shock. She turned to Francine. "Wait, *who* is your boss?"

"I work for Mr. Sidney Black. He's right there on the beach. Big house. Very famous house, it's been in magazines."

Antonia's jaw dropped. She looked at Francine aghast. "Sidney Black?"

"Yes," said Francine furrowing her eyebrows.

"The guy who runs BBK?"

Francine nodded. "You know Mr. Black?"

"Yes, I mean, no, no. I just heard his name for the first time today. This is so strange."

Antonia's mind raced and she tried to make sense of everything. What are the chances that she'd have Sidney Black's housekeeper in her car tonight, of all nights? She had to think of how to proceed.

"Francine, does the name Warner Caruthers mean anything to you?"

"Warner?" repeated Francine. "No, I don't think so."

Antonia felt a ping of disappointment. She tried another tack. "Did you hear anything about a documentary about rich people in East Hampton?"

"Oh yes!" she exclaimed with excitement. "I heard about that movie. Sheila, that is the ex-wife, gave a big interview to the guy who made the movie. Mr. Black was not happy."

She wasn't sure how, but Antonia felt like she was connecting the dots. She slowed the car down, eager to extend the trip and her conversation.

"And what is Mr. Black like when he's not happy?"

With this Francine smiled. "Mr. Black gets very angry. You can ask anybody, he has a lot of enemies. Last week he yelled at his next-door neighbor so loudly, I thought the police would be called."

"Does he ever become violent?"

"Oh no, not like that. Just mad, really mad."

"Francine," began Antonia. "The young man who made that movie, his name was Warner Caruthers, was found dead this morning."

Francine's hand flew to her mouth. "No! Terrible."

"I know."

Francine's eyes grew. "But you don't think Mr. Black . . ."

"No, no, sorry, I don't want to give you that impression. No one has said murder yet. It's still possible he slipped and fell in the bathtub."

"Horrible!"

"I know, a terrible accident."

Antonia paused. She should stop now; move on from the conversation. But anyone who knew her knew that wasn't her style. "I do think it is strange that there seem to be so many people who hated this young man. So many people who could become very angry."

Francine stared in front of her quietly. Antonia could see her mind was churning through the new information. "Do you think Mr. Black did something?"

"I don't think that. But you just told me he became upset about this movie, he has a quick temper and he mysteriously and abruptly sent you away last night so he could have a meeting."

"I shouldn't have said anything," said Francine, shaking her head.

"No, no, of course, I don't want to cause you trouble. I'm just thinking out loud. Who was the meeting with, do you know?"

Francine hesitated before she spoke. "No, I'm not sure."

Antonia could tell Francine was holding back and she felt that she had pushed enough. It was only right that Francine was loyal to her employer, even if he was a jerk. But Francine might be able to place the man with the briefcase with Sidney Black. She would need to gain her trust in order to further question her. For now, Antonia dropped her interrogation and turned right on Spaeth Lane. They continued in silence until Francine finally pointed at a driveway.

"This one."

There was a small white sign with the initials S.C.B. stenciled in black. Antonia started to pull in when Francine stopped her.

"I'll get out at the end of the driveway. I don't want to wake Mr. Black."

"Sure," said Antonia, putting the car in park. She was worried that she had gone too far and scared off Francine.

Francine opened the car door and then retrieved her suitcase. "Thank you for the ride."

"Listen, Francine, sorry if I stepped out of line. I was the one who found Warner Caruthers this morning. It shook me to the core and I suppose my mind is spinning with all those mystery novels I read. I don't want to suggest anything about Mr. Black."

"No, don't worry."

"Here's my card, if you ever need me," said Antonia, fumbling in her purse and pulling out a wilted card. She handed it to Francine, who put it in her pocket before pulling up the handle of her suitcase and walking up the driveway. Antonia watched as Francine disappeared into the darkness.

6

WEDNESDAY

Antonia walked along the beach as the foamy waves lapped at the edge of the surf, displacing shells and small stones. She strolled past the large mansions hovering on the cusps of the high sand dunes and drank in the salty air. Beach walks were like meditation and yoga and massage all rolled up into one. She was so lost in thought planning her strategy on how to deal with the lawyer with the briefcase that she didn't notice the two golden labs approaching her from behind until they were jumping all over her frantically. Their fat pink tongues hung eagerly out of their drooling mouths. Her heart quickened and she turned around.

"Hey you! Didn't you hear me calling your name?"

It was *him*.

"No, sorry, I was spacing out."

Antonia felt a familiar burning sensation rising up inside her. Nick Darrow was the reason.

The dogs continued jumping up at Antonia, their wet sandy paws making marks on her clothes. She leaned down to pet them, happy to avert her eyes from him for a moment so she could pull herself together. Genevieve always told her that when she felt anxious in the presence of a cute man she should chant in her mind: *I am a Goddess; I am a Goddess; Bend down and Worship Me.* She had laughed in her face at the time but now it was the only thing that popped in her head. She could throttle Genevieve at this moment. At least now it was easier to focus on the absurdity of the statement than the heat she felt emanating from Nick.

"Down, Ernie! You too, Maggie!"

"It's okay," said Antonia. "I don't mind."

"Well, they're definitely happy to see you," he said with a smile.

"I'm happy to see them," said Antonia, rubbing Maggie's forehead.

"And I'm happy to see you."

She felt herself blush. Dammit! Nick Darrow made her feel like a teenager in love. It was an infantile crush, but her feelings were utterly uncontrollable on this issue. He was charming and sexy with an intensity that she found irresistible. He had a full head of thick dark hair, penetrating blue eyes and delicious lips. He was also a mega movie star, who happened to be married to another mega movie star. Therefore all romantic feelings towards him were utterly ridiculous.

"Welcome back."

"Thanks."

"How was Australia?"

"Beautiful. Great country. But I missed this place. Four months is a long time to be away from home."

"I know. I can imagine."

"I felt so removed and out of it. Was on the set all day and then . . . well, it's very far away. I'm playing catch up on everything."

"Yeah, you didn't miss that much."

"Fill me in."

Antonia prattled on about local news, and Nick was such an attentive listener that she found herself telling him about her awful discovery of Warner's body in the tub. His face awash with concern.

"That's awful," said Nick.

"Yes, it's so sad," said Antonia, eager to change the subject. "So has Finn settled back into school?"

"He's thrilled to be back but now Melanie wants to take Finn with her to France while she shoots a film but I don't want to pull him out of school yet again, so she's all in a huff."

Melanie was Nick's wife. Hence, the utterly unrealistic emotions that Antonia felt for him.

"I see," said Antonia, staring pensively at the sand.

"He only has about six more weeks of school, I don't know why she can't wait. I'm here, I'm not working right now, and she can come back and visit for a weekend."

"You can't deny him, Paris, Nick."

"I'm not denying him Paris. . . ."

"We're talking *Gay Paree*! The Eiffel Tower, the Marais,

the Louvre! Not to mention the most fantastic food on earth. Close your eyes and conjure up the image of hunks of fresh baked sourdough bread smeared with gooey cheese. That is living. Now throw in a bottle of Bordeaux and you've got me!"

Nick smiled. "Okay, but Finn is seven and even though the drinking laws are more liberal over there, I don't think he'd be interested in a bottle of wine."

"You know what I mean!"

"I know, I know. France *is* great."

"Great? No. Finding a parking space on Main Street in August is great. France is *amazing*. I mean, you are talking to a cook. Those are my people there. They know food and wine and life. The coffee! The pain au chocolat! Fois gras! Oh, what I would do to have dinner again at L'Ami Louis. The chicken with duck fat potatoes is simply divine. The skin is crunchy on the outside, like a crust, then tender inside. And the salty potatoes, well . . ." Antonia glanced off at the sky, thoughts of Paris filling her mind. "Hey, forget bringing Finn, Melanie can take me!"

When she had finished her monologue, Antonia glanced over at Nick, who was looking at her with amusement. "I didn't realize you worked for the French Tourism Board."

"I get pretty worked up."

"To say the least," said Nick, shaking his head with a smile. "One thing we can all agree on is you certainly have a zest for life."

Antonia blushed and thrust her hands in the deep pockets of her sweater. They continued walking, and she stole a glimpse of him out of the corner of her eye. She tried to be critical: he wasn't as handsome as he used to be; his face was deeply lined and slightly puffy, as if he had been drinking heavily; his once lustrous dark hair was now salt and pepper; he was bulkier than he should be, especially now that he was in his late forties.

None of that really bothered her. Damn. What she also saw was a powerful man, full of strength and complicated emotions. He might not be physically perfect, like say, Sam, the chef she had met last night (not that she was looking). But Nick's passion and energy were undeniable. He was the most charismatic man she had ever met.

"You really think we should go with her?" Nick asked suddenly. He gave her a hard look, one that demanded honesty and truth. His intensity always took her off guard, and yet it was what she found the most thrilling about him.

Antonia's pulse raced. The idea of him going away yet again made her stomach turn; but it wasn't good to nurse this childish crush. She stole a glance at him. He was staring distractedly out at the water. Ribbons of white fluff cut up the blue waves, breaking in zigzag lines.

"I think you have to pick your battles."

"But it's the way she does it. She sets everything up like a battle. She's the most passive aggressive person I've ever met."

Antonia remained silent.

"Sorry, I don't mean to vent. Let's just say . . . Australia wasn't all fun and shrimp on the barbie."

Antonia smiled slightly. "It's okay, I know, marriage is hard."

"Were you ever married?"

Antonia paused. She glanced over at him, but seeing that he was still full of fury over his wife, she decided now was not the time to address it.

"Oh, ask me no questions, I'll tell you no lies," said Antonia slyly.

He eyed her curiously. "You play it coy, lady, but don't think I don't notice that you shut down every personal question I ask you. We walked on the beach together almost every day last November, with me babbling to you about everything. You barely mentioned that you almost got offed by the manager of your inn. You told me nothing of your past. And I thought I'm the one who's supposed to be protective of my personal life. Hell, if I do *anything* it ends up in one of those gossip rags. What is it about you that makes me tell you everything?"

She felt the blood race to her cheeks. It was one of those moments where she knew if she deflected the question they might never attain a deeper level of friendship. But it was scary, because is that what she wanted from him? Did he really care about her or was he just being nice? And could she risk making herself vulnerable? Finally, the words came out of her.

"I was married once. But he was a total jerk. And that's putting it mildly. *Sleeping with the Enemy* times ten. I suppose I deflect all of the personal questions you ask me because it's painful to think about him."

She felt relieved once she had told him. Nick was an emotional, passionate person, so he would not take what she said lightly.

"Antonia! I had no idea. I'm sorry."

"It's okay," she shrugged. "I am over it."

Nick gave her a long look. "You're strong. I'm sure you're okay."

"Yes, I am."

Philip had tried to make her feel weak, and succeeded for a long time, but then somehow she was able to fight back. Now, in reflection, it felt strange that she was ever with him. She couldn't imagine she would have allowed it. But she had been young. And in the beginning, she thought he was a knight in shining armor. He was handsome, confident, strong—a police officer, for lord's sake. He took charge, and made all the decisions for her, which at first she appreciated. But then he became all about control. And that's when her life really became terrible. It took a terrible trauma and the death of her father for her to finally muster the strength to leave him.

Antonia realized she was a million miles away and Nick was now staring at her quizzically. Finally, he spoke.

"Sometimes it's hard to understand how we end up with the people we do. It can take awhile to understand how wrong, or how right it is. But people make mistakes. It happens. It's what they do about it. How strong they are to change it."

She knew he was talking about him and Melanie but she didn't want to go down that road anymore. It was true, she and Nick had both married the wrong person for them. But he would probably stay, whereas she got out. They continued in silence towards the jetty, the dogs running in and out of the water, retrieving sticks and a chewed up yellow tennis ball. For just a moment, Antonia could imagine what it would be like to be in a relationship with Nick Darrow. Then the moment passed.

7

Antonia was in the parking lot shaking the sand out of her shoes when her cell phone buzzed.

"Who was the girl Warner was shacking up with?" demanded the voice on the other end of the line.

"What happened to pleasantries, Larry?" asked Antonia.

"Got no time, got no time, hot stuff. Deadlines, baby. Now talk to me."

Antonia sighed and unlocked her car door. She sat down and braced herself for another irritating conversation with Larry Lipper.

"I don't know what you're talking about."

"Come on! Be useful here. You must have some idea. I talked again to Len Powers at the Dune Club. He was pretty defensive about the possibility that it might be one of his members so I tried a different angle, that maybe it was someone else. That jogged his memory a bit. He remembered that after he told Warner to pack up and get the hell off club property, the cameraman bolted but a woman in a car pulled up. Warner chatted with the bird for a few minutes and she followed him in her car when he left."

"Rings no bells. I have no idea who he was associating with."

"Really? Come on."

"I swear."

"Geez, you're no help."

"What kind of car?" asked Antonia out of curiosity.

"Len only remembers German. Black. Said if his life depended on it he couldn't remember if it was a BMW or a Mercedes. Clearly not a detail person."

"Yeah. It's a pity," said Antonia sarcastically. She knew that Len would have no interest in helping a newspaper reporter; he was all about discretion. The old guard who were members of the Dune Club did everything they could to stay out of the paper, and away from prying eyes of any sort. As their head of security, they relied on Len to be the gatekeeper.

Suddenly, something Larry said struck her. "Wait, there was a cameraman?"

"What?"

"You said that there was a cameraman with Warner at the Dune Club."

"Duh! How else would he film the documentary?"

"Where is he now?"

"No one has a beat on him. Warner didn't introduce him to any of the people he interviewed, or at least the ones I talked to didn't pay a speck of attention to the guy's name so they don't know where to find him."

"But what about the police? Surely, they can locate him?"

"If they have, they ain't talking. I'm trying every angle to find this jackass."

"Because the footage is a motive," Antonia said more to herself. She thought of the lawyer. Why wasn't he trying to track down the cameraman? Was he unable to find him?

"I knew you were convinced he was murdered!" squawked Larry with delight.

"No, I am not. . . ." Antonia backtracked. "But I'm curious about what will happen to the documentary. Who even owns the rights to it now?"

"It depends on what sort of agreement he had with his cameraman. If they were partners, he'd receive a cut. But my hunch is Warner was the boss, which means probably Warner's parents retain the rights. Maybe they'll take on their son's cause in a last hurrah. He died while "seeking the truth" bullshit. What do the Mastersons say?"

"They're traveling in Europe. I only talked to Robert Masterson briefly."

"They have all the answers. So here are your marching orders: ask them or their son—the one who was friend's with Warner . . ."

"Luke."

"Whatever. Ask them who Warner was banging and who his cameraman was. Then we will recon and go from there."

"Larry, I'm not your partner on this."

"For God's sake, Antonia. Do me a solid. You owe me."

He hung up before Antonia could decipher what she owed him for. Was it for not sleeping with him?

* * * * *

Antonia returned to the inn and promised herself that she would chain herself to her office until she finished everything to which she needed to attend. This meant no Warner anything until she was done with work. It was time to push it all out of her head for now and focus on business. As it was, the surface of her antique roll-top desk was covered with various papers and spreadsheets that needed to be systematically filed, shred or discarded. The tan leather in-box was overflowing with a large stack of mail that needed her attention, including several big bills that needed to be paid, which was always a source of stress.

The Windmill Inn was usually at its lowest capacity on Wednesdays so it was a good 'maintenance day.' The restaurant was closed after the buffet breakfast (which meant no dinner service) and the kitchen shut for an industrial-strength scrub-down. Rosita and her team dismantled all of the common areas and every available room for a thorough cleaning. All of the light fixtures and silver candlesticks were polished, Oriental throw carpets were removed and dusted outside, the floors were waxed, curtains and bed skirts steamed and any necessary repairs performed. Large deliveries from the farmers and alcohol purveyors were received in the first half of the day. The sheets and linens were sent out to the laundry in the second half of the day.

Needless to say, it was Antonia's least favorite day of the week. She would always rather be in the kitchen cooking or chatting with guests. Desk work wasn't her skill set. She was a people person and a chef. She was definitely not meant to sit behind a desk. It had been torture for her during the slower months of January through March when the restaurant had only been open from Thursday through Sunday. (It had been a fiscal decision. Most of the restaurants in the Hamptons did the same during the winter months. The idea had actually been suggested to her by her former manager Lucy, who despite her flaws did have good business acumen. If she had only stuck to bookkeeping and managing and not murder, she might not be sitting in prison awaiting twenty-five years to life.)

At twelve o'clock the front desk bell interrupted Antonia's toils. As Connie, her front desk receptionist, was on her lunch break, Antonia was on call. She braced herself to greet the lawyer but instead found with relief that it was Bridget waiting at the reception desk. Once again Antonia was struck by how familiar she was. Maybe she was an actress? Her face was pretty enough, and she had that air of sophistication. She wore minimal makeup, which was already unnecessary, and simple jewelry. She had on a cream colored turtleneck and a long black cardigan that she held closed as if she was cold.

"Can I help you?"

She looked startled and turned abruptly to face Antonia. "Oh, yes, I wanted to make sure I didn't have any messages."

"Let me check," said Antonia with a pleasant smile. The front desk was a glossy walnut surface illuminated by a brass lamp with a green glass shade. Behind the desk was an antique post office cubby that she used to corral any correspondence for her guests.

"We usually indicate phone messages by a red flashing light on the handset next to your bed, but sometimes people don't want to leave a voice mail and want the actual human contact."

The girl didn't respond.

"Are you awaiting something in particular?" asked Antonia, glancing back at her.

"Just checking," said the girl.

Antonia discovered the cubby to Room Six to be empty.

"I'm not finding anything," said Antonia. "I'm sorry."

Bridget's face remained unmoved. "That's okay."

"But I will make sure if someone calls to put it right through or try to track you down. Is there anything else I can help you with?" asked Antonia pleasantly.

Bridget glanced at her evenly. "No, thanks."

And before Antonia could respond, Bridget quickly walked away.

Suddenly, a memory jarred her. Last week, Warner had stopped by the inn to ask for another copy of the key to the Masterson's house. He said he was sorry, but he had lost his copy. And she remembered that on his way inside he had stopped. Someone had stopped him. And he spent several minutes talking to that person, who was entering with her luggage. Bridget Curtis. They talked until she was led away to her room by Connie. What was the connection?

"You look lost in space," said Joseph.

Antonia had been so consumed by her reverie that she hadn't heard Joseph's scooter approach.

"I'm distracted. Come on into my office, I think it's time for a break."

Joseph followed Antonia. She pushed the armchair across from her desk to the side, and moved various piles of magazines and coffee table books out of Joseph's way. She took two blue mugs down from the shelf above the mini-refrigerator and with her instant kettle, made them each a mug of milky Earl Grey tea. After handing one to Joseph, she sat down at her desk and offered him the plate of savory muffins, roasted red pepper and feta, that she had left over from breakfast. He selected a small one, with Antonia taking a much larger muffin. She bit into the salty confection with relish. It was obviously a no-no in terms of her diet, but she tried to focus on the fact that it at least included vegetables, which added some nutrition.

"Tasty. New recipe?"

"Yes. Trying to branch out in my muffin making."

"Good idea. This one is a success."

"How's your work going?"

"Slowly as usual. I've spent the morning mired in hemophilia.'

"Hemophilia? Why?"

"I'm studying the Romanov family. Nicholas II's son suffered from it. They always thought that would be what killed him. But alas, he and his entire family were slaughtered in the cellar of their house."

"Joseph! Please, that is so depressing," said Antonia.

"True. But I find the Romanov dynasty fascinating," he insisted.

Joseph had written six acclaimed books of fiction centered around World War I. *The War That Changed Us* was his most successful, having been nominated for a Pulitzer Prize and landing itself on the bestseller list for forty-three weeks. The others were just as acclaimed. It took him several years to research each book, a slow and methodical process that Antonia believed he enjoyed more than the actual writing.

"I would so much rather focus on fictional murder that what's going on right here," sighed Antonia.

"You're right. Sorry to ask, but any news from the lawyer?"

"No."

Antonia took a gulp of her tea.

"Then you shouldn't look so troubled."

"Joseph, do you think maybe I should just go to the police and do a full mea culpa and hand over the Lysol can? I'll beg ignorance and that will be that."

She waited for Joseph's response with the assumption that he would agree. His response surprised her. "You could do that . . ."

"But?"

"But, and before I say anything, please react with calm and grace."

She frowned. "What is it?"

"I think you may have inadvertently taken an important piece of evidence."

"Why?"

"You told me you took a Lysol can, correct?"

"Yes."

"You're sure about the brand."

"Absolutely."

"I ran into Rosita this morning. She was cleaning the downstairs powder room. I glanced at her bucket of supplies and noted what disinfectants she was using. It wasn't Lysol . . ."

"That doesn't mean anything," Antonia interrupted, waving her hand in the air. "We're talking about the Mastersons' house, not what she uses at the inn."

Joseph nodded his head in accordance. "I realize that. And I recall that you had told me several times that they only use organic products. Wasn't there one day last winter when you were frantically trying to order some before Joan arrived . . ."

Joseph didn't have to finish. Antonia's face told it all. He was right. Joan Masterson was a maniac about that stuff. She never would have had a can of Lysol in her house. In fact, she was extremely specific about what she used: Shaklee products. Joan ate processed cheese, drank diet soda and flew privately but she was firm about one thing: only organic cleaners.

"Let me check something," said Antonia, rising. Before he responded, she dashed out of the office. She ran to her apartment to retrieve the illicit can and after a quick sweep of the downstairs, finally found Rosita polishing the banisters on the second floor back staircase. Rosita glanced up at Antonia who was now a sweaty, panting mess with her hair flattened against her head like a wet noodle. Antonia promised herself she would do more cardio.

"Rosita, I have to ask you something."

Rosita, a small, timid woman glanced up at her with worried chocolate-brown eyes. "Yes, Mrs. Antonia?"

"Don't worry, nothing bad. I just have a question. Did you ever use this Lysol can in the Mastersons' house? Don't be afraid, you're not in trouble if you did, I will never tell, I just need to know."

Rosita glanced at the steel can that Antonia clutched and shook her head. "No, Mrs. Antonia. Mrs. Joan only like organic."

Antonia swept a clump of hair out of her eyes. "But perhaps, just once, you did? In Eleanor's bathroom?"

Rosita shook her head. "No," she answered apologetically, sensing that was not the answer Antonia was hoping for.

"Have you ever seen this can in the Mastersons' house?"

Rosita looked at it again. "No."

Antonia sighed deeply. "Okay then."

"Everything okay?"

"Yes, of course. Thanks, Rosita."

"Soyla told me about the boy dying. I can't believe it! Very sad."

"Yes, it is."

"I talk to him once. He very nice."

"You did?" asked Antonia with curiosity. "What did he say?"

"He sat in the kitchen one day. He asked me if the Mastersons were nice and I say yes, very. He talked about rich people, how they bad. I don't say anything. But he said he wouldn't make a mess for me, he'd stay in his room and clean up. That's why I don't understand. Soyla said he was in Eleanor's bathroom? Why?"

"Had he been showering there all week?"

Rosita shook her head vehemently. "No. I came Monday and cleaned his bathroom. I put new towels and cleaned shower, because he used only his bathroom. There was nothing in Miss Eleanor's bathroom. I don't understand why he is there."

"I don't understand either. But don't worry. It was an accident."

Rosita took a deep breath. "You don't think I get into trouble, because he slipped . . ."

Antonia rested her hands firmly on Rosita's shoulders and looked intently into her scared eyes. "No way. Under no circumstances will you get into trouble. I promise."

*   *   *   *   *

"Well you're right," said Antonia, closing the door behind her. "Rosita didn't use Lysol."

"I was afraid so."

Antonia plopped down at her chair and slid the muffin plate closer to her. She shoved a large piece into her mouth. She took a swig of her now lukewarm tea before washing it down with yet another chunk of muffin. Joseph waited. Finally, Antonia leaned back in a food stupor.

"Carbs make everything better."

"How are you going to proceed?" asked Joseph, his gaze businesslike.

"Can I pretend I'm on an episode of a TV show and it was all a bad dream? I wake up tomorrow and it's all fine."

"I don't think that will help you much, however ideal that would be."

"Well, I'm not going to the police," said Antonia defiantly.

"Yet."

"No."

Antonia gave Joseph her most stubborn look to know she meant business. He smiled and with a fatherly sigh continued. "Okay, then. Here's what I think: in your absence I jotted down a few pertinent questions. Perhaps if we can figure them out we will have some answers."

"Alright, hit me."

"I know you said over and over again there was nothing that seemed amiss to you at the Mastersons' house. Are you sure?"

Antonia considered his question. "I felt something in Eleanor's room but then I realized it was the footprints. I mean, I think that's what it was, but could I say one hundred percent? No. Maybe it was something else."

"Alright then. Now, who has something to gain from Warner being murdered?"

"Aha! And I thought I was the suspicious one!"

"There are a lot of loose ends to this, and if we can eliminate some, we may have some answers. So, *cui bono*? Who benefits?"

Antonia flicked some crumbs off of her skirt while she pondered the question. "Well, let's see, it's almost like who *doesn't* have something to gain?"

"We'll get to that."

"Okay. Edward Hamilton and whoever else was in the documentary. Sidney Black . . . by the way, I can't believe I forgot to tell you! I gave a ride to his housekeeper last night. He had sent her away because he had a mysterious meeting. I think he might be a suspect . . ."

Antonia filled Joseph in on everything chatty Francine had told her about her boss.

Joseph nodded. "I did a little computer search on Sidney Black and Edward Hamilton last night and this is what I found."

"I thought you were researching hemophilia?" she teased.

"I had a lull."

Joseph handed Antonia print outs, which she perused. The first few pages were devoted to Sidney Black. There were several gossip items regarding Black's battle with the board of his co-op. Apparently he had illegally built a rooftop yoga studio on his penthouse and refused to take it down. The confrontation between him and certain board members became so vitriolic that a shoving match occurred in the elevator. One female resident even accused him of tripping her, causing her to gash her head on the marble floor of the lobby, an injury that required twenty stitches and the work of a plastic surgeon. The building was currently attempting to evict him.

There was more as well. An ex-girlfriend had come forward and sued him, citing mental distress because he had forced her to have an abortion. Antonia squinted at the woman's picture. Despite the demure suit and an attempt to appear abused, she still looked like one of Charlie Sheen's girlfriends— all long hair, big boobs and collagen lips. Antonia wondered if she had connected with Gloria Allred yet, patron legal saint of victimized women. On the following page there was a reference to a squash game where Black had thrown his racket into the face of his opponent when he lost the game. Joseph also included a *Fortune Magazine* article entitled "The Meanest Guy on Wall Street." No doubt about it, this man was trouble.

"Sidney Black is a bad, bad man," murmured Antonia. "I could tell Francine was scared of him."

There was less information about Edward Hamilton, but that was just as telling. The Google search had resulted in only a dozen mentions. For a man possessing so much wealth, it proved that he was still of the old guard mindset where money is better not seen and not heard. He was included on a roster of board members of a prestigious New York hospital and museum; there was a reference to his attendance at his Yale class of 1962 reunion. And at the bottom there was a blurb noting that he was a member of the Long Island Gun Club.

Antonia put down the papers. "Either one of these men has the means to hire the lawyer."

"Agreed."

"My money would be on Sidney Black. He tried everything to stop Warner from making the documentary, including restraining orders and harassment. And Warner was no angel, so I can see him going extra hard on Sidney Black. They're both kind of punks."

"Once again, I concur."

"But that said, at the end of the day, would it be worth it to kill Warner? And would they go that far? That's pretty extreme."

Joseph shifted in his seat. He pulled a cigar out of the breast pocket of his blazer and held it between his fingers. He would never smoke indoors but often found just the touch of a good cigar to be "a source of comfort and joy," as he put it.

"Once again, I agree. Sidney Black has dealt with bigger problems than Warner Caruthers. He has battled some of the most vicious men on Wall Street. I can't imagine that he would bother risking anything by killing Warner."

"Then maybe it was Edward Hamilton."

"Could be," conceded Joseph. "He is a private person. There could be very embarrassing revelations in the documentary. Enough to make him want to desperately protect his family image."

"But again, he's probably dealt with threat of exposure before. And why kill? He could sue. Or ignore and deny, which seem more probable."

Joseph nodded. "Yes, the man has probably never been involved in a lawsuit in his life."

"If we're ruling out homicide, there are still so many open-ended questions. Why would Warner be showering in Eleanor's bathroom? Rosita said he never did that before. And where does this Lysol can fit in? Is there some weird sex act I don't know about that includes this?"

"You're asking the wrong person."

Antonia laughed. "Supposing the can was Warner's, what

would he want with it? He probably never cleaned a bathroom in his life."

"Maybe it was a weapon."

Antonia paused to consider this. Her mind returned to the death scene. Images of the torn shower curtain, the bunched up bathmat and Warner's eyes came to her. She knew he was dead, but there was something about his final expression that had made her uncomfortable. She had detected . . . fear.

Antonia grew serious. "Maybe someone did kill him and used the Lysol can to clean up the crime scene. And the motive is the footage."

"I don't know," said Joseph lost in thought. "But if that is the case, perhaps it *is* best to go to the police about the can."

Antonia leaned back. Something didn't seem right. She wasn't ready to quit.

"No. Not yet. What I need to do is find the footage. That's my 'get out of jail card' so to speak."

"You mean you'd actually sell it to them?"

Antonia shook he head. "No. But it might lead me to the killer. Then I can turn him in at the same time as I turn in the can."

"Sounds like a dangerous plan."

"I got myself in soup, I need to ladle myself out."

8

The afternoon sun was slowly sinking down toward the horizon like an egg yolk dripping out of its shell. Patchy shadows were crisscrossing the patio on the north side of the inn where Antonia had decamped. In an effort to maintain a calm equilibrium she had decided to keep her routine as normal as possible. She busied herself cutting herbs from the overgrown clay pots that lined the slate wall. Antonia inhaled the fragrant basil and tarragon and tried to focus on the constant snipping of the scissors as she filled the wicker baskets.

As she worked, a rush of memories came back to her. When she was looking for Warner in the Mastersons' guest room, she had glanced at the cover sheet for his documentary. It had said the name of someone who was working with Warner. She put down her scissors to think. What was his name? It was one of those absurd names where the first name could be the last name. Rutherford something?

Antonia's cell buzzing jarred her. She glanced at the number and answered at once. Joan Masterson was on the other end.

"Antonia, I am so glad I caught you. Robert and I are just sick about this. Just sick. Warner's family is devastated. I tried to talk to his mother but she couldn't even speak. It is a *tragedy*. I don't know what to do. I feel responsible," said Joan, speaking with great urgency and stress.

"I know, Joan, it's heartbreaking. I can't believe it happened."

"Luke and his friends are shell-shocked. Simply shell-shocked. This is their first friend who died . . . well, it's so sad. Unbelievable. And I just hate that it happened at our house," said Joan.

"I know," said Antonia.

"Antonia, off the record, and I know it's terrible to say this, but . . ."

Antonia waited. She knew what was coming.

"But the bathtub wasn't . . . you know, it was normal, right? What I mean is, it wasn't exceptionally polished or anything, I mean, I hate to say it but in this day and age, with lawsuits . . ."

"I know what you mean, Joan, but there was nothing out of the ordinary. In terms of it being extra slippery. The same ladies clean for me, and we've never had that problem."

"Oh good! I mean, terrible to say, but I just don't want to be dragged into court . . ."

"Of course not," said Antonia.

"The police said he could have been drinking."

"They did?" asked Antonia. She hadn't heard that.

"Well, they alluded to it. They're waiting to receive the toxicology report."

Antonia slumped down on in a wrought iron patio chair, suddenly tired.

"One thing I wanted to ask, Joan, is the thing that did seem unusual to me was that Warner was in Eleanor's bathroom . . ."

"What?" exclaimed Joan in a piercing voice.

Antonia immediately felt the blood rush to her head. Did Joan not know?

"He had showered in Eleanor's bathroom . . ."

"You mean he was found dead in Eleanor's tub? Good lord! I can't let her know that. Why would he do that?"

"I don't know."

"But this is so odd. He loved his guest room. We even joked and called that part of the house 'Warner's Room' and 'Warner's bathroom.' He stored his shampoo there between visits . . ."

"I don't know, Joan. I agree with you, it's strange."

"Eleanor will feel violated. She simply can't know. Oh, I wish this documentary never took place! It caused so much trouble and all for naught. I should go on record saying I thoroughly disapproved of it. Had I known, I'm not sure I would have allowed him to stay. Young kids do these impulsive projects, just to become famous, and it comes back to bite them in the you-know-what. The tushie. There. I said it. We have a friend whose daughter put one of those videos up on YouTube where she's dancing around, partying with friends . . . just awful . . ."

Antonia temporarily zoned out while Joan continued her rant. When Joan arrived at the conclusion that the Internet was evil, Antonia finally couldn't take it anymore.

"Joan, I hate to interrupt, but was there a friend of Warner's working with him? Rutherford something?"

"Hayes Rutherford."

"Yes," said Antonia with excitement. "Where is he now?"

"Fortunately, Hayes had come to his senses. He was also supposed to stay with us but after the first interview, Hayes quit. He did not want to be in the business of ruining people's lives and causing a scandal. I've always thought him to be level-headed . . ."

"So, he wasn't the cameraman?"

"No. He's with Lukey and their friends in Greenwich right now, trying to stay close to Warner's family. The funeral's Saturday. The East Hampton police drove out this morning to interview them, but there was nothing much they could say. They all vouched for Warner's character. No one saw this coming."

"Joan, do you know *who* the cameraman was?"

"Hmmm . . . I don't think so."

"Could it have been another friend of Luke's?"

"I doubt it very much."

"Would it be possible to find out?" asked Antonia before quickly adding, "No one knows how to find him and as a courtesy he should be told about Warner, and funeral arrangements."

"Yes, absolutely. I'll ask Luke and he can ask Hayes. We're

boarding our plane soon—we're still in Nice—but I'll let you know sometime tomorrow."

Not soon enough, thought Antonia. "Or you could just give me Luke's cell phone number. It will save you the hassle."

"Wonderful idea. Although I think he said he was turning off the sound. It would be a little tacky to receive calls now . . ."

"I'll text him."

"Good idea. He loves that. All that LOL and BTW, I don't know what he is writing half the time . . ."

"Let me grab a pen."

With the phone still pressed to her ear and Joan prattling on about all of the acronyms young people use in their communication, Antonia ran into the sitting room and sat down at the English Regency desk. Atop of the leather blotter was a Windmill Inn pad where she scrawled down the number. As she was doing so, a movement along the patio caught her eye. She turned but saw nothing. After saying her goodbyes to Joan, Antonia texted Luke. She stared expectantly at her phone with the hope that Luke would instantly respond. Her eyes grew watery and she glanced up. When she did so, she saw with dread that the lawyer was now seated on the patio wall exactly where she had sat moments before.

He stood up as Antonia walked through the French doors towards him. He glanced at her expectantly.

"Don't get excited. I have nothing for you," she said defiantly.

He gave her a small smirk. "I'm disappointed."

Antonia put her hands on her hips in an effort to look more authoritative. "You can't threaten me."

The man looked amused. "I'm not threatening you Antonia."

"What about the manila envelope you left for me at the Felds' house?"

The man smiled, front rowing those Chiclet teeth again. "I have no idea what you are talking about."

Antonia squinted. "I don't believe you. You said you could find out anything, that your employer was powerful."

"He is."

"And that dossier was an effort to intimidate me. Well, I can't be intimidated. My past is my past and I will be held accountable for it. I want you to know I'm working with the police now. So this is over."

"I know for a fact you are not working with the police right now. But I want to make it clear, I am not threatening you. I just wish you had come to a different conclusion . . ."

"And I don't get it. Why are you coming to me? Shouldn't you ask the cameraman? He probably has it."

"*You* have it."

"I don't."

The lawyer clutched his briefcase and turned to move. "Well, then, we have nothing more to discuss now."

Antonia could have sworn he emphasized the word *discuss*. As if there was an alternative to discussing. Like maybe killing?

"That's a pity."

"And I would like you to cease and desist from bothering me or my friends and employers."

"You have my card. Contact me when you are ready to do business."

"I won't be."

Antonia dug her heels into the ground and folded her arms. He departed quietly, with only a final glance over his shoulder before he turned the corner by the wisteria bush. She could only hope that he had realized she had nothing to offer and would now leave her alone. It was all a silly misunderstanding, he would learn, and then move on. Good riddance, she thought.

*　*　*　*　*

"I'm here, and I am in full investigation mode, so let's do it," said Genevieve.

Antonia glanced at Genevieve's "full investigation mode" outfit: she was clad in skinny dark jeans and a shiny pearl gray top opened to reveal what little cleavage she had. She was wearing her high, chocolate, leather riding boots (she didn't ride, it was a 'look,' she said) and had layers of gold chains everywhere to be found and held a cape over her arm. Ralph Lauren had picked the right person to represent his store.

"I'm ready," said Antonia.

They walked out the back door to the driveway.

"Where's your car?" asked Antonia.

"Carl dropped me off," said Genevieve with a sly smile.

"Look at you," said Antonia.

"I know," said Genevieve, suddenly serious. "It's strange, and I know it's early, but I really think he may be *the one*, Antonia. It's like, he totally gets me. I think he finds me funny and amusing, which is exactly how I prefer to think of myself."

"I think of you that way also."

"I know and that's why I love you. And with him, it's just so easy. He's basically moved right in and it just feels *right*. There's a comfort level."

"I'm really happy for you. And I agree, he's a *man*. Most of the men that you've dated were *boys*. None of them were very serious, whereas Carl seems thoughtful and mature. And I like that he has a plan: he's traveled the world, now he wants to settle down."

"Oh my God, can you imagine?" asked Genevieve shaking her head in amazement. "How awesome would it be?"

"Awesome," said Antonia.

"It could be you, my friend. That hot chef last night seemed like he wanted to jump your bones."

Antonia reddened. "No, that was purely professional. Besides, he was probably married."

"Don't always sell yourself short, Antonia. Why wouldn't he be attracted to you?"

"Because he's a child."

"He's not."

"He looked like he was in his late twenties."

"Being a cougar is hot."

"I can't even think of that right now. We have more pressing business."

They were on their way to find the cameraman. Luke had returned Antonia's text with lightning speed. (That's what she amazed her about young people and their gadgets: even when they were in mourning, they still had time to text.) His response had been:

Hayes said Warner met some slacker dude at happy hour. Guy's name was Paul. He had camera experience so he took over the shoot.

Antonia had responded to query how she could find him, to which she received the following response:

Dude is a lush, day drinker accord to Hayes. Check local bars.

It wasn't much, but a few more texts back and forth with Luke gave Antonia a fuzzy description of this Paul and a hint that his watering holes of choice were usually in Amagansett, the next town over. Antonia had gone into her office and opened the Yellow Pages and proceeded to call every restaurant and bar (there weren't that many, fortunately) and ask them to check if there was a "Paul" at the bar. She hit pay dirt at Meeting House. The bartender confirmed there was a Paul drinking at the bar with his girlfriend. She annoyed him further by asking him to ask Paul if he was a cameraman. When he returned after several seconds with a positive answer Antonia was so startled that she quickly hung up. She reprimanded herself for proceeding without a plan. It was at that moment that Genevieve had called her, and on impulse, Antonia asked her if she was game for heading to drinks at Meeting House. Antonia had given Genevieve only a partial on the true reason they were heading to Meeting House. She explained that she was interested in finding the footage for Warner's documentary so that it didn't end up in the wrong hands, and to do that they needed to track down the cameraman, who may be reluctant to part with it. She didn't fill Genevieve in on the lawyer. Genevieve could have a big mouth and the less information she had to play with, the better.

"So, what's the plan?" asked Genevieve. "Surveillance or ambush?"

"You've got to be kidding me," said Antonia, maneuvering the car out of the driveway and onto the road. She pressed down firmly on the accelerator. She wanted to be sure she made it to the bar before Paul left.

"I was going to bring my binoculars, but they didn't fit in this handbag and I really wanted to wear it because we just got it in. Isn't it cute? The beading is incredible; they found these women in India who do all this amazing stuff."

Antonia glanced down at the bag. "It's nice, but how many handbags do you need? Every time I see you, you have a new one."

"And every time I see you, you have the same old boring one. You don't even use the one I bought you for your birthday."

"It's too fancy."

"It's chic."

"I *will* use it one day . . ."

"Whatever. The good news is I was able to fit pepper spray in my bag in case."

"Pepper spray?" said Antonia, nearly choking on her words. "I can't even believe you *own* pepper spray. What do you need it for?"

"You never know," said Genevieve flicking on the radio. She played with the dial until she got to 101.3. "This is the new Lady Gaga song. I love it."

"Well, I don't think we'll need the pepper spray, so just keep it in the car."

"Nuh-uh, you never know. Someone could be onto you.

They could know that you're snooping around. They get you in a dark alley and one blow to the head and you're dead."

"Right."

Meeting House Restaurant was in Amagansett, the next village on Route 27. Amagansett was still part of the town of East Hampton but had a much different energy. It was more relaxed, less fancy, but in possession of its own authentic low-key charm. There weren't a lot of daytrippers clamoring along the streets with piles of shopping bags trying to muscle their way into the latest designer boutique. That said, it beat East Hampton in the nightlife department, hosting some late night scenes and one of the only spots to hear live music in the area.

Antonia didn't allow Genevieve to take the requisite five minutes to reapply her makeup and instead rushed her out of the car. When they entered the restaurant, Antonia scanned the room for a "Paul". She observed several families with small children seated in the booths, as well as a couple in their fifties. She ruled them out immediately. That left a scruffy young man and woman in their early twenties that were seated at the far end of the bar. Bingo.

The man had stringy, longish hair, a puffy face that had probably ingested too much fried food for one lifetime, and a soft body. His mouth was adorned with an attempted goatee that instantly conjured up the image of scraggly cat whiskers. He wore a plaid shirt with the sleeves slightly rolled up. His girlfriend had long dyed black hair that made a shocking contrast to her pale skin. Her eyes were small but long lashed, and she wore heavy eyeliner and flaming red lipstick that was bright enough to be used as a signal to aliens in outer space. Several long beaded necklaces dangled atop her ratty black asymmetrical sweater. The couple was disheveled and insouciant, but Antonia thought their slovenly look appeared carefully cultivated rather than natural.

"That's got to be him," said Genevieve, pointing.

Antonia reached and grabbed her hand. "Don't point! We don't want to make it look like we're targeting them."

"But we are."

"But then it seems so shady."

Genevieve folded her arms. "So, how do you want to proceed, Miss Marple?"

Antonia pondered the question. Should she come right out and introduce herself? Probably that was the best course. "Okay, we'll go say hi. Then you'll engage the girlfriend in conversation and I'll try and elicit information out of Paul."

"In other words, you get the fun part."

"It's not the fun part! Remember, I'm trying to find this footage. For Warner's sake."

"You don't have to feed me that baloney. But fine. I will do it for the cause."

A young blonde hostess clutching menus approached Antonia and Genevieve. She was still in her teens and Antonia instantly felt old. "Two for dinner?" she inquired.

"Actually, we're just going to sit at the bar and have some drinks," said Genevieve.

"Of course," said the hostess, motioning them towards the bar.

When they approached, Antonia noticed that the couple had their legs linked in a bizarre Houdini-esque contortion. The girlfriend had her hand on Paul's inner thigh and Antonia had to avert her eyes for fear she'd see just a little more of Paul than she wanted to. Paul's beer glass was half full, but his girlfriend had almost drained a murky looking drink that had a shot glass floating inside it.

"Excuse me, Paul?" asked Antonia.

He twisted around abruptly, as if he had been caught doing something wrong. "Yes?" he asked gruffly.

"Hi, my name is Antonia Bingham. I, um . . ." Antonia hesitated. "I work for the Mastersons . . ."

Paul stared at her blankly.

"Warner Caruthers was their houseguest."

A flicker of recognition came across Paul's face. "Hey," he said softly.

Emboldened, Antonia continued. "And I'm so sorry about Warner, I'm not sure if you were close but," she paused hoping that Paul would interject the status of his relationship with Warner at this point. When he didn't, she continued. "Anyway, I take care of their house and I wanted to make sure that you didn't leave anything there, or if there is anything that you need . . ."

Antonia's voice trailed off.

"No, man, thanks," said Paul, wiping a lock of greasy hair out of his eyes. "I'm just like, totally freaked out. Drowning my sorrows right now with my lady."

Antonia glanced at his lady, who nodded in accordance. "It's pretty whacked," she concurred.

"You can say that again," interjected Genevieve. "Antonia's the one who found him."

Antonia turned and glared at Genevieve. She hadn't wanted to divulge details regarding the discovery of his body. It might take them away from the information that she wanted to gather from Paul. "Sorry I didn't introduce you, this is my friend, Genevieve Turner."

Genevieve stuck her hand out and Paul and his girlfriend shook it limply. He did not take the opportunity to introduce his "lady."

"You found him?" said Paul, shaking his head. "I'm so glad it wasn't me, man."

"You would have totally freaked out," said Paul's girlfriend with a snort. She took the moment to drain her glass. Antonia noticed that she had several earrings in each ear, including a small dangling Mickey Mouse in the left lobe next to a skull and crossbones stud.

"Yeah, I don't do well with blood. Makes me barf man. I'm really squeamish, if you can believe it."

Antonia stared at the sleeve of tattoos going up his wrist. He was obviously not squeamish around needles.

"Well, there wasn't much blood. But I'm sure you don't want to hear about that. He was, after all, your friend?" She purposely posed it as a question.

Paul took a sip of his beer. "Only just met him but he was a cool dude," said Paul. "Quality peeps."

The bartender approached and Genevieve and Antonia ordered drinks: A margarita for the former, a glass of cabernet for the latter. They slid up onto the barstools.

"Paul, listen, do you mind if I ask you a few questions?" Antonia queried.

Before Paul could respond, his girlfriend interrupted, her eyes narrowed to slits like a snake.

"Why? Are you the cops?"

"Do we look like the police?" asked Genevieve, slightly offended.

"No, but then neither does Mariska Hargitay," said the girlfriend.

"But Mariska Hargitay isn't a cop, she just plays one on TV," retorted Genevieve.

"Same thing," shrugged the girlfriend.

"We're not the police," Antonia said firmly. "We are friends of Warner's family, you can call Sergeant Flanagan to confirm . . ."

Paul waved his hand and announced firmly: "No need to call the cops."

Antonia gave him a quizzical glance. He shrugged with a guilty face. "We're not into law enforcement is all."

"They suck," added the lady friend. She punctuated the air by pointing her purple fingernail at them.

"I hear you," said Antonia. "But I'm here on another matter. This is obviously a very big tragedy for the Caruthers. They have asked me to piece together Warner's final moments. They have a lot of unanswered questions." God, she was getting good at this white lie stuff.

Paul drained his beer. "Alright," he said.

The lady friend still glared at Antonia, who shifted in her

seat awkwardly. There was something menacing about the girl's gaze, a sort of take-no-prisoners look.

"Before we get all somber, how about we buy you guys another round of drinks?" asked Genevieve.

Paul brightened. "Cool."

Antonia gave Genevieve a grateful smile. She winked in return.

"Alright," conceded the lady friend, as if she was doing *them* a giant favor.

As Genevieve placed the order and began flirting with the bartender, Antonia attempted to win the girl over.

"I'm really okay. Ask anyone. I have a restaurant in town, I own an inn . . ."

The girl perked up. "The Windmill Inn? That's *you?*"

Antonia smiled. "Yes, you've heard of it."

The girl nodded. She turned to Paul. "Aw, yeah, don't you remember Warner went by there to get his keys? She's cool."

Antonia was happy she received the stamp of approval. Now she could start her interrogation. She knew she had to be subtle.

"Paul, I was . . . along with the Caruthers family . . . we were wondering, why was Warner still at the Mastersons' house? He told me he was leaving on Monday."

Paul shook his head. "Dude, I don't know. He *was* leaving. He was going to head back to the city for a few days then we were going to recon in Southampton."

"What time did you last see him?"

"I saw him in the late afternoon. He said he was grabbing his stuff at the Mastersons before hitting it."

"Was Warner with his girlfriend?"

"He didn't have a girlfriend," said Paul. "He got play, but was uncommitted."

Antonia hadn't expected that answer. "Did he get play here, in East Hampton, I mean?"

Paul shook his head. "I don't think so. But I didn't know him that long. We met a few weeks ago, here, actually, and when he found out I was an expert with the camera he asked me to work with him 'cause his original guy flaked. I mean, we hung hard the past few weeks, in the trenches and all, and we'd have a few beers. I definitely didn't see him with a lady."

"Really?" asked Genevieve with skepticism.

"It's not like he was Chris Hemsworth," sneered the girl-friend. "I didn't even think he was hot."

"But what about a girl in a German car?" asked Antonia.

Paul shrugged his shoulders. "Don't know anything about that."

"Is it possible he had a lady friend?"

"Yeah, sure. But he didn't mention it."

"Were you with him every night?" asked Antonia.

"Pretty much," said Paul. "Except Thursday. I went to the city. Had tickets to The Exterminators."

"Is that a band?" asked Antonia.

"It's a way of life," he said solemnly. His lady nodded in accordance.

Antonia tried another tack.

"Was Warner drinking on Monday?"

Paul paused. "Naw, I mean, he had like three beers but no."

"That's not a lot for him?" asked Antonia.

Paul and his girlfriend laughed. "Three beers?" she asked.

"Three beers is nothing, Antonia," said Genevieve, tapping Antonia playfully. "This one is such a prude!"

Antonia smiled. "How do you think he could have fallen, then? Was he clumsy?"

"Not particularly," said Paul. "I think it was just one of those freak accidents."

"My uncle got struck by lightning," added the girl.

"That's awful," said Antonia. She decided to change course. "Tell me about the documentary. How did you find your subjects?"

"Warner would do research on each person and then find out what their hobby was and use that to entice them."

"You mean he told each one a different story about what the documentary would be about?" asked Antonia.

"Exactly," nodded Paul. "This one lady, total hottie, was way into horseback riding. Warner contacted her and told her he was doing a film about horses, and the world of showing, that sort of crap. She was totally game. And then once we got in the interview, Warner nailed her with his questions—like I said, he did his research—and she just didn't have a clue."

A woman? That was interesting. Antonia had not even considered that he would have included women in his documentary, but of course it made sense.

"What was her name?" asked Antonia.

Paul faltered. "Um . . ."

"Pauline Framingham," his lady said firmly.

"Right."

"Of Framingham Industries?" asked Antonia with an eyebrow raised.

"Yes."

"No wonder she didn't want the negative publicity," said Antonia.

"Powerful family," said Genevieve to Antonia. She wiggled her eyebrows for emphasis.

Framingham Industries was the largest privately owned pharmaceutical company in the country. The Framinghams were billionaires who had donated wings to dozens of museums and hospitals in New York and Palm Beach. Although they were not shy with putting their names on buildings, they shunned the press in general. It was possible the lawyer could have been working for her.

"Did Warner have any hesitation about doing this documentary?" asked Genevieve. "It's kind of biting the hand that feeds . . ."

Paul glanced off in the distance. "Warner was from that preppy world, but he didn't dig it at all. He was a serious filmmaker. He didn't want to do some dumb documentary like *The Real Housewives*; he wanted to win an Academy Award. This was his exposé. He knew that he had to get everyone in the first time, because once it came out people wouldn't want to participate anymore. And he was going to do it, dammit! For the common man, like every one of us! He was!"

Paul stomped a fist on the bar. His lady put her long, purple-taloned hand on his shoulder and squeezed. Paul turned and gave her the longest most erotic kiss that Antonia had ever seen in public, before he picked up his drink and took a long swig. Antonia and Genevieve both squirmed in their seats during the awkward moment. Antonia broke the silence.

"I'm sure it would have been brilliant. Paul, do you have any idea what happened to the footage? Where would Warner have kept it?"

Paul gave her a curious look. Then he started laughing, as did his lady.

"What?" asked Antonia.

"Duh, *I* have the footage," said Paul.

"He is the *cameraman*," interjected his lady.

"What!" exclaimed Antonia, before remembering she had to play it cool. "I didn't realize that. I thought it had gone missing."

"Are you kidding? I'm like Mr. Organization. And this was our Golden Ticket. I would never screw that up."

"Do you think we could come see it?" asked Genevieve quickly.

Paul turned to give his girlfriend a look. She whispered something in his ear and he whispered back. Clearly they were never given the memo that whispering in front of others was rude. Antonia waited. She noticed Paul's girlfriend's fingers squeeze his thigh. She prayed they would not be subjected to another pornographic interlude between these two slackers.

"Alright," said Paul finally. "But only because you are part of Warner's family."

Antonia didn't dare correct him.

9

Antonia followed Paul's blue Chevy Avalanche as it turned right off of Route 27 onto Oak Lane. They drove a short distance down the street before taking a left onto Schellinger Road. Paul slowed his car in front of the third house on the right and parked in the driveway. Antonia parked her car on the road. A small white sign pressed in the grass said "Levicky." A cluster of large bushes and one giant pine tree obstructed the view of the house.

Outside the air was cool. Antonia could smell the scent of barbequed meat wafting through the air from the neighbor's yard, and her stomach let out a small grumble. It was almost dinnertime. Antonia and Genevieve followed Paul and his girl-friend through a gate in an unpainted wooden fence. The grass in the yard was an inch or two overgrown and there were large clumps of rose of sharon bushes along the sides that separated the land from its neighbors. From a distance, the tiny one-story house had appeared neatly kept but upon closer inspection, Antonia could see chipped paint on the gutters and rotting wood panels below the front steps. There was a small attempt at cheer in the manner of a large urn filled with geraniums that stood next to the front door. A miniature American flag was propped in the soil.

Upon entering they were greeted by the zealous barks and licks from a Cocker Spaniel named Marilyn Manson who was relentless in his effort to make friends. Genevieve, in particular, was not a dog lover.

"Cute dog," said Genevieve flatly. Only Antonia could decipher that her voice was dripping with sarcasm.

"Thanks. Just watch your crotch. He'll make it his new home," warned Paul's girlfriend.

"Great," said Genevieve under her breath. She turned and gave Antonia an SOS look, which Antonia promptly ignored. Antonia was burning with anticipation to finally view the footage. What was in there that could be so important to the lawyer's employer? This was her moment to find out, and if Genevieve had to get molested by a dog, so be it. Sometimes you have to take a hit for the team.

They were ushered into the living room and offered beer, which was delivered to them in two tallboy cans. Antonia and Genevieve sat on the sagging tan couch while Paul fiddled with his filming equipment.

Antonia glanced around the room. It was cluttered with miscellaneous furniture of varying sizes. A leather chaise stood in the corner next to a reading lamp and a stack of newspapers. There were two large glass fronted display cases. One held framed photographs of weddings and graduations, as well as baseball trophies, a signed baseball on a pedestal, and a signed Mets jersey. The other held a large collection of porcelain figurines, with bunny rabbits a heavy favorite. The windows were covered in a gauzy white fabric. The room smelled like stale cigarette smoke, its presence confirmed by the overflowing ashtrays that were on several coffee tables.

During the time it took him to set up the footage they learned that Paul's girlfriend was named Heidi Levicky and before she came out here to help Paul and Warner with the documentary, she worked at a store called Top Shop in lower Manhattan while she pursued her dream of becoming a professional DJ. This was her parents' home that she "crashed at" when she was in town on the weekends "moonlighting" at CVS, but for the most part she lived in Chinatown. She and Paul (Brady) had been together for three years, and Paul had taken a summer program at the New York Academy of Film, before quitting because "it was all bullshit and he was better than that." He was "at the right place at the right time" when he met Warner which Heidi took as "a sign." They both had believed that this documentary with Warner would "score him a studio deal big time; Scorcese style."

"Okay, ready?" asked Paul finally, as a hazy image came on to the widescreen plasma TV. Antonia had noticed in life that no matter how financially challenged people were, they never skimped on televisions.

Finally, the footage came into focus. Antonia leaned in eagerly. This was her chance to see what was so important to the man with the briefcase. Alternatively, she had to find out what was missing that he had expected to find. Perhaps that is what held the answers.

The screen showed a sprawling perfectly manicured lawn with a large Tudor-style mansion hovering in the distance. Suddenly, a figure stepped on to the screen.

"Is that Warner?" whispered Genevieve.

"Yes," said Antonia. It was eerie to see him alive. He began to speak, motioning behind him.

"Here you have the home of a favorite member of society's old guard, Mr. Edward McKinley Hamilton III. A man who is respected for his expertise on family lineage and the history of New York society. Do all of his so called friends . . ." Warner punctuated the word *friends* my making quotation marks in the air—"know that his so-called prestigious family is full of Nazis and racists and former slave owners, wait a minute, cut, cut."

"What's wrong?" asked Paul's voice off camera.

"I want to wait until that lawnmower stops."

Warner walked off the screen. Antonia shuddered. Every part of the video felt sad and strange, especially the details: The fact that Warner was wearing jeans and a T-shirt; his ebullience in regards to his project; his aborted mission to renounce the millionaires who were part of the landscape from whence he came. Now he was dead. Part of a past that would never have a future.

The camera cut out and then reappeared. This time, Warner was seated in paisley armchair next to a roaring fire. He now wore khakis and a yellow ribbed cashmere sweater that made him appear very young. His hair was neatly brushed and he held an earnest expression on his face. Across from him sat a distinguished looking older man in a blue blazer and red ascot. He had thinning white hair meticulously combed back from his forehead. His eyes were watery blue with the glossy sheen that often accompanies old age. His skin was almost translucent. His tall frame perched on the edge of his chair in a complete upright position. Antonia felt there was something vaguely familiar about the man.

"That's Edward Hamilton," said Paul. He took a pack of cigarettes out of the breast pocket of his shirt and pulled two out of the pack. He put them both in his mouth and lit them with a green plastic lighter, before handing one off to Heidi and exhaling a long stream of smoke.

"He looks like a cliché," whispered Genevieve.

She was right, thought Antonia. An ascot? It was absurd. He was like a baby lamb walking into a lion's den with that outfit. Warner would have him for lunch.

"So, Mr. Hamilton, tell me exactly what you do," began Warner. His voice was tentative, definitely not as confident as he was when he was standing outside the house.

"I'm a philanthropist," said Mr. Hamilton in a firm voice.

"A *philanthropist*," repeated Warner. "So what does that entail?"

"I was fortunate enough to be born into a privileged family. I consider it both an honor and a duty to give away part of my fortune."

"Whom do you give it to?"

"Hospitals, museums, the arts. Our foundation donates to a variety of charitable institutions."

"Can you give me some specific examples?"

Antonia watched Warner while Edward Hamilton recited the recipients of his generosity. Warner would nod, but then glance down at his notes. She detected a small smirk on his face. He asked a few more follow up questions, focusing on his education, his time in the army, the manner in which his family earned their money (airplane parts) before moving on to his hobbies.

Antonia could tell Genevieve was becoming impatient. She would sigh, then cross and recross her legs.

"This doesn't seem so bad," said Genevieve finally. "Why was he all pissed off?"

"Just wait, it's coming," said Paul. He leaned forward and stubbed out his cigarette in the ashtray.

"Well, Mr. Hamilton. It sounds like you are a decent citizen," concluded Warner.

"I try to be," said Hamilton with great humility.

"Then how do you explain the illegitimate family?" asked Warner, with a dazzling smile.

"Excuse me?" sputtered Hamilton.

Warner's smile grew bigger. "You know, the two children you conceived with Cindi Lusk? During that extra-marital affair you had."

Hamilton's face reddened then became stormy. "I don't know what you are talking about," he said with clenched teeth.

"Does this help?"

Warner handed a stack of photographs that he pulled out from inside his notebook. Hamilton took them and flipped through them silently. He was seething. Antonia could see the vein in his temple throbbing as the camera zoomed in on his reaction. Warner watched with glee.

"You are skating on thin ice, young man," said Hamilton evenly.

"Does your wife know about your other family? Do your sons?"

Hamilton stood up. "I'm going to ask you to leave right now." He turned and faced the camera and held his hand in front of the lens. "Turn that thing off now."

Off camera they could hear Paul's voice protest. "Hey, don't touch the equipment, man." He took a step back and the scene came back into view.

"You've crossed the line, young man," said Hamilton. He was standing with his arms by his sides, but Antonia could see that his fists were clenched. "It's time to leave."

"But Mr. Hamilton, don't you think you should come clean? It is after all, hypocritical of you to ignore them, especially when you're spreading your money around to everyone else and you don't give them a dime."

"I have no further comment."

"Do you want to comment on the fact that it seems like most of your money came from doing business with the Nazis despite a U.S. embargo?"

With this, Hamilton exploded. "I don't know what you're talking about!"

"True or false: your grandfather sold airplane parts to . . ."

"Get out now! If you don't, I will call the police and have you arrested!"

Warner still sat in his chair. A look of amusement grew on his face. Antonia felt a chill. He definitely wanted to provoke Hamilton to the max. He was baiting him. Almost like he wanted Hamilton to hit him. It was hard to reconcile this Warner with the one she had met, who had seemed so enthusiastic and friendly. It was almost as if there were two Warners.

The screen went fuzzy.

"Heady stuff," said Paul, stretching his arms. As he did so his shirt rose above his belly button, giving everyone in the room a glimpse of his hairy untoned stomach.

"May I use your bathroom?" asked Antonia.

"At your own risk," said Heidi tersely. "It's over there."

Heidi's warning had been correct. The bathroom was filthy. Wet towels were dumped all over the floor, next to an overflowing hamper. The walls were a mosaic of mildew and mold and there was only a small strip of toilet paper remaining. Antonia bolted out of it as soon as possible. She stopped at the kitchen to wash her hands. The tap came on with a small choke and then a big spurt. Antonia glanced outside the window. The sky was trapped at that hazy hour when the light is filmy and visibility difficult. Clouds were scurrying across as if racing home to bed. She stared at the plastic white garden chairs that were lined up in a row of four next to a rusty swing set. A light breeze was swaying a swing back and forth as if a phantom child was pumping.

Antonia bent down to wipe her hands on a dishtowel. When she glanced up, she froze. There was someone standing in the shadows under the tree. Someone tall and big, most likely a man. She saw him take a step back into the hidden shade of the tree. Antonia cupped her hands against the window and peered out. It was impossible to decipher his face.

"It's back on."

Antonia turned around and found Genevieve standing in the doorway. Antonia quickly motioned for her to come over.

"What?" asked Genevieve.

"Do you see?" whispered Antonia. Her heart was pounding. When she turned around again, he was gone.

Genevieve stood on her toes and scanned outside. "What am I looking at? Confirmation that the yard needs weeding?"

"No, there was a man there."

"A man?"

"Yes. Standing in the bushes."

"Maybe a dog walker?"

"I didn't see a dog. He was just . . . watching."

"*The Watcher in the Woods*. Remember that movie?" asked Genevieve. "How do you feel about my pepper spray now?" She left the room without waiting for an answer.

Antonia glanced outside the yard again. It was empty. Had she imagined it?

She returned to the living room just as a very attractive brunette in her mid-forties appeared on screen. The woman and Warner were outside, perched atop a three-rail fence. A gorgeous chestnut horse stood next to them. The woman's hair was pulled back in a ponytail and she wore delicate pearl and diamond earrings in her ears. Her face was tan. She had hazel eyes with slight wrinkles around them, which, rather than making her look old, actually contributed to a mature sexiness. She was wearing a riding outfit.

"This is Pauline Framingham, I suppose?" asked Antonia.

"Bingo. The pharmaceutical heiress in the flesh. Well, not in the flesh, but on screen," said Paul.

"F.F. to the good part," commanded Heidi.

"Will do," said Paul. As the footage was fast-forwarded, Antonia watched Pauline Framingham carefully. Even though there was no sound she could tell that Framingham was a confident woman, who was neither insecure nor self-conscious. She gesticulated often, met the camera's gaze, and appeared composed. But suddenly Framingham's demeanor changed. She had been petting her horse, sliding her manicured hand back and forth under his neck, when she ceased doing so and abruptly whipped her head around and gave Warner an icy look.

"This is it, stop," said Heidi.

Paul rewound before pressing play. Antonia sat up straighter on the sofa and Genevieve leaned in.

"You seem pretty crazy about your horse," said Warner with that sly smirk that Antonia had noticed on his face when he interviewed Edward Hamilton.

"She's my baby, aren't you? Aren't you?" responded Pauline in the voice one uses on a small child. She nuzzled with her horse, rubbing their noses together.

– 133 –

"So you love animals?" asked Warner.

"I do. I have my horses and my dogs. They are my children, my babies."

"But you hate cats," said Warner.

"Cats?" she asked, still staring at her horse, whose neck she was now rubbing.

"Framingham Industries tests their products on animals. How many cats did you kill last year?" asked Warner, flipping through his notebook. "Oh yeah, thousands. Too many to remember, according to sources. I've also heard that you have killed your horses for the insurance money. So I guess you don't really like animals, Miss Framingham. You are benefiting from killing them."

"What?"

"You're a hypocrite, Ms. Framingham." He spat out her name.

This was when Framingham turned on Warner with indignation. She pointed her finger at him. "You are not a gentleman."

Genevieve turned to Antonia. "You are not a *gentleman*? That's all she could come up with?"

Antonia didn't respond, instead leaned closer to hear Warner. "So, are you saying, Miss Framingham, that *gentlemen* let you persecute animals? Do *gentlemen* let you illegally remove hundred-year-old trees from your property to build state-of-the-art barns? Do *gentlemen* let you do whatever you want?"

Framingham opened her mouth as if to say something, but

instead snapped it shut. "Interview over," she said, jumping down off the fence. The camera followed her as she led her horse down a muddy path next to a gated pasture. She dismissed Warner with a wave of her hand.

"Will I be hearing from your *gentlemen*?" asked Warner with a laugh. He then turned and looked into the camera. "And that, ladies and *gentlemen* is what we call a wrap."

The screen went dark. Antonia took a deep breath and let it out slowly. She turned and glanced at Paul.

"Did Pauline Framingham make any effort to obtain the tapes or excise herself from the film?"

Paul shook his head. "Not yet. We only shot that last week. Warner assumed she was getting her lawyers on it."

Antonia wasn't so sure. Maybe Pauline was calling her lawyers . . . or maybe she had something else in mind. Like sending an emissary.

"Paul, what happened with Sidney Black? Why did he take out a restraining order against Warner and vice versa?"

"That dude is Dr. Evil, man. He did not want to be included in this flick, did not want his ex in there. Said he'd sue Warner to death before this thing would see the light of day."

"Did Warner feel threatened by him?"

"Naw, but the turd was harassing us. He'd send his peeps in or show up everywhere to try and tell people not to work with us. He even followed us to Hamilton's house and hooked up with him after. We heard they were going to file a joint suit against us. Bullshit."

"Did he offer you money for it?" asked Genevieve.

"At first Sidney Black was like, how much do you want. But Warner said no. I'm telling you, they could have offered Warner a billion dollars and he still would have released these movies," insisted Paul. "He didn't need the money. His old man was loaded. He wanted the kudos, the film cred."

"This was his masterpiece," blurted Heidi.

"Can we see Sheila Black's interview?" asked Genevieve.

Paul glanced at his watch. Heidi leaned forward and tapped her cigarette on the edge of the ashtray. It was obvious they had plans or other ideas about how to spend the night, but Antonia needed to see as much as possible.

"Just a bit?" Antonia pleaded.

Paul sighed. "All right."

As soon as Shelia Black started talking it was clear there was something off about her, Antonia surmised. She was probably in her early fifties, and her stringy blonde hair was bobbed and pinned back with a velvet barrette. On her lapel she wore a giant Camellia broach. She was painfully thin, which had aged her, and caused the veins in her neck to protrude. She looked like one of those stick figures that children draw, where the eyes are giant round circles that bulged from her face, almost as if she had a thyroid condition. Those eyes kept darting around the room. Antonia wasn't sure what she was looking at, as the camera was held tightly on her face. Her eyes were blinking and fluttering, like a newborn baby adjusting to the light.

"What do you want me to do? Do you want me to sit here, is this okay?" she was asking in a surprisingly high-pitched tenor.

Warner's voice came on from off-screen. He was soothing. "Sure, you're perfect."

Antonia was instantly reminded of those bad TV movies she saw when the photographer lures a young pretty girl to his studio and coaxes her to take off all of her clothing for the camera. She had to hand it to Warner; he had been very skilled at manipulating people. It seemed like his was a misguided effort to reprimand people who possessed extreme wealth. He could have taken an entirely different direction; he could have enlisted these people to help the poor or unfortunate. But instead he had chosen to embarrass them. And it was possible that had been a fatal decision.

Sheila again spoke. "Oh, Sid is going to be so angry when he sees this! I hope you can premiere it at the Hamptons Film Festival."

"We were thinking of Sundance, but we'll see what we can do," said Warner off screen.

Sheila laughed. Her laugh came out of her nose, more like a snort. She darted her eyes back and forth. "How shall we start? Do you want to hear all about Sidney's idiosyncrasies? He doesn't like to be touched at all. Ever. It's very strange . . ."

"We'll get to that, Mrs. Black."

"Oh *you* don't have to call me *Mrs. Black*, Warner dear," she said flirtatiously.

It was at this moment that the front door open and Heidi's parents stepped over the threshold and into their living room. Every head in the room turned in their direction. The frumpy couple appeared surprised to find anyone in their house and immediately took on defensive stances. Their small mouths fell slightly agape and Mrs. Levicky's eyes instinctively darted around the room and to her glass enclosed cabinets as if to ensure that nothing had been stolen.

"What's going on?" Mr. Levicky asked suspiciously. He was a stout gray-haired man with a prominent jaw, sallow skin and deep-set eyes. Antonia instantly thought of one of those actors who played "the boss" in a fifties sitcom.

"We were just watching the documentary," said Heidi with a shrug.

"Okay," murmured Mrs. Levicky with uncertainty. Her many chins bobbled as her lips moved.

"I don't want my house turning into a movie theater!" bellowed Mr. Levicky. "It's already a revolving door!"

"This is the last one, Dad, we promise."

"Yeah, no more, Mr. L."

The parents grumbled and Antonia gave them a small smile but they didn't return her gaze and immediately trudged upstairs.

Antonia turned to Paul. "Has someone else watched this?"

"Yeah."

"Who? If I may ask."

"This jerkoff came by yesterday. He said he'd give us all sorts of cash for the footage but then as soon as he watched it, he bailed."

Antonia felt as if her knees were weakening. She opened and closed her mouth before speaking. "Was it a lawyer with a briefcase? Terry Rudolph?"

Paul nodded. "Yeah, that one."

"Who are you talking about?" asked Genevieve.

Antonia ignored her. "So he's seen all this," said Antonia pointing in the direction of the television. "Every interview you have."

"Yup."

"And he didn't want it?"

"Nope."

Antonia didn't know what to make of it. Here she had thought she had found the footage and could put all of this behind her. And now it turns out that this wasn't what he was after.

"Who is he?" Genevieve insisted again.

Antonia turned to her. "I don't know. All I know is he has asked me, and now Heidi and Paul, for the footage on behalf of his employer."

"Yeah, but the guy said this wasn't what he was looking for," Heidi chimed in. "He was like 'where is the rest?' and we were like, 'dude, what are you talking about?'"

"Believe me, if there was more, we would sell it. He was talking BIG money," said Paul, before backtracking. "I mean, of course I want to be a real artist and make critically acclaimed films . . ."

"But for now we could totally use the dough," interjected Heidi.

"*Is* there more?" Genevieve asked.

Paul shrugged. "Maybe. But if there is, Warner kept it hidden."

"Where?"

"I got no idea."

"Paul, do you have any idea why this man would think *I* had it? Did my name ever come up?"

"Sorry, but what's your name again?" asked Paul.

"Antonia Bingham, you douche bag," said Heidi. She turned to them. "See what I have to live with? He never listens."

"Antonia Bingham. Right," said Paul. He scratched his scraggly goatee. "I don't think so."

Antonia was discouraged when she left Paul and Heidi. Here she thought that either Sid Black or Edward Hamilton had paid the lawyer with the briefcase to retrieve the footage but he had seen these very interviews and rejected them. What was he looking for? Could there be footage of someone else? There had to be. And what was Pauline Framingham's role? Was she a suspect? And why did this man think Antonia had the footage? There were more questions than answers floating in the air. But Antonia was certain of one thing: she had to find out where Warner kept the missing footage. Before the lawyer beat her to it.

10

Antonia was quiet in the car, trying to process all of the recent events. This whole situation was building momentum that Antonia was having a hard time keeping up with. No wonder it had been so easy to find Paul. Here she thought she was such a detective, but the lawyer had not only approached Paul, but dismissed him. That was frustrating. Antonia had to be one step ahead of everyone in this investigation, not behind. She was loath to admit it, but she was excited by the puzzle pieces that were being thrown at her. Of course she wished Warner had not died; that was a true tragedy. But unraveling the circumstances appealed to every aspect of her character. If only she were able to find some answers.

"We're going to Fresno to meet Carl," announced Genevieve, fiddling with the radio dial. "And don't say you're dropping me off. It's only eight-thirty. You're not going home. Not yet."

The air outside was crisp and night had fallen. With few streetlights lining the road, and even fewer houses lit up, blackness overtook them. Antonia thought it would be the perfect time to sit down with a glass of wine and regroup. Before things had become unbearable with her ex-husband Philip she often listened to him discuss his cases, and she was actually quite good at putting together missing clues. One time she made the mistake of joking that she was a better detective than Philip and ended up with a bloody lip. That had ended her brief foray into investigations. But now however, there was no Philip, and the onus fell on her.

"I'm going home," said Antonia.

"Antonia, I can't let you do that," said Genevieve. "I'm sorry to say, but you act like an old lady. A grandmother. I would say *my* grandmother but that would be a lie. My grandmother has a raging social life. She's got Bingo, she's got shuffleboard, she's got bridge, she's got movie night. I swear, it's probably all a sex fest down there in Florida."

"I'm very happy for her," said Antonia, steering the car back on to Route 27. "But your grandmother, bless her soul, doesn't run an inn. She doesn't have to wake up early, cook breakfast for twenty people, check on houses, cook dinner for fifty, seventy people. She has time to relax."

Genevieve breathed out of her nose as if she was exhaling a cigarette. She shifted in her leather seat and paused several minutes before speaking.

"Antonia," continued Genevieve softly. "You're a hot chick. I mean, sure, we both know the way you dress sucks. You have some nice titties but you keep them camouflaged like they're hand grenades."

"Thanks," said Antonia sarcastically. She slowed down at the red light. The post office was on her far left, locked tightly for the night.

"Look, don't kill the messenger. I'm your friend. I truly want what's best for you."

"Uh huh."

Antonia pressed on the accelerator when the light changed.

"And what I want for you, above and beyond all else, is . . . for you to get laid."

Despite herself, Antonia couldn't resist bursting into laughter. "That's what you want for me above all else?"

"Above all else," said Genevieve solemnly.

"How very noble of you."

"So come on, I want to get laid, you want to get laid, so let's go to Fresno."

Antonia sighed. There was no point in arguing. One drink and a quick bite wouldn't kill her, and could possibly give her mind a break so she could process everything.

She made a right on Newtown Lane then cruised down past the store fronts and hung left at the railroad station. After a few short turns, she drove down the road where the restaurant was located.

Fresno appealed to both locals and regulars, and was one of the few restaurants that remained open year round, with a steady clientele. There was an outside patio, an indoor dining room with hardwood floors and wooden rafters along the ceiling, as well as a large mirrored zinc bar that was usually buzzing with customers.

As soon as they entered, Genevieve emitted an enthusiastic squeal. "There's Carl!"

Antonia had to hand it to Genevieve. She was not shy about going after what she wanted.

Carl was seated at the end of the bar talking with Cathy, the bartender, who Antonia would run into often at the library during the day. She was the type of woman that men loved: effervescent, athletic, strawberry blonde, with milk and honey skin. She generated a lot of tips, but even more come-ons. A quick glance made it apparent Carl was not immune to her charm. Upon hearing Genevieve shriek his name, he glanced up and for a flash second Antonia could swear that he grimaced. But then just as quickly, his face broke into a warm smile.

"Did you miss me?" asked Genevieve, wrapping her arms around him and planting a kiss on his neck.

"Absolutely," said Carl.

"Did you eat?"

"No, I was waiting for you."

"You're sweet."

Genevieve gave him a long kiss on the lips.

What is it with people necking at bars tonight? thought Antonia grimly.

"Hi, Antonia," said Carl, after Genevieve had pulled away. "How was your quest to find the cameraman?"

"We got to see some of the documentary but apparently,

the juicy part is missing," Genevieve interrupted before she could respond.

"Oh?" asked Carl. "What's the juicy part?"

"We don't know," said Genevieve, climbing aboard a barstool. "But maybe Warner was right, this movie would have been a big hit. There's all sorts of scandal and intrigue around it."

"He definitely tapped into a topic people are interested in," added Antonia.

Carl appeared pensive before speaking. "You two are playing it safe, right?"

"Of course," said Genevieve.

"No, I mean, seriously," said Carl. He spread his fingers on the bar and pressed them. Antonia noticed he did this when he was thinking. "I just want you to be careful. If this documentary was the reason Warner was killed then that means a killer is looking for the footage. That is serious."

"Don't worry."

"Genevieve, seriously. Sometimes the clichés are right: it's all fun and games until someone gets hurt."

"No one's getting hurt, silly," said Genevieve.

"We'll be careful," Antonia said firmly.

"You are so cute when you are over-protective," squealed Genevieve. She gave Carl another kiss. Antonia was regretting her decision to accompany Genevieve and play the role of third wheel, so she excused herself to go to the ladies room. She splashed water on her face and stared hard at herself in the mirror. A tired and stressed face returned her gaze. This is what they call burning the candle at both ends, she realized.

Everything over the past two days was catching up with her and it showed. She'd wait a little while in the bathroom to use the time to send Joseph a quick email regarding Pauline Framingham before she would slip out of the restaurant with a wave to Genevieve.

When Antonia exited the ladies room she was relieved to see Carl and Genevieve in deep conversation. She was about to wave goodbye when suddenly a voice next to her interrupted her thoughts.

"Can I buy you a drink?"

Antonia glanced to her right and was stunned to see Sam, the hot chef from the previous evening, sitting at a table. He had shaved since yesterday, revealing smooth, clean skin. He looked fresh and Antonia instantly felt slobby and caught off guard, at the same time angry with herself for feeling that way.

"Sure," said Antonia. "What a small world."

"That's what they say about this town. Come sit down, I just got here."

While Sam motioned for the waitress and ordered drinks, Antonia found herself examining him carefully. He was young and strong, that was for sure. The type of guy who could hoist her over his shoulders and carry her out of a burning building, if the need ever arose. Antonia stole a look at his hands. Was he wearing a wedding ring? The answer was no. When she raised her eyes, she realized that he had busted her.

"Sorry, just looking to see what time it was," lied Antonia. "Do you have a watch?"

Sam smiled and touched his left wrist. "I forgot it tonight. Why? Do you need to be somewhere?"

"No, just wondering. Thanks."

Antonia reddened with embarrassment. *Great, real smooth, Antonia.*

"I'm glad I got a chance to run into you again. I felt like a bit of a doofus going on and on about you last night," said Sam. "Remind me not to drink on an empty stomach."

"Oh, don't be crazy. I love compliments."

Sam smiled, and Antonia felt her cheeks reddening again.

"Are you from East Hampton?"

Antonia shook her head. "No. California. What about you?"

"California? Whereabouts?"

"Kind of in the middle, but more north than south," she said quickly. "What about you?"

"I'm from Boulder."

"Rocky Mountain man," said Antonia.

"Born and raised."

"Do you miss it?"

"Every day," said Sam.

The waitress came with their drinks and they suspended conversation. Antonia felt like it had never taken anyone as long to place cocktail napkins on the table. When she finally left, Sam continued.

"I like the energy of New York, I love the city. I totally bought into all that. But in my heart of hearts, I'm a country boy. I like to fish, camp, hunt. Outdoorsy stuff. I know I'll end up back there with a bunch of kids and a pickup truck."

For some reason Antonia felt jealousy curling inside of her. And that was the last thing she wanted.

"Oh, are you engaged?"

"Naw. I'm coming off of a bad break up," he confessed. "You ladies just destroy me."

"Hey, don't group me in that," said Antonia. "I do not destroy anyone."

Sam smiled at her but didn't say anything. Antonia looked away. She started fiddling with the diamond stud in her ear and despite herself became self-conscious about her outfit. Genevieve was right: she did dress like a dowdy old lady. She was wearing a blue peasant skirt and a red V-neck cashmere sweater with a paisley scarf wrapped several times around her neck. She could have at least accessorized. *Note to self: make an effort.*

"So were you a bad boyfriend?" she said finally. She casually unwound the scarf from her neck. Her sweater was V-neck, so at least she could show off some cleavage. "Is this something I should know about you?"

"What? Hell, no," insisted Sam. He leaned back. He was large, yet graceful, in complete control of his body. There were rumblings of cocky swagger underneath but it only made him more appealing. "I was used, abused, and excused. She had no mercy."

"Well, maybe you had no mercy," teased Antonia, somehow emboldened.

"Me?" said Sam. He leaned back towards the bar. "Not possible."

"Not possible? Maybe you're a jerk."

Sam stared at her with mock horror. "I am the best boy-friend a girl could ever have."

"*Oh really,*" said Antonia sarcastically.

"I swear to God," said Sam. "Scout's honor."

"Were you even a scout?"

"I was," said Sam.

"Well done then."

"Thank you."

"So, why'd the girlfriend leave?"

Sam leaned back in his chair. "She ditched me for another guy. A prepster."

"Despite your being 'the best boyfriend in the world?'"

Sam laughed heartily. "Touché. Maybe I was just too good."

"Maybe," said Antonia with disbelief.

"You don't believe me?"

"Oh, I believe you," said Antonia with a smile. "You brought her roses every day, drew a bath for her at night, cooked her gourmet meals . . ."

Sam paused and stared at Antonia. "Is that really your idea of the best boyfriend in the world?"

The conversation was now straddling that fuzzy line of flir-tatious and serious. "I guess not, no. Sounds a bit . . ."

"Pussy?"

"For lack of a better word," nodded Antonia.

"Yeah, I wouldn't do roses," said Sam with a thoughtful sigh. "Roses are too obvious. For someone like you I'd pick . . ."

Sam turned and stared at Antonia appraisingly. She waited in anticipation.

"Peonies," he said finally.

Antonia felt her stomach drop. She loved peonies. They were her number one favorite.

"Did I get that right?" he asked.

"Good choice," she said casually.

He cocked his head to the side and stared at her again. "And I wouldn't cook you gourmet meals. I'd make you something fried with a lot of butter."

Antonia laughed. "I led you to that one. Okay, so what about the bath?"

Sam nodded to himself. "See, I actually think that one you'd like. You seem like a bath person. So yes, probably I'd draw you a bath."

"You know me so well already," said Antonia, attempting humor to hide the fact that it was true.

"I'm pretty good, aren't I?"

"You are," she said.

"I bet I can guess your knives."

Antonia raised her eyebrows. The knives that a chef uses are very personal and can reveal a lot about that chef's process. "Okay."

"Misono."

Antonia swallowed. "Correct. But perhaps that was too obvious . . ."

Sam shrugged. "I got it right, didn't I?"

"Yes . . ." she admitted. "And yours are?"

"Wusthof."

"Aha, should have known."

"Why should you have known?" he laughed.

"You're a big guy. I don't see you with Japanese knives. German makes sense."

"I'll take that as a compliment," said Sam nodding.

"As well you should."

Genevieve abruptly stopped on her way to the ladies room, noticing Sam and Antonia for the first time. She gave Antonia a sly glance before greeting Sam.

"I didn't see *you* here," said Genevieve. "What a coincidence!"

"I know. How about that?" asked Sam.

Antonia watched as they made brief small talk. Genevieve thought she was extremely subtle yet in three seconds flat she asked him if he was married and how long he would stay in town, smiling at Antonia when she was pleased by his answers.

"Alright, I'll let you two finish your drinks," she said as she began to depart. "Antonia hasn't had dinner yet so you could also order some food."

Antonia shot her a withering look but Sam appeared amused. "We can do that."

There was an awkward pause when she left. Antonia was embarrassed by Genevieve's blatant matchmaking. At a loss for words, she was relieved when Sam suddenly spoke.

"Hey, did you hear about the dead body they found yesterday?"

"Am I aware of it? I found it!"

"No way!" said Sam with astonishment. He slapped his palms on the table. "You're kidding right?"

"I wish I was."

Sam cocked his head and gave her a sidelong glance. "For real?"

"For real."

"What the hell happened?"

Antonia filled him in on Warner until the waitress came to take their food order. Then she moved the conversation away from murder towards more pleasant topics like favorite recipes, travel destinations and movies. Antonia felt herself relax. She sat back in her seat, cabernet flowing through her veins, and stared into Sam's sparkling eyes imagining what it would be like to see him naked. Stranger things had happened.

After Sam paid the check he escorted Antonia towards the door.

"This was a lot of fun," he said.

"Yes, thank you again for dinner. It was so nice of you to treat."

"It was an honor."

Antonia lingered for a second by the front door. "Well, goodnight."

"To you too. Oh, and I hope you don't find any more bodies."

"Yeah, me too."

"By the way, do they have any leads? Was it murder?"

Antonia shook her head. "I know nothing."

Sam smiled. "Yeah, well, doesn't matter."

Sam held the door for her and then walked her to her car before getting in his own. Antonia turned and put her car in reverse when she glanced in her rearview mirror and saw Cathy, the bartender, come running out the door of the restaurant, waving at her. Antonia hit the brakes.

"Sorry, I didn't see you leave. The guy who was at the bar earlier asked me to give this to you," Cathy said, handing Antonia a piece of paper. "He was insistent."

"Carl? The guy who Genevieve was with?"

Cathy shook her head. "No, the guy who was sitting alone in the corner. Didn't you see him?"

Antonia felt the color drain from her face. "No, what did he look like?"

"He was wearing a suit. Dark hair."

"Is he still there?"

"No, he was only there fifteen minutes. He was staring at you the whole time. You, my friend, are a popular lady. But I have to say, I'd go with Sam. He seems much friendlier."

"Thanks, Cathy."

"You betcha."

Antonia took the piece of paper from her and unfolded it. The handwriting was scribbly but clear.

We are very eager to do business with you.
We're increasing our offer to $100,000.

11

THURSDAY

By the time the sun peeked out on the horizon and unfurled its light across East Hampton, the fragrant smell of coffee was already wafting its way through the kitchen and dining room of the inn. As was their routine, Antonia and Soyla had risen early to prepare the buffet breakfast for the inn guests. (Antonia used to have an intern Liz who helped out in the morning, but she had gone back to culinary school so Antonia had asked Soyla to take over her duties.) Antonia had made a batch of cheddar chive muffins and a golden almond coffee cake filled with thick chunks of apricot. Soyla plated fresh bagels, salmon and cream cheese. The scent of cinnamon and sugar hung thickly in the air.

Antonia was in the mudroom off the kitchen and had just removed her apron to head out to the beach for her walk when Soyla told her that there was someone asking for her in the dining room. Antonia was prepared to find the lawyer, but it was not him.

Instead, a thin, tall man in his late fifties with faded reddish hair that was turning white, pale skin and cool blue eyes awaited her. He wore a forest green windbreaker with a club logo on the pocket, chinos and penny loafers. He raised his chin as she approached and with a mixture of sadness and dread, Antonia knew at once who he was.

"I'm Townsend Caruthers, Warner's father," he said, stretching out his hand.

Antonia held it with both of hers. "I'm so sorry for your loss."

"Thank you. I was wondering if we could talk for a minute?"

"Of course."

"I appreciate it. I know it's very early but I've been up for hours and I have to get back to Connecticut."

Antonia led him into the sitting room and closed the door. Soyla brought in coffee and pastries but Mr. Caruthers didn't touch anything. He sat down in the armchair with his body erect and his hands holding on tightly to the arms, like the Lincoln Memorial. Before he spoke, Antonia experienced a split second of panic that he was there to accuse her of manipulating Paul Brady by pretending she was acting as an emissary on behalf of the Caruthers family. But one look at Mr. Caruthers alleviated her anxiety. His face was awash with pain, frustration and anger, the simmering emotions so palpable that Antonia could feel his distress.

"Warner looked like you," she said, breaking the silence.

"Yes, he did, didn't he?"

"Same eyes."

He nodded.

"I drove up this morning. I came alone; my wife didn't make the trip. She's . . . not taking it very well, as you can imagine. But the police needed to talk to us, so I came."

Antonia nodded sympathetically. "Of course."

"It's very strange. They asked me if Warner had any enemies. I'm afraid I could tell them very little. You think you know someone, your own son, and yet they have a life that you know nothing about."

Antonia nodded. She could tell Mr. Caruthers wanted to talk, and she was prepared to listen. He continued, nervously fondling the arms of his chair as he spoke.

"The police told us that we weren't allowed in the Mastersons' house until the toxicology reports were back, but I was hoping they'd make an exception. I'd like to figure this out myself. But I'm afraid they're holding firm on this one."

"It must be very frustrating."

"Right, right."

He crossed his legs. His left foot remained on the floor, tapping softly as if to an imaginary beat. "I know it's their policy and they have to wait to make sure that there was no foul play. But I think that in this case the situation is obvious. No one wanted to kill my son, Miss Bingham. I'm certain he fell in that bathtub. He was probably drinking . . . I respect police protocol but it seems a little silly . . ."

Antonia nodded. "I will absolutely make sure that when the house is unsealed I will retrieve Warner's possessions as quickly as possible and return them to you."

He looked up startled. "Oh yes, thank you. I didn't even think about that . . ."

Silence filled the room. She could tell Mr. Caruthers was restless but she didn't know how to help him. He was engulfed in sorrow of the sort that no one can penetrate. When Antonia's mother died of cancer when Antonia was only ten she felt as if the wind had been sucked out of her. And when her father died, it was more traumatic. She experienced panic attacks for months. But it seemed so wrong to bury a child. So heartbreaking.

"When is the funeral?"

"Saturday. We have to wait for his brother to return from Australia. It takes Morgan awhile to get his act together. But he'll make it."

"That's good."

Again, they descended into quietude. Antonia felt as if she was an actor in a dress rehearsal where no one knew their lines. Each sentence came out stilted and weighted, as if they were clumsily stumbling their way through.

Mr. Caruthers glanced around the room before returning his gaze to Antonia. "I'm not here to place the blame on anyone. My son is dead and there is nothing I can do about it. I told the Mastersons they don't have to worry about a lawsuit. Even if they were liable, and I know in this day and age, everyone is, I would never pursue that path. That's not how we are."

"That's very nice of you. I'm sure they are very grateful."

"I suppose I just have . . . questions. That's really why I'm here. Not about what happened, hell, I don't even really want to know what happened. More about Warner's final days; I heard he was causing a lot of problems with his documentary. The whole thing was ill-advised, if you ask me. But Warner was not the kid you could talk to on things like that. He was headstrong. Chip off the old block, I suppose . . ."

He stared off into space. Antonia prayed he would not cry. That might unleash her own floodgates. She waited a beat before speaking.

"I have been in contact with Paul Brady, the cameraman. He has the footage of the interviews Warner conducted. I am sure legally they belong to you. Would you like me to retrieve them?"

"Right, I hadn't really thought of that . . ."

Antonia didn't want to tell him that the interviews would probably end up on *TMZ* if Paul Brady had his way. "Unless you want him to continue on with the project."

He shook his head. "No. I don't want that documentary to see the light of day. If you can write down the contact info for the cameraman, I'll have my lawyer send him a letter." He paused before adding, "I don't want to turn on the television one day and see Warner making a fool of himself."

"I understand."

"Too bad he wasted time on this."

"Mr. Caruthers, was there another documentary that Warner was working on?"

"Not that I am aware of."

"Had he done any interviews in New York or elsewhere?"

"I'm not sure. He was in California visiting friends before

he came out here so I don't think so. But I don't know. I really tried to stay out of it."

"I understand," said Antonia. "I happened to watch some of the interviews that Warner conducted including the one with Sheila Black, Sidney Black's ex-wife. It's true it was incendiary, but it hardly contained new information that the tabloids hadn't already picked up. I know that Sid Black was particularly enraged by the documentary, but there seems to be little reason for it. Did Warner ever mention anything to you?"

"No. He would never confide in me about that. He knew that I thought the whole project was junk. Such a waste of time. And you know what kills me? That's his mark on the world. All that is left of him . . ."

He didn't finish. Antonia felt very sorry for him.

"Mr. Caruthers, I agree that this documentary might have been controversial and perhaps not the sort of thing that you or I would watch, but I do know is that he truly believed with conviction that he had a role in exposing the hypocrisy of the upper classes in his attempt to defend the common man. Maybe he felt guilty that he was brought up with privilege and this was his way of atoning for it, but however he demonstrated it, he tried to make a mark for justice. I think that should bring you some comfort."

Mr. Caruthers nodded. "Yes, yes it should."

Antonia nodded. He abruptly stood up. "I won't take up any more of your time."

"It's no bother at all."

His eyes darted around the room and fell on the desk. "English Regency. I also collect it. That's a nice piece."

He walked over and ran a hand along the top.

"I bought it at Hampton Briggs Antiques in Bridgehampton."

"Beautiful."

They began to walk towards the door.

Mr. Caruthers thrust out his hand.

"Thank you for meeting with me. I appreciate your time. Warner said you were very helpful to him."

"Me? I barely did anything. Just gave him the key."

"Well, he specifically mentioned you. Antonia Bingham. Said you were very helpful."

Antonia's opinion of Warner shot up tenfold. Perhaps he was a better person that she realized. Or maybe he just thought of her as the 'common man.'

* * * * *

The air was brisk and fresh and the sun was climbing up the sky when Antonia finally left the inn. She zipped up her fleece and walked over to her Saab. There were three cars parked next to Antonia's. One was a rented silver Honda that belonged to a German couple who had checked in a few days prior. Another was a green Volvo station wagon with Connecticut plates that belonged to an older man and woman who were staying at the inn celebrating their anniversary. And the final car was a black 2010 BMW that belonged to Bridget Curtis. The staff parked their cars in the back lot around the corner. Parking was tight so Antonia encouraged employees to carpool.

Antonia was distracted with rehashing the events of the morning but suddenly stopped abruptly and turned around. Bridget drove a black German car. Len, the security guard at the Dune Club had seen Warner and a woman in a black German car. Antonia had seen them talking at the front door of the inn. What was the connection? Antonia realized she still hadn't had a chance to ask Bridget about it. She put that on her 'To Do' list, which was now a dozen pages long.

When Antonia pulled into the Main Beach parking lot she noted that the surf was rough, the water a murky blue. She scanned the beach. Two women were walking with a small white Maltese. There were several surfers bobbing in the waves. Antonia noticed a man walking towards the jetty and her heart did a leap, but then she realized it wasn't Nick. There were no dogs with him, and upon closer inspection this man was taller and thinner than Nick. What did she expect? He would have been there an hour ago.

She kicked off her shoes and made her way down towards the edge of the water. The sand felt cold and damp under her feet. Little pools of water had formed near the break and Antonia avoided them. The water was still frigid this time of year. The sky was blue and bright, but the sun was cold and hard. Gaggles of noisy geese dappled the skyline, eastbound. Antonia watched the waves crash and then recede. Two men were standing on the surf with fishing rods and a bucket.

Antonia let out a deep breath that was louder than she had expected. She couldn't help it but she felt a surge of disappointment. She knew she was later than usual, but why couldn't

Nick have waited? In the past he had been late and she had dawdled until he finally came. Usually if he was away he told her in advance. Mostly, she was mad at herself for caring.

An image of Sam the Chef popped into her mind. He was definitely cute and they had really hit it off last night. He was so easy to talk to and comfortable in his own skin that it made her feel relaxed. She could imagine falling for him. But the negatives already had started to creep in her brain, cracking all images of fantasyland. The fact was Sam was young and transient. He was in town to set up his restaurant and then leave. She knew those types. Chefs were even more dangerous than actors. It was the hunger that drew them to their professions and that instilled in them an eternal quest to be sated, both by food and romance. She could see potential heartbreak written all over it. Not that her obsession with Nick made it any better, but at least she had come to terms with the fact that he was unattainable. Or at least she had tried to. The reality was that she had failed in that department as well. Oh, when was she going to learn? Antonia chided herself. She was a failure when it came to her love life. She was thirty-five and she still didn't know better!

Upon reaching the jetty, Antonia turned around. She pulled her phone out of her pocket and saw that it was nearing eight o'clock. Time to return to work. She walked towards the parking lot. As she approached, she noticed a figure standing near the dunes. The person was facing Antonia but was too far away for Antonia to make out whom it was. Antonia squinted. From a distance, and she couldn't be sure, it looked like it was

Bridget. It was definitely a woman, and she had long dark hair. Antonia quickened her pace. This would be a good opportunity to casually ask Bridget if she had known Warner.

Antonia started a light jog. She was definitely not used to exertion but she wanted to catch up with Bridget—at least, who she thought was Bridget. Suddenly, as if noticing that Antonia was about to get a better look at her, the woman turned quickly and stepped back into the parking lot, out of Antonia's line of vision. Determined now, Antonia began to run. Huffing and puffing and cursing every cream puff she had ever eaten, Antonia made it to the parking lot. Her eyes scanned the area. No Bridget. No one. She reluctantly entered her car.

As Antonia cruised down the road, she decided to do a drive-by of the Mastersons' house. She wasn't allowed in but no one said she couldn't stop by to check on it. She put on her left blinker to turn left on to Lily Pond Lane and had to wait until several cars and trucks passed. Already the roads were thickening with commercial traffic. Most of the gardeners and construction workers who serviced the houses in the Hamptons commuted from up island where the cost of living was cheaper. Their twice-daily commute that thronged Route 27 was nicknamed the "Trade Parade."

Antonia let her car idle outside of the Mastersons' driveway. The house was bathed in sunlight. If Antonia had expected it to seem inauspicious or nefarious, she was wrong; it looked as it always did, as did all of the neighbors' properties. Around her there was movement everywhere. The hum of lawnmowers rang out behind her. The man with the Wheaten terrier was accompanying his dog on their usual morning walk. A white pick-up truck drove past Antonia and pulled into the neighbor's driveway. Something occurred to Antonia and she turned to watch the man with the terrier as he grew closer. Her pulse quickened.

It was *Edward Hamilton!* No wonder she recognized him when she saw the footage! Here he had been right under her nose the entire time. Antonia quickly dialed a number on her cell phone.

Larry Lipper's voice barked a demanding hello.

"It's Antonia. Question. Where does Edward Hamilton live?"

"Hang on a minute, did you talk to the cameraman?"

Antonia didn't have time to fill him in. "I did, but he said Warner didn't have a girlfriend here. Didn't know anything about a lady in a car."

"Hang on, start from the beginning," interrupted Larry.

"Larry, I promise I will call you later and fill you in on the details. I'm in a rush now and have an urgent question: where does Edward Hamilton live? And don't pretend like you don't know."

"What do I get in return?"

Antonia sighed in exasperation. "A blow job."

"Really?"

"No. Of course not. But you get to be a good person. Now tell me."

Larry sighed. "He lives on Lily Pond Lane."

Antonia nodded. "All coming together."

"You think he offed Warner?"

"No."

"Liar."

"I don't."

"Hang on a sec, my other line," Larry demanded.

"Can't wait. Goodbye, Larry."

Antonia paused, her hands on the steering wheel. Should she stop Edward Hamilton and say something? This was her chance after all. Edward Hamilton was coming closer and closer. Antonia rolled down the window.

"Good morning!" she called out.

"Good morning," he responded brightly.

"Out for a walk?" Antonia asked, before kicking herself for saying such a dumb and obvious thing.

"Yes, Samantha enjoys a brisk morning lap around the neighborhood," he said, patting his dog. Samantha impatiently lurched forward, but Hamilton held her tight.

"I'm *Antonia Bingham.*"

She waited for his response. Would it ring any bells?

"Edward Hamilton," he replied.

"I look after the Mastersons' house. I'm not allowed in right now because of what happened, you know."

Antonia watched Edward Hamilton's face very carefully. He remained composed, his watery blue eyes blinked several times as if focusing, but that was all. If Antonia had hoped to see flashes of anger or fear she was unrewarded.

"Yes, I saw all of the police activity here the other day," he replied.

"Sad, right? A tragedy."

"Yes," he said.

Samantha was becoming increasingly impatient, pulling forward, eager to continue her walk. Antonia tried to think of something else to say. "Did you happen to know . . ."

Before she could finish, Samantha pushed forward, yanking Edward Hamilton with her. "Sorry, I'm afraid we must keep moving," he said.

"Okay," said Antonia with disappointment. "Have a great day."

Well, that was a failure, thought Antonia. Although what did she expect? Was she really going to ask him if he had killed Warner? Or put his lawyers on her case to find the footage? She tried to remember some of the tactics that she had gleaned from her ex-husband regarding interrogating suspects. She recalled that he had said to isolate a suspect. Well, that was impossible. Was she supposed to grab Edward Hamilton and shove him in her car and drive away? She was an overweight, 5'6" woman; she doubted she could have physically hoisted him into the car. That was for law enforcement, people who had guns and badges. Philip had also mentioned the clichéd good-cop-bad-cop theory. Of course, that wouldn't have worked either, as she was alone. Other ideas were to have the suspect tell his side of the story and search for inconsistencies. Again, she failed on that front. She blamed the dog on that one. The only thing she had really done was to scan his face for signs of stress when she mentioned Warner. But Edward Hamilton had been a blank.

Antonia felt defeated. She had come to fancy herself as

something as a sleuth, seeing that she solved a murder in the fall. But maybe that was just luck. She put her car in drive and began her journey home. As she passed the neighbor's house she glanced in the driveway and saw the white pickup truck that had passed her. A man was pulling a large hose off the roof and one of those giant vacuums they use on pools. *The pool man.*

Antonia made a quick turn into the neighbor's driveway. The pool man froze and glanced at her expectantly.

"Hi," said Antonia, closing her car door.

He was in his mid-thirties, Latino, with a small mustache and a t-shirt emblazoned with the moniker *Roselli Brothers Pools.* She quickly surmised that he was not one of the Roselli brothers.

"Hi," said the man nodding.

"I work at the house next door. I think you talked to my friend the other day, the man from the newspaper?"

"Yes," said the man cautiously.

"You told him you saw Warner Caruthers going through the bushes?"

The man cocked his head to the side. "I think I saw the man. I'm not sure it's the guy who died."

"What did he look like?"

'I didn't have a good look. He wore a baseball cap. He went through the bushes to the house behind."

"Was that the only time you saw the man?"

"Your friend asked me that the other day and I said no, but I forgot something. Last week, and I'm not sure if it was the same guy, but a guy came out of the Mastersons' house, then a girl. They kissed and the girl drove away."

Antonia's pulse quickened with excitement. "What did the girl look like?"

He looked up at the sky as if it held her picture. "Dark hair, skinny."

"Long or short hair?"

"Long."

"Well dressed?"

The man gave her a quizzical look. "I think she was wearing jeans."

"Did you happen to see her car?"

He shook his head. "No. Just her."

The pool man stood still, awaiting further questioning. He was carrying a large hose and several buckets. Antonia felt guilty putting him through the third degree.

"Thank you. You've been a real help."

Antonia crunched back down the driveway. She felt a little bit better about herself as she now had a lead. A girl with dark hair had been spotted with Warner at the Mastersons' house. A girl who had not yet come forward. The question was, why not? What did she have to hide?

Antonia noticed with dismay that she had a new nick on the side of her car door as she opened it. Her beloved Saab was coming to the end of its life. It had done her right all these years and she felt a little sentimental about it, especially since they weren't made anymore. All good things come to an end. As she sat down she glanced in her rearview mirror and saw a black car lingering outside the hedges. Antonia quickly craned her neck to have a better look, but as soon as she did so, the car zoomed away. Her pulse quickened. Was she being followed? Or was she just paranoid?

When Antonia finally pulled into the inn's parking lot, she saw Bridget's car parked exactly where she had seen it before. Antonia must have been delusional when she thought she saw Bridget at the beach. She walked towards the back steps and took them two at a time, in a hasty effort to return to the kitchen for an early start at dinner prep. With everything that was going on these days, she needed to prepare in advance lest some stranger show up at her doorstep and demand her time. She opened the screen door but not before peeking back at Bridget's car. She couldn't help it; it was calling her. She was already behind, what did another minute or two matter? She ran back outside and rested her hand on the BMW's hood. It was warm.

12

Joseph was perched in a green Adirondack chair by the garden. A pitcher of iced tea was sweating on the wrought iron table, alongside two glasses of crushed ice that was slowly melting. He was chatting with Hector, who pulling dead leaves off the carrots. A green rubber hose lay flat on the ground and emitted a small trickle of water onto the patch of dirt. The smell of damp earth hung in the air.

"Hector and I are excited to attempt growing Japanese eggplant. Last time I tried at my own house I was less than successful, but I know with Hector's skill we will be a success," said Joseph when he felt Antonia's presence.

"Hector is the best. Last year the garden was bountiful."

"Maybe too much zucchini," Hector admitted. They had experienced a bumper crop the previous year.

"It was wonderful! I was up for the challenge. I had to devise so many innovative ways to prepare zucchini."

"They were delicious," said Hector.

"I should write a cookbook."

"I've been telling you that for months," said Joseph.

"Good idea!" said Hector, before gathering his tools and moving towards the back of the lawn.

Joseph squinted up at Antonia and smiled knowingly. The midday sun cast a strong light across the sprawling yard. Antonia plopped down in the chair next to Joseph. She began by detailing the dinner menu but quickly switched to filling him in on the recent developments. Joseph listened quietly. His only motion was to remove a cigar from his breast pocket and tap it against the arm of his chair.

"So, what do you think?" asked Antonia, when she had finished her account.

"I'm concerned. If you're being followed, it's now becoming dangerous."

"I was afraid you might say that."

"You have to be careful, don't forget all that has happened to you, Antonia. Despite having a talent for detective work, you are not a trained professional."

"I know, I know. And I am. But isn't it interesting about the girlfriend? Do you think it was Bridget? She has long dark hair. She was seen with Warner. I'm going to have to ask her. It's not very polite considering she is a paying guest in my inn, but there's something she's hiding. I'm sure about that."

"It doesn't hurt to ask. Just don't accuse her, please."

"Come on, I'm a little more subtle than that!" she chided.

"And don't forget that most women have dark hair. It

would be a little too easy for it to be someone who is staying right under your nose."

"You're right," sighed Antonia.

"I have my own news," said Joseph, taking a sip of his iced tea. "I did follow up on your email about Pauline Framingham, the pharmaceutical heiress from Warner's documentary."

"And?"

Joseph nodded. "Now of course I am familiar with the name Framingham and Framingham Industries. You'd have to live under a rock to not know who they are. In recent years they have not received as much press, perhaps because the family members are not as flashy as other billionaires, but once upon a time they were followed and remarked upon in the papers. When you said the name Pauline Framingham something rang a bell."

Joseph paused to light his cigar.

"I'm dying here," said Antonia.

"Sorry," said Joseph, blowing a large puff of smoke. "I found very little on the Internet, so I went back to the old periodicals in the East Hampton Library."

"And . . ." prompted Antonia.

"And I found a few slight articles about Pauline Framingham. Apparently, at the age of seventeen, she was almost tried for manslaughter for killing her best friend."

"What?!"

"Yes. The charges somehow disappeared; of course this is going back thirty years ago when the rich and powerful were more powerful. I'm certain that the Framingham family had undue influence . . ."

"How did she kill her?"

Joseph ashed his cigar, turned and glanced at Antonia. "With a tennis racket."

"You're kidding?" asked Antonia, practically jumping out of her chair.

"The facts of the case are fuzzy. Pauline always maintained her innocence. The confirmed reports are that Pauline and her friend Susie were playing tennis on the courts at Pauline's estate on West End Road. And this is where it got vague; Pauline said she left to get a pitcher of lemonade and when she returned Susie had been killed. But the police maintain that the girls had been sparring and Pauline whacked her friend on the head with a racket. They had a witness even. They did everything to coerce her to confess, even suggesting that perhaps Pauline was practicing her swing and the friend stepped behind her. Which is also not plausible, considering there was severe head trauma. But Pauline never confessed and the charges went away. However, the 'cloud of suspicion' has always hung over Pauline's head."

Antonia didn't know what to make of these revelations. She had not thought Pauline Framingham a serious contender in the murderers' gallery, but perhaps the stealth kind are the likeliest suspects.

"This is becoming even more bizarre." Antonia stood up and began to pace.

"The plot thickens, as they say." Joseph lit his cigar and puffed away.

* * * * *

Antonia was so lost in thought pondering her next move that she nearly walked right into Genevieve's new beau, Carl when she rounded the corner in the parlor. He put up his hands and clasped her wrists to prevent her from mowing him down. For a brief second it felt like a weirdly intimate exchange, with Carl so close to Antonia that she could feel his breath on her forehead. She took a small step back.

"I'm so sorry," said Antonia, embarrassed. "I'm a little distracted these days."

Antonia moved to drop her hands and Carl unwrapped his long thin fingers from her wrist. There was a certain elegance to his moves, as if he were a dancer. He was wearing a dark suit and a red and blue striped tie that Antonia had seen on a recent Brooks Brothers catalogue cover.

"No worries, I know those days."

Antonia smiled slightly but must have given him a quizzical look as to what he was doing there because he quickly continued.

"I was just showing the house two doors down. It's a real beauty, three story, shingled, diamond-paned windows, in perfect shape. Only the location is a bit of a problem for most people, right on the highway."

"Oh, I know that house. It's very pretty. Did the people like it?"

"Yes, actually they were very enthusiastic. It was a very wealthy couple from the city, he's one of those hedge fund guys."

"Well, that's great."

"I guess," he said, looking less than excited.

"Are they being difficult, haggling over the price?"

"No, it's not that. It's just that I don't see them in this house. It's all wrong."

"How so?"

"They're too nouveau. I don't think they'd appreciate it ultimately. I know most realtors would love a quick transaction, but that's not what is most important to me. I like to believe what I am doing is almost like matchmaking. I'd rather fit the correct family into the correct place. So that things may be in order."

"Almost like feng shui?"

He shrugged. "Sort of. What I mean is that the universe makes up its own mind about things. You can't impose yourself. Things have to happen."

Antonia wasn't sure what to make of Carl's attitude. "Well, I'm just glad my realtor didn't impose his opinion on me when I bought this place. I knew the second I saw it that it was perfect, even though it was in horrible condition."

Carl glanced around carefully. His eyes moved over everything.

"And now it's a gem."

"Thank you."

"Actually, that's why I stopped by. I have a business proposition."

"Oh?"

"Yes. The couple I showed the house to today drove all the way out here for the day. I would have liked to have shown them a few more houses but they had to rush back, which isn't ideal. My thought was perhaps my real estate company could do some sort of arrangement with you here at the Windmill Inn. We promote your inn and in return perhaps our clients receive a discounted rate, something to give them incentive to stay here."

"I'd be happy to look into that," said Antonia. "What's your company called?"

"Star Properties."

"Hmm. I haven't heard of that one."

"We're very low-key. We cater to a discreet audience."

"I hear you. Well, I'd love to work with you. We have arrangements with several companies and we're always looking for ways to generate business."

Carl nodded slowly. He ran his fingers through his hair. "Great. I'll run it by some of my colleagues."

"We're just getting ready for tea. Can I offer you anything to eat?"

"No, thanks," said Carl. He pulled out his cell phone and looked at the time. "I should run. I want to stop by and see Grandmother before my next meeting."

"Did you make an appointment this time?" Antonia said teasingly.

Carl smiled. "I tried, but there was no answer. I'm going over anyway to check on her. She hasn't been feeling very well."

"Oh, I'm sorry to hear that. I got the impression before that she was in good health."

"Well . . . there are some health issues there that she denies.

And the fact is, she's old. When you're in your eighties it's day-to-day."

"True."

"It's sad to see people age. I don't know what's worse, losing them in their prime or when they can barely remember you."

She sensed a flicker of unhappiness behind his dark eyes. Antonia didn't want to mention that having lost both her parents, she could definitively attest that she would have preferred to have kept them on this earth a bit longer.

But before she could respond, Jonathan hastily entered the room.

"Oh, Antonia . . ." Jonathan began before freezing when his eyes fell on Carl. "I'm sorry, I'll come back later."

"It's okay, did you have a question?"

Antonia noticed that Jonathan's eyes flitted to Carl and a look of discomfort fell across his face.

"Just some wedding party details. We can discuss later."

Before Antonia could respond, Jonathan hurried out of the room. Antonia turned and gave Carl a skeptical look.

"Do you two know each other?"

Carl wrinkled his face. "I didn't know he worked here."

"Yes, he started in November. My last manager moved upstate for the next twenty-five years."

"I don't really know him but I've run across him. I didn't get the best impression."

"Really?" asked Antonia with surprise. "What happened?"

Carl glanced up at the ceiling. He sighed deeply. "Look, I don't want to go into details, and I'm sure he does a brilliant job here. Perhaps we just met on an off night. We took an instant dislike to each other."

"I'm so surprised to hear that. He's a wonderful person. I think you probably just got the wrong first impression."

"I'm usually pretty good at reading people."

* * * * *

After Carl left, Antonia sank into the velvet armchair. She wondered what Carl had against Jonathan. She hoped that it was some sort of misunderstanding. It would become very awkward if there was animosity between the two of them. Particularly since Carl had just expressed interest in a business relationship. It would be Jonathan who handled that sort of thing. When Antonia finally heaved herself off her plush pillow she was startled to discover that Bridget was seated in the large wingback chair on the far side of the room. Far enough to remain out of sight but close enough to eavesdrop.

"Oh! I didn't see you there!" exclaimed Antonia.

"I hope it's alright," said Bridget evenly.

Antonia regained her composure.

"No, of course it's okay for you to be here, you just surprised me. I thought we were alone."

Bridget held her gaze but said nothing. Antonia bent down to tuck the lamp cords underneath the skirted table all the while feeling Bridget's eyes boring into her. She had to figure out how to finesse the question of Bridget and Warner.

"So, what brings you to East Hampton this time of year?" Antonia asked.

Bridget appeared surprised by the question. "I work in fashion. I do location scouting for catalogues."

"Oh, well East Hampton is a photographer's dream. We have a lot of shoots out here."

"I know, that's why it's tricky. I'm trying to find some new venues. I've been driving around all week."

"Well, please let me know if you need help."

"Thanks."

"You know," said Antonia. "I wanted to ask you about Warner Caruthers."

"Who?" asked Bridget.

"Warner Caruthers?" repeated Antonia. "You were friends with him, right?"

Bridget placed a bookmark inside her novel and closed it. "No."

"Are you sure?"

Bridget spoke carefully. "I don't know anyone named Warner Caruthers."

"Oh," said Antonia not sure how to proceed. The room felt suddenly quiet. Should she press her? She was a guest at the inn and it really was none of Antonia's business.

"You said 'were,'" asked Bridget. "Is he dead?"

"Yes," said Antonia. "Unfortunately, he died earlier this week."

Bridget grimaced. "That's horrible."

Antonia watched her face carefully. She seemed genuinely surprised. Either that, or she was a very talented liar.

"I know," concurred Antonia. "We're just trying to locate the young woman he was keeping company with."

Antonia purposely let her sentence trickle off. Bridget remained expressionless.

"Wouldn't the police know?"

Antonia shook her head. "No."

Bridget nodded. "I hope they find her."

"Me too."

Antonia paused, staring at Bridget. She'd done everything by the book: isolated her, studied her face for signs of stress, tried to pump her for information but still she received no reaction. For a second she wished Genevieve was with her so she could be 'bad cop' but she realized that was too aggressive. Joseph was right; there were lots of women with dark hair that Warner could have been with.

"Anyway, sorry, never should have brought it up. I thought you knew him. On the positive side, the news says we will have spectacular weather this week."

Antonia picked up a vase of tulips off the coffee table and moved it over to the side table against the windowsill.

"That's good," replied Bridget. She watched Antonia carefully before sliding her marker out of her book and prepared to resume reading.

"I'm off to make dinner," said Antonia with fake cheer. "Will you be joining us this evening?"

"Definitely," replied Bridget.

* * * * *

Sergeant Flanagan was standing by the reception desk. He was a wiry man in his forties; fit but lean, of medium height, with short dark hair and brown eyes. His build was average and his frame unassuming, but upon closer inspection, taut muscles rippled under his skin as he moved. He was the type of man whose strength was probably under-estimated by hardened criminals. Antonia had seen his kind before, men with a deceptively sinewy body that contained enormous potency. She took a deep breath when she first saw him, but wasted no time ushering him into her office. His eyes took in the small space, consuming every detail and making Antonia slightly embarrassed by the plates of half-eaten sandwiches and chocolate chip muffins. She could tell he would prefer to stand, but he politely sat down across from Antonia with reluctance.

"What can I do for you?" she asked.

"I had some questions."

"Oh. Can I get you anything to drink or eat? Coffee, donuts?"

He smiled slightly. "No, thanks."

"You must get that a lot. Coffee, donuts."

"Everyone thinks they're the first."

Antonia hoped he couldn't tell how nervous she was. She aligned the papers on her ink blotter but then realized that it might make her appear guilty. She glanced up and smiled at him.

"You know, before you ask me anything, I'll just jump in. Recently, some information has come to my attention that I think should be turned over to the police in regards to the death of Warner Caruthers."

Sergeant Flanagan leaned back in his chair and smiled.

"The other day I had the opinion that you were not exactly forthcoming."

"Really?"

"Yes."

Antonia froze her face into a smile. Her second impression of Sergeant Flanagan confirmed her first: this man was no dummy. He was alert and intelligent; not someone to be dismissed. It was apparent in his eyes alone.

"Well, now that you mention it, I was thinking about my statement, reviewing it, if you will. And I wondered if I had forgotten to mention that I found a Lysol can in the bathroom where Warner was discovered. I knew it wasn't important at the time, I thought Rosita, the cleaner, had left it. But then I recalled that the Mastersons only use organic products."

The sergeant's eyes grew slightly wider and he shifted in his seat. "And what did you do with this can?"

"I accidentally took it. I have it upstairs."

"Miss Bingham, removing something from a possible crime scene can make you guilty of hindering and obstruction."

"Oh, but I didn't realize it was a crime scene," Antonia said coyly. "The first responding officer on the scene said it appeared as if Warner slipped. And besides, if I *unknowingly* removed something from a crime scene, and I had no culpable mental state, I won't get into trouble if I return it in good faith."

"This is tampering. I should cite you."

"I didn't do it on purpose. I was just cleaning up a little, so the police had a clear path to Warner," lied Antonia.

Sergeant Flanagan shifted in his seat. "I don't like it."

Antonia put her hand to her heart. "I am so sorry."

He sighed deeply. "Give me the can."

"I will give it to you at the end of this meeting."

Sergeant Flanagan gave her a quizzical gaze. "You know the law well."

"I watch a lot of TV."

"Now, can I assume there is a reason you decided to tell me about the can? Or was it just because I showed up on your doorstep."

"Well, at first I thought everyone was being silly when they thought that Warner had been murdered . . ."

He interrupted her. "That is still not a confirmed fact. Autopsy reports are not in yet."

"I know, but you know how people gossip. Friends of mine who are also drama seekers were promoting the theory."

"Yes, a lot of people are."

"But now I have my doubts about what happened . . ."

"And?"

"I think this situation is more complicated than I thought. I think it is possible Warner *was* murdered. And I know the motive."

She launched into an explanation about the lawyer who had first offered her $50,000 for the missing footage before upping his offer to $100,000 after he tracked her down at Fresno. She presented Terry Rudolph's business card as well as the note that had been given to her by Cathy the bartender. Sergeant Flanagan took both gingerly and copied the information into a worn brown leather notebook that he produced from his pocket. Antonia noticed he wore a very thick gold band on his ring finger. When he glanced up, she continued.

"The fact is, I think he's following me."

"Why's that?"

"Well, he found me at Fresno."

"How do you know it was him?"

"Isn't it obvious? 'Upping the offer.'"

Sergeant Flanagan remained unmoved. "Is there another reason you think he is following you?"

Antonia and the cop locked eyes. She didn't want to tell him about the file that was left for her at the Felds' because it would lead to all sorts of questions about her past. Questions she wasn't willing to answer. In addition, if she mentioned that she had seen someone in Paul Brady's bushes, Sergeant Flanagan might tell her to stay away from potential suspects or witnesses. It was better to remain silent.

"No, just a hunch."

Sergeant Flanagan continued to hold her gaze. He knew she was holding out on him again. Finally, he sighed. "Miss Bingham, I want to be helpful here, but if he's made no threat to you, only presented you with a business card and an offer, technically he's done nothing illegal."

Antonia nodded.

"Unless there is more you want to add?" asked Sergeant Flanagan.

"That's all. I just hope you look into it."

He smiled. "We will. And Miss Bingham, let me please add that you have to let the police do our job. If this ever ends up becoming a criminal investigation, you might be called as a material witness. Therefore, it is of the utmost importance that you steer clear of this investigation. Do you understand?"

Antonia nodded. If she spoke her agreement and then continued her inquiry into Warner's death, it would mean that she lied. But nodding was vague, wasn't it?

Sergeant Flanagan eyed her sternly. "Now if you will please bring me the Lysol can."

13

After seeing the detective out, Antonia breezed through the parlor where afternoon tea was in full swing. The room was perfumed with the scent of peppermint and chamomile and there was a hum of happy chatter. Antonia loved formal tea. When she first opened the inn, she had offered it every day. But she soon learned sadly that it didn't make much financial sense and she was hemorrhaging money. (Every aspect of running an inn was trial and error.) So to compromise, she offered tea on Thursdays for the bargain price of fifteen dollars a caddy. She actively recruited members of the Ladies Village Improvement Society, the Village Preservation Society as well as whatever book club, bible group and retirement program she could reach. She used her finest lace napkins, silver trays and delicate china, and made sure to have a fire blazing at all times, creating a cozy and intimate atmosphere. It was much more popular than the daily tea, and as the attendance grew week after week, Jonathan rewarded Antonia with his highest accolade, confirming that her idea was "sheer brilliance."

Antonia recognized several people and stopped to greet them. The ladies who knew Antonia well sat upright and inquired with somber faces about her discovery in the Mastersons' guest bathroom. They clucked when she detailed the loss of Warner Caruthers, marveling that he was "so young" and it was "such a loss." Just as Antonia would excuse herself, they would lean in with a mischievous glint in their eyes and whisper if Antonia thought it was "murder." She smiled, but ultimately remained evasive about the details. She noticed that two of her favorite ladies were seated in their usual corner table and she moved over to them as quickly as she could.

Ruth Thompson, aged seventy-five and an active retiree who swam thirty laps at the Rec Center every day of the year was joined by her friend Penny Halsey, aged seventy-two, an expert bridge player. Both women were old-school East Hampton. Ruth's family, on her maternal side, had been among the town's founding families, and had several streets named after them. And Penny's husband's family had been there for centuries and still owned many houses on Main Street. Antonia knew both women well from their work on the East Hampton Historical Society, as well as the library committees.

"I heard there were quite a few people popping champagne around town when they learned of this young man's death," said Ruth. She sat completely erect in her plush armchair, fiercely buttering a raisin scone.

"You're terrible," said her friend Penny. "But it *is* true, I'm afraid. This documentary caused quite a stink."

"Well, the young man I met was lovely," assured Antonia. "I can't reconcile the Warner I knew with the one I am hearing about."

"Split personality," said Ruth, popping the scone in her mouth.

"Probably drugs," added Penny. "I just watched a news show about crystal methadone. It's a narcotic very popular with young people."

"I don't think he was into that," said Antonia.

"I wouldn't be so sure," said Penny. "Apparently, everyone is doing it."

"Oh, Penny, maybe we should try it," said Ruth when her mouth was no longer filled.

"Hilarious!" responded Penny before dissolving into a fit of giggles.

Antonia joined in the laughter. Ruth and Penny, along with their friend Nancy, were always an amusing addition to tea. They had a no-holds-barred outspokenness to them, and could often be quite shocking.

"Where's Nancy today?" asked Antonia, when the laughter subsided.

"We don't know, but she said she was coming," replied Penny.

"She's been getting dotty lately. She probably forgot," said Ruth.

"You're terrible," said Penny.

"I'm *honest.*"

"Well, tell her I missed her," said Antonia.

Penny's eyes widened as she stared behind Antonia.

"*There* he is!" said Penny loudly.

"It's about time," agreed Ruth.

Antonia glanced in the direction of the doorway, where Joseph had just entered. He nodded and waved to the ladies, who chanted greetings as he rolled towards his usual table. Jonathan joked that Joseph was treated like a rock star performing at Wembley Stadium when he showed up for afternoon tea. The ladies *loved* him, and it always seemed like a competition between them as to who could move over to his table first. Joseph would never confess but he adored the attention. He liked to put on a fresh boutonniere and regaled the ladies with the latest historical anecdotes he had uncovered. He had a way of making war stories scintillating and gossipy.

"Stay out of trouble," Antonia warned with a smile when Joseph approached.

"My dear, I am just here to have some Earl Grey," he replied with a wink.

"Joseph, you *must* join us today," said Ruth firmly. "And we have an extra place as Nancy didn't show."

"I would love your company," said Joseph.

Antonia laughed and moved towards the kitchen. On her way, she noticed a blonde woman sitting alone at a table by the window. Antonia recognized her immediately.

"How is everything this afternoon?" Antonia asked.

"Fine, although I really don't like watercress sandwiches. I think there were a disproportionate number of watercress sand-wiches on my plate. I prefer the others." Her voice was a high-pitched whine.

"Well, we can definitely fix that," said Antonia brightly. She picked up the top plate of the caddy with the offensive sandwiches and motioned for Soyla. "Can you please bring this lady more cucumber and egg salad sandwiches."

"Sure, Antonia."

Antonia returned her gaze to the woman. She was very petite, with bones that appeared so brittle they might snap at any moment. As Antonia scanned her outfit, she noticed that the woman was covered in what appeared to be dog or cat fur. She also had the camellia pin clipped to her Peter Pan collar.

"Thank you," the woman said, twisting her scarf. "I hate to be a bother about the sandwiches, but what's the point if I don't like it? Customer satisfaction is the most important thing, right?"

"Absolutely. I'm Antonia Bingham, by the way. The inn-keeper."

"Sheila Black."

For a split-second, Antonia debated if she should say any-thing. It was perhaps indiscreet. But as always with Antonia, curiosity trumped all. "I actually recognize you. You see, I saw the interview that Warner Caruthers conducted with you for his documentary."

Her face brightened. "Oh, really? Yes, how do I look?"

"You look . . . great," said Antonia.

Sheila pushed her thin hair behind her ears and smiled. "I

wasn't sure. Some people don't photograph well. But I have a suspicion that I look good on camera. Actually, I've been told that."

"I'm sure."

"This documentary will be groundbreaking. I'm sure Warner told you. Did he ever receive a response from Sidney? Oh, I would have liked to see the look on his face when Warner confronted him! Sidney's beady eyes must have popped out of his head."

"I don't know."

"He *promised* he would call me and hasn't. I have a real bone to pick with him . . ."

"With who?" asked Antonia with confusion.

"*Warner.* He hasn't returned my calls!"

"Warner?"

"Yes, Warner. I'm certainly not talking about *Sidney.* We only talk through lawyers. Or Page Six."

"Mrs. Black, I'm sorry but I guess you haven't heard . . . Warner is dead."

Sheila's face betrayed no emotion. Antonia was not even sure she was processing the information. An awkward silence hung in the air until Sheila finally spoke.

"Did Sidney kill him?"

"Why do you think that?"

"Because that's what he does. He kills anything that gets in his way."

"Has he ever told you he killed someone?"

"He didn't have to," said Sheila. Her eyes were darting all over the room, from the floor to the ceiling. "I saw him do it."

"You saw him!" gasped Antonia.

"Yes," said Sheila. Her eyes were now everywhere. "Once, we were driving at night, and up ahead was a raccoon. I said, 'watch out for the raccoon!' and you know what Sidney did? More like what he didn't do. He didn't slow down! Squashed the poor animal to death."

Antonia regained her composure. "They don't know what happened to Warner. It may have been murder, or he may have just fallen in the bathtub. We can only . . ."

"What's going to happen to the documentary?" interrupted Sheila.

"I'm sorry?"

"It *is* going to see the light of day, isn't it?"

"I-I don't know. I don't think so," stammered Antonia.

"That's awful!" said Sheila, stomping her fist on the table. "It had better. This was my chance. Warner was going to pull the lid off Sidney. He said so himself. He said he had some juicy stuff that would make Sidney wish he'd never been born. It better see the light of day! That man is a monster!"

Sheila embarked on a rambling tangent for several minutes while Antonia stood there mutely, nodding like a sidekick on a late night talk show. It was clear that the woman was unstable. After a vehement diatribe against her ex-husband, Sheila descended into a morass of non-sequitors like the fact that her favorite color is purple; she has a young British lover who knows how to 'pump' her; she never takes off her camellia pin; and she does all of her grocery shopping at CVS. (The latter was particularly offensive to Antonia, who as a chef, took umbrage at the fact that someone would consider a pharmacy a culinary destination.)

It was Jonathan, with his sixth sense, who intuited that Antonia was in dire need of salvation and called her into his office for a faux-emergency.

"Thank you!" exclaimed Antonia as she closed the door firmly behind her. "I thought she would never stop."

Jonathan's eyes sparkled from behind his glasses. "She wouldn't have. She's obviously very lonely."

"Agreed. And very crazy. I can't tell if anything she says is true. Her ex-husband is no prize but now I see why he divorced her."

"From what little I witnessed, how could he have married her?"

"I know. She's trouble," said Antonia, shaking her head. "I think I need a Tylenol."

"You've had an eventful day." Jonathan opened his desk drawer and produced two pills. He poured a glass of water from the pitcher on his windowsill and handed it to Antonia. "Here."

Antonia swallowed both quickly. "It has been crazy, hasn't it? First Warner's father, then the police, then Sheila Black . . . what next?"

Jonathan smiled. "It's always something."

"It is," said Antonia. She placed the glass down and wiped her mouth. "And now the kitchen beckons."

"Just remember, it's your favorite place on earth and you'll do brilliantly."

"I'll try."

Antonia opened the door. She started to exit when Jonathan called to her.

"And Antonia, you did the right thing by returning the Lysol can."

She froze. "Excuse me?"

Jonathan had a guilty look on his face. "I'm so sorry, I didn't mean to eavesdrop. But I couldn't help but overhear the other night when you were talking to Joseph. I was outside cleaning up those overflowing ashtrays that Kendra and Marty never deign to take look after. I didn't want to say anything, really none of my business, but when I saw you hand it to the detective today, I was quite relieved."

"Um, yes. I'm glad I returned it."

Jonathan nodded. "I'm sure you'll sleep quite well tonight."

And here Antonia had been thinking herself the only one at the inn who knew *everything* that was going on. Now it appeared she had some competition.

14

A good twenty minutes later, Antonia was up to her elbows in food. The kitchen was the most fulfilling place in the world for her. She enjoyed caramelizing, braising, roasting, frying and baking. The aroma of chopped onions cooking in butter was her favorite smell (although she primarily used shallots these days.) It reminded her of when she was very little and would help her mother prepare Thanksgiving dinner. Despite having taken cooking classes, Antonia did not consider herself a classically trained chef. She had never worked the line at a four, or even a three, star restaurant. She had never apprenticed under a master chef. She had come to her current status through a route that is often looked on with derision: catering. For true food devotees, that's like saying you were a cook in the army.

In stressful times, the kitchen was a sanctuary to Antonia. She threw on her apron and forgot about everything else other than the new pork chop recipe she was fiddling with. Several hours ticked by and Antonia didn't even notice. Therefore, it came as an utter shock when Glen popped his head into the kitchen and announced breathlessly:

"They're here."

"Who's here, jerk-off?" sneered Marty.

"Nick Darrow and Melanie Wells," said Glen purposefully, as if he couldn't believe how clueless Marty was. "I seated them at table four."

Antonia felt as if she had been shot. It was a strange, primal feeling. She had often wondered if Nick would ever come to her restaurant. In some ways, she was surprised that he never had. She had the best damn restaurant in town! Secretly, Antonia had reasoned to herself that it was because Nick would have to bring his wife, and that would somehow seem offensive to Antonia. She couldn't believe that he was finally here. And this week, of all weeks.

"Actors are the pickiest goddamn eaters in the world," Marty said in his flat Brooklyn accent.

"I didn't know they had booked a table," said Antonia, wiping her hands with a dishtowel.

"They didn't. But they're *famous* so I made room for them," said Glen, his eyes widening. He quickly scurried away to return to his maitre d' post.

Soyla, who was plating the amuse bouche (a white bean and truffle 'cappuccino'), glanced up from her station. "Antonia, if you want, you go, we'll be okay."

Antonia shook her head vigorously. "I have no need to go suck up to celebrities."

Soyla stared hard at Antonia, but quietly resumed her work. Soyla was one of the most intuitive employees Antonia had ever had—Antonia sometimes felt that she knew *everything*.

"*She* doesn't need to go suck up," sneered Marty as he brought up the flame on the burner. He threw two pork chops on the pan, which sizzled as they landed. "Glen's already got his lips glued to their asses for sure. He's probably out there right now humping their legs. He'd take either of them as long, as he could get away with it."

"Oh, Marty, you have a way with words," laughed Kendra, who placed two entrees on the dock.

"I have a way with a lot of other things, Kendra. Take me up on my offer and let's have a roll in the sack."

"How could I turn down a come-on like that?" asked Kendra rhetorically. She put her hands on her wide hips and did a little jig. Her fat rolls wiggled like a dish of Jello.

"Why waste time on compliments and all that bullshit? We both know what we'd be after. It would be memorable for you."

"You're very confident in your abilities," said Kendra.

"They don't call me tripod for nothing."

Antonia and Kendra groaned in unison. "Lovely," said Kendra.

"Don't let those ice cream scoops go to waste. Let daddy lick them."

"Okay, enough," said Antonia. Sometimes she felt as if her job description was more den mother than executive chef. Marty and Kendra always engaged in this sort of R-rated sparring.

Antonia saw Kendra's large frame sidle up to her station

and stand next to her expectantly. She glanced up. Kendra had soft doughy features and eyes hidden by layers of chubby cheek rolls. Her weight gave her the deceptive appearance of someone soft and gentle, but in fact she had a fiery temper. "So, are you going to do a special tasting menu or anything for them?"

"For who?" asked Antonia.

"The movie stars!" said Kendra, wiping her forehead with a red bandana. She always carried one in her pocket and wore one on her head.

"I don't think so," she said.

"They may expect it," said Kendra. "When I was at Caché we were always making special courses and dishes for celebrities. It was all white truffles and caviar and fancy stuff, and it was all comped."

"Well, that's not my style," said Antonia. "If Nigella Lawson or Julia Child walked in here, they could eat for free. Other than that, they have to pay."

"Julia Child is dead," said Kendra.

"Then I guess she won't be receiving a free meal," said Antonia, throwing some chopped chive as a garnish on top of the baked lobster special.

"What about the President, would you make him pay?" asked Kendra.

"I don't know. Did Dan Barber make him pay when he went to Blue Hill?" asked Antonia, cleaning her board with a dishtowel.

"I think politicians have to pay," said Kendra.

"They don't pay for jack," said Marty. "They steal everything. A bunch of thieves."

"It's true, a bunch of crooks. Look at East Hampton. The goddamn town went bankrupt because of the former town supervisors. Stole all the money and put it where? God knows. All these fancy houses paying enormous taxes, we shouldn't be bankrupt," said Marty.

"Just keep your money under your mattress," laughed Antonia.

"Oh, I do, sweetheart."

"I don't know, I think Nick Darrow and Melanie Wells will expect something. Just wait and see," said Kendra, bringing the conversation around.

Antonia sighed and scanned the kitchen. Perhaps she was right. Maybe Nick Darrow would expect something. She had to look at it objectively. He was her friend, *sort of*. If she had other friends visiting who had never been to her restaurant she would send them a free course, wouldn't she?

"Alright. Slip something in there," Antonia said finally. "Either the chicory and pecorino salad with the Meyer lemon vinaigrette or the jicama 'tacos'."

"Sounds good," said Kendra.

Glen returned five minutes later with their order. Antonia took it in her shaky hands and read it over and over, as if it held some mysterious message for her. She finally hung it up on the board and set to work, summoning all of her expertise to help her.

"Don't worry, it will be great," said Soyla quietly.

* * * * *

Antonia breathed a sigh of relief about ten minutes after Nick and Melanie's desserts went out (another free course dispatched "with compliments from the chef." They had ordered only coffee and mint tea but Antonia could not bear the fact that they might not sample the Valhrona chocolate panna cotta with dulce de leche sauce or the rustic caramelized apple tart with honey mascarpone.) If they had anything to complain about then they were just picky eaters. Nick's rack of lamb had been cooked perfectly; Melanie's halibut steamed to perfection. She had, of course, requested sauce on the side and vegetables instead of potatoes, but Antonia stealthily cooked the fish in butter sauce. There was no way she was sending out a dry piece of fish, no matter what diet Melanie Wells was on.

"Antonia, someone would like to say hello to you," said Glen gaily. He stood half inside the kitchen door, while someone stood behind him out of view.

This is it, thought Antonia. Nick Darrow would finally come to her kitchen, her safest spot in the world. She felt more naked that she did if she was actually naked. "Okay," said Antonia. Despite her best efforts, her voice wobbled.

"They can come in," said Antonia. She turned so that her body was completely facing the door. She felt frozen in place.

Glen smiled and opened the door all the way and in walked . . . Sam.

Sam!

Sporting a corduroy blazer and even a tie, he sauntered in with a large grin on his face. That is until he saw Antonia's face, which had fallen when she realized he wasn't Nick.

Noting that something was wrong, Sam's eyes darted around the kitchen. "Bad time?" asked Sam sheepishly.

Antonia quickly recovered. She wiped her hands on her apron and walked over to the door. "No, no, please. Come in."

Sam's smile returned. "I just wanted to say thank you so much for a delicious meal. My buddies were right; you can cook your butt off."

"I didn't even know you were here! I would have really turned it on."

"You did turn it on," he said. "It was delicious."

"But had I known . . ."

"I never reveal myself when I'm going to a pal's restaurant. I don't want any of that fake stuff like complimentary courses and all that jazz. And you didn't disappoint."

Antonia flushed with pride. She hoped Nick had felt the same way. "You are too kind."

"Not sure about kind. But definitely experiencing some professional jealousy here. I may have to steal that pork chop recipe. That lime chutney on top was off the charts."

"That's a good one, isn't it?" asked Antonia.

The other workers in the kitchen had resumed their duties, completely disinterested once they realized that Sam was not a movie star. He moved closer to Antonia.

"I was wondering if you can steal away for a nightcap?" he asked.

Antonia's eyes gave him an appraising look. Once again, she was drawn to the large muscular body underneath his clothes. She had never been a body person, obviously, or else she would have lost the twenty extra pounds attached to her ass, but in this case, she had a physical reaction to Sam. He was sexy. And yet . . . he was cute for sure, but he was more like the guy you have a crush on that you assume nothing will ever happen with, whereas Nick Darrow was the guy who you love. It actually didn't make sense, as it was usually the movie stars that were unattainable. This was the reverse.

"I don't know," said Antonia, looking up at the wall clock. It was almost ten fifteen; dinner service was coming to a close. She could slip away if she wanted.

"Come on," coaxed Sam. "Even if we just go out to your dining room and have a drink."

She hesitated. Nick was out there. What would he think if he saw her with Sam? Maybe he would be jealous, Antonia thought suddenly, with a rush of adrenaline coursing through her body.

"Sure," she said finally. "Let me just take off my chef's jacket. I'll meet you in there."

Antonia kept an emergency "presentable" outfit in the mudroom to dazzle VIP's when she had to make a hasty change. Now was the time to put it to use. She gathered the magenta DVF wrap-dress, chocolate leather boots and a small Estée Lauder cosmetic bag (free with purchase of a sixteen ounce jar of "body glow' sea salts) and moved into the small powder room, where she changed and put on fresh makeup. After the final mascara application, she slid the elastic out of her hair and ran a brush through it, before fluffing it with her hands. There was no doubt about it, she had what Genevieve referred to as '80s hair,' woefully out of date.

Oh well. At least Marty whistled as Antonia walked through the kitchen on her way to the dining room.

"Mama mia, that guy is one lucky son of a bitch. You got that roll around with me look, sweetheart."

"Enough," reprimanded Antonia, rolling her eyes.

She placed her hand on the swinging door. This was it. She would finally meet Melanie, her imaginary rival. She would see Nick Darrow, but on her own turf. Antonia had this strange certainty that when she opened the door, her destiny would change forever. It was completely irrational, she knew. Deep down she felt that she had won tonight's battle. She had poured all of her love into the meal that she made for Nick. He had to have sensed that. And what can be more luscious than being fed by someone who cares for you? He would have to see that all of his sparring with Melanie was a vicious cycle that had to end. Not that Antonia would ever break up a marriage, especially when a child was involved. Hadn't this marriage been dead for years? Isn't that why Nick came to see her every morning and poured out his heart?

Antonia opened the door. She smiled with expectation. Her eyes scanned the room. Bridget was alone at table one, stirring her cappuccino. She looked up when Antonia entered the room. Antonia smiled distractedly. Sam was seated at table ten, against the wall. He was leaning back in his chair, his legs outstretched with his feet crossed, a bottle of beer in front of him. He rose as she approached. Antonia glanced around the rest of the room. Table four was empty. Her heart sunk. Where was Nick? It was then that she glanced at the front door. She froze, the gleeful expression fading from her face.

Nick was helping Melanie on with her jacket. He waited while she put both arms in then pulled out her long straight hair that had gotten caught underneath. She was more petite in person than she appeared on screen, and more ethereal. She had beautiful green eyes that were set wide apart, giving her an almost feline quality. Worst of all, she had that celebrity aura, where she appeared to be bathed in a shimmering light that emitted a glow, like a hologram from a sci-fi movie. Antonia felt as if everything started to slow down and the room began to spin. There was something very tender and gallant about the way Nick attended to Melanie. Not like a husband who was at his wit's end with his wife. On the contrary.

At that moment, Nick turned and met Antonia's gaze. She held her breath. Was she ready to receive his compliments? Would it be awkward to meet Melanie? Nick expression brightened. And then . . . he waved at her. She watched the corners of his mouth curl and he mouthed "thank you" before taking Melanie's arm and escorting her out the door.

15

Antonia felt as if she had been slapped. A mouthed *thank you?*
That's all she got for the meal of her life? Nick didn't even
have the dignity to come over and say it to her face—he made do
with an off-hand, across the room brush off? Antonia continued
walking over to Sam, her mind bursting with embarrassment.
How could she be so stupid? So ridiculously naïve? At the same
time, she also wanted to blow his effing head off.

"Is everything okay?" asked Sam, putting his hand on Antonia's shoulder. His touch was gentle, but she felt as if she had
been stung. When Nick walked out that door, Antonia zipped
up her emotions like a cocoon and planned on denying entrance to anyone who asked.

She looked up at Sam as if she had never seen him before.
His eyes returned a quizzical, worried look. *Get a hold of yourself, Antonia. Take deep breaths. This is absurd. Don't collapse in
front of everyone in the restaurant.* Antonia straightened up.

"Wonderful," she said.

"You sure?" asked Sam, cocking his head to the side. His air was watchful and concerned.

"I'm sure," said Antonia firmly. She sat down at the seat across from him. "It's just been a long day, and I need a drink."

Sam remained staring before returning to his own seat.

"I know the feeling."

The waitress brought Antonia a glass of Stag's Leap cabernet and a plate of chocolate biscotti. Sam watched Antonia pensively, while she in turn took a long sip of her drink in an effort to compose herself. She picked up a cookie and took a bite.

"Ah, chocolate and red wine, there is no greater combination for soothing the soul," said Antonia. "You know what I mean? One of God's best pairings."

"A dark ale beer and fried shrimp po' boy soothes *my* soul," said Sam.

Antonia nodded. "I hear you on that. Riesling and blue cheese salad with Anjou pears can also do the trick nicely."

"Too complicated. I'll take a vodka shot chased by herring on a thick piece of dark buttered bread with a dash of salt."

"We could play this game forever," mused Antonia.

"I know, and I wouldn't get bored."

They sat in silence for a moment. Antonia couldn't help but think that Nick and Melanie would be in their car now, driving home. Would they discuss their dinner? Was it one of those meals that stay with you forever, that you refer to as one of your top ten? Perhaps they were immune to sensational cooking.

"So, did you see Nick Darrow and Melanie Wells?" asked

Antonia. She was attempting to be casual and hoped Sam wouldn't see through her.

He shrugged. "Yeah."

"Not impressed by movie stars?"

"He seems like a jerk to me. Isn't he the one always making those political statements? I hate it when famous people pontificate. He should just shut his pie hole."

Antonia felt defensive of Nick. "I think he feels like it's his responsibility because he has a forum."

"His responsibility is to entertain me," said Sam, taking a sip of his beer. "Other than that, he can pipe it. When you or I cook for people it's also a sort of performance. We don't have to shove our political views down their throats."

Objectively, Sam had a point. Nick did make some pretty wild statements about the government, and was such a vocal critic of the previous administration that he swore to leave the country if they remained in power. She had admired his conviction. Hearing it from Sam's standpoint, coupled with Nick's snub, Antonia felt maybe she should reevaluate. At times, Nick did come off as a blowhard.

She chose to change the topic. "Well, what about Melanie Wells? She's beautiful."

Again, Sam shrugged. "I guess."

"What? Not your type."

"She's fine, of course, beautiful, but she looks high-maintenance. She also could use one of those po' boys we were just talking about. Don't forget, I'm a chef, I like to feed people. It's a total turn off for me when people don't eat."

Antonia wanted to jump up and hug Sam. *Take me to bed now!* She thought. Okay, the silver lining was starting to emerge. "So, if she made a pass at you, you'd just be like, sorry, sweetheart, you ain't my type?"

"I don't know," said Sam with seriousness.

"Really?" asked Antonia, shaking her head. "I thought she was a goddess to men."

"Not to me."

Antonia got the impression he wanted to dead end the conversation.

"You don't like to conjecture about that stuff," said Antonia, feeling instantly embarrassed that she had even brought it up.

Sam looked up from his beer bottle. "What's the point? Melanie Wells is off with her husband and I am right here, exactly where I want to be."

His eyes bore into her with laser-like intensity. Antonia shuffled in her seat. "Would you like another drink?"

Sam motioned to his bottle. "I'm all set."

The bartender had brought over the entire bottle of red wine before he departed and now Antonia took the opportunity to refill her glass for the third time.

"I don't always do this, you know."

"What?"

"Drink a lot of red wine."

"That's okay," said Sam. "You've had a rough week."

"I know!"

The wine had definitely made Antonia tipsy and she regarded Sam in a blurry light. He was so sweet and handsome.

And that body. She wasn't sure she had ever been with someone who had muscle definition. Should she just go to bed with him? It was amazing how benevolent alcohol made one. All of Antonia's inhibitions were slowly falling by the wayside, replaced by a warm and cozy sense of lust. In the corner of her mind, she was still unable to completely erase the vision of her naked body against his rock hard abs. She shuddered despite herself.

Sam leaned back. He had a drink straw in his hand that he had been fiddling with, and Antonia watched as he made a knot out of it with only his index finger and thumb. He definitely exhibited dexterity.

"Antonia, do you want me to wait for you to close?" Glen had appeared out of nowhere. She glanced around and saw that the entire room had been cleared and prepped for closing. Only Antonia and Sam were slowing the process.

"That would be great, Glen."

"No problem," he said. He didn't leave and Antonia could tell something was up.

"Anything else?" she asked.

"I don't want to interrupt," said Glen, his voice full of excitement. "But did you hear there was another dead body found right near the one you found? This one was on Lee Avenue."

Antonia's face paled. "What? You're kidding."

Glen held up his hands dramatically. "Don't worry. It was an old lady. Like eighty something, died in her sleep. Natural causes. Was in poor health. Normally, wouldn't be a big deal but in light of Warner Caruthers' death, the town was in a tizzy! The police said it was nothing to worry about, but no one is having that. I tell you, people are *freaking* out."

"Who was the woman?"

"Nancy something?"

Antonia connected the dots quickly. "Oh my God, Nancy Woods?"

"Yes! That's it," said Glen."

"I don't believe it," said Antonia.

"Did you know her?" asked Sam.

"Yes! She usually comes to afternoon tea. She didn't show today . . . She's lovely . . . well, usually. She can be cranky, says outrageous things and you can't tell if she was joking. For example, she just had a birthday a few weeks ago and her entire family came, even 'the undesirables.' She actually said that. But wow, I know she was old, but this is so sad."

"Sorry to be the bearer of bad news, Antonia," said Glen who did not look sorry at all. "But I just thought you should know."

"Thank you."

"The police had to close off Lee Avenue this afternoon because there were so many voyeurs trying to get a glimpse of the body being carried out. Next thing you know, riots on the street!"

"Oh, don't say that!"

"Sorry. It's two in one week, practically next door to each other! This is crazy."

"Don't people die every day?" asked Sam.

Glen crinkled his nose. "I suppose. But not in the rich part of town. This is major news."

When Glen left, Antonia remained deep in thought.

"Are you okay?" asked Sam.

"You know what, Sam. This makes me uncomfortable. I feel like I should go check on the Mastersons' house. It sounds weird, but if there are all those people around . . ."

She didn't have to finish before Sam interrupted her. "Let's go."

"Seriously?" Antonia was relieved. She did not want to go alone.

"I'll drive."

* * * * *

Antonia directed Sam from the passenger seat of his blue 1985 Land Cruiser. She had the window rolled down and was inhaling the crisp air. She was already regretting the wine. That, compounded with the news of Nancy's death, made her feel sick. She glanced over at Sam. He drove effortlessly and comfortably. That seemed to be his way with most things. Antonia had always been attracted to men who were passionate and volatile and somewhat on the edge. Sam didn't seem to be like that. Maybe this was what she needed instead.

The roads were dark "south of the highway". Very few of the houses were lit off season, as this was summer people territory, and the streetlights were few and far between. The wind whispered through the trees and the branches quivered from its touch. Sam's SUV was the only thing on the road as it zoomed towards its destination.

"These houses are incredible," said Sam, impressed.

"If you didn't hate celebrities so much, I would show you which one is Bon Jovi's."

"Bon Jovi lives here?" asked Sam in amazement.

"Yup."

"But I thought he was a Jersey boy?"

"I suppose when you make that much money you can be both a Jersey boy *and* an East Hampton boy."

"Nice."

They continued up the road towards the Mastersons' house. Despite the fancy addresses, not all of the houses in the Hamptons had gates or any other type of foreboding structures blocking entrance from the outside world. The split rail fence or the tall privet hedge was the most popular barrier. Most residents did as little as simply strategically place a few bushes and deep, lush trees on the property line. And if there was any sort of fence it was primarily to prevent deer, which had been attacking people's gardens at an alarming rate, or to comply with the swimming pool laws, and not to prevent robberies. People were generally lax about security and the crime level was low in this part of town. That fact might have contributed to the police's unwavering belief that Warner's death was an accident.

"It's the driveway on the right, next to the red reflector on the tree," directed Antonia.

Sam made the turn. The car crunched over the gravel and the house loomed in front of them. The exterior was veiled in darkness. There was no timed lighting to give the false impression that someone was home.

"Nice crash pad."

"I know."

Sam put the car in park. They stared at the house.

"Well, everything seems okay," said Sam.

"Yeah, I guess."

"What, is something off?"

"No, I don't think so. It's just . . ."

"What?"

Antonia turned to face Sam. "I just remember that when I first entered the house the other day, the day I found Warner, I had a funny feeling, as if something was off. And I sensed the same thing when I was in Eleanor's room—she's the Mastersons' daughter. I had thought it was the footprints that Warner had left but now . . . I don't know. Maybe I did see something else."

She thought of Eleanor's room. She ran through the images of her frilly décor, the desk, her bed, her chair, but nothing jumped out at her.

"Like what?"

"I wish I knew. It's been bugging me."

Sam glanced at the house. "What are you saying?"

"I need to go in the house and check it out. Will you come with me?"

Sam stared at her closely. "I'd love to."

"Thanks. Now stay here a second with the lights on and I'll call you when it's time."

"Okay."

The fresh air slapped Antonia in the face when she exited and she nestled further into the fleece that she had thrown over her dress. In the distance, she could hear the waves crashing against the shore. Her eyes darted around. The garage appeared tightly secured; the garden supply shed was also locked. The wind pushed some errant leaves across the grass. She walked over to the door. The police had not put a padlock on the door but instead a large East Hampton P.D. sticker ran across the hinges. Antonia knew she could unseal it with a penknife, that the police would rarely check, but that would be a blatant crime and besides, she had a better idea.

She scurried alongside the house until she reached the laundry room. One of the windows was unable to be properly locked and did not signal the alarm when it was opened. Joan and Robert Masterson didn't know this. However, their children did, because they were the ones who had rigged it years prior so they could sneak in and out of the house. Antonia had discovered it one wintry Saturday in February when the window blew open. She had mentioned it to Eleanor Masterson, who was at the house that weekend, and Eleanor asked her not to mention it to her parents and said she would take care of it. Antonia suspected that she hadn't done so. She was planning on giving Eleanor another month to tell them, but once Robert and Joan were at the house for the summer she would give them the heads up.

A planted fern was strategically plopped near the window and doubled as a stepladder of sorts. Antonia dragged the planter closer to the window and stepped on it.

"Hey, do you need help?" asked Sam from the car. Realizing what she was doing, he exited the car and moved towards her.

"I got it."

"Do you really think this is necessary? Can't we just go in through the door?"

"This way I'll feel a little bit better about breaching the crime scene."

The window stuck at first attempt, but Antonia smacked it on the sides and it swung open. Bingo. She knew Eleanor hadn't dealt. Antonia clipped off the edges of the screen and pulled it off, careful to retain her balance. Sam took it from her.

"Steady now."

He placed his palm on her lower back. She felt like her entire body had received a warmth transfusion. Antonia put her hand through the window and felt for the cool surface of the washing machine. Pressing down with her hand, she swung her leg over the window ledge and hoisted herself in. Her legs splayed ever so slightly. She was glad it was dark so that Sam could not get a crotch shot. A wrap dress was probably not the right outfit of choice for this endeavor. Carefully, Antonia slid across the washing machine to the dryer, the red light on the alarm panel in the laundry room acting as her guide. When she reached it, she hastily punched in the code. At once, the red light turned to green.

"Mission accomplished," Antonia announced to the darkness.

She leaned out the window. "Hang on a sec, Sam."

She jumped down off the dryer and felt for the drawer next to the sink. She opened it and removed two flashlights. After testing that they both worked, Antonia peered out the window and motioned to Sam.

"Your turn."

Sam strode back to the car and killed the engine. Antonia illuminated the window for him and waited while he pulled himself through the window in one deft move. She noted that his ass looked very nice in his pants.

"So, here we are," said Sam.

Antonia handed him the larger flashlight. "Let's do it."

The house was chilly. A cold, impersonal draft hung in the air. Antonia followed as Sam led them out of the laundry room. The burst of adrenaline made her feel alert.

"Go left."

When they turned the corner into the kitchen Sam stopped so abruptly that Antonia bumped into him.

"What is it?" asked Antonia anxiously.

"Sorry," said Sam. He turned and patted her arm gently. "So sorry. I didn't mean to startle you. I just can't believe this kitchen!"

Antonia's emitted a deep breath. "Sam, don't do that!"

"Sorry, but man, this kitchen is unbelievable! Are these people in the biz?"

Antonia smiled. She glanced around, her eyes following the spots that were lit up by Sam's flashlight. "I'm not even sure they cook. They have a private chef in the summer."

Sam turned to Antonia with a look of amazement. "Maybe I have to apply for that job."

"I know. Good gig."

With his flashlight lighting his path, Sam walked over to the massive Viking stove and ran his hand along the side of it appreciatively. He opened the oven door and peeked his head in, using his flashlight to illuminate all of the corners, before closing it gently. He lifted the fryer out of its resting place and stared at it before silently moving along the counters, surveying all of the kitchen equipment, including the wide array of appliances that met every need. He paused to stare up at the throng of copper pots hanging from the ceiling, as if lost in thought. Antonia watched him with pleasure. It was the first time she had brought someone here that would have as much appreciation for the professional kitchen as she did.

"I'm feeling like a real hick," said Sam finally. "I didn't know people lived like this."

Antonia nodded. "And for some of them, this is not only their second home, but their third or even fourth."

Sam whistled quietly. He continued glancing around the room with wonder. For the first time, Antonia felt the age difference between them. It was clear that he was young enough to still experience marvel and allow it to show all over his face. Whether it was a factor of his youth or his lack of exposure to the world, Antonia wasn't sure, but the raw genuine amazement he was exhibiting seemed like a sensation that Antonia had been denied for years. It made her nostalgic.

"Look at these," said Sam.

He had walked over to the large chopping block that contained dozens of professional knives. He removed one and fondled the blade.

"This is a beauty," he murmured, his eyes locked on the knife.

"I know."

Sam ran his finger along the tip of the knife. He returned it with reluctance.

"Do you want to see the rest of the house?" Antonia asked.

Sam glanced up as if remembering that she was there.

"Yup," he said decisively.

Antonia poked Sam in the direction of the hall and accompanied him on the route that she took when she did her walk-throughs. Normally, the daylight would seep in through the endless windows and light her way, but tonight she had to find her way in the inky darkness, with only their two little flashlights assisting them. Antonia kept moving from room to room, but several times had to stop and retrace her steps when she realized that Sam was no longer with her. She would then return to the dining room or the living room and find him studying every element from the furniture to the framed pictures and paintings.

Tonight, everything felt sinister. The portrait of the lady sitting on a bench that hung over the fireplace in the living room was eerie. Antonia felt the lady's eyes boring into her with disapproval. She quickly left the room and returned to the hall. Antonia noticed the tracks that the gurney had left in the front hall carpet when they had carried Warner's body out to his final resting place. They were so ingrained into the carpet that she could imagine their journey.

"This house is hardcore," said Sam softly, coming up behind Antonia.

She turned to face him. "This has always been my favorite house, but tonight it feels creepy."

At that moment a car passed by and Antonia grabbed Sam's arm and stood frozen. They both glanced out the windows, watching the car's lights flash past. Once they ascertained that the car kept driving, their bodies relaxed.

"I think we're freaking ourselves out," said Sam.

"I know. Let's go upstairs."

Sam gave her a concerned look. "You sure?"

Antonia nodded decisively. "I'll lead the way."

16

The flashlights' small circles of light danced across the striped wallpaper and curled around the banister. Antonia and Sam walked slowly and tentatively up the stairs. They paused when they passed the picture window. The moon cast sparse light on the covered pool, which was sealed still as a tomb. The iron garden furniture, stripped of its cushions until the summer, was scattered around the patio, ultimately ignored. The Mastersons' property possessed a very narrow backyard. The neighbor's house was situated so close to the hedge that one could see into its large second story windows. There was a light on upstairs, as well as several on the ground floor. She couldn't see anyone. Antonia believed it belonged to a family named Harkin. It was another lovely old house, although bereft and run down.

Antonia thought for a moment that she saw something in the bushes. A deer? A person? She pressed her nose closer to the window.

"Did you see anything?"

Sam held his flashlight down so it made a circle on the carpet. He scanned the backyard. "No, did you?"

"I thought for a second . . ." her voice trailed off. Perhaps her mind was playing tricks on her. "Nothing."

They continued up the stairs.

"Do you think we should turn on the lights?" asked Sam. "I pretty much doubt that the police will happen to drive by during the exact five minutes that we have them on."

"No," said Antonia. "I don't want to worry about being discovered by the cops and being arrested for trespassing. I'd rather just take my chances."

"Your call," said Sam. "Which way?"

Antonia pointed the flashlight down the hall to the right. It seemed to die in the darkened abyss. "This way."

Antonia was comforted by Sam walking next to her. He was powerful. It was strange but it was as if she could actually *smell* his strength.

"The bedroom is on the left," said Antonia.

They moved in that direction. Antonia stopped on the threshold of Eleanor's room. Sam approached and stood next to her. Their bodies were slightly touching.

"Do you want to turn on the light here?" Sam whispered.

"No," said Antonia. "I might be able to figure out what specifically was bothering me if I just spotlight one thing at a time."

Her flashlight traced the corners of the room and flitted from spot to spot, searching for a clue. Could Warner have hidden the footage in here? Was that what had struck her? She scanned for it, but found nothing that looked like a tape or disc or video camera. The carpet, however, now looked like four thousand people had walked across it, and would almost certainly need professional cleaners to attend to it. Antonia scanned the bed, which was still perfectly made up. She moved her flashlight towards desk. The pens were still neatly aligned. She felt no comfort in the fact that almost everything appeared normal. That was almost more disturbing.

"Anything with the pictures?" asked Sam.

"No."

They were staring at each other in the charcoal wash of darkness. Antonia had the feeling that if she kissed Sam now he would not refuse. She couldn't do that, though; not here. She casually turned back to the room.

"Hmm . . ." said Antonia.

Antonia's flashlight darted around the room frantically. What had given her pause? What was here? She was looking for some sort of camera equipment but maybe that was wrong. Maybe it was something else?

Suddenly, a cold chill ran down her spine.

"The watch," Antonia said finally.

"What?"

Antonia trained her light on the watch that was sitting in the dish on Eleanor's dresser. "That doesn't belong in here."

"How do you know?"

"I know. I come in here all the time. Eleanor wears a gold Cartier tank watch."

"Maybe it was Warner's?" offered Sam.

An image of Warner floating in the bathtub popped into Antonia's head. He had on a Rolex watch.

"It wasn't Warner's."

She turned and stared at Sam. "Whose was it?"

"The police?" Sam asked hopefully.

This time, Antonia felt a conviction that she hadn't felt before. For the first time in days, she experienced a harrowing clarity.

"The killer."

Sam let her words hang in the air. The room was dark. Antonia had her flashlight facing downwards, blazing on a small patch of trod-upon carpet.

"I thought you said it was an accident."

"I don't think so anymore."

"What do you want to do?" Sam asked finally.

Antonia took a deep breath and entered the room, making her way towards the watch. The silver felt cold to the touch. The watch was heavy. She couldn't imagine Eleanor wearing it.

"Definitely a man's."

Sam came up behind her. She could feel his breath on her neck. "Recognize it?"

"No."

Antonia turned it over but there was no inscription or monogram. "I didn't think this was what I would find."

"What were you looking for?" asked Sam, moving closer.

She didn't want to tell him about the footage. "I'm not sure."

They stood in silence. Finally, Sam spoke.

"What are you going to do with it?"

"I want to take it, but I shouldn't in case the police come back for it."

"Good idea. Let's check the bathroom," said Sam. "Maybe you'll find something in there."

Antonia replaced the watch in the dish. There was no way she was removing anything else from this room, not after the debacle with the Lysol can. She didn't think Sergeant Flanagan would take kindly to her if she did it a second time. She moved towards the bathroom. The door was ajar. Sam pushed it further open, his flashlight scanning the room. There were muddy footprints all over it. The bathroom mat was shoved to the corner behind the sink. The towels were no longer on the rack, but heaped in a careless pile on the floor near the toilet. The shower curtain had come off, but the shower rings remained, dangling in the darkness. Sam glided his light down to the edge of the porcelain tub. There was a large bloodstain where Warner's head had rested, as well as a tiny trickle that led down towards the drain. There were also bloodstains on the side of the tub, presumably from when they moved the body. The room smelled strange.

Like death, thought Antonia.

"What happened here?" she whispered.

Sam turned and met her gaze. She turned back out of the bathroom, shaken. Sam followed.

Sam put his hand on Antonia's shoulder. "You okay?"

Antonia took a deep breath and nodded. She felt completely lucid now, no longer in that tipsy red wine fog. Revisiting the house had definitely sobered her up.

"You know, I never got to examine Warner's room after I found him," said Antonia. "Let's go check it out."

"Sure," agreed Sam.

Their small flashlights lit their way down the hall to the guest quarters.

The guest room was the final doorway, the suite that had been home to Warner during his final weeks. Antonia shone her light in the room. It flitted across the twin maple four-poster beds. The duvet covers were white, the white pillows framed with blue trim. Above each bed was a poster of a David Hockney collage. The other walls held framed posters from Guild Hall. Joan Masterson had bought out most of the stock from the poster store on Main Street when it shuttered.

Antonia's flashlight slid left, revealing a window seat. To the right, there were two French doors that led to a Juliet balcony. As far as Antonia knew, no one used the balcony. It overlooked the driveway and was merely a design decoration, rather than a functional element. The roller shades that hung over the doors were drawn.

Antonia walked over to the dresser and began opening the drawers one by one. They were empty. She ran her hand under each panel as if she might find a loose board where Warner could have stashed something. She quickly lifted the dust ruffles of the beds and scanned underneath with her flashlight. She opened the closet and found nothing.

"What do you think you might find?" asked Sam.

"Not sure yet," replied Antonia.

She glanced over at Warner's duffel. Perhaps in there? Might be too obvious but worth a shot. Antonia dumped everything out. Wrinkled shirts and balled up shorts fell to the floor. She felt through everything but there was nothing of interest other than dirty laundry. She hastily shoved everything back inside and walked over to the desk. The folder was gone. The police had obviously taken it. And no sign of a phone or camera or anything that might contain the missing footage.

"Let's check the guest bathroom," said Antonia.

The Mastersons had done a complete renovation of their bathrooms two years prior. This bathroom was slightly smaller than Eleanor's, but essentially the same infrastructure. Once again, Antonia was confounded as to why Warner would bathe in Eleanor's.

"I think I can turn the light on in here. We're facing the back of the house. The police won't be able to see."

"Okay," said Sam.

Antonia flicked the switch on. It took them several seconds for their eyes to adjust. They glanced around the room.

"Well, the police are right, it doesn't look like anyone used it," said Sam.

"Why do you say that?"

"It's spotless. Look, the toilet seat is down, the towels are all still folded neatly, the window shades haven't been pulled down for privacy . . ."

"I don't know," said Antonia. "Maybe he put the toilet seat down himself?"

Sam looked at her askance. "Do you know any guy living alone who would put the top lid down? That's a total courtesy for the ladies. If this guy was using this bathroom, the toilet seat would be up."

"Wait, the toilet paper!"

Antonia walked over and lifted up the metal casing that covered the toilet paper. The cleaning ladies always made a triangle with the ends when they finished a bathroom, and Antonia expected the paper to be torn, confirming that Warner had used it. But she was wrong. Her shoulders sagged.

"You're right. The toilet paper is folded at the ends."

"Like in a hotel?" Sam asked moving closer to glean a better look. "Geez, these people are fancy."

Suddenly, something caught her eye. Antonia inhaled loudly. Sam straightened up and noticed Antonia's face was ashen.

"What is it?" he said, fear in his voice.

Antonia was too stunned to speak. She slowly raised her hand and pointed at the towel rack.

"What?" asked Sam.

"The towels," whispered Antonia. "Look at the towels."

Sam stared at them. He walked closer to have a better look. He started to move his hand to feel one when Antonia yelled out.

"Don't touch! Evidence."

"I'm missing something here," said Sam. "What is it?"

Antonia walked over and pointed to the cream towels stenciled with white monograms. "This one. It's backwards."

"Okay," said Sam.

"The cleaners would never have left the towel backwards. The inscription says GUEST on it. They are meticulous. They would have absolutely noticed that the stitching is going the opposite way."

"But what if they made a mistake?"

Antonia shook her head. She was certain. "No, they *never* make mistakes. That was recently confirmed to me."

She remembered how silly she had been to think Rosita would have been careless enough to leave the Lysol can. What had she been thinking? Rosita was an expert cleaner.

Sam sighed. "Okay, giving you the benefit of the doubt. What does it mean?"

"Rosita told me that Warner used this bathroom. She cleaned it on Monday morning. She replaced the towels, cleaned the shower, etc. He had been using this bathroom all along. Eleanor's bathroom was always clean. But then he is found dead in Eleanor's bathroom."

"The question is why?"

"Yes, why? It doesn't make sense that he would suddenly switch bathrooms. But something happened and he ended up dead in Eleanor's bathroom."

"Maybe he brought a girlfriend over and kept all that activity in Eleanor's room and something went awry and he ended up dead," offered Sam.

"Maybe," said Antonia.

She walked over to the window and looked down at the yard. It was quiet; the only movement was the breeze. She raised her eyes and stared into the back of the Harkin's house. She could see through the bushes that a light was on in the downstairs, but she detected no movement. The curtains were drawn in the upstairs bedrooms. They were probably asleep, which was where she should be. Antonia was suddenly tired.

She felt Sam approach her and pause right behind her. She could feel his energy so close to her that it was as if they were touching. Antonia slowly turned around. The moon's light cast jagged shadows against Sam's face, making him look like a sinister circus clown. A chill crept down Antonia's spine.

"We should go. I suddenly feel strange here."

"Are you sure you got everything you needed?" asked Sam. He didn't move.

"Yes."

He stared into Antonia's eyes for a second before moving.

"Let's do it then," he said. As she stepped out of the shadows, Sam's face returned to its usual handsome expression. He took her hand and led her downstairs.

17

They drove down Lily Pond Lane in silence. Antonia was nervous, unsure as to how to proceed with Sam. She was wildly out of practice with men. The stoplight was green, which meant that they were only two minutes away from the inn. Should she ask Sam up for a nightcap and recap? It didn't seem right. She felt odd. Earlier, she would have sworn that she was receiving romantic vibes from him; now she wasn't as confident.

Sam pulled up the driveway of the inn and put the car in park. Antonia turned and smiled.

"This was a wild night, Antonia," he said. He leaned over and gave her a quick peck on the cheek. "Let me make sure you enter safely."

Antonia was glad that they both had to turn in different directions to open their car doors so Sam couldn't see her face turn instantly red. Was this a blow off?

When she got out of the car, Sam was standing next to her. She started walking to the back door. He walked along side her.

"Well, thanks for coming on the wild goose chase with me."

"Anytime," he said, sinking his hands in his pockets. "But the highlight of the night for me was still your kick-ass dinner. That'll go down in the history books."

"Thanks," said Antonia, quickly adding, "and I'd love to sample your food also."

Sam laughed. "Yes, that's definitely on the agenda."

He opened the screen door for her and held it, while she fumbled in her bag for the key. There was so much crap in her bag that it took her extra long to find the key, and she made a note to herself to clean out all the junk. Sam waited patiently. Finally, she found it and unlocked the door. She twisted the knob and held it. She turned to Sam.

"Good night, Sam."

"Good night, Antonia," he said. "See you again real soon."

He gave her a small salute before backing down the path and turning to walk to his car. Antonia didn't wait for him to drive away; instead she made her way inside.

When she reached her apartment door, she found a Post-It note stuck on from Jonathan.

Francine "Sidney Black's cleaning lady" rang you. Said she had something v. important to tell you re: what you discussed the other night. She wouldn't exp. (sounded very nervous.)

Antonia was instantly filled with curiosity. But one glance at the clock reminded her that it was way too late to return the call. Drat, she'd have to wait until the morning. She unlocked her apartment door and made her way to her room to collapse in bed. She was asleep within minutes.

* * * * *

Antonia sat up in the bed with a start. What had woken her? There was almost no visibility in the room with the blackout shades down. She leaned over and turned on the bedside lamp. A glance at the small alarm clock next to her bed revealed it was two-thirty two a.m. She hadn't been asleep very long. Her eyes scanned the room. The window curtain fluttered gently, almost imperceptibly. Was there someone behind it? Antonia's eyes bore into it as if she had x-ray vision. She could almost hear her heart thudding as she waited. Once again, the curtain moved softly, the right side flapping every so slightly open. Antonia gave a start. Then just as abruptly, the curtain flapped back. It was the wind. Antonia's shoulders relaxed slightly, but her eyes studied every crevice of the room before confirming she was alone. She was certain of one thing: it hadn't been a dream. She had heard something. A thump.

Antonia cocked her head to the side and waited. The night was still. The occasional passing car was the only break in the silence. She took a sip from the water bottle next to the bed. The cool liquid rushing down her raw throat produced a calming effect.

Suddenly she heard it again. It came from the other side of

her wall— the wall that was adjacent to the back stairs of the inn. Antonia stood up, grabbed her bathrobe and tied it tightly around her. She crept out of her bedroom to the kitchenette. Her fingers clasped the largest knife she could find from the top drawer. Clutching it in her hand she returned to the front door and slowly opened it.

It was dark. A lone table lamp produced a hazy illumination in the hall, but one that barely penetrated the blackness. From her somewhat skewed angle, Antonia could decipher the bottom of the stairs and the back door. She quickly glanced right at the door that led to Joseph's elevator, and squinted. The hall was empty. Antonia twisted her head to the left and that was when she noticed them. In the reflection in the mirror above the table she saw two legs clad in black, standing on the back staircase.

They weren't moving. They were waiting; as if they knew they had been heard.

Antonia waited. The feet stood frozen. Was it the lawyer? If he had been truly following her, he might have known she went to the Mastersons' house this evening and perhaps he thought she had found the footage.

The headlights of a passing car cast a flicker of illumination in the hall but disappeared as quickly as they had come. The hairs on the back of Antonia's neck were standing up at full attention. She couldn't take it anymore; it was time to make a move.

"Who's there?" Antonia whispered hoarsely. Her voice felt scratchy and foreign.

There was no response.

Antonia fondled the knife in her hand. She raised it slightly, prepared to use it.

"I see your feet in the mirror. Who's there?"

Suddenly, the legs started moving down the stairs. Antonia watched the body form in the reflection of the mirror. The footsteps pounded in unison with her heartbeat. Finally, Bridget's face came into view. Antonia brought the knife down and hid it in her bathrobe pocket.

"Bridget!" exclaimed Antonia. "You scared me."

Bridget's hair was back in a ponytail, and she wore no makeup or jewelry. She was dressed in head-to-toe black.

"I'm sorry," she said. "I didn't want to wake anybody."

"That's okay," said Antonia, her shoulders relaxing. She walked towards the stairs and met Bridget on the bottom. It was then that she noticed Bridget's large suitcase next to her.

"Sorry, this thing is heavier than I thought," said Bridget. "I tried to carry it but then I had to drag it down."

"Are you leaving us?" asked Antonia, her eyebrows arched in a manner that displayed both surprise and consternation.

"Yes, unfortunately, I have to go," said Bridget before adding, "I spoke to the woman at the desk the other day. I said I may have to check out quickly and gave her all of my credit card details for additional charges."

Antonia studied the suitcase. It was awfully large. It must have been the cause of the thumping. "I'm sorry you have to leave us like this. You can't wait until morning?"

"No."

They stood in an uncomfortable silence. Bridget gave her a somewhat defiant glance, prompting Antonia to blurt out the first thing on her mind.

"I just have to ask you. I know you said you didn't know Warner Caruthers. But I saw you talking to him when you checked in. It didn't seem like it was the first time. Are you sure you didn't know him?"

There was a brief pause before a flicker of recognition came across Bridget's face.

"That was the guy who died?" asked Bridget with surprise. "Yes, then, I did meet him. I was totally lost trying to find my way here and I asked him for directions outside of the Dune Club. He said he was heading over here to pick up some keys and I could follow him. That was it. I've never met him before or seen him after. Except when I was pulling my luggage in and he was leaving."

Antonia was stunned. She actually believed Bridget was telling the truth. "You weren't his girlfriend?"

"What?" Bridget was surprised. She shook her head. "No."

Antonia was at a loss for words. She should have handled this more gracefully. Interrogating witnesses was all about having a plan. She clearly failed that one.

"Oh. Well, then, let me help you with your bag."

Bridget gave her a strange look. "No, that's okay. I can do it myself."

She moved her body in front of the suitcase to bar Antonia from touching it. When she saw Antonia's expression, she attempted a smile. "Thanks anyway."

There was nothing more Antonia could say. She could try to barricade the exit, but that would be both insane and useless.

"I'll hold the door for you, then."

"Thank you."

Bridget picked up the suitcase, an obvious effort judging from the grimace on her face. Antonia glanced down and saw that her knuckles were white. She wondered why she didn't want any assistance. Instead of protesting, she turned and unlocked the back door and held it for her. A burst of damp, chilly air came wafting in.

"Well, good luck to you. Come back and visit us again."

Antonia noticed Bridget falter, as if she wanted to say something. Her eyes were sad. But instead of talking, she quickly turned and dashed down the steps. Antonia was tempted to run out and question her but a voice in the back of her head commanded: *Let her go*.

FRIDAY

18

Antonia did what she always did when she'd had a rough and sleepless night: made herself a kick-ass breakfast. It was a riff on a dish she'd had at the Regent Beverly Wilshire Hotel in L.A.: scrambled eggs with lobster and truffled hash browns. It had the beautiful medley of salt, grease and carbs. It took her two minutes to devour it. After baking a few batches of peach muffins for the guests at the inn, she left the kitchen with Soyla running the show.

Antonia debated whether or not she should head out to the beach for her morning walk, but she still felt too raw to be face-to-face with Nick. Fortunately, the bridal party that was staying at the inn for the weekend arrived early and demanded Antonia's attention. Antonia accompanied them upstairs to settle into their rooms. Wedding parties were good business but high maintenance. Tensions ran high and expectations even higher. It wasn't five minutes before Antonia found herself enlisted by the maid-of-honor to stuff fourteen goody bags. Antonia was on her hands and knees tying red ribbon bows when Connie told her Larry Lipper was downstairs to see her. For once, it was a relief that he had come calling.

"Larry, to what do I owe the pleasure?"

"I thought I'd brighten your day, hot stuff."

Antonia smiled. "Somehow I doubt it. Let's step into my office."

Moments later Larry had his feet up on Antonia's desk and was reclining in the chair across from her. He had been pumping Antonia for more information about Warner, trying to glean what she had learned over the past few days, but Antonia remained evasive.

"What have *you* discovered, Larry."

"I'm only telling you stuff to get your mind pumping. A connect the dot thing. Like I say something and it might remind you of something . . ."

"Got it."

"Okay, this theory of Warner having a girlfriend is picking up. He was apparently at Rowdy Hall last week and left with some chick."

"How do you know that?"

"The bartender told me. He said Warner was pretty wasted and obnoxious. He was sitting next to some guy, talking to him. Bartender couldn't tell if they were together or not, but one minute they're drinking together and the next, the guy tells Warner to knock it off or he'd take out his teeth. He said Warner was heckling some old man at the end of the bar."

"Why?"

"Bartender didn't know. He thought perhaps over the base-ball game that was on TV."

"Then what?"

"Well, as soon as Warner's lady friend showed up, he split."

"Hmmm . . ." Antonia wondered if Warner had been with Paul Brady.

"It was probably his cameraman he was talking to. You could ask him."

"It wasn't."

"How can you be sure?"

"I've been doing this a long time, sweetheart. I know enough to print out a picture of Paul Brady from his website. Yes, this a-hole has a website. And the bartender said it defi-nitely wasn't him."

"What did the girl look like?"

"Bartender said dark hair. Didn't get a close look."

Antonia thought of Bridget. Had she been telling the truth?

"What's that look on your face?" asked Larry.

"What? Nothing."

"I know when you're withholding. Don't you think I'm used to that look by now?" Larry cocked his head and gave her a skeptical look. His face was actually handsome, with a chis-eled jaw, beautiful blue eyes and dark eyebrows. If only it wasn't the cherry on top of such an obnoxious little package.

"Come on, I give you everything, you give me nothing."

He was right. That was irritating. Antonia did owe him

something. She'd give him this little nugget and then he could be on his merry way. "I talked to the pool guy again. He also saw Warner with a brunette."

"Hot damn!" said Larry slapping his hand down on the table. "Details."

Antonia filled him in on the little she knew. Larry started whistling with glee, jumping around in his seat like an excited schoolboy. When she was done, he announced. "We need to find this chick."

"How?"

"I need to lean on his friends. Hard."

Larry's phone rang. He answered with lightning speed and barked a hello. Suddenly, he sat bolt upright and dropped his legs to the floor.

"You're kidding me!"

He listened for a few more moments, scribbled something down on his pad before adding, "I'll be right there."

He closed his phone and stared at Antonia. "Sheila Black was found dead this morning. Murdered."

Antonia's hand flew to her mouth. "Oh my God!"

Larry's eyes gleamed with excitement. "I'd say someone really doesn't want this documentary to see the light of day!"

* * * * *

After Larry flew out of the office, Antonia suddenly remembered Francine's call and immediately dialed her number.

"Black residence."

"Francine? It's Antonia Bingham."

"Yes," came Francine's voice in a heady whisper. "Hold on one minute, please, one minute?"

"Sure," said Antonia.

Antonia waited for what seemed like ten minutes but was probably more like two. There was a beep on the other line and she glanced at her caller I.D. and saw that it was Genevieve. She'd have to call her later. Antonia tapped her pen against her desk and inhaled two cookies and almost an entire cup of milky coffee before Francine finally returned to the phone.

"Sorry, Mr. Black was leaving." Francine spoke into the phone as if she had her mouth pressed firmly into the receiver.

"Where's he going?" asked Antonia with urgency.

"Out to his boat."

Antonia shifted in her seat. She didn't like this at all. "How is he acting today?"

"The same . . ."

"Is he nervous? Appear agitated?"

"Not more than usual."

"Hmm . . . did he receive any calls this morning?"

"Calls?" asked Francine. "Not that I know of. Maybe his cell phone. Did something happen?"

Obviously, the police hadn't contacted him yet about Sheila, Antonia concluded. This was perhaps a good thing. She could get more out of Francine.

"Doesn't matter. Is everything okay with you? I know you called."

"I feel a little bad saying anything."

"It's okay, Francine. It will be in the strictest of confidence with me."

"Mr. Black is difficult, but he is a good employer."

"I understand. But maybe you just need to get something off your chest? Is anything concerning you?"

"You said to call if I had anything . . ."

"Absolutely. Is everything okay?"

"Yes, everything's okay. But Mr. Hamilton was here last night."

"Edward Hamilton?"

"Yes. And I heard him talking to Mr. Black."

Antonia leaned forward in her chair and rested her elbows on the desk. "Mr. Hamilton was there? Did they leave together?"

"No. Why? You're worrying me."

Antonia had to keep her thoughts to her self. Right now it was about control. Let Francine do the talking so she could pump as much information out of her as possible. "No, sorry to interrupt, go on," she urged.

"I can't remember the exact words. But they talked about Warner, the boy who took the film, and they said they were happy that he was gone. Mr. Hamilton laughed when he said that."

"He laughed?"

"Yes. Sort of 'ha, ha, now the boy is dead'."

"Hmm . . ." said Antonia. Unfortunately, rejoicing at someone's demise is hardly a confession of guilt. "What else did they say?"

"They said . . ." Francine faded off.

"What?" prompted Antonia.

"They said now that Warner is dead, they have to take care of the cameraman."

"What do you mean?"

"I think they mean . . . something bad."

"Like murder?"

Francine was quiet and Antonia was sure she could almost hear her nodding. "Francine, do you think they meant murder?"

"Yes," whispered Francine.

Antonia's pulse raced. She slid a plate of linzer torte cookies across her desk and selected the largest one, licking the raspberry jam with her tongue.

"Why do you think murder? They may have just meant, we have to take care of him, like talk to him, make sure he never makes the film, that sort of stuff," she said with her mouth full.

"No, because they said they may need a gun."

Antonia sat up in her chair. "A gun? Are you sure?"

"Yes. They said they would need a gun. And Mr. Hamilton, he said he had one."

Antonia's mind raced. If Hamilton and Black were talking about this last night, there was no reason to believe they didn't hop over to Sheila's and kill her.

"Are you sure, Francine? I mean, what were you doing when you heard them? Maybe they knew you were there."

"No, they didn't know. They were in the study and I was in the kitchen. But then I thought maybe I should hear them, because I remembered our conversation, and you said maybe the boy was murdered. I thought, maybe I can find something out. So I crept quietly, I am very quiet, and I pretended I was dusting something in the hall in case they found me, but they didn't know I was there and I heard them."

Antonia had a feeling Francine was the type who spent extra time perusing her boss's file cabinets and medicine cabinet. She had that collector-of-information, a.k.a. snoop, vibe about her. *Takes one to know one*, Antonia thought guiltily.

"Are you certain?"

"Yes, Mr. Black trusts me. I do feel a little bad telling on him . . ."

"Well, it is your responsibility to tell if you think he's going to break the law."

I'm such a hypocrite, thought Antonia. *I should practice what I preach.*

"I know what I heard. Mr. Black, he saying, 'we have to take care of that little punk.' He kept saying 'little punk' 'little punk.' And Mr. Hamilton, he said, 'one down, one to go.' And Mr. Black said, 'I thought it would be easier. These kids today are so greedy.'"

"Wow, you have tremendous recall," said Antonia, impressed.

"As soon as I heard them, I rushed into the kitchen and wrote everything down."

"Make sure you hide your notes. Anything else?"

"They talked a lot about Mr. Black's ex wife."

"They did?" exclaimed Antonia. She tried to tone down her excitement. "What did they say?"

"He always says the same thing. He hates her."

"Did he seem more passionate or angrier about her than usual?"

"No. It's always the same."

"Did he say he wanted to kill her?"

Francine paused. "I don't think so. He just complains a lot about her. He hates that he has to give her all that money."

Not anymore.

"Back to the gun, did they make it seem like they were really going to use it? Maybe just threaten Paul?"

"Who's Paul?"

"The cameraman."

"Oh, I don't know. I think, yes. They said, they need a gun. They need to take care of it."

It didn't really make sense to Antonia. If they did indeed kill Warner, they did it in such a manner that no one would know. But a gunshot? There was no hiding that. Antonia tried to conjure up the image of Edward Hamilton and Sidney Black on a murdering spree. She pictured them crouched in the bushes, stalking Paul, Edward Hamilton's ascot flapping in the wind. Something didn't sit right with that. It would be too risky, and their part in it too obvious. Now Sheila was also dead, though; it couldn't be a coincidence.

"When do you think this will happen?"

"I'm not sure, but Mr. Black leaves on his boat on Monday."

"Where's he going?"

"He's sailing down the coast. I'm not sure where."

Suddenly, a thought occurred to Antonia. If they shot Paul,

they could dump his body at sea. It would be a very convenient final resting place.

"Francine, try and keep tabs on Mr. Black's movements, particularly if he says that he's going to meet Mr. Hamilton. And let me know as soon as you think something is up. Call anytime."

"Okay."

When she hung up, Antonia kept her hand on the receiver. She wasn't sure if she should call Paul Brady and warn him. She didn't want to set off the alarms before she had solid proof. She took another bite of her linzer cookie. Flakes of powdered sugar flittered down on her shirt like fresh snow.

Something wasn't right. If the lawyer was working for Sid Black and Edward Hamilton, why were they about to go and kill Paul Brady themselves? Wouldn't they have him do it? And why Paul now? He had already offered to show them the footage that he had. Did he suddenly discover the missing piece? And now Sheila?

Antonia sat down and tried to make a chart of everything she knew. She put Warner's name on one side of the column and Sheila's on the other. She wrote down everyone who had a motive to kill Warner. The list was long. Under Sheila's name, she wrote *Sidney Black*. She paused before writing *Edward Hamilton* under Sidney's name. Why not? Maybe it was like that Hitchcock movie where they each agreed to kill the other person's nemesis? Who knew? She stared hard at Sheila's name on her list. There was something else, someone else, but she couldn't quite remember. Who else should go there?

She started drafting other charts, putting down theories of murders. Each time she came to a roadblock, she balled the paper and aimed for her trash. Sometimes she was successful, other times it landed on the floor. Her office was becoming a mess. Suddenly, a knock on the door interrupted her.

"Come in."

"Hi, Antonia. Can we talk?"

Nick Darrow's hair was damp as if he had just showered, and he was wearing the emerald green turtleneck that she had once complimented him on. He looked fresh and clean and . . . movie star-ish.

Antonia glanced around her messy office before her eyes landed down at her shirt, which looked like Jackson Pollack had gone crazy with a box of powdered sugar. She dusted it off with her hands, but that only made it press further into the fabric. It was a no-win situation.

"Sure. Let's go outside. I could use the fresh air," replied Antonia.

She didn't wait for an answer, but instead walked briskly out of her office to the front door, furiously rubbing the sugar off her blouse, erasing the evidence. The temperature was in the high fifties. The air was moist and the clouds hung low, clumped together in long, ominous strips. The forecast had called for rain later in the day and it appeared to be accurate. As it had been a relatively mild spring, the dried grass could definitely benefit from a shower. Antonia stopped in front of the pair of chairs that were nestled in the corner by the elm tree. It was a serene spot, partially hidden by azalea and wisteria bushes. She flopped herself down on the chair.

"What can I do for you, Mr. Darrow?" asked Antonia when Nick had caught up. Her voice was neutral, not overly friendly and not rude.

"I was wondering what happened to you this morning, so I stopped by," said Nick, sitting down in the chair next to her. He glanced around at the flowering cherry tree that provided shade. "This is a nice spot."

"I like it too."

Nick turned and stared at her, but Antonia remained fixed straight ahead. The basement screen door had a hole in it and would need replacing, she noticed with dismay. Yet another expense. She wasn't sure she had the energy to deal with Nick today, after everything that was going on, but she could feel his presence burrowing into her. He had that effect on people, the larger-than-life charisma that could fill up any space— including the outdoors. Finally, Nick broke the silence.

"I'm sorry I didn't stay to talk with you last night. I wanted to thank you personally for a fabulous dinner. It was delicious."

"You're welcome," said Antonia.

"For fear of sounding like a seventh grade girl, are you mad at me?"

Antonia turned and looked at Nick. "Mad at you? Why would I be mad at you?"

"You seem it."

Antonia gave a short fake laugh. "No, not at all. I was just busy. I had a lot of stuff going on this morning. You can't even imagine. Plus, I didn't sleep well last night."

"I'm sorry to hear that. I slept like a baby. Really, that lamb dish was off the charts. All of it, the amuse bouche on down, was fantastic."

"Thank you," said Antonia. "I hope Melanie enjoyed it as well."

The second it came out of her mouth, she regretted saying it. She could tell that her tone was not genuine, and Nick would be able to pick up on that. She had no reason to act betrayed or scorned. She and Nick talked about his wife all the time; he had never given her any false hopes that he had a romantic interest in her. She had developed feelings for him in spite of, rather than in the absence of, his complete honesty. These irrational feelings now made her jealous and vindictive. She had to stop.

"She liked it very much. She wanted to tell you herself, but we had to get home to relieve the babysitter."

Antonia nodded.

"The babysitter is fifteen. We couldn't find anyone last night and our live in sitter is on vacation. And I had to drive this girl home to Springs after. What a nightmare," continued Nick. "This town is so over-staffed with police I thought I'd be pulled over. Had too much wine last night. But it was all delicious. A perfect evening, except for driving the babysitter home. I asked Melanie why she couldn't find someone who could drive . . ."

Nick stopped when he saw that Antonia did not appear

sympathetic. He stood up and glanced at her curiously. "I know you're not being straight with me. Something's wrong."

"Nothing's wrong."

"Are you mad because I left without saying goodbye?"

She was about to deny everything when she stopped herself. "I was surprised that you didn't stop in. Disappointed."

He sighed deeply and ran his hand through his hair. "I thought so."

"I just thought we were friends, and it would have been nice to, you know, get a hello."

Nick moved over and put his hands on her shoulders. He gave her one of those penetrating looks that he used on his co-stars.

"I know. I'm sorry. It was rude of us to leave without saying anything. I apologize. The dinner was wonderful, thank you."

His voice was intimate. His eyes remained on her face, searching hers for answers. His laser beam intensity took Antonia off guard. She had always been dazzled by his attention; now that he had touched her, the sensation was magnified. It was time to grow up, Antonia told herself. He apologized, now she had to move on.

"You're welcome," said Antonia finally, adding a small smile.

"Are we square now?"

"Sure," said Antonia.

"Because, you of all people. I couldn't take it."

"Me of all people? What does that mean?" asked Antonia in a voice that couldn't hide her surprise.

Nick's eyes bore deeper into her. "It means that you're the

person in my life who doesn't tell me the crap they think I want to hear. I don't want our friendship to end."

She wanted nothing more than to collapse in his arms, embrace him and make passionate love to him, like the kind they do in movies, soundtrack and all. But Antonia realized that his was not a declaration of love. This was a declaration of friendship. A confession in which he acknowledged that Antonia was a great sounding board, who wasn't one of the obsequious sycophants that he was used to spending time with, and that meant something to him. She couldn't go on this way. Just being the straight man, the reminder to someone, the person who puts someone in his or her place— that wasn't good enough.

"I don't want our friendship to end either," Antonia offered. "But just be normal. *Be* a friend."

Nick nodded. "Fair enough."

Antonia shook off his arm gently. "Okay, I do have to get back though."

"I know," said Nick.

They started walking towards the porch. Antonia had just taken the first step onto the old wooden staircase when Nick spoke.

"She's jealous, you know."

Antonia turned her head to glance back at him. He still radiated intensity that almost threw her off balance. "Who?"

"Melanie," he said, throwing his hands up in the air. "That's why we left. When she realized it was your restaurant, you were the chef; she wanted to get the hell out of there. I waited until the end of the meal to tell her."

Antonia's head started swimming with all sorts of questions but the only one that popped out was "What about the babysitter?"

"I did have to take her home. But you're right. She could have waited five more minutes."

Antonia was confused. "Why in the world would Melanie be jealous?"

Nick smiled. "She thinks I'm in love with you."

Antonia felt the blood drain from her head. It was if something inside her was cracking, as slowly as an eggshell, but peeling off the armor that held her together. "That's crazy."

Nick didn't respond. He kept his watchful eyes on her. Antonia felt naked and exposed.

"How does she even know we know each other?" she asked, searching for something to say to break the awkwardness.

"I've mentioned you here and there in the beginning. She's very jealous. After one fight when she brought it up, I stopped. But she has kept on it. It's a bit of an obsession for her."

"Me?" asked Antonia, her mouth dropping in shock.

Nick nodded.

"Well, you can tell her I said she's nuts. She has nothing to worry about. I'm not a force to be reckoned with."

"That's not true."

Antonia wanted to ask more. Like, *Does Melanie have something to worry about, Nick?* And, *Why are you telling me this?* But she couldn't. This was real life, and there are formalities and proprieties and secrets that needed to be kept. It would not be helpful if she asked Nick if there was any reason why Melanie should be worried. He was a married man with a son. And in her heart of hearts, she knew that he was playing with fire, experimenting just a little to see what it was like out there. She didn't want to be the guinea pig that ended up on a dissecting slab with her heart and guts ripped out.

They stared at each other in silence for another minute before Antonia turned. "I've got to get back to work."

"Okay," said Nick. "We'll talk later."

She felt his eyes on her and wished she had not devoured the plate of cookies.

19

"Everything all right?" asked Joseph when Antonia re-entered the inn. He was sitting on the red bench in the foyer, one that afforded him a perfect view of the front porch.

"Yes, sure," said Antonia quickly.

Joseph's eyes flashed behind his glasses. It was difficult to keep anything from him, Antonia knew. He was a writer: an observer by trade.

"Sheila Black is dead," whispered Antonia.

"Oh my."

"I know," nodded Antonia.

"And I'm sure you heard about Nancy Woods, as well," said Joseph.

"I did."

"She was a cantankerous lady, but she played a mean gin rummy," sighed Joseph.

"I can't believe it. First, Warner, then Nancy, now Sheila.

They say bad things happen in threes so let's hope we're done."

"Agreed. And in the meantime, is it still convenient for you to take me to my eye doctor's appointment this morning?"

"Yes, of course!" said Antonia hurriedly. "I totally forgot."

"Are you sure?" said Joseph. "I could scooter myself to town and take a taxi back if it doesn't work for you. It's those darn eye drops they put in my eyes that blind me. I don't want to be cited for reckless scootering."

"No, it's perfect, I'll just grab my purse and we'll go."

Ten minutes later, Antonia pulled out of the driveway. On occasions such as these, Joseph would forgo the scooter and use his crutches instead. In those circumstances they required the assistance of Hector to help Joseph sit down in Antonia's car. She promised Joseph that her next car would not be so low to the ground.

He smoothed the creases on his oxford shirt. Joseph was always immaculately dressed; he had been so from the day Antonia met him. His clothes were perfectly ironed and starched by Soyla, who completely doted on him. "It's dreadful about Sheila. What happened?"

"All I heard was she was found murdered. It's so odd."

"What is going on in this town?"

"I have to tell you, I did something illegal last night."

"Again?"

"Yes. I can't stop. Promise you won't turn me in."

"Of course not, my dear. How would I eat?"

Antonia spent the short drive updating Joseph on everything that had transpired in the past twenty-four hours including her trip to the Masterson house. She explained how she led Sam through the rooms, and discovered the watch and the upside down towels. When Antonia reached the parking lot, they sat in the car in silence.

"Thoughts?" asked Antonia finally.

Joseph scratched his chin. "Do you think you should inform the police about Sidney Black and the gun?"

"I don't want to get Francine in trouble."

Joseph became suddenly serious. "Antonia, I know you've had bad experiences with law enforcement, but it doesn't mean all cops are bad. You don't have to take the weight of the world upon yourself and do their job. You have to trust them."

Despite herself, Antonia's eyes filled with tears. At times like this Joseph reminded her so much of her father that she could cry. They were both compassionate and thoughtful men, with giant hearts. Joseph had definitely filled a hole in her life, stepped into the role of parent, which was immensely reassuring to Antonia.

"Sorry, I'm just over-tired," said Antonia, wiping her eyes.

"It's a lot to take. And you are in the thick of it. Perhaps it conjures up bad memories for you. But don't forget that what happened to you happened to you in California, not East Hampton."

"I wish I could, Joseph. But the last time I put faith in the police, they destroyed my life."

"I know," said Joseph softly. "You've only told me bits and pieces about that night, but I know it changed your life forever."

Tears streamed down her face. She hated crying. She put her hands over her eyes and wiped away all the tears. After a moment, she began to speak in a voice so soft that Joseph had to lean in to hear her.

"Philip didn't reveal his true colors until a year into our marriage. In the beginning, it was bliss. I had been floating along, aimlessly, and he set us up in a nice home, in a nice town. Things went well. But then little by little, I realized how controlling he was becoming. He didn't want me to work, so I quit my catering business. He didn't want me to have friends, so little by little they dropped off. He'd come home, and we'd talk about his cases, which were very interesting to me. But the work stress started to get to him. He was cited more than once for excessive violence at work, and then ultimately relegated to counseling due to anger. That was a joke. And the more frustrations he had at work, the more he took it out at me. He drank more, became physical with me. And just mean. I asked his colleagues to help me, but they just closed ranks and didn't listen."

Antonia paused. Joseph put his hand on her arms.

"About four months before I left him, I went back to catering. I didn't tell him of course, but I had to do something. That's where I met Genevieve. It worked out well because Philip had to work the night shift on the weekends, and that's when I was busiest. But one day he left work early, and I wasn't home when he got there. He waited for me, and he became very violent. We fought. He finally took off and went to a bar. I called my father who came over to stay with me."

Antonia had to stop to compose herself. She hated thinking about the past. Joseph waited patiently, his face awash with concern.

"When Philip came back my father asked him to leave. He refused. Philip was like a maniac, on a tirade. He kicked my father in the stomach and he fell . . ."

Joseph patted her hand. She glanced up at him.

"My father had always had a bad heart, but this blow killed him. And the police did nothing. Didn't charge Philip. Nothing. He got away with it. I tried to do everything to get back at him, but the only thing I could do was sue him civilly. His money bought the inn. It's dirty blood money, but at least I made him suffer a little bit. Not a fraction of my pain . . ."

"I'm so sorry."

Antonia wiped her eyes. She attempted a smile. "I know. So that's the reason. I know that was L.A. and we're in East Hampton, but it's hard to move on."

Joseph nodded.

They sat in silence for a solid five minutes. After she stopped crying, Antonia felt as if a giant weight had been lifted off her chest. She realized that horrible part of her life was over. She had regained the strength to move on and live her own life, full of wonderful friends, in a town that she loved with a job that she loved. Philip had no hold on her anymore.

Joseph finally broke the quiet. "Just promise me you'll be careful."

Antonia nodded. "I promise."

"Good. Because I couldn't bear it if anything happened to you."

"Likewise."

They exited the car and walked slowly towards the curb. After Antonia had helped Joseph into the eye doctor she went outside to sit on a wooden bench. She was drained and tired after crying. The day felt heavy and morose. She glanced at her cell phone and noticed she had missed a call from Larry. With a sigh, she dialed him back immediately.

"How'd it go?" asked Antonia with anticipation. She had almost forgotten all about Sheila Black.

"Yeah, she's dead."

"Do they have a suspect?"

"If they did, they didn't tell me."

"What do you think?"

"They don't know if it's the same man who possibly killed Warner. The guy who killed Sheila made a mess. There was nothing fussy about that kill. It was more like rage."

"You think Sid Black did it?"

"Maybe. Could have gotten a mob guy in there. Problem is no one saw anything. Neighbors are all weekenders, hadn't come out yet."

"That sounds absurd . . ."

"Listen, gotta fly. I'll get back to you . . ."

Larry hung up before Antonia could say anything. A second later her cell phone buzzed again. Antonia picked it up.

"What now?"

"ahisohihihio," said the voice on the other end.

"Larry?"

"Get over here now!" hissed the garbled voice.

Antonia became instantly tense. She glanced around. "Who is this?"

"It's me, who do you think?"

"Genevieve!" sighed Antonia with relief. "You scared the dickens out of me."

"I scared the dick out of you? What are you doing?"

"Dickens, never mind. Where are you?"

"I'm at work," said Genevieve. "Why haven't you called me back? So much to discuss."

"Can you speak up? I can barely here you."

"I can't speak up. I need you to get over here now. It's *an emergency.*"

"I'll be right over."

Antonia replaced her phone in her pocket and rose. She walked briskly down Newtown Lane before making a right on Main Street, and into Ralph Lauren. Antonia wandered past the faceless mannequins dressed in eveningwear. Genevieve was ascending the stairs, clutching cashmere capes in colors with fancy names like "eggplant" and "dusty rose." Antonia gave her a quizzical look.

"What's up?"

Genevieve grabbed Antonia's elbow and escorted her to the front. She spoke in a low, urgent voice.

"Do you know who is in this store at this very minute? Do you know who is trying on suede culottes and white prairie blouses, as we speak?"

Genevieve's heavily made up eyes blinked rapidly.

"Who?"

Genevieve looked furtively around before leaning in to Antonia. "Pauline Framingham. The woman from Warner's documentary."

She leaned back, nodded her head, raised her eyebrows and appeared quite pleased with herself.

"Really?" said Antonia.

Pauline Framingham, the equestrian pharmaceutical heiress. She was still someone who had to be considered. She had enough money and clout to send a lawyer to buy footage. And perhaps all those times the lawyer referred to his employer as "he" was just a ruse to throw Antonia off the path.

"I am looking forward to a visual."

"That's why I called you. Follow me."

Antonia walked behind Genevieve towards the dressing room. It was then that she had a full vision of the outfit Genevieve was wearing. She wore a newsboy hat, a pin striped double-breasted suit with cropped pants, replete with gold watch chains tied to her vest, and blue and white stiletto heels. The absurd part was that she was totally able to pull it off. Some people were just born with that *je ne sais quoi*, thought Antonia. She was not one of them.

"Ms. Framingham, I have the capes," said Genevieve as she stood outside the dressing room. There were no doors; the only shield was a printed fabric curtain.

"Just a second," said a voice.

Genevieve turned and raised her eyebrow at Antonia. Antonia felt the anticipation. Pauline Framingham should not be discarded as a suspect; there was that business with the friend she had killed.

A second turned into several minutes. Antonia felt suddenly tired, and went and sat down on the armchair outside of the dressing room. The past few nights of roaming and fitful sleep were catching up with her. She closed her eyes and let her mind go blank.

"Alright, I will take these and return these."

Antonia sat up with a jolt. Pauline Framingham, in the flesh, was standing in front of her handing a bundle of clothes to Genevieve. She was taller than Antonia had thought she would be, broad-shouldered and what one would describe as 'athletic.' She wore brown pants, a blue button-down shirt, an Hermès scarf knotted at her neck, Gucci loafers and a blue blazer. She exuded that rich, waspy aura.

"I'll ring you up," said Genevieve. She shot Antonia a look, her plump lips curled upwards in a perplexed expression.

Antonia was not sure how to proceed. She watched as Pauline Framingham moved to the checkout counter and pulled out a blue, quilted wallet.

"And you'll order the boots for me," Pauline said, as she handed Genevieve a black American Express card.

"Yes, I already ordered them. Size 9," said Genevieve, running the card through.

"Perfect," said Pauline. She turned and glanced around the store as Genevieve rang up her order. She smiled at Antonia as her eyes darted past.

This is my chance, thought Antonia. *What should I do?*

"Genevieve, I'm going to run," said Antonia finally.

Genevieve gave Antonia a questioning look. "Okay," she said with uncertainty. She was wrapping Pauline's selections in tissue paper.

"Yes," said Antonia, moving closer to the checkout. "I have to go back to the Mastersons' house. Do some follow up with the police. It seems that Warner Caruthers' death may not have been an accident."

Antonia remained facing Genevieve but her eyes slid to Pauline. She felt Pauline stiffen. Genevieve, clearly delighted with the initiative Antonia had made, smiled slightly.

"Oh, right. Yes, I heard that guy, *Warner Caruthers*, might have been murdered."

"Yes, it's very sad."

"He was a good guy," said Genevieve, swiping Pauline's credit card.

"I'm not sure why anyone would want him dead," said Antonia.

"I am."

Antonia and Genevieve turned and stared at Pauline with surprise. Her eyes flashed with anger.

"That guy was not a good person. I'm sorry to have eavesdropped on your conversation, but I couldn't help it. Warner was a little punk who was out to ruin people's lives. It's no surprise he was murdered. Hell, if I had thought of it, I might have done it myself."

"Did you?" asked Genevieve before Antonia shot her a look.

"Genevieve!" she reprimanded before turning to Pauline. "Of course she's kidding."

Pauline smiled. "No, I was at a riding competition in Florida earlier this week. But I can tell you that I applaud whoever did it."

"Do you have any idea who that might be?" asked Antonia.

Pauline replaced her credit card in her wallet and closed it. She picked up the Ralph Lauren bag with her purchases and smiled. "No. But if you find out, let me know and I will buy them dinner."

And with that, she sauntered out of the store.

For once, Genevieve and Antonia were speechless. Antonia couldn't believe it had been that easy to get a reaction from Pauline Framingham. She made a note to follow up and find out if she really was at the riding competition.

"Holy moly," said Genevieve.

"I know."

"Well, what do we do now?" asked Genevieve. She leaned over the counter and put her elbows down, resting her head on her hands.

"I need you to ask your friend Tanya, the one who works for Edward Hamilton, what he is up to these days, and if he is acting strangely. Also, ask her if he has access to a gun."

"A gun? Ooooh," said Genevieve. "The plot thickens."

"It does, because Sheila Black is dead."

"You're kidding me!"

"No. Murdered last night."

Genevieve shook her head. "This is surreal. Warner, Carl's grandmother, Sheila Black . . ."

"Wait, Carl's grandmother?"

"Yes, it's so sad. That's why I called you this morning! Carl's grandmother died."

Antonia's mind raced. It suddenly hit her. "Nancy Woods?"

"Yes."

"Nancy Woods was Carl's grandmother? You are kidding me? How did I not know that?"

"Did you know her?"

"Yes! She came into the inn all the time for tea with her friends Ruth and Penny."

"She did?"

"Yes. Wow, horrible. The three of them were so much fun together. All very proper on the outside, but sassy and outspoken when you got to know them. Oh, what will Penny and Ruth do without her?"

"What will Carl do without her is the question?"

"Of course, you're right. How is Carl?"

Genevieve shook her head sadly. "He's really freaking out. They were super close. And you know he hadn't checked on her for a few days. Apparently, she had been dead awhile."

"How awful! But he can't blame himself, she told him not to come. And I knew Nancy, she was pretty firm. I liked her a lot, but she was a force to be reckoned with. I imagine she could be very difficult, and what she wanted, she got. If she didn't want him to come and help her, forget it."

"But still, he feels bad. Not to mention that I'm upset because I couldn't reach him all yesterday and I was so pissed off and screamed at him and then he told me he was dealing because he found his grandmother dead. Total guilt attack."

"It's not his fault. I'm sure there's nothing he could have done."

"No, he said actually she'd been pretty sick but didn't want people to know. That's why he moved here. He knew it was the end."

"Carl and Nancy Woods," said Antonia in disbelief. "It really is a small town."

"Yup. And with the rate people are dying, getting smaller every day."

"Please give Carl my condolences."

"For sure."

*   *   *   *   *

Antonia then made a brief stop to run an errand at Village Hardware on her way back to pick up Joseph. There she ran into Len Powers, who provided her with a few more details about the deaths of Sheila Black and Nancy Woods. His son Matt worked as an EMT in East Hampton but was at Marder's Garden Center when the call came in so he was one of the first responders to Sheila's house. Len said Matt was pretty shook up and hadn't seen anything like the scene of her crime before. Fortunately, Nancy's death seemed pretty straightforward.

Afterwards, Antonia picked up Joseph and filled him in. They were quiet on the drive back to the inn, their thoughts consumed with all of the tragedy that the week had brought. When they made their way up the steps to the inn, Joseph took Antonia's hand suddenly.

She turned to stare at him. "Do you think it's me? Have I brought bad luck to this town?"

"Don't be silly . . ."

"But there were no murders until I came to town . . ."

"Don't be absurd. It's a coincidence."

"I hope so. A bad one." She felt such relief to have him in her life.

"Oh, and one more thought I had while getting my eyes poked at," said Joseph.

"What?"

"I thought about the watch in Eleanor's room. Find the person who is missing a watch. Then you'll have your killer."

20

Antonia was in the kitchen finishing up her prep work but even the monotonous rhythm of chopping that she usually felt so comforting couldn't assuage her restlessness. She wasn't sure what, but she felt a sense of impending doom. Something bad was about to happen, she was sure.

At around five o'clock a flustered Jonathan entered the kitchen and asked to speak with Antonia.

"Uh oh, is the wedding driving you nuts?" asked Antonia with concern.

The bridal party had been monopolizing Jonathan's time. Their list of requests was endless and their nervous energy torture. Jonathan had maintained his patience with them, but Antonia could tell they were grating on him. His usual calm, unflappable British manner was certainly being tested.

"More guests arrived this morning and were seen to their rooms. I put the bride in touch with the Monogram Shop for her last minute demands. They're working overtime personalizing cosmetic kits for the bridesmaids, as we speak."

"High maintenance bride."

"Yes, to say the least. But I didn't want to burden you with all that. I just wanted to say that we had a phone call from your friend Carl . . ." Jonathan winced when he said his name, "asking if we could have the reception for his grandmother here after her funeral. I said of course and tried to discuss the details with him, but he insists on talking to you exclusively. I'm sorry about that."

Antonia remembered that Carl had said he didn't care for Jonathan but wouldn't disclose why. It didn't seem like a good time to bring it up. "Thanks, Jonathan. I'll give him a call."

"Here's his number," he said, handing Antonia a slip of paper.

* * * * *

Antonia returned to her office. Better to get it over with and talk to Carl. She owed it to Genevieve at least. On her desk was a stack of printouts that Joseph had left for her, including pictures of Paul Brady's website, featuring dozens of pictures of him with friends, a dog, and with Heidi. Antonia studied the pictures. Warner didn't appear in any, but then they were recent friends. Ah, Warner. Now with everything else going on, she wondered if Warner's death would slip to the backburner. She hoped not. At least she knew it wouldn't with her.

Before she could try Carl, the phone rang and Genevieve was on the other line.

"Tonight's the night."

"What do you mean?"

"My friend Tanya who works for Edward Hamilton called me. She overheard him saying on the phone that, and I quote, 'Tonight is the night the rest of the Warner Caruthers situation will be taken care of.' I kid you not. Can you deal?"

"Wow," said Antonia. She knew it was coming, but the fact that it was imminent filled her with dread.

"So what do you think, check it out or call the cops?"

Antonia was pensive. She had promised Sergeant Flanagan she wouldn't get involved. But a friendly tip off wasn't getting involved. On the other hand, no doubt he would press Antonia about what else she knew, and then the floodgates would open. She had fooled him once; she didn't know if she was a good enough actress to do it a second time.

"I suppose I have to check it out."

"We, you mean."

"What about Carl? His grandmother just died, don't you have to be with him?"

"He wants to be alone. He has to call the family, deal with all the stuff. He said he'd prefer to do it on his own. I tried to help, but whatever. I can help you instead."

"Okay, if you think that's fine with Carl. I think the best thing to do would be to head to Paul's house and wait outside. I'm hoping this is all a giant misunderstanding. However, if for a second we believe there is a legitimate danger we call the police anonymously."

"Sounds like a plan."

"It is except for one problem: I have a job that happens to get in the way of this little project."

"The restaurant? Come on, you yourself said Marty could run that kitchen without you! Take a night off. Well deserved."

"It feels decadent. But I'm useless today anyway. I'll pick you up in twenty."

"You got it. Oh, and I'll dress incognito. You do the same."

*   *   *   *   *

Antonia almost laughed when Genevieve opened her front door and revealed her interpretation of "incognito."

"You're kidding me," said Antonia.

"What?" asked Genevieve.

"The outfit?"

Genevieve glanced down. She had on a tightly fitting black "military jacket" (as interpreted by Ralph Lauren) with swirling gold embroidery, cord braiding and fringed epaulets. Underneath was a cropped and belted camouflage jumpsuit tucked into patent leather high-heeled riding boots. Dog tags were roped around her neck.

"What's the problem?" asked Genevieve innocently.

Antonia gestured towards her outfit. "That's what you wear for a possible stake out?"

"What, I'm supposed to dress like you?" she asked, motioning to Antonia's baggy black pants, black ribbed turtleneck sweater and running shoes.

"Well, although I'm not the most stylish person right now, I'm nondescript."

"I just don't think I have to dress like one of the Indigo Girls when I want to spy on someone."

"I'm hardly dressed like an Indigo Girl! I can at least run in these shoes."

"I run better in high heels. I have high arches."

Antonia heard the crunch of the gravel in the driveway and turned to see Carl pulling up in a silver SUV. He wore a grimace on his face when he exited, and nodded hello as if it was the last thing he wanted to do. He was holding a wilting cardboard box in his hand.

"Everything okay, sweetie?" asked Genevieve. She gave him a kiss on his cheek.

"I'm so sorry about your grandmother," said Antonia. "I actually knew her. She was a lovely woman, with lots of friends. She will be missed."

"Thank you," said Carl. He loosened his tie roughly, before jerking it off.

"I tried to call you back today about the reception. Of course we can have it at the inn."

"Yeah, that's not gonna happen . . ." he said brusquely.

Genevieve gave Antonia a worried look.

"Oh?" asked Antonia.

"You know, I tried to plan it, give her a nice sending off, but what always happens is my damn family gets involved and wants to do everything *their* way."

"I'm sorry, sweetie," said Genevieve. She tried to kiss him, but he recoiled somewhat.

"Family politics are so intense. I understand your frustration," said Antonia.

"If only you knew the crap I was dealing with."

"Well, don't worry about anything. Even if you decide at the last minute, I'm sure we can work something out at the inn," said Antonia.

"Thank you," said Carl. He shook his head in frustration, brushed behind Genevieve and went inside.

"He's like, freaking out. Can you see why I was happy that he didn't want me around?" asked Genevieve.

Antonia nodded. The death had definitely taken a toll on him, judging from his demeanor. "He's a little wound up."

Before Genevieve could respond Carl reappeared clutching a bottle of Heineken. He took a large chug, his Adam's apple bopping up and down as he did so, before breaking to wipe his lips with the back of his hand.

"Sorry, ladies. You know how family is. They drive you nuts! Here I am, the one who moved back to look after my grandmother, because nobody else in the family would lift a finger, and then they come marching back to town and boss everything. Insist the funeral will be in the city—moved her body there without even asking me and then left town. They didn't give a damn about this woman. Not a damn!"

Carl took another swig of his beer. His forehead was sweaty and the rims of his eyes red as if he had been crying.

"Babe, I'm so sorry. I know how much you loved her."

"Doesn't matter," he practically spat out the words. "They don't care about that at all."

Genevieve rubbed his back and made clucking noises while Antonia stood there feeling awkward and out of place. It was clear that it wasn't a good idea for Genevieve to leave Carl alone in this state.

"Gen, I'm going to go. You should stay here," said Antonia.

"You're sure that's okay, Antonia?"

"Don't stay on account of me," said Carl. "I'll be fine."

"No, it's okay. This was a bad idea anyway," said Antonia. "It's not really our business. I'm going to head home."

"You sure?" asked Genevieve.

"Absolutely."

* * * * *

Antonia was comfortable in her decision to return to the inn. Dinner service had started and she could be there to oversee everything. It was actually insane of her to slip out on one of the busiest nights of the restaurant (although deep down she knew Marty would be fine without her.) But still, spying on Paul Brady would have to wait. She only hoped *he* wouldn't die. It sounded absurd but not in this climate. She consoled herself with the fact that if she knew this information, the cops must also.

When she reached the intersection of Newtown Lane and Main Street, she stopped at the red light. Friday nights always brought the weekenders through town, and this evening was no exception. SUVs full of parents and sleepy kids cruised by behind sportier cars driven by young, upwardly mobile couples. The congestion would thicken on a consistent basis over the next few months. Traffic cops barely out of their teens would try and direct crowds but would end up making a mess of things. Ah, summer.

Antonia glanced down at the passenger seat where she had

placed the pictures from Paul Brady's website. She had brought them in case there was a lull in their stakeout. Paul Brady and Heidi Levicky's images stared up at her. He had his arms draped around her possessively in most of the shots. In others, she wore a pouty look on her face as if she was very pissed off. An idea sparked in Antonia's head.

The car behind Antonia honked, signaling that the light had turned green. She proceeded with the traffic but instead of continuing back towards the Windmill Inn, made a right into the parking lot. She was here in town, so no time like the present to act on a hunch. As she approached, she felt a large sense of clarity. The answer was right in front of her, how could she have not seen it?

Rowdy Hall was tucked away in a mews off of Main Street. The restaurant, meant to resemble an English-style pub, was one of the few places open year-round. The décor is what one would find in the English countryside: a long hammered-copper bar fronted by several backless wooden bar stools. Two flatscreen televisions with images of a sporting events bookended the bar. There were tables scattered around the room for the dinner guests. And contributing to the authentic feel was a rack with various local and national newspapers.

Antonia bypassed the waitress station and approached the bar. She was friendly with the bartender and knew he would be candid with his recollections. When she inquired if he'd been working the previous Thursday he directed her to his colleague, a thirtyish Irishman with pale skin and jet-black hair. After a brief introduction, Antonia got down to business.

"I know you spoke to my friend Larry Lipper about the fight here last Thursday between Warner Caruthers and another man."

"Aye. Heard about the guy dying in the tub. Can't say I'm broken up about it, though may he rest in peace."

Antonia nodded. "I know. I heard he caused problems. Do you mind telling me what happened?"

The bartender scratched his neck and glanced up at the ceiling as if it held the answers.

"Your man, Warner, came in at about six o'clock or so. He had a few pints. There's a baseball game on, and Warner gets a bit loud. An older man on the other end of the bar, clearly rooting for the other team, tells him to pipe down. Warner recognizes him somehow—I think he works at the Dune Club—and starts yelling at him. Clearly, they had gotten into it before. I only get a scattering of conversation cause I'm working back and forth but enough that I know it's bad. I give him a warning but as I do another bloke comes up and tells him to stop yelling at the old man. Warner yells at him also. Finally, I told Warner he had to leave. And just as he got up, his girl shows, and they take off together. Just in time too."

"His girl? What did she look like?"

"Dark hair. I didn't get a good look. I just wanted him out."

Antonia pulled out the pictures from Paul Brady's website. "Was this the girl?"

He took the papers from her and nodded. "Yes."

Antonia again tapped her finger on the picture of Heidi. "Are you sure?"

"That's her. She was the one that Warner was waiting for. I remember thinking they were an odd pair, she sort of goth and he very clean looking. But you never know about people."

Antonia shook her head. "You're right. You never know."

21

Antonia gripped her steering wheel, wracked by indecision. This was a new twist. Warner had been having an affair with Heidi. Right under Paul's nose. Did he find out and kill Warner in a jealous rage? That would make sense. Perhaps he came back early from the Exterminators concert—or didn't go at all—and found them together. He bashed Warner in the back of the head in a heated fit. Then maybe both he and a guilt-ridden Heidi cleaned it all up and made it look like it was an accident. They probably had no idea which bathroom Warner was using and just dumped him in Eleanor's.

This was a major development. Antonia had to talk to Paul and Heidi. If she confronted them without warning, he might confess. She dialed the cell phone number that Paul had given her.

"Yup," answered Paul after several rings.

"Hi, it's Antonia Bingham."

"Oh, hi," he said tersely.

"Listen, Paul. I have something I want to ask you and Heidi."

"Heidi's at work."

"Well, then I'd like to talk to you. Is it possible for me to come over?"

"No. Not possible," said Paul firmly.

Antonia was surprised by his stern tone. Definitely a marked change from the last time they talked.

"It will only take a second . . ."

"No," interrupted Paul. "Don't come by. I'm not home. Just forget you know me."

He clicked off. There was something definitely not right. Paul sounded stressed, and his voice forced. Could he have been speaking under duress? Were Sidney Black and Edward Hamilton already there? She had no choice. She had to move.

*   *   *   *   *

Antonia's car moved slowly down the block, crunching twigs and crushed leaves along the way. There were more houses illuminated tonight than the previous time she was there, but the road still felt dark and somewhat desolate. Right away Antonia noticed that the Levicky's living room light was glowing and Paul Brady's truck was in front. She didn't see any other cars around, but that meant little. Sidney Black and Edward Hamilton would probably be too smart to park in front.

Antonia exited the car and softly shut the doors. The air felt heavy with impending rain. It was damp enough that Antonia's hair would be a clumpy mess when she returned home. Salty sea air was a terror for anyone with her thick hair type. After inspecting the area, she noted that both neighbors' houses were dark. No one home. The Levicky's living room faced the house on the left. That would be the way to go.

Antonia cut across the road and moved stealthily through the shadows of the trees. She thought it ironic that she was shading herself in the very area where the man had been watching her from her previous visit. If indeed he was watching her. In the area that marked the property line, the bushes thickened into a tangled mess that was difficult to maneuver. Antonia found herself wading through twisted and snarled rose of sharon and holly bushes. Sharp holly leaves pricked through the thin layer of her pants.

Antonia strained to see inside the Levicky's window while remaining concealed. It was improbable that whoever was in the house would see her through the chalky darkness, but she didn't want to take chances.

The room appeared even shabbier from the outside. Paintings on the wall were slightly askew as if put up in haste. The sofa sagged even deeper. Antonia was imagining a *House Beautiful* makeover when Paul Brady came striding through the living room clutching a bottle of Amstel Light. Without thinking, Antonia dropped flat to the ground to avoid detection. She pressed her entire body to the cold ground. The grass was damp, and it felt itchy smashed against Antonia's face. The grass blades were like daggers poking into her fresh cuts from the thorns. A musty odor of damp earth floated into her nostrils. So Paul was home drinking a beer. He had told her it wasn't a good time. Why? Was he hiding something? After waiting a few beats, she peeked up and watched as Paul plopped himself on the couch and flicked on the television. Marilyn Manson came bounding in and jumped up next to him. Antonia was pissed. He was merely blowing her off. She was about to stand up and go ring the doorbell to confront him when she felt something on her thigh. It was a buzzing. For a split second her heart pounded before she realized that it was her cell phone.

"Hello?" Antonia whispered into the phone.

"Hey, It's Sam. I heard you weren't feeling well. They said you weren't working tonight."

Antonia had called in "sick" to the restaurant. Liars are always called out.

"Sam?" said Antonia with confusion and surprise. "Right. Yes, I'm not feeling well."

"Do you need anything? I could come by . . ."

"Oh my gosh, sorry, bad time. Um, can I call you back?"

There was a slight pause before he responded. "Sure. No problem."

"We'll talk later, bye."

Antonia clicked off. Time to talk to Paul.

A car's headlights flashed in the distance. The purring murmur of the motor indicated it was approaching. Antonia crawled into the furthest corner, one that was still shrouded in shadows and would wait until it passed. If the car saw her appear from the bushes, they might alert Paul, especially if it was the Levickys. Better to wait.

The car was moving at a leisurely pace, or at least it seemed to Antonia, who was growing impatient. She should have just rung the doorbell. All of this cloak and dagger stuff was foolish. Get things out in the open with Paul and then move on.

The car was fast approaching now, and the lights cast a larger net. Then it stopped . . . right in front of the Levicky house. It remained idle but the motor was running. The wait felt endless. Was it Heidi's parents? Ugh, could they just get a move on so Antonia could go home? A light mist in the air had turned into scattered raindrops. They were still few and far between, but the drops were plump and heavy. Antonia hoped that the rain would not pick up before she could discover why Paul Brady had blown her off.

All at once, Antonia heard two car doors slam.

"This is it," a male voice said.

"Who the hell is Levicky? I thought you said his name was Brady," said another male voice.

"It is. This is where he's staying."

"I'd say not for long after the gift we're bringing him," said the other voice with a wicked chuckle.

The two shadowy figures approached the front door. From Antonia's angle, only their backs were visible. She expected to see Sidney Black and Edward Hamilton but when one turned towards the outside lamp to press the doorbell, she saw at once that it was the lawyer, Terry Rudolph. Antonia recoiled into the bush. Of course. Hamilton and Black wouldn't do it themselves; they would send a henchman. But hadn't he already been to Paul Brady's house and dismissed the footage

Paul had? Antonia hadn't really believed that Edward Hamilton and Sidney Black would send someone to kill Paul . . . but now it felt possible.

Antonia had to think. She pressed down further into the web of branches. By now, the scratchy leaves left an impression on Antonia's cheek. She had a flashback to a leaf-rubbing project she did in elementary school. The assignment was to put white paper over a leaf and rub on top of it with a crayon, tracing the spindly veins to make creepy images. She felt like that piece of paper now. She held her breath until she finally heard a door open.

"Come on in."

She heard footsteps before the door shut.

Antonia remained low to the ground. She slithered up towards the Levicky's living room window, feeling like an army commando. A quick peek through the dingy glass revealed the three men standing in a semi-circle. The lawyer's arms were folded and he wore a look of impatience. The other man—short, muscular, with a strong nose—stood with a neutral look on his face. Antonia quickly ducked back down. A glance to the left revealed the window on the other side was ajar. She slid against the house and planted herself underneath. She was concealed but able to hear their conversation.

"So, let's see what you got."

"It's kind of grainy."

"Hold it sideways."

"Can we fast forward to the part we want?"

Antonia popped up and took another quick peek through

the gauzy curtains in the window. From this angle she could see Paul. His face betrayed neither fear nor ease. The lawyer and the other man were holding up a small camcorder and watching the screen. None of the picture was visible to Antonia. She crouched back down.

There was silence and Antonia waited. All she could hear was her own heart. The scattered raindrops had turned into a light shower and were gently pelting Antonia's body.

"Where is the footage of Mr. Black?" asked the lawyer's voice.

"Right there."

"What, you mean this?"

"Yeah." Paul's voice had a nervous lilt to it.

"That's not him."

"What do you mean?"

"Come on, you really thought we'd believe that was Sidney Black? That's you, you moron."

"Oh, no wait, see there."

"You're joking. Mr. Brady, either you have it or you don't."

"This is the stuff," whined Paul.

"You've wasted my time," said the lawyer with irritation. "And worse, you've wasted my associate's time and Mr. Black's time."

"Listen, okay, so this might not be *exactly* what you want, but I can get it. This is like, a teaser."

"Not good enough, I'm afraid," said the lawyer. "I don't think you understand who you are dealing with."

"Come on now, we can work this out."

"I doubt it. Frank, let him have a look at what we brought for him. He'll see how serious we are."

Antonia twisted her head and took a quick glance. The lawyer's 'associate' opened the briefcase. Antonia watched as Paul peered in it. His face looked pale. He shook his head.

"Dudes, please, let's work this out."

The lawyer shook his head. "Take a look in the briefcase and say goodbye."

For the first time, real terror seized Antonia. This must be the gun that Francine was talking about. They were showing it to Paul Brady before they killed him. It was sick. Had they shown Warner the murder weapon first, too? Were they so twisted?

Antonia fled across the lawn. She lurched past the hedge, down the path, across the road and to her car.

Her hands were shaking so badly it was difficult to dial her cell phone.

"911 what's your emergency?"

"I think a man is about to be murdered! Come to 3400 Schellinger Road. Hurry!"

"Who's going to be murdered ma'am?"

"A man named Paul Brady. You have to get here fast. Please call Sergeant Flanagan. I think it's related to the death of Warner Caruthers."

"Ma'am, may I have your name please?"

"Antonia Bingham."

"Are you at the house now?"

"I'm outside the house."

"How many individuals are in the house?"

"Three. A lawyer, Terry Rudolph, and his associate Frank are the other two. I think they have a gun."

"We're on our way."

Antonia collapsed back against the seat. "They're on their way. Thank God."

22

The rain was coming down hard. A steady beat pounded on the roof and dripped down into the gutters. Large drops slapped against the windows before disappearing down into the darkness.

"You haven't touched your tea," reprimanded Joseph. "Are you quite certain you wouldn't want a shot of bourbon instead?"

Antonia shook her head glumly. She was curled up on her sofa, her fluffy pink and white throw blanket atop of her. The blanket was so old that it shed all over her clothes like a large Persian cat. Antonia clasped her hands around the steaming mug as if it would provide her with the warmth she craved. Joseph was perched in the deep upholstered armchair across from her.

"How could I have been so stupid?" she asked miserably.

"You were carried away."

"Worse than that. I became the town idiot."

"Don't be so hard on yourself."

Antonia gave Joseph a wary look. "I spied on a man, then I called the police and told them he was about to be murdered. *Six* squad cars arrived at the scene, and it turns out it was all a false alarm. They were planning on paying him off! There wasn't a gun in the brief case; there was a contract and a pile of cash! It was all legal, or at least sort of, until Warner's father had his lawyer send a letter demanding the property back. But that's beside the point. I now have the police department thinking I'm a hoax and a lunatic. As do Paul Brady, Terry Rudolph, and his muscle-man associate Frank! I made an utter and complete fool of myself. This could kill my business. I should just leave town now."

Joseph put down his mug atop the Louis Vuitton steamer trunk that doubled as Antonia's coffee table. He put his hand in the air as if waving away Antonia's words.

"Yes, you made a mistake. But it was all in good conscience. The police understood that once you explained it to them . . ."

"Sergeant Flanagan thinks I am insane. I could tell by the look on his face. I *requested* him at the scene. They pulled him out of the movie theater. He was with his *son*. And all for nothing." Antonia smoothed the throw blanket over her knees. "I could go to jail for a false call . . ."

"Did they say that?"

"No. But still." Antonia buried her face in her hands. "You should have seen the lawyer's face when the police showed up. And Paul Brady was scared out of his wits. He probably has a secret pot stash somewhere in the house and thought he was getting busted. The only thing I can hope for is that they bought my excuse. I told them that when I arrived on Paul's doorstep I saw two sinister men standing over him, and Paul seemed agitated. After Warner's death, I thought something was afoot."

"That seems reasonable enough."

"But Sergeant Flanagan pressed me. I swear he knew I was fishing around. He wanted to know why I thought that these men would kill Paul Brady."

"What did you say?"

"This was my one mistake. I said that I had heard from someone that they were going to bring out a gun. I realize now how stupid I was. Sergeant Flanagan talked to the lawyer who said his employer referred to him as 'the big guns.' Of course, Francine lost that in translation. This was all about a payoff. I was totally wrong about a murder."

"Antonia, I don't think you have to worry that much. Yes, you made the call. But now the police are on to the fact that there are very interested parties trying to track down the missing footage. It's pure motive for Warner's death. And in regards to the lawyer, what you did was an inconvenience. What Paul Brady did was lie and mislead him. That's worse."

"I suppose."

Antonia leaned back on the sofa. She was exhausted, physically and mentally. Worst of all, she was mortified. Gossip like this could spread all over town. She'd have to sleep with Larry Lipper for a year in order for him not to print it in the newspaper.

"I'm done. It's over."

"You're quitting the investigation?"

"I am retiring. I'm in over my head. I think it all must be my imagination run amok."

"What about the towels? What about the Lysol can? The watch?"

Antonia shrugged. "Who knows, maybe Warner moved them. Maybe he did want to shower in Eleanor's bathroom. And maybe he was a clean freak who wanted it perfectly sanitary before he did so. I don't know this guy from Adam, why am I conjecturing on what he would and would not do?"

Joseph didn't respond. He pulled a handkerchief out of his pocket and removed his glasses. He began wiping the lenses pensively. Antonia flopped around on the sofa. She felt restless, anxious and agitated.

"You agree with me, right? I should quit this all. It's all rubbish."

Joseph finished wiping his right lens before returning the glasses to his nose and the handkerchief to his pocket.

"I agree, maybe let the police solve the murders of Sheila Black and possibly Warner. But don't you think you need to find the footage? It must be somewhere?"

"I don't have any idea where it is or how to find it. I've just proven that I am totally pathetic when it comes to solving puzzles."

"I don't ascribe to that at all," said Joseph, unusually emphatic. "You have achieved a great many things because of your passion and your convictions. I think you have an instinct about the circumstances surrounding Warner's death that others don't possess. You see people come and go all day. I know that you study them, notice things about them that others don't notice. You have to trust yourself. I say, don't throw it all away."

"You mean, despite being totally humiliated, I should try and find out what really happened to Warner?" asked Antonia.

"What have you got to lose?"

"You're appealing to my vanity by flattery and persuasion."

"I'm making a cogent argument. If it strokes your ego, all the better."

Antonia sighed. "What would I do without you?"

Joseph laughed softly before switching the topic. "By the way, I checked. Pauline Framingham was telling the truth. She *was* down in Palm Beach. And it doesn't look like she's made any attempt to retrieve missing footage. I'd remove her from the list. But I still think you need to have a conversation with Heidi Levicky."

"You're terrible," teased Antonia. "You want me to kick back into private eye mode."

Joseph smiled but didn't respond.

"You do!" insisted Antonia.

"Maybe," said Joseph. "It's a welcome distraction to the usual routine around here. Listen, try something for me. It is what you would call 'New Age' but hear me out. I want you to lie down and close your eyes. Yes, like I'm a psychiatrist, or hypnotist, or whatever charlatan you think of."

"You're serious?"

"You know I am always serious."

Antonia was surprised. She hadn't seen this side of Joseph. Perhaps this murder had awakened something in both of them.

"Are you sure?"

"When I interviewed older or tricky subjects for my articles, I often used this device. It actually works. But you need to relax."

"Okay," said Antonia. She did as was told.

"Good. Now think back to each interaction you had with Warner. Try to remember every exchange you had. Even if it was mundane."

Antonia closed her eyes firmly and let her mind wander back in time. Life could be so frustrating. It was all about living forward but thinking backward. Using the past in order to help decisions with the future. But mistakes were always repeated. People rarely learned from their errors.

"Focus, Antonia," cooed Joseph.

"I am."

Antonia conjured up images of Warner. They came more as flashes rather than a linear memory.

"Okay, he arrived at the inn about mid-morning. Connie, from reception, told me I had a visitor. He was leaning against the table reading a brochure that we have on fishing in Montauk. I introduced myself, and he told me he was Luke's houseguest and he had come to get the key."

"That's great. Go on . . ."

"We talked about fishing briefly. Then he said he was here to make a movie. I said that I loved movies, I have hundreds of DVDs downstairs in our lending library. But he said his was a *documentary*. I said I was more of the romantic comedy type. This is all boring . . ."

"No, go on."

Antonia sighed. "Okay, I told him I watched "When Harry Met Sally" every few weeks. He said maybe his movie would change my tastes. I asked what it was about and he said 'the Hamptons.' But then he quickly added that he hated when people called it 'the Hamptons.' And I agreed. Lumping a bunch of very different villages and towns into one generalization drives me nuts. Then we talked about Luke, how he's working at an investment bank now. I think Warner thought he had 'sold out.' Then I gave him the key and told him when Rosita comes and when I come by and he said he would be very respectful, he loved the Mastersons like family, and that was it."

Joseph nodded. "Good. What about the next time?"

"The next time was when he came in hastily. He was in a big rush, and he asked for the key, said he had lost his, he was very sorry. I went to get another spare key in my office, and when I came back, he was gone. Jonathan asked me to come into his office to check on something, so I did, and when I returned to the front desk Warner was there again. I gave him the key. And he left. And on the way out, he stopped and talked to Bridget Curtis . . ."

Antonia sat bolt upright.

"What is it?" asked Joseph.

"Where did Warner go between the time when I went to get the key for him and came out of Jonathan's office? Was he handing off something to Bridget? I can't understand it. I still think she must be somehow involved."

"He could have gone anywhere. He could have used the time to hide the footage at the inn."

Antonia stared into Joseph's eyes. "Where?"

"I don't know. But it's got to be here."

SATURDAY

23

The rain was torrential on Saturday morning. A walk on the beach would be an exercise in futility. The relentlessly pounding raindrops promised a beating to everyone who dared challenge them. Antonia was relieved that she would not have to face Nick this morning. She was still feeling awkward about their last conversation. How should she react? Should she act casual as if he had said nothing? She was not good at that. Not at all. This was why she had opted out of the love game long ago. It was better to remain virginal. She'd live like a saint from now on. She'd always enjoyed reading about them in religion class. They didn't have to do very much and yet still ended up worshiped.

After making breakfast and addressing members of the wedding party's inquiries about where to get manicures and a blow-out (the Salon in Amagansett), Antonia was able to retreat and address the real issue at hand. Her first mission of the day was to find the footage. She started at her office, yet a thorough search only resulted in finding the Naturopathica Spa gift card that she had been looking for since the day after Christmas (it was a present from Genevieve.) She then moved to the front desk, where another brisk exploration revealed nothing of interest. From there she rummaged through the parlor and the living room with no success, before being seized by the idea that Warner hid the footage in her kitchen. It would make sense; he would know that it was her domain. But after opening every single cabinet and drawer, sifting through all the bags of flour, sugar, corn, and even opening boxes in the freezer, Antonia realized she was wrong. Warner would never have hid the footage in a place that was available to so many. She was way off. And at this point Antonia was tired, so she decided to call it a day on her investigation. Instead, she sequestered herself in the kitchen with the several new recipes that she was eager to try.

On the savory side, she was exploring a new grilled lamb dish, one that would require a labor-intensive marinade that she had not yet perfected. For several hours she crushed peppercorns, coriander and mustard seeds. She chopped garlic, thyme, rosemary, mint, cucumber, basil and sage. She fiddled with dollops of yogurt, hoisin sauce, hot sauce, soy sauce, raspberry vinegar, a medley of wine varietals and grenadine. She prepared about twenty marinades, but none was quite what she had in mind until the concoction she finally created at ten-thirty in the morning. Developing recipes felt like lab work to Antonia, bringing her tremendous satisfaction when she nailed something. After wiping down her mise-en-place, she commenced work on her caramelized banana bread pudding. She wanted to incorporate all of her favorite flavors: peanut butter, pretzels, chocolate, banana, caramel and marshmallow to create a decadent dessert. It was difficult work, but anything to avoid thinking about the embarrassing events of the prior evening.

At twelve-thirty, Antonia retired to her office with a steaming bowl of pureed white bean soup garnished with bacon, alongside a hunk of crusty baguette, oozing with melted fromage d'Affinois. She then nestled into her chair to dine in silence. The gray light floating through the windows was static and harsh, as if the world was paralyzed between daytime and nighttime. The rain continued pounding. Antonia flipped through the stack of notes that she had retrieved at reception, and checked her emails and voice mails. Genevieve had left a rambling message expressing anger that Antonia had gone to Paul Brady's without her. Gen had a heart for drama, regardless of whether or not she was the catalyst. Antonia believed it was actually an aphrodisiac for her.

In addition, there was a message from Larry Lipper. He had most likely heard about what happened last night on his scanner or from one of his contacts and was calling to gloat. Antonia picked up the phone.

"Hang on a sec," said Larry when he answered.

She heard him bark orders at someone in his newsroom. She had a big spoonful of soup while she waited.

"I heard about your big screw up yesterday."

"I'm sure you did."

"Why didn't you call me? I could have been your wingman."

"I don't know. Obviously, the plan was ill-conceived."

Then Larry surprised her. He moved on and didn't rub it in.

"Listen, I heard something about Sheila Black. The police want to talk to her lover. Someone overheard them together said he was British. Know anyone who fits that description?"

"Hmmm . . . the only British guy I know here is Jonathan, my manager."

"Was he porking her?"

"I would doubt it."

"Alright, well, if anyone comes up let me know."

"Will do."

*   *   *   *   *

Antonia sat back down at her desk when he left. That's right; Sheila had mentioned that her lover was British. Maybe Jonathan knew another Brit. She should ask him. Suddenly, she thought of the weird interaction between Jonathan and Carl. She was curious as to what had transpired between them but she thought she shouldn't pursue it; too awkward. Better to let it go. Instead, she sent an email to Genevieve asking her if she knew any British guys around town. If there was anyone who had a beat on the men in the Hamptons, it was Genevieve. Antonia began sorting through the papers on her desk, but her mind was filled with all things Warner. She knew it wasn't good for her. Suddenly, she remembered that Sam had called her last night. As far as he was concerned, she had blown him off.

Without even hesitating, she picked up the phone and dialed his number.

"Hey, Sam, it's Antonia," she said after he answered.

"Hey," he said cheerfully. "I didn't think I'd hear from you."

"Why's that?"

"I don't know," he said.

This emboldened Antonia. "I was wondering what you're up to now? I have a few hours before I need to start cooking and I'm bouncing off the walls a bit over here. Are you working? Is it a bad time? We can talk later . . ."

"No, no, it's a great time. I'm actually at home, well, I mean, my cousin's house, where I'm staying. Do you want to come by? I can make us lunch . . ."

"I already ate. But I'll come by. Just give me the address."

After hanging up with Sam, Antonia marched into her apartment with determination she had not experienced in years. If her entire life was falling apart with craziness, she may as well take advantage of it and act out of character. She stripped, showered, blew her hair dry and put on makeup, taking extra care to put on mascara and dramatic eyeliner. After spraying herself with perfume, she went to her top drawer to pull out some 'sexy' lingerie. She forgot that she didn't really have any sexy lingerie. The closest thing was a lacy thong that Genevieve had given her as a stocking stuffer at Christmas—which was still coiled in a cylinder and wrapped in its packaging—and a white silk camisole. Antonia donned them, and topped them with a long sleeved v-neck shirt that accentuated her breasts and a black skirt. She pulled on her high leather boots and pushed gold hoop earrings through her lobes. She turned to survey herself in the mirror. She was ready.

* * * * *

The house Sam was staying at was in the Amagansett Dunes, an area south of the highway, close to the beach. Unlike beach-front property in other villages, the mostly one-story houses in the Dunes are clustered together on tiny slivers of uneven land, cramped so close as to almost touch. The landscaping is untamed, consisting of thick clumps of patchy Bermuda grass running wild on every surface that isn't paved or built upon. Despite the proximity of one's neighbors, there was something very carefree and relaxed about the area; like Venice Beach in the 1970s. Antonia loved the beachy feel, that sense that no one would become apoplectic if you dragged sand into his or her house. There was an appreciation for the elements; importance was not placed on status or formality.

Antonia found Sam's car parked outside of a brown one-story ranch style house. Two surfboards were leaning against the garage door, the tips still sandy. After parking on the road, she checked herself out in the rearview mirror. She reapplied lip-gloss, and ran her tongue across her teeth. It was now or never. She opened the car door. The ocean was loud, pounding violently. The wind was gusty, which caused the rain to blow laterally. Antonia had brought an umbrella but it was of little use. She made a mad dash for the front door and shook the drops off her raincoat and hair.

"Hey," said Sam, opening the door. His hair was wet and he

was barefoot, clad in blue jeans and a Harley Davidson T-shirt. It was the first time Antonia had seen his arms and she noticed he had a large tattoo of a dragon on his right bicep.

"Hey," said Antonia. She smiled at him. His eyes scanned her appraisingly, and she knew at once that her primping attempts had been effective.

"Come on in."

Antonia followed Sam inside. The house appeared to have been decorated in the seventies. There was a blue shag carpet covering most of the linoleum floor. To the right, there were two sofas: one encased in brown velvet and the other in a tan houndstooth pattern. Both had various psychedelic throw pillows adorning them. A glass coffee table encrusted with sea glass separated them. On the wall, was an enormous rock fireplace, with a driftwood mantle, atop which were lava lamps and a large hexagonal mirror. Sliding glass doors led out to a long deck with a dining table and four chairs, as well as a chaise. Scraggly grass and a brown fence blocked the view of everything but the neighbor's rooftop.

"I'm having a total *Brady Bunch* flashback," said Antonia, after surveying the room. She put her handbag down on the hall table. "This place is groooovy."

"Isn't it? They were going to redo it when they bought it, but then it all sort of started to come back in fashion and now they think it's really kitsch."

"I guess it's the perfect décor if you don't really care about those things. The air is so salty down here, a magnet for mildew and mold. It's kind of nice to not worry about that. I have to say, the inn and the houses I look after require a fortune to maintain the antiques and outdoor painted trim."

"Here, let me take your coat."

Antonia unwrapped herself and handed him the coat. She saw him take in her boots and linger on her breasts. She knew Genevieve would be proud of her.

The living area was all one room with the kitchen at the far end, separated by a counter and two high barstools. Sam walked over and opened the refrigerator. He leaned down to glance inside and Antonia could see his back muscles rippling through his shirt. She watched the curve of his arm as it bent. She had formerly thought tattoos were tacky, but now she reconsidered. There was something sexy about them.

"What can I get you? Coke? Beer? Coffee? Wine? I also have some good parmesan. I can whip us up some pasta."

"I'm all set, thanks."

Sam turned and stared at her. She felt a jolt of electricity. She parted her lips, but didn't say anything. Sam got the message. Something had passed between them. He straightened up and closed the refrigerator door. He turned his back to her and opened one of the cupboard cabinets.

"I have something perfect for today."

"Oh yeah? What's that?"

Antonia walked towards him. He removed two mismatched glasses from the cabinet—one had a whale emblem on it, the other a crest of some sort—and took out a bottle of whiskey. He poured a generous portion into each glass and handed one to Antonia.

"Good stuff here."

"It's the middle of the day!"

"Yeah, but it's a rainy day. There's nothing else to do. And you're going to like this."

"I am?" she said, cocking her head to the side.

"Trust me."

She kept her eyes on his. He returned her gaze. He smelled good, like soap and shampoo. Very clean.

"Bottoms up then," said Antonia, clinking her glass with his.

She poured the liquid down her throat. It burned at first, but then a warm aftertaste filled her mouth.

"Yum."

He raised his eyebrows. "Good, right?"

Antonia leaned against the counter. Sam was close to her now, the fission between them palpable.

"How about another?"

"Why not?" she asked coyly.

He filled up both of their glasses. Antonia noted that he had filled hers higher than his own. She didn't mind and reached out her glass and clinked his.

"Wait," he said, putting his hand on her arm to prevent her from drinking. "What are we toasting?"

"Hmmm . . . I don't know, what do you think?"

"I don't want to toast to all that bullshit like world peace and crap like that. Let's toast to us."

"Yes, world peace is crap."

"You know what I mean. Nothing generic. More intimate."

"Refreshing," said Antonia with a laugh. "Sure, to us."

Sam waited a beat before releasing his hand from Antonia's arm. The spot he had touched tingled. She raised the glass to her mouth and swallowed the golden whiskey. This time it didn't burn, it melted.

He twisted the bottle on the counter so that she could see the label. "I got this baby in Scotland."

"It's good," said Antonia. The alcohol was hitting her now, flowing gently through her blood, and warming her entire body. "It melts in your mouth."

"It does," nodded Sam. It was almost imperceptible, but he took a slight step towards her.

"I like things that melt in your mouth," said Antonia. She shocked herself when she said it.

"You do," said Sam. It was more of a statement than a question. "Me too."

Sam took another step towards Antonia and scooped her into his arms. His mouth found hers and she felt his soft lips pressing against hers. The kisses were gentle at first, soft and romantic. They slowly became more urgent, as if they both wanted to take as much from the other as possible. What started as a slow tango turned into a frantic cha cha. They took turns hungrily ripping each other's clothes off, attacking one another with desperation, as if this was the long awaited culmination of a lifetime of lust. Antonia rubbed her hands over Sam's chest and arms, tenderly caressing his rock hard body. Sam deftly lifted Antonia's sweater, and used his mouth to sample everything she had to offer. After several panting moments, Sam grabbed Antonia's hand and led her into the bedroom, where he pulled her down onto the sateen comforter and made love to her not once but twice, the thumping rain drowning out their moans.

*   *   *   *   *

They lingered in a dreamy haze. Sam had his arms wrapped around Antonia, his body pressed against her back. Antonia noted that their breathing had become unified, their chests rising and falling in harmony. After several more languid moments, Sam finally extracted himself gently and sat up on the edge of the bed. He was still undressed; his firm body completely exposed. Antonia remained lying down, her body now covered by the blankets. He glanced down at her, a wide smile creeping across his face.

"That was really nice."

"I know," agreed Antonia.

Sam leaned over and kissed her forehead. Even though they had just been intimate, Antonia felt embarrassed that he was naked. As if sensing this, Sam pulled on his boxers. She watched with admiration as he slipped each muscular thigh through. He turned and stood up and walked out of the bedroom. Antonia fumbled for her thong, which she found curled up on the floor under the bed and quickly put it on. She retrieved her camisole on the bottom of the bed and donned it. She took a second to scan the room. She knew that it was only temporary quarters, but she wanted to glean if there was anything in the room that conveyed Sam's personality. A biography of Abraham Lincoln was on the side table with a bookmark slid between the pages.

There was a hamper in the corner overflowing with laundry. She noted boxers, button downs and a gray Union College t-shirt. Stacks of *Sports Illustrated* magazines were in a pile next to the bed.

Sam returned with two bottles of water, one of which he handed to Antonia. He took a sip of water and kept his eyes on Antonia. She felt embarrassed, as if he had noticed that she had been checking out his stuff.

"Any update on Warner's death?" asked Sam.

Antonia rolled her eyes. "No, it's a mess."

"Have you told anyone about what you found?" asked Sam, taking a sip.

Antonia watched as he drank. Everything about him was sexy. "You mean about the towels and the watch?"

"Yes."

"Only Joseph."

"He's the man in the wheelchair, right?"

"Scooter."

"Right," he said. "But no one else?"

Antonia shook her head. "No. Why?"

Sam shrugged. "I just don't think it's a great idea if people know we broke into the Mastersons' house."

"Good point." Antonia glanced out the window and realized the sky was becoming even darker with storm clouds. "God, I need to go."

She needed to dress but didn't want to walk to the kitchen in her skivvies. She knew it was irrational to be modest now, after what they had just done to each other, but she felt self-conscious. Once again, it seemed as if Sam read her mind.

"Your clothes are in the other room, I'll get them."

"Thanks."

He returned with Antonia's clothes and held them out to her. "Cool boots."

"Thanks," she said, retrieving them.

Without removing the sheets, she started to get dressed. It was awkward, and she felt slightly ridiculous, as she knew Sam was watching her.

"You have a great body, Antonia."

She blushed. "Yeah, right."

"Cut that out. It's true."

"Yeah, well . . ."

She had one arm in the sweater and one out before Sam jumped over on top of her. He pinned her arms down and pressed his chest against hers and stared straight into her eyes.

"I'm not letting you go until you acknowledge to me that you have a great body," he said, half teasing, half serious.

Antonia tried to extract herself, but his arms were powerful.

"Okay, Okay," she giggled. "I have a great body."

He pressed her down harder in the bed. His strength was overwhelming.

"Say it like you mean it."

"I have a great body!" she shouted.

"Thank you," he said, finally releasing her. "Now stand up, show me that kick-ass ass of yours, and get dressed like a real person."

Antonia did as she was told. He was right; she was stupid to be ashamed. It had just been so long since she had been with another man that she felt out of practice. Not to mention the fact that Sam was in such good shape, and was younger than she was. She went into the bathroom to refresh herself, and found Sam in the kitchen upon her return. He'd slid on his jeans, and was leaning against the counter reading the sports section of *The New York Post*. He gave her a bright smile when she reentered.

"Well, this was fun. But duty calls. What time is it anyway?"

"I don't know," he said with a mischievous smile.

"You don't know?"

Sam pointed to the clock above the stove. "There. It's three o'clock."

Three o'clock. Time to return to the restaurant.

"I gotta dash."

Sam walked over and kissed her eyelids. "When can I see you again?"

"I'm working tonight . . ."

"Great, I'll stop by."

"Don't you need to work?"

"It's a weekend, baby. Day off. Tomorrow also. Maybe we can go to Montauk and prowl around."

"Sure."

He moved towards her and slid his hand down her neck gently. He pulled her in for a languid kiss. She hadn't felt like this for a long time.

"You sure you have to go?"

Antonia nodded. As if to prove the point, she went over to retrieve her bag on the front hall table. She felt dizzy, but in a warm and cozy way. Nothing like an afternoon of loving to set you on course. She checked her phone quickly before closing her bag. There were a few emails but they could wait. Out of the corner of her eye, Antonia spied a dish full of miscellaneous junk. It held loose change, safety pins, a Golden Pear coffee card, and matches from Rowdy Hall. An unsettling feeling hit Antonia like a ton of bricks. She picked up the matches and held them between her fingers.

"You smoke?"

She turned around to face Sam. He had moved closer to her. He glanced down at the matches and shrugged.

"Naw, I just grabbed those up when I was at Rowdy Hall one night. Been there a few times." He put his hands on her hips and kissed her again. "Man, I can't get enough of you."

A sickening feeling was growing inside Antonia. She pulled away slightly. "Do you frequent Rowdy Hall?"

"I've been a few times."

"Did you ever meet Warner there?"

Sam glanced up. "I don't think so." He stopped before adding, "What did he look like?"

"You know, thin, strawberry blondish hair."

"I'm not sure," Sam murmured. He bent back down and kissed Antonia again. She watched as his hands slid down her body. His watch-less hand. Antonia felt herself stiffen. She continued talking over his shoulder.

"He got into a fight there one night. He was harassing an old guy from the Dune Club. The bartender was going to throw him out but someone else stepped in.

"I don't know." Sam was kissing her neck.

"Really? You never saw a fight there."

Sam pulled himself back abruptly. "Wait a second, that was Warner?" said Sam.

"Yes . . ."

"I did meet him," he said with a shake of his head. "Or not really. The guy was a jerk. He was yelling at this old man for kicking him out of some place or another. But really mouthing off. I think he was wasted. Anyway, I told him to lay off, and he wanted to take me out to the back and fight me."

"Really?"

Sam was pretty heated. "Yeah. He was a punk. But I didn't have to lay a finger on him. He left when some girl showed up."

Antonia nodded. She felt slightly dizzy and didn't know what to think. "Can I use your bathroom one more time?"

"Sure," said Sam.

Antonia made a beeline into the bathroom and locked the door. She felt a sense of panic. Was it all just a coincidence? Sam *met* Warner. He had gotten into a *fight* with him. True, he admitted it; but only because she had found the matches. What about the watch? She had never seen him wear one, even when they were at Fresno and she asked him what time it was because he busted her checking out his ring finger. Antonia's mind raced. She had to calm down and think. Surely, Sam wouldn't kill someone over a bar fight. Would he?

She suddenly remembered the T-shirt in Sam's laundry basket. It was from Union College. Warner had gone to Union College. Antonia was nauseous.

Everything started to come together. Sam wasn't interested in her; he wanted to know what she knew. That's why he kept showing up everywhere. Had he been the man in the bushes watching her? Oh God, and she had led him to the crime scene. Sure he made it seem like it was her idea, but was it? And then there was how he kept pumping her for information about the investigation. He was on to her, and she had her head so far up her ass, she had no idea.

Antonia felt hot and clammy. She flushed the toilet to buy her some time and turned on the water in the sink to splash on her face. After dabbing her eyes with a towel and fixing her runny mascara she took a deep breath. What to do now? *Just stay calm. Don't worry.* She told herself. The other side of herself answered with contempt: *Don't worry? You may have just slept with a psychotic killer, you slut! And now you're in his bathroom and he may be sharpening his cooking knives getting ready to julienne you!*

Antonia put her hand on the doorknob. She took one last look at her reflection in the mirror. She would pass. Her eyes slid down to the sink and fell on the cabinet underneath. Something in her mind clicked.

She went over to the cabinet and opened it. There was a toilet brush, three sponges and . . . a can of Lysol bathroom cleaner. Antonia wanted to throw up.

Sam smiled at her when she returned to the living room. All she saw now was the cold sinister look of a killer. She had to get the hell out of there.

"I've got to go, I'm really late."

"I'll walk you out."

"You don't have to!" Antonia practically screamed.

Sam appeared startled. "It's okay."

"I mean, it's raining. It's so nice of you, but I don't want you to get wet."

Sam smiled. "I don't mind."

He escorted her to her car and she gave him a peck on the cheek and promised to call him. Once she was sure she had the car started she decided to make a move.

"I didn't know you went to Union College."

"What?" asked Sam with confusion.

"I saw your t-shirt in the laundry."

Sam looked up as if he was trying to remember. "Oh, my ex-girlfriend did. She gave it to me."

Antonia nodded. "The one who left you for another man?"

"The very one."

Antonia didn't say anything.

"Maybe it's time to get rid of it," admitted Sam.

"Maybe," said Antonia.

"Where did you go? I'll wear one from your college."

"Ha ha," said Antonia with a fake playful laugh.

She lurched back in reverse, narrowly missing a parked car, and pushed down on the gas, leaving Sam's house in the dust.

The rain was thick and Antonia's windshield wipers were working overtime to scrape the rippling cascades of rain off her window. She had to drive slowly, with her lights on, in order to see clearly. The short walk to the car had chilled her bones: so she turned the heat on full blast. Antonia's heart was doing somersaults. She had escaped from Alcatraz. What was she supposed to do now? She had to think. There were still so many questions . . .

Antonia knew one person who may have some answers.

24

The small parking lot abutting CVS Pharmacy was glutted with cars. Rain was a catalyst for traffic congestion in town. Everyone became eager to escape their houses and scurried out to do all of the errands that they neglected when the sun was beaming. Antonia waited patiently while a harried mother in a yellow slicker loaded her bags into a Honda Civic. Her screaming child was locked into a metal cart, his fat legs thrashing against the bars with the rage of a prisoner on death row. It took an abnormal skill for the mother to keep him in place while hoisting the overstuffed plastic bags into the backseat of her car. After a solid five-minute effort she finally pulled out, releasing the parking spot.

When the CVS electric doors slid open, the blast of air-conditioning that greeted Antonia was an affront to her damp and chilled body. How is it that stores get temperature control all wrong? She shook the raindrops out of her hair and brushed them off of her jacket. A quick glance at the front checkout counter revealed Heidi Levicky manning register five. If Antonia had any trouble envisioning Heidi as a clerk, it dissipated as soon as Antonia noted that Heidi maintained the bored cynical look that seemed to permanently adorn her face. As the line was snaking around in a U shape, Antonia decided to pick up necessities while she was here. She trolled the makeup aisle, selecting goodies that promised "thick, luscious lashes" and "sexy, pouty lips." After hitting the shampoo section, she made her way to the front of the store, which had cleared slightly.

Heidi's hooded eyes remained neutral when Antonia approached her counter. A black concert T-shirt peeked out under her CVS apron.

"Remember me?" asked Antonia. She placed her basket on the counter.

Heidi immediately started removing items and scanning them methodically.

"I should be mad at you. My parents were super-pissed when they arrived home and found the cops at our house. Now they've given us three weeks to move out."

"I'm very sorry," said Antonia with genuine concern. "It doesn't matter, I know, but my intentions were good. I really did think his life was in danger."

Heidi shrugged. "Yeah, I can see that. And you know what? That guy is so stupid that maybe it would have been. I can't believe he told that lawyer dude that he had the footage! Who did he think he was dealing with? Morons? Of course they would have found out that he was lying. He's so dumb. He knew I would never go for it, that's why he purposely did it when I wasn't there. What an ass."

Heidi continued pulling items out of Antonia's basket and sliding them across the scanner.

"Listen, do you have five minutes? I really need to ask you something."

Heidi glanced up and gave Antonia a look. Finally, she shrugged. Antonia took that for a confirmation.

"Give me a sec," commanded Heidi.

While Heidi helped other customers, Antonia idled by the racks of sunscreen in the front of the store waiting for Heidi. Sunscreen was always something she forgot to buy. She'd have to remember next time. Sometimes the sheer volume of miscellaneous junk carried in drug stores amazed her. Perhaps that's why Sheila Black did all of her shopping here. Antonia shuddered slightly, an image of Sheila conjuring in her mind. She wondered if the police had made any progress in the investigation into her death.

"So, what's up?" said Heidi.

She had snuck up on Antonia so quietly that she startled her. "Oh, okay. Do you want to talk here?"

"It's raining outside," Heidi responded flatly.

"You're right."

Antonia moved towards the wall of the drug store, setting off the electric doors as she did so. She took a few steps backwards and Heidi watched her with disdain. Finally, she walked towards her.

"Heidi, I wanted to ask you about Warner."

"Yeah," said Heidi with uncertainty.

"I know you were sleeping with him."

She was probably a very clever poker player, but Antonia saw a tell in Heidi's face. Her bottom lip quivered ever so slightly.

"That's not . . ."

Antonia put her hands up. "Don't even deny it. I have more than one witness."

"Okay," conceded Heidi. She shrugged her shoulders defiantly. "So?"

Antonia had not expected her to admit her transgressions so freely. "So, what about Paul?"

Again a shrug. "I like to keep my options open."

Antonia's eyes widened. "Does he know?"

"No."

"Is it possible? Do you think he might have found out and killed Warner?"

"No. Paul's not the jealous type. He's too lazy."

Antonia was willing to believe that Paul was lazy; but that didn't mean he wasn't jealous. "You never know what could set someone off."

"The guy can barely get off the couch!" laughed Heidi. "And besides, Warner was his ticket. If Warner was still alive, this documentary was going to be seen around the world. Paul could get a Hollywood gig. And I . . . I could get my DJ career hopping. You know, I was going to do the soundtrack and even have a cameo. But now Warner is dead and the film will never see the light of day. Warner would have been really disappointed."

"Yeah, I guess you're right," conceded Antonia. She had to admit, but what Heidi said made sense. Two slackers don't suddenly become killers. She knew Heidi had to get back to work but she felt like there was more information to be learned from her.

"Heidi, do you have any idea *what* the missing footage is?"

She hesitated for a split second.

"*Heidi*," pressed Antonia.

"I know Warner caught Sidney Black on tape doing something embarrassing. That's all I know."

Suddenly something occurred to Antonia. "Heidi, why does the lawyer think I have the missing footage? Did *you* tell him something?"

Heidi ripped off a black lacquered hangnail on her index finger with her teeth. She started chewing on it before she spoke. "Yeah, okay, so what?"

"Why would you tell him that? I don't have the footage!"

"Yes, you do," insisted Heidi. She spat out the nail on the floor. "Warner told me. He said he left the footage with Antonia Bingham. That's how I recognized your name the first time I met you."

"Where?"

Heidi shrugged. "It's with you somewhere. Check around."

"But why would he leave it with me?"

"I guess he trusted you."

Antonia felt exasperated. "Heidi, if Warner trusted me and left the footage with me, then why in the world would you tell that to the lawyer?"

"The guy's the devil! He had this whole file on me. Look, there's some stuff I did and my parents would flip if they found out! He knew everything. That man sucks. He is pure evil."

* * * * *

Antonia steered through the back roads, circumventing town. So, she was right about the lawyer: if he had produced the file on Heidi's background, there was no doubt that he had left the file on Antonia's past at the Felds' house. And she couldn't blame Heidi for caving; there was something menacing and threatening about him. But now she had to think: if Warner left the footage with her, where would he have put it? The Windmill Inn was too big to tear apart. She'd already looked through the kitchen and her office. Where could it be? Antonia's cell phone tore into her thoughts and she saw it was Mrs. Joan Masterson calling.

"Antonia? Antonia?"

"Yes, hi Joan."

"Hi there, am I catching you at a bad time?"

"No, just driving."

"Sorry to bother you. We've just come from the funeral. It was awful. Very, very sad. Luke gave an exceptional eulogy though. I am proud of him. But the poor family. They are devastated."

"I'm so sorry to hear that."

"I know, I know. Headed back to the city. Listen, I know it's raining cats and dogs out there and I'm sorry to ask this. But my neighbor Annabel Fellowes, who lives down the block, just drove by the house and she thought she saw an open window on the side of the house."

Oops. The laundry room window. She must not have closed it tightly.

"A window? She was sure?"

"Yes. I was wondering if you wouldn't mind terribly popping over to check on it. You know how when the rain gets in and the mildew, and the carpet starts to smell and it all stinks like wet dog, I just hate the smell of wet dog. That's really why we never got a dog, I just couldn't imagine what would happen when it rained, it would come inside and smell awful. Disgusting."

"Of course, Joan. I'm on my way."

"Thanks, Antonia."

It was getting late and Antonia knew she should return to the inn to greet the wedding guests before they set out for the ceremony. But now here she was guiding her car through the slick roads during a rainstorm that didn't appear to be letting up. And it was her own damn fault; she should never have snuck into the crime scene. Particularly with the possible killer.

Her thoughts again drifted back to Sam. Was she being irrational in suspecting him? Was it one of her typical post-coital freak-outs? She'd been known to have those. On the very rare occasions when Antonia hooked up with a man, Genevieve usually had to talk her down after the first time. She was always mortified afterwards, self-conscious of everything, especially as the extra pounds on her body increased every year. But this time was different. This time she had reason to feel anxiety. She had the checklist in her head: Sam had met Warner; he even had a Union College t-shirt, Warner's alma mater, which perhaps suggested a longer term relationship than Antonia knew about. There was also the fact that Sam didn't wear a watch, owned Lysol cleaner, and was a drifter who had recently come into town. Ah, what was Antonia thinking sleeping with a guy like this? Abstinence was the way to go, for sure.

* * * * *

The Masterson house stood idle, enduring the rain stoically. Harsh pellets beat down on the roof and dripped off the gutters. The gray and stormy backdrop gave it the appearance of a house in a horror movie. The reality was that in some ways the place *was* now haunted. Warner had died there, his final breath gasped in the second floor bathroom. Forever more, Antonia would feel his presence there and remembering his bloated face in the bathtub. His death was now an inextricable part of the fabric.

Antonia retrieved her umbrella from the back seat and opened it. She ran over to the side of the house where the laundry room window was indeed flapping it in the wind. Antonia pressed against the slippery window with all her might, securing that it was now sealed. She was about to return to the warmth of her car when she heard a loud bang. At first she thought it was thunder, but then she realized it was coming from the Harkin house behind her. Antonia walked over to have a closer look.

She hadn't noticed before how part of the privet hedge had

thinned out entirely, allowing for a gaping hole between the Harkins' house and the Mastersons' house. It was almost as if done on purpose, as if two star-crossed lovers wanted access between the two properties. This must have been where the pool guy had seen someone (Warner?) climbing through.

Antonia glanced through the hole in the hedge and saw a figure carrying planks towards the corner of the yard and dropping them into a pile. She could only make out his silhouette, but something about him was familiar. Antonia closed her umbrella and slid through the gap. The raindrops on the leaves pressed against her as she did so, chilling her more.

When she made it through the fence, she cut between two thick bushes obscuring her view of the house. After she cleared it, she glanced up at the looming manor and tripped over a rusted wheelbarrow. She knocked it over, sending a bag of soil and several spray cans to the ground. Antonia quickly replaced the cans and wiped herself off. Lovely, she noted. She was now streaked with wet mud.

Antonia noted that the backyard was in a serious state of disarray, the garden overgrown and neglected. She spied several piles of miscellaneous junk—old lawnmower equipment, paint cans, broken ladders and such—dumped along the back hedge. There were green plastic tubs of soil that had most likely held some plant life before they were discarded. A lone fountain stood in the corner, featuring some sort of nymph holding an instrument. The hydrangea bushes flanking it were still spiky and leafless. There was also a smattering of rusting animal cages near a decaying woodshed. It was amazing to Antonia how rich people could let their houses rot out from under them. Some-one had told her once that the status symbol for the old mon-eyed crowd in the Hamptons was not what you had *now*, but what you had *then*. That's why WASPs never spent money on shiny new cars or fancy updated houses. That was *new* money. They kept the old Mercedes and the old weather-beaten man-sions—in effect, the *old* money. It declared, *"I got here first!"*

Antonia walked across the mushy grass towards the figure. His back was to her, his body stiff as he carried a shovel over towards the corner of the yard next to the planks. Antonia stopped short with surprise.

As if he suddenly sensed her presence, he turned abruptly towards her.

"Antonia!"

"Carl?"

She walked through the mushy grass towards him. Water was slowly starting to seep into her boots despite their claim that they were waterproof. Or maybe they were water resistant? Either way, they were failing her.

He leaned his weight on the shovel and wiped a wet clump of hair from his eyes. "What brings you here on this miserable day?"

"I was going to ask you the same question. What are *you* doing here?"

He motioned towards the mansion. "This was my grand-mother's house."

Antonia was stunned. "Really? Your grandmother, Nancy Woods? But I thought it belonged to someone named Harkin . . ."

"That was my grandmother's maiden name. It had been her father's house before her, so it was always called the 'Harkin House.' That's how it works around here; houses are always referred to by their previous owners."

"I had no idea she was the Mastersons' neighbor."

"But I told you that the first night we met."

Antonia nodded. "Right. You said the same neighborhood. I just didn't connect the dots."

Carl glanced over at the Mastersons' yard. "Well, their property is in a lot better condition than ours. Unfortunately, my grandmother was old and the people who worked for her really took advantage of her condition. I'd been coming round trying to clean up since I returned to town, but the list of stuff that needed to be done is endless."

Antonia peered up at the house. She had never examined it closely. It was a large, top heavy shingled cottage, taller rather than wider, perched atop a foundation high enough so that the basement windows peeked out from the ground like shark teeth. The salty air had left the house weather-beaten. The roof was dilapidated. There were patches of missing shingles crawling along the back of the house and the white paint trim was chipped.

"It could use some love, but can't it wait? I mean, why do it today when it's raining?"

"I know, it seems crazy. But no one wants to look at real estate in this weather so I found myself with free time. The memorial service is on Tuesday, my usual day off, so I thought I would seize the chance when I could. And actually, it's therapeutic. Manual labor takes my mind off things."

"Yes, you're right. The kitchen is my go-to place for that," said Antonia, studying Carl's face. Despite his calm demeanor, she felt tension bubbling under the surface. "I imagine this must be hard for you. I know you were close to your grandmother."

"I was. Everything I have done was because of her. She was a strong woman. It's strange without her."

Antonia reached out and touched his wrist, pressing softly. "I'm sorry."

There was a crack of thunder and the rain intensified. Carl and Antonia both glanced up at the darkening sky. "Hey, maybe that's her saying hello."

Antonia glanced at the sky. "Yes, could be."

Carl turned and stared at her intently. "Sorry, do you think it's strange that I believe something like that? I think the dead try to contact us. I know, it sounds odd. But I've always felt like that."

"I don't think it's strange. Both of my parents are dead and I feel their energy around me often."

"Really? We should talk about that sometime. I am very interested. Genevieve doesn't like to talk about things like that. But I do."

There was another smack of thunder, followed by a flash of lightning.

"I'd love to talk anytime. But right now, I think I should get back to the inn. And you should go as well! Don't get caught holding that shovel or you may get struck by lightning."

"Good point," said Carl. He pressed it so hard down in the earth that his jacket bunched up around him.

"Well, I'll leave you to it."

"Thanks."

Antonia sludged through the yard, retracing her steps towards the Mastersons' house. The mud stuck to her boots and made a thick sucking sound with each step she took. An image of a mug she used to have with Winnie the Pooh sticking his feet in honey came to mind. It was a sticky mess. Antonia pushed her way through the bushes and crawled through the space in the privet hedge. When she crossed the property line, she glanced up at the Mastersons' house. It was definitely a loved house, in much better condition than the neighbors'. Her eyes moved up to the guest bathroom window, where she and Sam had peered out of only two days before. Funny that she hadn't known then that she was staring into Nancy Woods" house. Antonia shivered slightly and returned to the warmth of her car.

25

Dinner preparation invoked the usual swirl of frenetic activity, but tonight the mood was injected with a sour feeling. Marty was grumpier than usual due to the fact that the kitchen had to prepare several trays of sandwiches and snacks for the anticipated late returning wedding guests. He loathed any culinary endeavor that hinted of catering and not fine dining. As a result, he channeled his anger by snapping at the wait staff and making increasingly vulgar, caustic remarks to Kendra. Every part of her anatomy was a ripe target for him, and Antonia had to step in several times to diffuse the tension. And like a food chain, this caused a trickle down effect where Kendra would greet every request from Jonathan regarding the wedding guests with a barrage of obscenities. The normally unflappable Jonathan appeared slightly shaken, and was even curt with sweet Soyla.

Antonia was also in a fairly foul mood. She was feeling

great remorse over the fact that she had slept with Sam, a potential suspect. The after-sex guilt caused a tsunami of stress.

Glen was the only one who was floating through the restaurant, enjoying the dinner crowd, until seven-thirty when he stormed over to Antonia in a huff, his face now contorted with anger.

"Antonia, you didn't tell me that you needed a table for your friend. I can only seat him at the bar and he refuses," scoffed Glen.

Antonia glanced up from the halibut that she was encasing in razor thin slices of potato. "My friend?"

"That odious troll."

"Who?" asked Antonia, confused.

"Larry Lipper, from the newspaper."

"I didn't know he was coming tonight . . ."

"He said you gave him carte blanche to come whenever."

Antonia groaned with exasperation. "I'm sorry Glen. He *is* odious, perfect word choice. You are so astute it amazes me. Do you think you could find a place for him? It's always good to have the newspaper columnists on our side. And you're so great about figuring all the seating out . . ."

Glen had to be massaged. He responded well to positive reinforcement rather than negative. That's why his relationship was so much better with Antonia than it was with Marty.

After sighing as if he had just been asked to solve the crisis in the Middle East, he acquiesced dramatically. "Alright, I'll see what I can do."

"You're the best. That's why I love you."

"I know!" said Glen, playfully wagging a finger at her. "Oh, and he wants to see you as soon as possible. Don't make me do the dirty work, come on out and say hi to him."

"Will do," said Antonia. "Thanks."

"What a goddamn drama queen," snapped Marty when Glen had left the kitchen. "His sole job is to seat people, place their fat asses in chairs, and he has to be a goddamned baby about it all the time. You'd think it was difficult. Just pick up a menu, lead the person ten feet to the table, pull out the chair for them and you're done. The guy makes almost as much as me, and I'm breaking my ass cooking them their food, on my feet all night, and he's bitching."

"We love you too, Marty," said Antonia with a smile.

Marty grumbled from his station. He also required constant praise, although his song and dance routine was different from Glen's. Whereas Glen would pout and demand appreciation, Marty preferred to have unsolicited accolades heaped on him that he would then resist as if he hated the attention from a crowd so frivolous and far beneath him.

"Antonia, if you want to go out and say hi to Larry, I can cover for you," offered Kendra.

"Me too," said Soyla softly.

"That's okay, I can let him percolate. Let him whine and whimper all he wants. I've got work to do."

"That's right!" cheered Marty. "Let Glen deal with it! Make him work for his money for once."

The whirl of activity continued. Jonathan needed extra tables to hold the buffet for the wedding guests in the parlor, but he was unable to find the key to the storage. It was out of character for him to misplace something, but then everything about this evening was off. After a back and forth dialogue, Antonia excused herself from the kitchen to assist him in his search. But her efforts proved futile; the key was not on her usual hook in her office. In order to accommodate everyone, Antonia sent Jonathan into her apartment to borrow her own dining room table. It would have to do. Most of the time, Antonia thought with a sigh, her job was about trouble-shooting.

On her way back to the kitchen, she stopped in the dining room. Light from flickering candles and the crackling fireplace reflected against the diners' cut glass wine goblets and silverware and made warm shadows on the walls. Delicious aromas from each plate wafted through the room, creating a savory trail of sizzling steak, truffle oil, and cheesy soufflé. The pounding rain outside highlighted the intimate atmosphere inside, and the low hum of conversation rumbled cozily. It was nights like this that Antonia wished she were a guest and not the chef.

Joseph was on his way out of the dining room. "Delicious as always my dear. I had the roast."

"I'm glad you like it, are you off?"

"Yes, I have a slight headache, I believe from the rain. I think I will take a Tylenol PM and retire early this evening."

"Feel better."

Apparently, not everyone was repelled by Larry Lipper because he was at the bar having a very snug tête-à-tête with a woman she recognized as a salesgirl from Calypso. Antonia watched with amusement as he slid his tiny breakfast sausage fingers along her thigh. Further down the bar, Antonia noticed Nick Darrow perched on a barstool. He had on a tweed blazer and a blue button down and was sipping Maker's Mark. His gaze was fixed on Antonia, and he nodded to her. His face looked tired, but his eyes were liquid and alert. He watched her carefully as she proceeded towards him, brightening with each step she took.

"Antonia, I want to tell you something," said Larry as she passed him.

She gave him a momentary glance. "Later."

Larry watched with curiosity as Antonia approached Nick. Nick stared up at her and his face broke into a smile.

"I like the chef uniform," he said once Antonia reached him.

Antonia glanced down at her jacket as if she had forgotten what she had on. "Right. Work clothes."

"Suits you," he said appraisingly.

"Thanks," she said quickly. "So, to what do we owe the honor? You're making our little inn the new Hollywood stomping grounds."

Nick chuckled. He ran his finger along the edge of his glass. Then he stopped and glanced around the room. "I like it here."

"Yes, it's a nice spot," said Antonia. She slid into the barstool next to him. She wanted to be calm, not think too much of the fact that Nick was here. Back again. Alone. Why this sudden burst of attention? Maybe she was over-thinking it; maybe he really did just like the restaurant.

"Are you done cooking tonight?" asked Nick.

"I think so. I want to give myself the rest of the night off."

"Good," said Nick. He leaned in towards Antonia and his voice took on a level of urgency. "Because I needed to talk to you."

"Trying to avoid your buddy Larry Lipper?"

Nick smiled. "He talked my ear off until that girl showed up. The only thing that can distract Larry is ladies."

"Right."

"But seriously, we didn't finish our discussion the other day."

In an effort to neutralize her emotional state, Antonia distracted herself by pulling the bowl of fried chickpeas dusted with Indian spices towards her. She selected a handful before responding. "I thought we had."

"Not really. I pretty much laid my cards on the table and you didn't react."

"I don't understand, what cards?"

Nick ran his hand through his hair with frustration. "You want me to spell it out? About Melanie. About how you are a factor in our relationship. In fact, when I returned home from telling you all this, Melanie of course gleaned where I had been and raised hell."

Antonia shook her head. "I'm sorry."

"I'm used to her histrionics, that's par for the course. But I thought I would get more of a reaction from you. I told you how much our friendship means to me, and you didn't respond at all. Antonia, you have to realize that you give very little of yourself. It doesn't go unnoticed that you deflect almost every personal question and shut yourself off. It's taken me months to pry anything out of you."

"Nick . . ."

He leaned in closely. "Who hurt you this badly? Why do you seal yourself off?"

"I . . ."

"Look, don't even deny it," he said, pulling back. "I know it has something to do with your ex-husband."

Antonia felt her face flush. She wasn't sure she wanted to hear what he was about to say. "Listen, Nick. I don't want to talk about this here. Now."

He took a sip of his drink. There was something frantic about him tonight. A side she had seen before in the roles he played in movies but never with her. She had thought that their relationship had always been genuine, and honest. But now there seemed to be something almost theatrical about this scene. As if he was thriving on the drama of the situation.

Nick put his glass firmly down on the bar. "I understand. Sorry, you're right. This is not the time or place. I'm on edge. Melanie is riding me, and I wanted to make sure things were cool with you."

Antonia gazed at him evenly. "They are. It's all good."

"Okay," he said, taking another drink. "I know I'm agitated. It's been a weird week. A woman I was on the board of Guild Hall with was murdered."

"Sheila Black?" asked Antonia with surprise.

"Yes, I'm sure you heard someone hacked her up. What's happening to this town? First the guy you found, then her. The reason I don't live in Los Angeles is because I wanted to live in a safe, little town. Now this."

"Wait, how did you know Sheila Black?"

"She's a theater buff. Came to all of our shows out here. Bored lady, wanted to get involved so we let her sponsor some. She was a handful, though. She had me stay in character whenever we were in meetings. Last time I met her, she made sure I spoke with a British accent."

"Really?"

"Yeah, she was nuts."

Antonia thought of Sheila's British lover. She must have had a thing for the Brits. She wondered if the police had tracked him down. Before she could ask, she was interrupted.

"Antonia."

She turned around.

"Sam!" she said, startled. She hadn't prepared herself for how she would react if she saw him again. Somehow it didn't occur to her that he would just show up. And now that he was here, looming over her, she realized just how big of a guy he was. He was taller than she remembered and his muscles popped out of his shirt as if he were Popeye. A glance at his large hands confirmed her suspicion that he would have no problem squeezing the life out of Warner or Sheila.

"How are you?" he asked.

"Good," answered Antonia. "I wasn't expecting you."

Her face must have conveyed everything she was thinking because Sam's expression immediately changed.

"I hope I'm not interrupting," said Sam quickly. His eyes

darted between Nick and Antonia. He squinted a little, as if trying to discern the subtext of what was going on.

"Not at all," said Antonia quickly.

"No, you're not interrupting," said Nick quickly.

It was only an extra beat, but everyone felt it. They remained silent for a moment longer than normal, making the situation morph from normal to awkward.

"I'm Sam Wilson." He extended his hand to Nick.

"Nick Darrow."

"Sorry!" said Antonia, flustered. "I should have made the introductions."

There was another awkward pause. Antonia felt Nick's eyes drilling into her, his intensity seething. She didn't know how to diffuse the situation. She wanted Sam to disappear, wanted to continue talking to Nick but instead she sat paralyzed, unable to do anything.

Sam turned to Antonia. "I thought I'd come by and say hello, maybe steal you away for a nightcap."

Antonia squirmed with discomfort. She did not want Nick to glean that anything had transpired between herself and Sam. "That's nice. Do you want to order food? I can get you a table."

Nick waved the bartender over and pulled out his wallet. "You can have my seat, I've got to go."

"I don't want to push you out," protested Sam,

Nick rose. He took a last swig of his drink, finishing it. "Not at all. It's late. I need to head home."

"Are you sure?" asked Antonia.

Nick nodded. He turned to Sam. "Has it stopped raining?"

"No, still cats and dogs out there."

Nick nodded distractedly. "Alright then. Have a good night."

Sam slid down into Nick's seat. Antonia had to force herself not to watch Nick depart. She felt a lump growing inside her of both anger and disappointment. She turned to look at Sam who was staring at her curiously. How was she supposed to talk to him?

"I didn't realize you were friends with him," said Sam evenly.

Antonia shrugged. "Not friends exactly, but I know him."

"I'm sorry, then."

"Sorry?"

"Remember the other night? I was bashing him and his colleagues. All the Hollywood people."

"Oh right," said Antonia softly. "That's okay, I didn't take it personally."

Antonia tried to smile but it felt flat. Sam continued to give her a penetrating gaze. "I can't help but feel I interrupted something," said Sam finally.

"No, what do you mean? We were just talking."

"Is there something going on between you two?"

"Why would you say that?" asked Antonia quickly.

"I got a vibe."

"No," said Antonia. "He's married."

Sam curled his mouth in disdain. "That doesn't mean anything. At least not to celebrities, for sure."

"No, there's nothing."

They sat in silence, Antonia avoiding his gaze. Was he a murderer? She debated whether or not by asking him outright. The restaurant was crowded enough with people so that she could safely accuse him. Finally, Sam stood up. "Look, I'm going to go."

"Why?" asked Antonia.

"I feel like, I don't know, like, you're not psyched to see me."

"That's not true . . ."

Sam put his hand under Antonia's chin and raised it so that she had to make eye contact. "I don't know what's going on."

"Nothing's going on," said Antonia. She knew it was a lie.

Sam continued staring at her, holding her face. Finally, he bent down and kissed her on the forehead. "Today was really nice. I just want you to know that."

"Thanks. I'm sorry, Sam, I just . . ."

"It's okay. You know how to find me."

26

When Antonia returned to the kitchen she handed the proverbial reins to Marty and changed out of her chef's clothes in the mudroom off the kitchen. It was only nine o'clock and the dining room was still buzzing but Antonia was spent. The cherry on top was the last conversation with Sam and Nick. And then as she was exiting the dining room Larry Lipper tried to engage her by making a snide remark and she snapped at him before fleeing the room.

Sleeping with Sam had been a bad idea. That's why she avoided sex as a rule. You may just end up sleeping with a killer, or at the very least, handling the post-coital interaction in a very awkward manner. And why had everything with Nick become so complicated? Was he just using her to play his wife? He clearly thrived on drama, and he loved over-analyzing everything. It was the actor in him, but also the guy who has sat on the couch in a shrink's office too long. Antonia was skeptical of therapy. She'd had tough times and knew it could be useful, but she also didn't want to examine herself so much that she started her sentences with 'I'm the type of person who . . . ' It bred too much self-reflection and frankly, she didn't want to reflect. Nick Darrow was the opposite, he could scrutinize his own every move down to a tee, a true method actor. And maybe that's what this was all about, he was just ego-stroking, searching for affirmation. But despite that all, and perhaps this proved just how naïve Antonia was, she still felt that he did genuinely care for her and needed her in his life. He said himself that he confided things in her that he couldn't in others.

Antonia went into the reception area to collect her messages. Jonathan's light was on and his door ajar. She gently knocked. He was standing over his computer, shutting it down, watching the screen as it evaporated into darkness.

"How's it going?" asked Antonia.

"Brilliant. I think we're in good shape."

"Any of the wedding guests return yet?"

"No, I think it will be a late night. But that's okay; I've got it sorted. We're all set with a cold buffet in the living room for them upon their return. It will be self-serve, of course. I insisted Soyla retire for the evening. She will be on call early."

"Yes, absolutely. Besides, who knows what time the wedding will end? We once had people who strolled in for breakfast."

"I agree," concurred Jonathan. "Oh, and here's the key from your key chain. It doesn't work."

"You tried the yellow one?"

"Yes. The one that's marked 'storage room,'" he said wryly. "It was not a match. But don't worry. We'll suss it out in the morning."

"I'll go through my bag later. I thought I had returned it to the hook on my wall, but my purse is such a war zone that maybe it got buried in there."

Jonathan swung his raincoat off the back of his chair and donned it. He grabbed an umbrella from the stand in the corner.

"I'm over and out for tonight, Antonia."

"Goodnight. Survive the rain."

"Will do."

He let Antonia out of his office before switching off the light and walking towards the front door.

She wandered into her office and sat down at her desk. Jonathan had left a stack of bills for her to glance over but instead she pulled out a piece of white paper from the stack in the printer drawer. With a black felt tip pen she drew two columns and wrote *Warner* on one side and *Sheila* on the other. Off the top of her head she wrote down everything she could think of that connected them. There was the obvious: they were both dead (murdered) in East Hampton and both had been involved in the documentary. But what else? What had Sheila told her when she had talked to her during tea? In the midst of all those non-sequitors, she revealed that she did her shopping at CVS. Heidi worked at CVS, was that another connection? Antonia was unsettled. She was missing something. What if she took out the documentary, was there another reason they were dead?

As she was chewing on the back of her pen cap, Antonia heard the soft twinkle of the front door bell, followed by footsteps.

Out of the corner of her eye, she saw someone standing on the threshold of her office door.

"Did you forget something, Jonathan?" she asked.

But when she glanced up she realized it wasn't Jonathan at all. And just as the slap of cool air that came in with the open door curled around Antonia, she found herself almost at a loss for words.

"Hi! I didn't expect to see you again," said Antonia with surprise.

Bridget Curtis was drenched from head to toe with rain. Small drops dripped down from her face to her toes. If she stood in the same spot any longer, a puddle would form underneath her. Her expression was as stormy as the night, and she glanced at Antonia with a mixture of reproach and disdain. There was a momentary pause as if Bridget experienced a split second of indecision, but when she finally spoke, her voice was firm.

"I'm not who you think I am."

Antonia leaned back in her chair and threw her pen on the desk. "Oh?"

Bridget's face remained stern. "Yes. It's not important who I am or why I'm here right now. But I feel compelled to tell you that you're being followed."

"What do you mean?" asked Antonia.

"There's a man . . . I've seen him watching you."

"Who?"

"I don't know who he is. Only that he's followed you to the beach and to that house where the guy died."

"Wait a minute." Antonia put a hand up. "If you know all that, it means that you were watching me too."

Antonia saw Bridget's resolve falter before she composed herself. "I can't reveal that to you now. It would only distract you."

Antonia was annoyed. "Distract me? That's really lame. You come here and tell me that you've been watching me and you can't tell me who you are or why you're here? This all sounds bizarre."

Bridget nodded. "I agree. I'm sorry, I don't want to sound like a freak. To be honest, this conversation was never supposed to happen. I didn't plan on coming back. But I was concerned about this man. And then I heard about that other murder."

"Well, now that everything is changed, I'd appreciate it if you told me who you were."

Bridget bit down on her lip, as if she was conflicted. She glanced up at Antonia. "Not yet. I'm not finished with what I need to do."

Antonia waved her hand in the air with impatience. This girl was really something else. Did she really think Antonia would beg it out of her? "This is ridiculous. I don't have time for this."

Bridget sighed deeply. "I know you don't, but when I can tell you, I will come back, and you will understand. I'll leave now, but I wanted to warn you about this man. He could be dangerous."

"I know all about the man. His name is Terry Randolph and he's a lawyer who is trying to blackmail me into giving him something that he thinks I have. But I don't have it, don't know where it is, and if I did have it, I'd turn it over to the police right away. And I really wish he'd stop hiding behind doorways and in backyards and trying to spook me."

Bridget was surprised. "I didn't know you knew . . ."

"Yes, I do know. There's a lot of strange stuff going on, but fortunately, I think I'm on top of it. So if you want to tell me why you are really here, please do so, otherwise, I have no time for you."

27

Antonia returned to her apartment feeling both irritated and exasperated. The events of the past few days were taking their toll and even though she had much to muse upon, she announced to her empty living room that she was on an official brain strike. She didn't want to think about Bridget, the odd and strangely broken girl who seemed to have some dark secret. She supposed she should have sympathy but right now she had no patience for that. She didn't want to think about Sidney Black, that mean little man, or Warner, whose death had catapulted her into a strange series of events. And most importantly, she didn't want to think of her love life. Everything was giving her a headache. If she'd been a prescription pill popper, now would have been the time to take one, but that was not her thing, fortunately or unfortunately. So, as she was too agitated to sleep, she nestled onto her sofa with a giant bowl of cayenne popcorn on her lap, and flicked on the TV.

She momentarily debated going downstairs to retrieve *When Harry Met Sally* from the lending library, but she was too tired. Instead she made do with a Lifetime TV movie about a teenager from a seemingly pleasant family in the suburbs who had a double life as a prostitute.

After a while of mindless watching, Antonia felt relaxed, and comfortable, safely tucked in her quiet little cocoon. The inn moved when there were people upstairs; floorboards squeaked, doors banged; windows rattled. It was like being on a cruise ship. But with the wedding guests still out celebrating, right now the only sound that Antonia heard was the rain pounding on the roof and trickling down the gutters.

Antonia shook peanut M&Ms into her popcorn bowl and pressed play on the remote. The TV movie was formulaic, but harmless, as if the writers just slapped a train of thought together and ran with it. They should have spent the last year with Antonia and witnessed all of the murders she was subjected to—then they would really have something to write about!

After the conclusion of the movie, a glance at the cable box revealed that it was eleven-seventeen. The wedding guests had still not returned. The pouring rain was obviously not enough of a deterrent to make them pack it in for the night. After stifling a yawn, Antonia went into the bathroom to brush her teeth. She stared at her reflection in the mirror. Her face was puffy, and she had slight dark circles under her eyes. Lack of sleep, stress—anything could be a contributor to this unattractive mien. Warner dying, Sheila Black dying, Nancy Woods dying, sleeping with a possible murderer.

She turned on the tap and began spreading soapy cleanser on all over her cheeks. She thought of Bridget. There was something about her that unsettled Antonia. Of course because Bridget had revealed that she had been following her, but it wasn't only that. She couldn't quite put her finger on it. There was something familiar about the girl. Antonia tried to think back to a time she may have met her before, but nothing came to mind. It would come to her, though. She didn't have immediate recall, but she knew one day when she wasn't concentrating, she'd remember who Bridget was.

After patting her face dry with a washcloth, she scooped a generous dollop of face cream and began massaging it into the deep wrinkles on her forehead. Antonia leaned down and retrieved a new bottle of peppermint foot cream from the cabinet under the sink. Her eyes swept the contents of the cabinet, confirming that her addiction to products was becoming overwhelming. She was a few purchases shy of ending up on that show 'Hoarders.' After applying the cream, she opened the cabinet again and pushed aside her bucket of cleaning supplies to place it next to other specialty creams for various body parts (hands; elbows; eyes; thighs; stretch marks.) She flicked off the light and returned to her bedroom.

Antonia yanked back her comforter cover and froze. It was as if something that had been hovering at the back of her mind came forward and announced itself, solving the puzzle that she had been pondering over for days. *It couldn't be*, she told herself. *But it had to be.* In her mind, images clicked, one after another, as if she were flipping through one of those picture books that looked like a movie if you turned the pages fast enough. She wasn't sure, but she thought she had found the missing page.

"Oh my God," said Antonia out loud. She surprised even herself that she had spoken with such conviction. But for the first time in days, she experienced utter and complete conviction that she knew who was behind everything.

Antonia walked over to her chest of drawers and pulled out a pair of jeans that she rarely wore. After changing out of her nightgown into a long sleeved shirt and a UCLA sweatshirt, she put on her raincoat and Wellies and grabbed a flashlight out of the bottom drawer in the kitchen. It was a miserable night to leave the house, but she had no choice. Once Antonia felt like she had clarity there was no stopping her from proving it. It was as if fear, hesitation and reason left her body and she became hell-bent on finding the truth. And it wasn't something she could assign to someone else—she had to see for herself.

*   *   *   *   *

The rain was teeming down with renewed vigor. The pellets were hard and fierce, bouncing off of surfaces with determination. The gusty wind was frantically dragging towards the east, hauling along leaves on its journey and anything else not tethered to the ground. Antonia pulled out of the driveway carefully, avoiding the small ditches that were now mud baths. The town green had become a giant pool, the wet grass no longer visible under the murky pond of rainwater. Antonia's car splashed through the puddles that made up half of the road, her wipers working overtime to keep the ripples of water cascading down her windshield at bay.

The road was slick and Antonia had to drive slower than usual. Visibility was low. The raindrops that had accumulated on Antonia's coat during her short walk to the car were now dripping onto her cloth seat and melting into the butt of her jeans. Antonia felt damp and chilled. She reached over and turned up the heat. The chilly air blasted through the tiny filters, emitting a low whistle. She knew she was certifiably insane to go out at this hour in this weather, snooping around no less, but for some reason she didn't feel worried, but rather had a sense of steely resolve.

Antonia lurched through the giant puddles. Her car was old, and at times like this she felt that there was very little that separated her from the outer elements. She may as well be driving a tin can. She glanced up at the corners of her window to make sure no raindrops were escaping inside. As she splashed down the road, she noted that there were several houses with outside lights on, confirming that weekenders had arrived and this part of town was not so desolate. That said, the houses here were spread so far apart that it was very possible that a neighbor wouldn't hear anyone else, especially with the rain pounding so hard.

"Here it is," announced Antonia aloud, to no one.

She was outside the Harkin house. She slowed her car and craned her neck to glance inside. Of course, Nancy Woods was dead, and as far as she knew, no one else was living there, but she wasn't sure. But from this angle, all she could see was the house was enveloped in a shroud of darkness.

She paused at the stop sign and debated her next move. She could make a left on Hedges Lane and another left on Lily Pond and park in the Mastersons' driveway. Or she could pull over to the side of the road and walk back to the Harkin House. She decided that the former would draw the least attention. Cars weren't just parked on the side of the road here. If a police cruiser passed by, it would most certainly stop. Better to risk 'trespassing' at the Mastersons' house.

Antonia killed her lights and pulled into the Mastersons' driveway as slowly as possible. The gravel crunched softly under the weight of her Saab. She wished for a moment that the Mastersons had paved their driveway with silent blacktop, but she knew that was in vain. Paved driveways were a no-no south of the highway. They were regarded with the same contempt as tacky lawn ornaments or above-ground pools.

Antonia drove as close to the garage as possible and parked at an angle to prevent detection from a passing car. The rain was bad enough, but it was the wind that was as potent as ever. Before she exited, she quickly dialed Genevieve's number from her cell phone. It rang and rang but then went to voice mail. Dammit. Where was Genevieve? Even if she was at the movies, she was one of those irritating people who would answer and have an entire conversation during the climax of a film. Her phone was her life. If Antonia could just talk to her, she might not need to go on this little fishing expedition.

The weather was mean. Branches were beating against each other violently, creating foreboding sound effects. She turned on the flashlight and scanned the back yard to find her bearings in the inky blackness. Fortunately, she knew the place like the back of her hand; otherwise she would have been disoriented.

She walked towards the edge of the property with determination. Her boots sunk into the wet grass, the muddy ground suctioning her down. Pools of water had gathered by the rose garden along the hedge, flooding the flowerbeds. Streams of raindrops were running down her face and Antonia felt her nose starting to run. Antonia could only imagine how lovely she looked right now. Like a real femme fatale.

The small streak of light emanating from her flashlight found the hole in the privet hedge. Antonia paused, scanning the edges. It appeared smaller than it had earlier; less of a gap and more of a keyhole. After squeezing the flashlight in her pocket, she hurled one leg over the side and squirreled her body through the narrow patch. The jagged branches scratched at her jacket like a cat's tiny paws clawing an armchair. As she pulled herself through to the other side, she felt as if she was whipped cream being squeezed out of a pastry bag. She landed with a plop and let out a deep breath, unaware that she had been holding it. After walking through the thick cluster of rhododendron bushes that bordered the hedge, Antonia paused on the threshold of the Harkin property. She stared up at the back of the house where a pale light flickered through a slit in the curtains of an upstairs bedroom. Someone was there. Carl? Or maybe one of the grandmother's caretakers? Carl had said they were using and abusing his grandmother. Maybe they had set up house? Could it be the British man?

It was a minor glitch, Antonia told herself. She should have expected that, and indeed she did initially, but she had been fooled by the lack of lights on in the front of the house. She would be quick. A glimmer in the distance provided minor guidance, allowing Antonia to turn off her flashlight. In case someone took that moment to glance out of his window, she didn't want him to spot her.

Antonia glanced around furtively for the wheelbarrow she had tripped over earlier in the day. It was no longer in its spot by the edge. A setback. She continued on, fumbling through the yard in the smoky wash of darkness. The rain was being blown sideways by strong winds and dripping down Antonia's cheeks. The musty scent of damp wood and wetness hung in the air.

With her hands in front of her for protection, she walked with all the grace and ease of a zombie. Squinting through the blackness and stumbling blindly, Antonia slowly moved forward. Fuzzy images became buckets and bushes as she moved closer. She could have sworn she saw a gun leaning against the house but when she came closer she deciphered it was a rake. Antonia took a step and her leg caught on something. She pressed forward. Whatever it was resisted her. She kicked her leg forward. There was a slight bang. Before she knew it, she had fallen over flat on her face, landing in a wet puddle. Her leg hurt like hell and she fought all of her temptation to scream. She turned on her flashlight for a quick second, allowing its sparse light to reveal what had tripped her. It was the wheelbarrow. Antonia shone the light on her leg. Part of her jeans had torn above her calf. She slowly rolled up the bottom of her jean and saw a bloody gash in her leg. It stung.

After taking a moment to pull herself together, Antonia mustered up her energy and rose. Her leg throbbed. She could feel the gash reopening as she moved, and new blood spurting out. The wet jeans flapping against it didn't help either. Hobbling forward, she bent down and peered into the wheelbarrow. The sparse light from the flashlight scanned the inside. Antonia's heart thudded with her discovery. Inside was the stack of spray cans that Antonia had seen earlier. She felt a wave of nervous agitation. She turned one of the cans over. Lysol. The same exact one that had been found near Warner's body.

Deep in the back of Antonia's mind, a hypothesis burgeoned. The killer had been at the Harkin house. The wheelbarrow had been near the hole in the hedge. For some reason, he grabbed a Lysol can and ran over to the Mastersons' house. There he killed Warner. Was it Carl? And if so, why?

Antonia had to get in touch with Genevieve. She replaced the Lysol can and turned to retrace her steps and make her way back to the car. She limped slowly, her hands in front of her so as not to trip over anything again. The rain had reinvigorated itself and was pounding steadily. A flash of lightning glistened across the sky followed by a rumble of thunder. The ground was sloshy and slippery. Antonia took a misstep and her gait faltered. She tried to reach out and steady herself but there was nothing to grab onto. Instead, she slid into a puddle.

"Damn!" Antonia exclaimed, before cupping her hands over her mouth in horror. How could she have yelled out? She glanced up at the window, but there was no movement.

She had to get the hell out of there. Antonia planted her

hand in the mushy earth and hoisted herself up. Her leg was throbbing and she was a mess. She moved as quickly as possible towards the hedge. She passed through the bushes but then got turned around. Antonia felt around for the hole in the hedge, but in the darkness, she was becoming disoriented. She took a few steps back so that the streetlight in the distance could alert her to where she was. She glanced at the bushes, but was unsure. After a glance around, Antonia quickly turned on her flashlight. She scanned the back and found the gap in the hedge. She flicked off the flashlight and glanced up at the house behind her. And froze.

There was someone staring down at Antonia from the upstairs window. The curtain shrouded his face, but Antonia could see the outline. Oh My God. Could he see her? She wasn't sure. Her heart beat so hard she could hear it. If it was Carl, she shouldn't be afraid. Or should she? Antonia was paralyzed. She waited, holding her breath, her entire body motionless but wracked with panic. Finally, he disappeared from the window. Antonia expected a front door to open any minute, so without further ado, she leapt through the bushes, through the hole in the hedge. When she reached the Mastersons' backyard, a flash of lightning streaked across the sky. She glanced up at the back of the Mastersons' house, at the guest bathroom window that Warner had been using. Something dawned on her. If the killer was in the Harkin house, on the second floor, he could easily have seen Warner in the guest bathroom. Did he see Warner do something that caused him to run over and kill him? Was there some sort of communication between the killer and Warner?

A loud clap of thunder sounded and Antonia didn't wait anymore. She hobbled as fast as possible to her car. Her cold hands fumbled in her pockets for the keys. Antonia's eyes kept darting to the backyard. Any minute now the person from the window could come out, shine a flashlight on her and kill her. Was it Carl? She didn't want to wait around to find out.

Finally, locating her key, Antonia opened her door and started the car. She tore out of the driveway, this time not caring if anyone heard.

28

Antonia drove as fast as possible to Genevieve's house, while trying her on her cell phone at the same time. The cell phone miraculously found a signal and connected, but then it rang and rang. There was no answer.

"Dammit, Genevieve!" said Antonia, banging it on the steering wheel.

The light at the intersection of Main Street and Newtown Lane seemed to take an eternity. When it changed, Antonia peeled out as fast as possible towards Genevieve's. Despite her soggy state, she was sweating and burning with adrenaline.

Antonia considered tonight's discovery. If Carl was the killer, she wanted to know why and how. He was never mentioned as being in the documentary. What could he have had against Warner? Maybe Warner just got in the way somehow. She had to find the link. Antonia went through her checklist. Carl was new in town, having returned here only three weeks ago. Since his arrival, three people were dead. It could be a coincidence of course, but there could be a connection. The first death was Warner Caruthers. His guest room and bathroom faced Carl's grandmother's house. The Lysol can found near his body was exactly the same one found in the backyard of the Harkin house. The second one dead was Carl's grandmother, Nancy Woods. It was believed she died of natural causes, because she was old, and her friends confirmed that she was losing it. But what if she didn't? What if she was murdered too? Then there was Sheila Black. How did she play into this? She was in the documentary that Warner was filming. Had she seen something? Antonia didn't think so, because Sheila didn't even know that Warner had died when she saw her. Sheila had a British lover that the police were looking for. Could he have been the tie between all of them?

In the meantime, Antonia wanted Genevieve to clear something up. She said that she and Carl had been together the night Warner was murdered. But did Carl leave at all? Was there a time gap?

Antonia made a right into Floyd Street and pulled into Genevieve's driveway but the lights were out. She was unprepared what she would say to Carl if she saw him, but she knew she needed to get to Genevieve and tell her everything. Antonia ran through the rain up the brick path to the front porch. She rang the doorbell and waited on the step but there was no answer. Even the outside light was off. She cupped her hands and pressed her face against the living room window, but could see nothing.

Genevieve had one of those fake rocks with a spare key underneath it and Antonia turned it over to pull it out. But the key wasn't there.

"Genevieve?" Antonia yelled.

There was no answer. A quick walk around the house in the pouring rain revealed nothing. Perhaps Antonia was wrong. Perhaps Genevieve and Carl were out to dinner somewhere and this was all a mistake. If only she hadn't already played her card with Sergeant Flanagan when she called him to Paul Brady's house. She couldn't try him again. What if it ended up that Genevieve was at a restaurant or something? The police would lose their patience with her. She had no choice but to return home.

* * * * *

It was almost midnight and the inn was quiet when Antonia returned. There were no cars in the driveway. Outside, the lightning and thunder had picked up, grumbling and groaning like an old man with indigestion constantly turning on and off his bedside light. Antonia swiftly reentered her apartment. There were no messages on her voicemail and yet another attempt at calling Genevieve proved futile. Antonia changed out of her wet clothes. She inspected the cut on her leg. It was purple and raw and promised a lovely bruise. She wiped it down before applying Neosporin and a thick bandage. Hopefully, it would only cause her a day or two of discomfort. Instead of her nightgown, she put on cozy sweats and furry wool socks. She was tempted to take another hot bath, but due to the late hour, decided against it.

Antonia once again dialed Genevieve's cell. This time it was answered.

"Hello?"

Carl.

"It's Antonia," she gulped, trying to sound casual. Her heart hammered in her chest. "Hey, is Genevieve there?"

"Hey Antonia. Crazy weather we're having. Everything okay?"

"Yes, sorry to call so late. I just . . . had to ask Genevieve something. Is she around?"

"She's in the shower. Shall I have her call you back?"

Antonia paused. Should she mention that she just saw someone in his grandmother's house?

"Where are you guys?"

"We're at Genevieve's. Why? Do you want to come over?"

"You are? I was just there."

Damn. She shouldn't have said that.

"We just got back from the movies. Everything okay?"

"Yes, fine, thank. Just have her call me back, please."

"Will do."

Antonia hung up and felt a surge of relief. She had been right; they were out at the movies. But then if Carl was with Genevieve, then who was at his house? Was it an employee or perhaps a relative?

She put on a kettle for tea. She plopped a bag of chamomile in a mug and waited for the water to boil. She felt like someone had taken a cheese grater to her nerves. Had the person in the window spotted her? The thought made her shiver. And if he did, would he know why she was snooping around?

The phone rang.

"Genevieve?" asked Antonia hopefully.

"No, Antonia, it's Jonathan. Did I wake you?"

"No."

"I'm terribly sorry for ringing so late, but when I returned home, I had a sudden fear that I had forgotten to leave the box of favors for the wedding guests on the banquet table with the sandwiches. Did the wedding guests already return? I do apologize . . ."

"No, they're not back yet. I guess the wedding is a rager."

"Yes, it is late. Although they did mention that they had the DJ until one am."

"They did look like a crowd the enjoyed a party."

"Yes. I hate to trouble you but would you mind terribly checking if I put the favors out? If they're not there, they are in my office behind the door."

"Sure, it's no problem."

"Thanks very much. I would hate for them to be forgotten."

"Yes, after all that hard work."

"Right. I don't know where my head is. But I'm glad I caught you at home. Thanks."

"No problem."

"Cheerio," he said before he hung up.

Cheerio. Antonia liked how the British spoke. Antonia rose and exited her apartment and walked down to the front door of the inn. The halls were hushed except for the forlorn ticking of the grandfather clock. She went into the parlor. The sandwiches were lined up, but there was no box of favors. Antonia turned towards the offices. She went into Jonathan's and flicked on the light.

The bright overhead buzzed slightly, and Antonia blinked. She peeked behind the door and found the box, the brightly wrapped silver picture frames with the couple's entwined initials engraved on them. She picked up the box and made her way back to the parlor, the floorboards squeaking under the carpet behind her. After laying the favors out on a side table and throwing the box out in her office, Antonia paused in the entryway. The coziness felt compromised by a sudden draft floating through the inn. Antonia glanced at the front door. It appeared shut, but she pressed hard against it and she heard the latch click. She wanted to lock it, but she couldn't because of the wedding guests. Instead, she went back into her apartment, just in time to turn off the wailing kettle.

After pouring herself a mug of piping hot tea, Antonia curled up on the sofa, back where she had been just an hour and a half ago. She was too wired to go to sleep. The rain was tapping on the roof with gravitas, the approaching thunder clanging along ominously. It was late. Antonia was tense. She wished Joseph hadn't gone to bed early. She would love a little glass of sherry and some stinky cheese to top off the evening.

Antonia flipped on the TV again and watched a reality show for several minutes. Suddenly, there was a flash of lightning followed by a loud clap of thunder. The lights in Antonia's apartment quivered and went off, as did the TV.

"Great," said Antonia.

At least once a year the electricity went out during a storm.

The Hamptons often experienced blackouts. Antonia had a backup generator that sustained all of the downstairs rooms of the inn, but it could take several minutes to kick in. It wouldn't normally matter at an hour like this but with all of the wedding guests still not back, it could be a problem. Antonia picked up the flashlight that she had used earlier and exited her apartment. She had to go downstairs to the basement to check to make sure the generator was viable.

The hallway was dark and cold. Antonia moved across the Oriental carpet runner towards the front door. It became colder as she approached, a frosty wind blowing through. When Antonia reached the front hall, she realized the culprit: the front door was ajar. Could the wedding guests have returned?

"Hello?" Antonia asked.

She cocked her ear to listen, but there was no response. Certainly returning revelers would not be so silent.

There must be a problem with the latch. Antonia again walked down the hall and pressed it shut before retracing her steps. The blast of cold damp air that had been released into the inn curled itself into every corner. It could take several minutes for the heat to reassert its control of the temperature. Frustrated, Antonia trained her flashlight along the walls, illuminating her path. The solemn oil portraits that hung in the foyer appeared more sinister and severe in the darkness. Despite the fact that this was her home, Antonia felt a nervous chill run down her spine. Her heart pounding, she moved towards the basement door and fumbled to turn the knob. The door swung open and the stale basement air burst forth and greeted her.

The basement was damp and in the blackness it felt as if the walls were perspiring with moisture. She walked down the wooden steps, each one creaking in her wake, and drank in the rank odor. She was still limping slightly from the cut on her knee, and used the thin wooden railing to steady herself. As she penetrated the frowsy, dank underbelly of her home, a sense of foreboding welled inside her.

The generator was buzzing which was a good sign. Antonia used her flashlight to trace the panel alongside it. All systems were a go, so it was only a matter of time. Her flashlight scanned the rest of the basement, finding everything in order. Antonia turned around to walk upstairs. She shone the flashlight upwards, towards the basement door and stopped dead in her tracks. The door was shut.

Maybe it was the wind, Antonia told herself. Mustering up all of her courage, she marched up the steps. She turned the handle on the basement door and was gratefully surprised to find that it was not locked. Her mind was playing tricks on her. And heck, it was only a few months ago that Lucy Corning, her former manager, had locked her in a storage closet.

Antonia opened the door and peered out into the hallway. Nothing seemed amiss. She ran her flashlight over all the walls.

Stifling a yawn, Antonia walked back down the hall and opened the door of her apartment. She walked over to her phone and saw that she had missed a call from Genevieve. Antonia picked up the phone and pressed redial.

Suddenly, Antonia heard a phone ringing in the distance. She walked to her front door with her cell pressed against her ear. When she opened her door, the ringing became louder then stopped. Antonia glanced down at her cell. Genevieve's phone was ringing inside the inn.

It was then she realized that her instincts had been right.

He came lunging towards her. His gloved hand covered her mouth and shoved her inside her apartment. Kicking the door shut behind him, he pinned her arms behind her body, so tightly she thought they would snap. The flashlight dropped out of Antonia's hand and rolled across the rug before landing against the leg of the coffee table. Its dim light was the only illumination in the room. She flailed and tried to kick him with her legs, but with enormous strength, he pressed on her knee with his own and felled her. Antonia started to collapse. She was unable to breathe with his hand on her mouth and she felt dizzy. Fear clenched her throat, seized her entire body.

He produced duct tape from somewhere, which he deftly stripped across her mouth with one hand. Then he threw her onto her sofa. He picked up the flashlight and placed it on the coffee table so that its light made a circle on the ceiling. It was close enough to illuminate him and for the first time she could finally see him clearly.

Carl's eyes were wild and feverish. His hair was matted down on his head and his Adam's apple bobbed up and down with agitation. The last time she had seen someone look this enraged was when her husband Philip attacked her for the very last time.

"You just couldn't leave it alone, could you?" he demanded.

Antonia tried to speak but the tape prevented her from doing so.

Carl produced a long knife from the pocket of his jacket. The edge caught the pale light from the flashlight and glinted.

"I'll let you speak, but you had better not scream or I will kill you at once."

Antonia nodded in accordance. She felt a choking fear that her life was about to come to an end regardless of whether or not she screamed.

He slowly and meticulously placed the knife on Antonia's neck. It was cold, and instantly Antonia's body froze with terror. Carl twisted the tip of the knife ever so slightly, making a small puncture wound, as slight as a paper cut but just as painful, under Antonia's chin. She winced.

"That's just the beginning. I'm warning you. Do not scream."

Antonia nodded. Her eyes were now pooling with tears of anguish, fear and pain. She anxiously glanced around the room searching for an escape route, but knew it was futile. She could only pray for the wedding guests to return and have some urgent need to wake her up, or perhaps Joseph? What use would he be?

Carl yanked the tape off and Antonia recoiled. It was like getting a lip wax from an aggressive spa employee. She blinked several times.

"Where's Genevieve?"

"Don't worry about her."

Fear curled inside Antonia.

"What were you doing in my yard tonight?" he demanded.

Antonia didn't speak. He jerked her arm.

"I-I remembered the Lysol cans," she stammered. "They were the same type I found in the bathroom where Warner died. I had a hunch and I went over to your grandmother's house to check it out . . ."

"Who else knows about this?" he demanded.

"Everyone. I told everyone," she lied. She wouldn't be stupid enough to present him with a clear motive to kill her.

"I don't believe you," said Carl.

"It's true. I told my buddy on the police force. Larry Lipper from the newspaper . . ."

Carl's eyes narrowed into slits. "You're lying."

"I'm not," she said defiantly.

"I heard you talk on the phone. You said nothing about it."

Antonia's mouth snapped shut. Fear was engorged inside her. "I called them in the car before I got there."

Carl shook his head and chuckled nastily. "No, you didn't. Not one minute ago, you said you had a hunch and you went to check it out. You are not telling the truth."

He pushed Antonia back hard on the sofa so that her head jiggled back and forth like a bobble head. Antonia snuck a look at Carl. His eyes were dark and stormy. She knew she was face-to-face with the devil. He had morphed into an entirely different person; even his features seemed darker and more terrifying. His expression was enraged, his brows furrowed, his mouth contorted. This man was going to kill her.

She knew she just had to stall him, buy herself more time . . .

"Why did you do it? Why did you kill Warner?"

A slow smile crept across Carl Harkin's face. He glanced at Antonia as if debating if he would confide, then ultimately couldn't resist.

"He was collateral damage."

He paused but Antonia didn't want to encourage him. Let this take as long as possible and maybe I will live, she thought. Carl turned and gave Antonia a look as if he knew what she was thinking of before resuming. She was struck again how evil he looked. How had he fooled them all into thinking he was a good guy? Or wait, maybe not everyone: a memory surged back into Antonia's mind of Nancy talking about her family's "undesirables." She'd been talking about Carl!

"My God," Antonia said. "Your grandmother, she told me about you. She said—"

"My grandmother!" Carl sneered. "It always comes back to her. Everything always did. It was time for her to go, but she just wouldn't die! The old bitch planned on living forever."

Antonia wondered if he was adding himself into this equation.

"But, that couldn't happen. I was tired of waiting. Tired of living abroad. Tired of dating old ladies with lots of money. I deserved someone hotter."

"Like Genevieve."

He turned his milky eyes towards Antonia. They appeared glassy and far away.

"Genevieve was convenient. She gave me a crash pad. I like Genevieve, but actually, you're more my type."

Antonia squirmed with discomfort. She had to get off that topic. "What happened with Warner?"

Carl continued as if he hadn't heard her. "Grandmother was such an evil bitch. She punished me all the time when I was a child. Locked me up. Terrorized me. She used her money as a weapon. Doled out minor parcels to me when I was desperate, but made me beg like a pig for it. As if she'd ever done anything to deserve that money! She inherited it from my grandfather and lorded it over the rest of us. And they called me the family pariah? Those morons. I've had to live a horrible life doing menial jobs while she sat pretty on top of her piles of dough. I was tired of it. It was time for her to go. No one would notice if an eighty-three year-old died in her sleep . . ."

"No one except Warner?" said Antonia. It was starting to come together.

Carl turned. His tone became vindictive and angry. "It was all planned. I went to see Grandmother and told her I had something special for her. Then I took the pillow and walked towards her. She said, 'I don't want the extra pillow, I need to sleep.' I said, 'You need it tonight, Grandmother.' Then I put the pillow on her face and I pressed down. I pressed down as firmly as I could and waited. I counted to one hundred. She thrashed a bit, but actually, she didn't really resist. Maybe she knew I had finally bested her . . ."

His voice trailed off. He had balled up his hand and pressed it against his thigh as he reenacted his grandmother's final moments. It was as if he was doing it all over again.

"And Warner saw you do it," said Antonia meekly. "Through the window, right?"

Once again, Carl turned to her with surprised eyes, as if

still bewildered by all that had transpired, despite being the catalyst for everything.

"I had met Warner a few days before. I dug a hole in the Mastersons' fence—the one you came through today—so that I could enter my grandmother's house unnoticed. I didn't realize anyone was staying at the Mastersons' but then Warner happened upon me when I returned. I told him we did it as kids, going back and forth, and he didn't care, wasn't his house. But now he knew me, and knew my face. It wasn't going to be a problem . . ."

"Until . . ."

"Until I caught him spying on me. When I was sure it was over and Grandmother was dead, I happened to glance out the window. And I saw Warner staring at me through the Mastersons' window. Clear as day. Mouth agape, expression of shock. He was naked, about to take a shower. I'm quite certain he just happened to glance out of the window at the wrong time. Perhaps he was closing the shades. But he had seen me do it. He was a witness. A witness I couldn't afford to keep."

Those very words made Antonia's heart leap: *a witness I couldn't afford to keep.* Isn't that what she was? She had to keep him talking, delay this monster from not affording to keep her.

"So, then what?"

Carl was talking as if on autopilot. "I went downstairs. I was calm, but quick. As you saw, my grandmother's back yard is a mess so it was only a matter of grabbing the can of Lysol. I thought I would spray it in his eyes like mace. The Mastersons' back door was unlocked. I found him upstairs, hiding like a pussy, calling 911. I sprayed him and smacked the phone out of his hand. Then I dragged him to the bathtub and smashed his head against the porcelain."

"And then you staged the rest," Antonia added. "You didn't want anyone to know that he was in that back bathroom. You didn't want them to connect the dots."

Carl shook his head. "I cleaned it all up, put it back together and made it look like he had showered in that bathroom. Then I went back to the bathroom where he saw me at Grandmother's and fixed it up."

"You didn't put the towels back correctly."

"What's that?"

"The towels. One was inside out."

Carl stared into space. "The towel was inside out," he repeated, more as a rhetorical question. "Is that what tipped you?"

"Partly. And you also forgot the Lysol can. The Mastersons use purely organic."

"I was rushing. Genevieve was calling. Waiting for me. That's why I forgot my watch."

"The watch!" said Antonia.

"Yes. But I came back to fix it all up early that morning. But you were already there . . . you've been a problem since the beginning."

The fleeting movement Antonia had seen in the yard. She knew she wasn't being crazy.

"See, Antonia. Twice you almost foiled me."

"And Sheila?"

Carl laughed maniacally. Antonia watched as his long fingers clutched the knife in his hand. She couldn't believe this was the same person that she had actually liked and been excited that her best friend was dating. This was a true psychopath.

"Sheila was my sugar mommy. I met her a few weeks ago also. She gave me money and an alternate crash pad."

"But I thought her lover was British?"

"She liked to role play. Turned her on. She was a crazy bitch."

"Why did you kill her?"

Carl ran his hand through his hair. His eyes were far away. "She was demanding. I earned every penny I made from her. She was a nag. No wonder that ex-husband left her. Needy bitch. She started to follow me. Found out about Genevieve and threatened to expose me. I couldn't take it anymore . . ."

Carl stopped and shifted slightly to scratch his chin. It was a split second falter, but Antonia made her move. She would never again allow herself to be a victim. Never. Antonia summoned up all of her energy and kicked his hand away, sending the knife flying. She pushed him with all of her might so that he fell backwards and leapt off the sofa.

"Stop, you bitch!" protested Carl.

But Antonia didn't stop. She summoned all of her energy and ran out her front door. Her leg was burning and her body was sore but she knew she had to escape now or she never would.

The inn was still pitch black; the generator hadn't yet kicked in. Antonia ran to the foot of the stairs. "Joseph!" yelled Antonia with desperation.

She craned her neck to stare down the hall at her apartment door, which Carl banged open with explosive force. He came hurling towards her, his face contorted, hell bent on pursuing her. Undaunted, Antonia ran up the stairs. But just as suddenly, she tripped on the edge of the rug. She pressed her hands on the carpeted stairs to pull herself up. Her cut was throbbing and her whole leg was weak but she was too terrified to think about that.

"Joseph!" she yelled.

She scrambled up to resume her ascent when Carl grabbed her ankle. He yanked her with force, thrusting her onto her face in the stairwell.

Antonia screamed in pain. Her nose was burning, possibly broken. She was momentarily disoriented. Carl took the opportunity to drag her down the stairs. Her head was banging against each step as he yanked her. From somewhere deep within, Antonia gathered her strength and screamed on the top of her lungs.

"JOSEPH!!!!!!!" she had never yelled so loudly in her life.

"Shut up or I'll kill you now," hissed Carl. He was dragging her towards the front door. Antonia clung to the banister, wrapping her arms around it as if it was a buoy and she had been in a shipwreck.

"What's going on?"

Antonia glanced up at the top of the stairs. There was enough moonlight streaking through the window to illuminate Joseph. He had propped himself on his crutches and was looming in the distance, staring down at Antonia and Carl. It was a surreal moment, as if the sky had opened and God himself parted the clouds of heaven to help her.

"Help me, Joseph!"

"He can't help you!" snapped Carl. He took a final yank and pulled Antonia. She thought she heard a snap, and she felt as if her knee had been dislocated. A warm sensation flooded her body, as if she was taking a hot bath. Carl dragged her towards the front door.

Antonia heard Joseph's footsteps clunk down the stairs. The crutches making it sound like a four-legged creature was coming towards her. "Let her go!" shouted Joseph.

Antonia glanced up at Carl, but he paid Joseph no heed. He was frenzied, determined to drag Antonia out of there.

"I said, let her go!" bellowed Joseph.

Carl ignored him. He opened the front door with one hand, letting in a large gust of wind and rain. The raindrops actually felt soothing to Antonia, as if reminding her she was alive.

Antonia heard Joseph's footsteps continue as Carl dragged her. She rolled her head back to stare at the diminishing figure of Joseph, who had now made it to the middle of the stairs. Then suddenly the strangest thing happened: Joseph lifted one of his crutches, and with the precision of a javelin thrower, hurled it directly at Carl. The crutch smacked Carl straight in the chest, sending him falling through the door backwards. Antonia heard his head hit the brick patio.

With all the strength she could muster, Antonia reached and grabbed the crutch. As Carl started to stir, Antonia raised the crutch. She began whacking him repeatedly over the head. She paused.

"Where is Genevieve?" she demanded.

Carl's eyes were rolling. He shook his head. Antonia whacked him twice on the head.

"Where is she?" demanded Antonia.

When he wouldn't answer, she raised the crutch again. Finally, he put his hand up.

"In the hole."

"Which hole?"

"The yard . . ."

Antonia remembered the shovel. Carl digging in the rain. Was Genevieve buried alive or dead? Antonia whacked two more times, until he no longer moved. She heard Joseph calling her name over and over. She glanced up at him and said: "Get Genevieve from the Harkins' yard . . ."

Before she passed out.

MONDAY

29

Southampton Hospital has a bad reputation. It is the East End's punching bag, a place ridiculed for being inefficient and incompetent. But Antonia found the derision undeserved as she had received excellent care. Her leg had been set, her wounds tended, and most importantly, her body drugged up enough so that she would feel no pain. As long as they continued bringing on the Vicodin, she was one happy lady.

Sergeant Flanagan was her first visitor; he came to take her statement.

"You're lucky to be alive," Sergeant Flanagan scolded.

"I know," said Antonia.

"And you're even luckier that your friend is okay."

He was referring to Genevieve. When Antonia regained consciousness, her first questions had been about the fate of her friend. Thankfully, Genevieve had been found alive. Carl had indeed dug a hole in the backyard and placed Genevieve there, but didn't have time to kill her, perhaps because he was interrupted when Antonia went by the house earlier. Fortunately, Genevieve was rescued in time to only suffer a bad bruise on the head and a case of serious heartbreak. Her biggest lament, she said when she visited Antonia, was that it would be "back to the drawing board in the dating game."

"I know. What would I do without her?"

"You were a big help, but it was too dangerous. Don't get yourself into trouble again. Let the police handle their own business," warned Sergeant Flanagan.

"Absolutely," promised Antonia.

"You know, you really pummeled Carl. He's going to be in the hospital for a long time. If this innkeeping doesn't work out, you have a second career as an American Gladiator."

"I will reserve my brutality for serial killers. Isn't that what he is?"

"A classic psychopath. We're right now talking to other police forces in other states trying to map together the crimes this man committed. There was no way that these three were his first. This is where he started unraveling. Unfortunately, I think he did a lot of damage before we found him."

Antonia felt chills. To think she had been that close to a sociopath. "I hope he'll be locked away for awhile."

"Don't worry. Just get better."

"They said in four to six weeks I will be fully recovered."

"That is if you stay out of trouble."

"I'll try."

After the Sergeant left, Joseph entered. He had been with

her most of the night, but upon Antonia's insistence had been driven home by Hector in the early hours so that he could take a short nap and change clothing.

"I'm so glad you are okay, my dear," he said, patting her hand gently.

"What would I have done without you?" asked Antonia. "You saved my life."

Joseph waved off her gratitude. "Does this mean you will waive all of my dietary restrictions forever?"

"Not a chance!" teased Antonia. "But I will make you your favorite meal, cholesterol be damned, as soon as I get out of here."

"Sounds delightful."

For the rest of the day Antonia received a steady stream of visitors. Larry Lipper came in, whipped open his notebook and demanded an exclusive.

"You owe me, babe," he demanded.

Antonia (not the way he really wanted!) sighed deeply and told him everything she could remember. Their meeting was fortunately cut short by Soyla, who was so intuitive about when Antonia needed her help. Later Glen, Marty, Kendra, Soyla and Hector all came to check in. Marty told her she looked "sexy as hell" in her hospital-issued gown.

In the afternoon, Jonathan stopped by.

"I knew that man was bad news," he said as he pulled up a chair next to Antonia.

Antonia propped herself up. "I never even asked you. How did you know each other?"

"I didn't really know him. I was at a bar one night about two weeks ago and he was sitting behind me with a woman pontificating about culture and class, all the while speaking in what was clearly a fake British accent. When he started to go on and on about his years at Oxford, spewing all sorts of erroneous facts, I couldn't help myself. I turned around and corrected him. He was furious and his date was not amused at his deception."

"Wow. I wish I had asked you earlier."

"I know. But I probably wouldn't have said anything. I thought you were friends."

"Yeah."

"Speaking of which, I have something for you."

Jonathan handed her a tin. "It's from your friend Sam."

"Aw, that was sweet."

When he left, Antonia opened the tin and found bacon and fig muffins. She read the note that was attached to it:

Antonia—

Wishing you a speedy recovery. As we both agreed, bacon heals all, so eat these as if the doctor prescribed them! I'm heading out of town, hoping one day our paths will cross again.

Sam.

The note and the gesture were classy. She had to hand it to Sam. He was a nice guy. It made her wonder, had she had totally blown it with him on purpose on some subconscious level? Maybe she wasn't ready for a nice guy. Maybe she still felt she didn't deserve it.

After the visiting hours ended, Antonia dozed off into a fitful sleep. This was one traumatic week that would leave her with nightmares for awhile. But even so, she was grateful that she had so many close friends around her. Sometimes it took a crazy thing like this to happen in order to realize what you have. Antonia vowed to take more time to appreciate everyone and everything.

When Antonia opened her eyes, Karen, the nurse, poked her head in the door. Her face was animated.

"*Nick Darrow* is here to see you," she whispered with excitement.

Antonia stared at her with glassy eyes. She tried to sit up a little.

Karen handed her a small mirror and a brush with a wink. Antonia did the best to make her wild mop presentable, but she was suffering from a severe case of bed head and the fact was there was very little she could do about it. Her reflection also confirmed the presence of swollen eyes from hours of remaining horizontal and an alarmingly pale complexion. *Ah heck with it*, she thought. She couldn't exactly look like a beauty queen when she'd recently been attacked.

"It is what it is," she said finally, before asking Karen to send him in.

Of course, as was his manner, Nick Darrow swooped in and made a grand movie star entrance. He wore a coat and tie and held an enormous arrangement of flowers, which he placed on the table next to her, then he leaned in and gave Antonia a kiss on the cheek.

"You look incredible for someone who took down a serial killer," he boomed. "Remind me to hire you as my stunt double next time I do a movie."

Antonia smiled and sat up. She still felt somewhat weak and the blood rushed to her head, but there was no way she was going to let on. "Thanks. I think I'm retired from all that now."

"I hope so."

Nick swung a bench towards the edge of Antonia's bed and sat down. "Seriously, Toni, let's not do this again. You had me worried."

Antonia smiled. She hadn't heard anyone call her Toni since her father died. It was sweet. "I don't plan on it Nick. I swear."

Nick put his hands on hers. He gave her a long look. "How are you really? Are you okay?"

"I'm going to be."

Nick nodded, pensively. "Okay, because I need you to stick around."

"Oh, I'm here for the long haul," said Antonia.

"I like to hear that," said Nick. "I like to hear that."

SIX WEEKS LATER

30

The restaurant was buzzing. Antonia smiled and waved at Sergeant Flanagan, who after much cajoling had finally taken her up on her offer to bring his wife by for a special dinner. From the looks of it he was enjoying everything, including the special course that she sent out for her "celebrity guests." She was glad.

As she checked on various diners and made the requisite small talk, Antonia realized how much better she was feeling these days. Only yesterday, she was finally able to ditch her crutches and could now use a cane as her knee had almost healed. She had been determined to get back on her feet as swiftly as possible, and with the help of thrice weekly visits to Matt Powers, the physical therapist, she had achieved her goal.

She approached table twelve with a big smile. A young blonde woman in her twenties faced her, seated with a man. The woman had a wide Scandinavian face, cornflower blue eyes and flaxen hair. She was striking because of her Nordic looks, but basically nothing special upon closer observation. Antonia said hello and put her hand on the back of the man's chair. She turned to introduce herself to him and her mouth dropped open. It was Sidney Black.

He gave her a wicked smile, more like a smirk, that let her know that he acknowledged her discomfort and would not be quelling it. He put down his knife and fork and wiped his mouth with his napkin, before reaching for his glass of wine and taking a large sip.

"When are we going to do business?" asked Sidney. He scanned Antonia top to bottom, the way a lion would examine his prey. Antonia's chef jacket was buttoned to her neck but she still felt naked.

"Mr. Black . . ." she said, her voice trailing off.

"This is one woman who won't give me what I want," he said to his date, while motioning towards Antonia. "She is one tough negotiator."

"I wouldn't say that . . ."

"I got rid of the lawyer after that mess with the cameraman. I decided to handle it myself. What's your number?'

"My number?"

"How much are you holding out for?" He picked up the fork and knife and resumed cutting into his steak. It was seared perfectly on the outside, Antonia noted, and rare on the inside. Usually she considered that a perfect execution of the dish, but watching Sidney Black tear into the meat made the blood red of the steak seem almost obscene.

"I can assure you I'm not holding out for anything. I don't have it."

He gave her a cold stare, before motioning for her to lean in towards him. She did so awkwardly. He pulled her towards him by her scarf and whispered in her ear. "If I see that tape played anywhere, you are in deep shit. Your business will be in deep shit. I will squash you."

Antonia could definitely see why people feared and detested Sidney Black. He had cold, hard eyes; small and beady, but most of all, mistrusting. "I understand."

He gave her a wicked smile before releasing her.

"Okay then. Bring us some desserts on the house," he said, before waving Antonia away.

Antonia's face was burning as she moved away from the table. How dare this man act this way? Accuse her, treat her like scum? He was an asshole. A true asshole. She walked over to the maitre d' table and began furiously reorganizing the stack of menus to calm herself down. Glen was busy chatting with customers and the service staff was coming to and from the kitchen.

She glanced around the room, calming herself down. Deep breaths, in and out. She felt her equilibrium restoring. Sidney Black was evil, but she couldn't let it ruin her night. She had so much to be grateful for these days, especially considering everything that had happened a month ago. It was as if she had been given a second chance, or even a third chance considering the fact that she had also escaped her ex-husband Philip. Warner was not as lucky as she had been. She wondered why she had been spared. Part of it was luck; she lived at the inn and could scream loud enough so that people could rush to help her. Maybe the other part was some sort of plan by a higher being. In any event, from now until eternity, her life would be inextricably tied to Warner Caruthers', which was strange. There was now an entire cast of characters that played a large part in her life, people she knew for a very short time, like Sheila Black and Carl.

Then of course there was Bridget. Bridget and Warner had even met each other that day at the inn when Warner was dropping off the key. Suddenly a thought occurred to Antonia. The key. Bridget and Warner. She recalled that Warner's father had told her that Warner 'specifically mentioned' her. He said she was 'very helpful.' Antonia felt as if she was seeing pieces of a puzzle in her mind, but by shifting them slightly they were slowly coming together.

"Oh my God," Antonia said under her breath.

She abruptly hobbled towards her office with determination, her cane clicking across the floor. After flicking on the light, she made a beeline towards her file cabinet and quickly opened the drawer. It was where she kept her keys, including the extra keys to the Mastersons' house and the storage room at the inn. Jonathan had been unable to open the storage room with the key. The last person who had used the keys on that chain was Warner when he had bumped into Bridget. Then he had disappeared. His behavior that day had been strange; his premise for coming back to the inn very flimsy.

Antonia clasped both keys. They were identical, except one was marked "Mastersons' House" and the other "Storage

Closet." Antonia took both and walked down the dark hall. She put the key to the Mastersons' house in the door of the storage room and turned it.

The door opened.

Stale air filtered hungrily out of the room and poured into the hallway. Antonia pulled on the hanging cord to illuminate the space. It was actually more of a room than a closet, although crammed to the brim with a variety of things. Miscellaneous furniture, old filing cabinets, extra banquet tables, tools, boxes of formal china, extra linens, stacks of paper towels and various discarded junk crowded the area. Antonia's eyes flitted around the room. Where would Warner have hidden it?

Suddenly Antonia smiled. Warner did have a sense of humor.

Amongst everything else in that room, there was the lending library of DVDs that guests could sign out. She walked over to the shelf on the wall and picked up the DVD of *When Harry Met Sally*. Inside she found a small disc inside marked *Too Rich to Behave*. Bingo.

Antonia made her way to her apartment as fast as she could with her injured knee. Her heart was pounding and her mind racing. She put the disc in the television and pressed play. There was a long pause before a picture came on the screen. It was dark and the film work was jumpy, as if from an uncomfortable, low angle. The camera abruptly zoomed into focus through a fence and revealed an Olympic sized swimming pool, flanked by small cabanas with yellow, blue and white awnings. Antonia knew at once that it was the Dune Club. She watched as a man walked towards the edge of the pool and dropped his towel. He was stark naked.

"Oh my God," said Antonia. Her hand flew to her mouth.

It was Sid Black. Antonia watched as he took a large belly flop into the pool and began paddling around. The camera made sure to capture his face, before panning around and zeroing in on a sign that said: *No Trespassing*.

So this was what Sid Black desperately wanted. Francine had said he would do anything to get into the Dune Club. If Warner had this footage and showed it to the appropriate members, there was no way it would ever happen.

Antonia watched the entire video, which lasted about ten minutes and culminated in Sid Black extricating himself from the pool and standing at the deep end. Then suddenly, Sidney Black took a giant piss in the pool. Warner would definitely have leverage with this.

Antonia took the disc in her hand and returned to the dining room, eyeing Sid Black. He possessed the most obnoxious arrogant air of anyone she had ever met. Even the way he speared a piece of his molten chocolate cake and shoved it in his mouth was repellent to her. She walked over to him.

"Are you enjoying your dessert, Mr. Black?"

"It's fine," he said. He appeared annoyed at the intrusion.

"Oh wait, we forgot to put a cherry on top," said Antonia, glancing at his plate.

"What?"

And with that, Antonia smashed the disc into his chocolate dessert.

He glanced up at her in shock.

"This is the footage you've been harassing me for." She leaned down, speaking clearly and as menacingly as she'd ever managed. "It's yours now. But you have no idea if I made a copy. And you have no idea who else has seen it. So I suggest you be nice to everyone around you, because you will never, ever know if they have seen you in your birthday suit pissing in the Dune Club pool. Time starts now. Running out of patience. Tick Tock."

And with that, Antonia walked away. It felt great to be in control of her life again.

She went over to Joseph's table and plopped down. She gave her sore knee a rub, and recognized that she would have to take it easy for the rest of the night. He glanced up at her curiously.

"What was that all about, my dear?" he asked, wiping his mouth delicately with his napkin.

"It was about nice girls finishing first after all."

Joseph smiled. "Well done, my lady."

Antonia told him about her brainstorm, remembering Bridget and Warner's exchange before linking him to the key and the footage. Afterwards, they sat in silence for a few minutes. Antonia was feeling relieved and pleased with herself. Things would get back to normal.

"You know, we never did find out why Bridget came to the inn," said Joseph finally.

Antonia sighed deeply. "I know. I suppose some cases are never closed."

"But she said she would be back, didn't she?"

"She said she was working on something that she would reveal when the time was right. I tried to get it out of her, but she was a stubborn girl. Extremely head-strong."

"Sounds kind of like you," said Joseph.

"Ha!" said Antonia. She smoothed some stray breadcrumbs off of Joseph's tablecloth.

"In fact, she kind of looks like you, too," said Joseph.

"I'm not going to worry about her, right now. All I'm interested in is returning to the quiet life of an innkeeper. No more dabbling in crime."

THE END

ABOUT THE AUTHOR

Carrie Doyle is a best-selling author who lives in New York City
and East Hampton with her husband and two sons.

Visit Carrie's author site at **WWW.CARRIEKARASYOV.COM**
or learn more about Carrie (and Antonia and the Hamptons!) on
WWW.DUNEMEREBOOKS.COM.

ALSO BY CARRIE DOYLE (WRITING AS CARRIE KARASYOV):

The Infidelity Pact

WRITING AS CARRIE KARASYOV WITH JILL KARGMAN:

The Right Address
Wolves in Chic Clothing
Bittersweet Sixteen
Summer Intern
Jet Set

CHECK OUT THESE OTHER THRILLING HAMPTONS MURDER MYSTERY BOOKS:

Coming Soon!

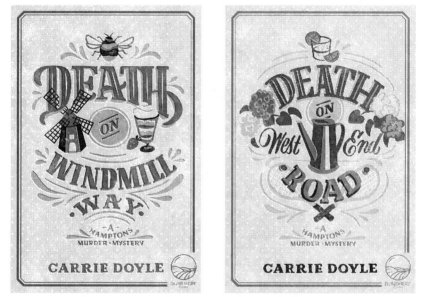

Please visit

WWW.DUNEMEREBOOKS.COM

to order your next great read or just to
hang out with Antonia and hear what
she says about the Hamptons!

DUNEMERE
Books

WWW.DUNEMEREBOOKS.COM

CPSIA information can be obtained
at www.ICGtesting.com
Printed in the USA
LVOW11s2033090917
548177LV00001B/76/P